Snow, Ice, and Spice

Grant Siblings Series book 2

Sarah Smith

For my Aunt Mary. Thank you being my biggest cheerleader.

Chapter 1

Maya

"**M**aya, babes. Don't freak out, but Aaron is here. And he's, um...he's not alone."

It takes a second for my best friend Ingrid's words to sink in through the pounding EDM music in the background and the two vodka cranberries coursing through my bloodstream.

When they finally do, I'm confused. I haven't heard from Aaron in days. But I can tell by the worried look on Ingrid's face and the way she paused before she said, "he's not alone" that this isn't going to be good news.

"What do you mean he's not alone?" I ask.

She opens her mouth, but nothing comes out. She quickly clamps shut her ruby-rose lips before taking a breath. "Well, um, he's...at the bar with someone. And they're, um...well, they're making out."

Fury steamrolls my insides. As hard as I'm trying to keep my expression from turning into pure rage, I'm doing a terrible job judging by the way Ingrid looks. Her angelic face turns pained as she stares at me, her periwinkle eyes shining with concern.

She sets her cocktail on the standing table we're next to and grips my hand in hers. "I'm so, so sorry, Maya. I don't know how he found out about my New Year's Eve party. I didn't invite him, I swear."

I sigh and give her hand a soft squeeze in return. "I know you didn't."

Ingrid's family is one of the wealthiest in Denver. She's a party girl who lives her life on social media and has amassed a million followers on both TikTok and Instagram. Every time she hosts anything from a housewarming party to a rave, every person under the age of thirty-five in the Denver area scrambles to get in. I have no doubt that's how Aaron slithered his way into Ingrid's Gatsby-themed New Year's Eve bash at a random warehouse in this industrial neighborhood of Denver.

Ingrid's eyes shine bright with concern. "I'll get my security guys to throw him out right now."

I shake my head. "No, that would just cause a scene. It's okay, really."

Her perfectly arched eyebrows crash together. "It's not okay. It's absolutely not fucking okay." She punches her free hand at the ground, causing the delicate gold sequins of her flapper-style mini-dress to sway with the movement.

The tidal wave of anger inside of me pauses and I start to soften. It means everything that my best friend has my back. She's been like that ever since we became friends in middle school.

I glance around at the crowded warehouse. It's essentially a giant open dance floor save for the DJ on the stage and the bar in the center. Everyone is decked out in 1920s-style outfits smiling and drinking, having the time of their lives as they count down the minutes to midnight. I don't want to ruin the vibe by making Ingrid's bouncers march in here just to throw Aaron out...no matter how satisfying that would be.

My gaze screeches to a halt when he comes into view. There he is standing a dozen feet away from me, making out with some blonde I've never seen. My jaw plummets to the floor as I watch him grope her boobs. When his hands travel south to her ass, I make a disgusted noise.

"Oh my god..." Ingrid says when she turns to look.

For a few seconds, all I can do is stand there and stare. I think back to the last time Aaron and I met up a week ago. That was the last time I had heard from him before he stopped answering my texts and calls. He met me at Sweet Cheeks, the ice cream shop owned by my older brother Gage's girlfriend Becca. He was twenty minutes late to our date—and he had forgotten his wallet. So I paid for it like I have for the majority of our dates.

Irritation bubbles through the anger just from thinking about it, but for the briefest moment, I wonder if I have any right to be angry with Aaron right now. We've only been seeing each other for a month. And we never actually had an official chat about making things between us exclusive. But he was the only guy I was seeing. And he could have at least told me that he wanted to break things off instead of meeting me for a date and acting like everything was all good, then ghosting me.

This is why I don't date or do serious relationships—and why I'll never, ever get married. Every time I do anything other than hook-ups—every time I try and date someone—it always ends in disaster.

That tidal wave surges inside of me once more. Just because we weren't official doesn't mean he can treat me like crap at my best friend's party of all places.

I swipe Ingrid's cocktail from the table and down it.

"Oh, Maya..." She looks at me, her eyes huge.

Anger and adrenaline collide inside of me as I stomp over to Aaron.

"What the fuck?" I bark. Aaron, the woman he's with, and a half-dozen people around us jolt at my shouted words.

His brow hits his hairline. "Whoa, Maya. So weird running into you here."

"Is it? This is Ingrid's party. You know she's my best friend."

The woman he's with aims her confused expression at me, then Aaron.

He frowns at me. "Oh. Right."

"So you think you can ghost me, then hook up with another woman at my best friend's party, RIGHT IN FRONT OF ME?"

I'm shouting, but I don't care. Aaron is just the latest jerk in a string of insensitive assholes I've dated for the entirety of my twenties. And I'm fucking sick of it.

He waits a beat before huffing out a breath. Then he shrugs at me. "We were never exclusive."

For the second time in five minutes, my jaw is on the floor. I can't fucking believe the nerve of this guy, using a technicality to make an excuse for his shitty behavior.

I tug both hands through my hair, ruining the delicate wavy curls that took almost two hours to style for this party. But I'm too pissed to care how I look like right now.

"Are you fucking serious, Aaron? So just because we weren't exclusive means you can act like an insensitive asshole?" I manage to bark the words instead of screaming them, and I'm strangely proud of that.

Just then the music stops and the DJ's voice booms over the speaker system.

"Thirty seconds to midnight, everyone!"

4

The entire warehouse starts counting down, but I'm still frozen in place, in pure shock at Aaron's behavior.

He shakes his head at me. "Sorry, Maya," he mutters before turning back to his date. Clearly, he's done with our conversation and is getting ready to kiss his new girl as soon as the clock strikes midnight.

And he's not one bit torn up about this. He expressed as much remorse in that muttered "sorry" as he would have had he bumped into a stranger.

"Ten! Nine! Eight!" the crowd chants around me. My head spins. Maybe it's the cocktails, maybe it's the rage steamrolling through me, maybe it's shock, but I feel a sudden surge of adrenaline.

I'm not ending this year staring at my ex while he makes out with the woman he replaced me with like some pathetic loser.

I look past him and see a tall, handsome blond guy standing alone at the bar, downing a shot. Perfect.

I run up to him, grab him by the lapels of his jacket, and turn him to me. Holy...

This guy is gorgeous. Like, ridiculously hot. I take a half-second to admire his square jaw, plump lips, broad shoulders, and muscled frame that's evident despite the tailored suit he's wearing.

His whisper-blue eyes are wide as he looks at me.

I stop ogling him and refocus. "Are you here with anyone?" I ask.

He shakes his head.

"Good." I plant a kiss on this handsome stranger as everyone shouts, "Happy New Year!" around us. Confetti and streamers rain down around us.

As I press my lips against his, he makes a shocked noise. But a second later he sinks into the kiss. It's not long before his tongue teases my mouth open and the two of us fall into a rhythm.

I breathe and instantly get a lung full of his cologne. A blend of pine, citrus, pepper, and a hint of smoke. Damn if this isn't the most intoxicating mix of scents I've ever smelled...

His hands fall to my waist and he grips me tighter the longer we kiss. He laps his tongue against mine, like he's tasting me, savoring me...

I moan into his mouth. Holy hell, this guy is a dynamite kisser. This is the best first kiss I've had since...ever.

Behind me, someone cheers, then falls into my back. I stumble forward, breaking our kiss.

The handsome stranger catches me.

"You okay?" he asks.

I still at the sound of his voice. I know that voice. That deep, guttural, melodic tone.

Instead of answering him, I straighten up and narrow my gaze on his face. I register now that he looks familiar. I've seen him before, I just can't place him. Is he a celebrity? He's as good-looking as one.

It's not until he smirks that the alarm bells start ringing in my head.

Theo Thompson. Ingrid's cocky cousin who I can't stand...who I haven't seen since my twenty-first birthday when he crashed my party and spent the entire night hitting on me before giving me an unwanted lap dance.

I stumble back, horrified at what I've just done.

That doesn't deter Theo though. That smug smile remains plastered on his face as he gazes at me.

"Well damn, Maya. It's nice to see you again."

Chapter 2

Theo

It's a struggle not to laugh as I gaze at Maya, her expression growing more horrified by the second.

I start to reach for her, but she steps away.

"Aww, no hug?" I grab my chest in mock pain. "I figured a hug would be fine after that kiss you forced on me."

Fury flashes in those gorgeous deep brown eyes of hers. "I did not force anything on you."

"Oh really?" I lean against the bar, enjoying just how cute Maya gets when she's all worked up. "Correct me if I'm wrong, but didn't you just grab me and kiss me a second ago?"

She opens her mouth but nothing comes out. She purses those luscious bee-stung lips that are somehow still glossy after laying one hell of a kiss on me.

"Okay, fine. I kissed you. But don't act like you didn't enjoy it. You were pretty into it."

I laugh. "Hell yeah, I was into it. It was fucking hot having you manhandle me like that." I let out a low whistle and lean down so our faces are just a few inches apart. "If you'd like to manhandle me some more, I'm all for it. Your place or mine?"

She levels me with a murderous glare before shoving my shoulder. I chuckle as I stumble back and right myself.

"Not in a million years, Theo."

I don't even try to hide it as I do a slow once-over of Maya. The last time I saw her was on her twenty-first birthday, like, six years ago. She was gorgeous then, but fuck me, she's stunning now. She's wearing a glittery dress with these long silver needle things that are blinding even in the low lighting of this warehouse. But it's the short hemline and low neckline that's grabbing my attention. I do a scan of her mile-long legs. *Fuck.* I forgot how tall she is. I'm six-two and she's almost eye-to-eye with me with her heels on. That means she's gotta be around 5'8" or 5'9" barefoot. I rake my gaze along the length of her legs again. I can't help it. I've always had a thing for tall women.

I tear my eyes from her stunning legs and take a long moment to admire her flawless cleavage. She smacks my arm.

"Are you fucking serious?" she says through gritted teeth.

"You look hot. Sue me."

She rolls her eyes and groans before looking off to the side. "I can't believe I just kissed you," she mutters. "Out of all the people in this room."

"It's a sign," I tease. "We're meant to be together."

Maya aims her fiery gaze on me and I have to bite my tongue to keep from teasing her even more. Yeah, I'm being an asshole. But she's fucking hot when she's mad. The way those big, beautiful brown eyes get even bigger when she's pissed, the way the tan skin on her chest and cheeks flushes red, the way her voice turns hard, it all drives me wild. I've always been a sucker for a fiery woman who isn't afraid to fight with me. Keeps things exciting.

"Let me make this crystal clear: never, ever in a billion years will we ever be together, Theo." She says it without even blinking.

Ouch. Not that I blame her for saying that. I've been giving her shit since she kissed me. It's been like that since the moment we met. I still remember that night years ago, how I was hammered when Ingrid introduced me to her best friend, how the first words I uttered to Maya when she smiled at me and said, "It's nice to meet you," were, "Holy fuck you've got nice boobs."

Her scowl will forever be burned in my brain. With that godawful first impression I made, I knew Maya would always loathe me. I deserve it.

Still though. It always sucks when someone looks you straight in the eye and tells you just how much they can't stand you. And if I'm being brutally honest with myself, I know damn well that Maya isn't the only one who wants nothing to do with me.

"Wow. A whole billion years, huh?" I say, a smile on my face despite the sting piercing my chest.

"A billion times a billion years," she bites back.

Just then Ingrid runs up to us. The second she spots me, her mouth falls open.

"Theo! What are you doing here?"

I almost laugh. "You invited me, remember?"

"Oh. Right." She flashes a smile that's far too tight to be genuine. "I just didn't think you'd show up. I thought you'd be resting for your game tomorrow."

That sting intensifies. I should have told her.

I swallow back the tightness in my chest and hope my smile is still convincing. "Still recovering from my injury so

I've gotta sit it out." I point at my left knee. "Sorry, didn't mean to crash the party."

"You didn't!" My cousin's smile turns natural this time as she pulls me into a hug. I soften the slightest bit as I squeeze her back. "You're always welcome. You know that. I just figured my famous hockey player cousin had more important things to do tonight," she teases.

The bartender drops off a trio of champagne flutes on the bar top for us. I grab one and down it. "I'm off to bed."

"Do you still have to show up for the game if you're injured?" Ingrid asks.

"Nah, I get to get my ass kicked by the Bashers team physical therapist instead," I lie.

"You sure you shouldn't be resting?"

"That's professional hockey for you. No rest for the weary." I give Ingrid another hug and promise to meet up soon before turning to Maya. "Kiss goodbye?"

She flips me off, which makes me want to cackle, but I hold it back.

I hold up my palms. "Fine. Call me whenever you feel lonely, Maya. I'm always down to keep you company."

I wink at her, relishing that glare she levels me with. As I walk off, I run my tongue along my bottom lip, savoring the taste of her kiss. I smile to myself and realize that this is the first time in weeks that I haven't ended the night feeling like absolute shit. And it's all because of Maya.

Chapter 3

Theo

As I sit across from my agent Javier in his office in downtown Denver, I take in the slight frown on his face as he stares at his computer screen. He hasn't said anything in the thirty seconds since he greeted me and told me to have a seat in his office.

Fuck. This isn't good.

That stab of anxiety in the side of my gut intensifies. I've felt it all morning, since the moment I woke up. I should be at the arena with my team, the Denver Bashers, playing against the Detroit Warriors, but because I was a horny dumbass, my knee is messed up and now I'm sitting in my agent's office waiting to hear if my future as a hockey player is over.

I take a quiet breath and steel myself for the shitty news he's about to give me.

"Listen, Theo." He folds his hands on his mahogany desk and sighs, his blazer-clad shoulders sinking with the movement. "I don't want to beat around the bush. It's not looking good."

"What do mean? Is Coach Porter still pissed that I hurt my knee?"

Javier huffs out another sigh. Another long pause. Dread settles at the pit of my stomach. Shit. This is gonna be worse than I thought.

"The Bashers are dropping you, Theo. And no other team in the league is interested in picking you up."

I grip the arm of the plush chair I'm sitting in as my stomach bottoms out. I let out a chuckle that's pure shock and disbelief. "Javier, what are you talking about? I wasn't trying to switch teams. I've played for Denver for the past five years. I'm not interested in going anywhere else."

His brow furrows. Javier's always been a straightforward, no-nonsense guy. He's almost always frowning. The permanent wrinkles in his brow and forehead are evidence of that. But I can't remember the last time he's looked this... serious. No, serious isn't the right word. More like defeated.

"Here's the thing, Theo. When you injured your knee, that was the last straw for Porter. He's done with you."

I open my mouth, but I can't speak for a solid ten seconds. "What the...how? Knee injuries happen all the time in this sport. Players have to take time off to recover constantly."

Javier tilts his head at me. He raises a single salt-and-pepper eyebrow. "You didn't injure your knee playing, Theo. You injured it when the Bashers assistant coach took a hockey stick to your leg after he walked in on you in bed with his wife."

"Y-you know about that?" The entire Bashers coaching staff and my teammates know, and that's humiliating enough...I was hoping Javier wouldn't find out too.

He lets out a heavy sigh and nods. I shrink into my seat.

What the hell was I thinking, hopping in bed with the wife of Assistant Coach Marquez?

"No one bought your story that you injured it while training," he says. "Plus, it was all over TikTok. And Instagram."

"Oh…" A hot flush creeps up my neck and face.

"For as much as you post on your social media accounts, you don't notice when you're trending, do you?"

I shrug and clear my throat. "I've turned off notifications. I've got a lot of followers. Hard to keep up with all the comments," I say quickly.

Javier lets out a sharp exhale. "I'm gonna be straight with you, Theo. You're a great player. Really damn good, actually. You're in the top twenty-five forwards in the league, no question. But even that's not good enough for you to get away with this bullshit in your personal life."

"'Bullshit in my personal life?'"

"Yeah. You're a hell of a left winger, but off the ice, you're either staying out all night getting wasted or you're hitting on reporters in the middle of an interview or you're sleeping with the significant others of coaches."

"You say it like it's a bad thing." My try at a joke falls flat judging by the deadpan look on my agent's face.

"That thing with Estella happened one time," I say defensively.

Javier closes his eyes, like he's trying to be patient with me. "That's one time too many, Theo."

"She told me they were separated." As soon as I say it, I regret it. Javier shakes his head at me, like he's annoyed. I suddenly feel like a misbehaving teenager who's whining while being told off by my teacher.

"Clearly things between them were more complicated

than she presented. You should have been more careful," Javier says in a you-can't-be-that-stupid tone.

"I didn't think Coach Marquez was with the Bashers anymore. I thought he took that job in Toronto after...what happened." I clear my throat. "I figured since he left I could just go back to the team and pretend nothing ever happened."

Christ, I sound so pathetic and desperate, but that's exactly how I feel right now. I'm about to lose my hockey career because I couldn't keep it in my pants.

"He did, but it's not that simple," Javier says.

My shoulders slump as I deflate even more. Everything he's saying is true. I acted like a horny dumbass that night Estella and I ran into each other at that club a couple of weeks ago and she started flirting with me. When she mentioned that she and Assistant Coach Marquez were separated, that was all I needed. I was down to fuck.

I fight back a cringe as I think back on that night. I should have been thinking with my head, and not my cock.

"I don't care what you do in your private life, Theo. I never have. And honestly, if you had been more discreet, we wouldn't even be having this conversation," Javier says. "But the fact is that your private life isn't very private because it almost always ends up trending on social media."

He pauses for a second, like he's trying to choose his next words carefully.

"When I heard back from Coach Porter, I put some feelers out to the rest of the league. But it was a no-go. No one I spoke with wants you on their roster," he says. "They think your reckless life choices make you more trouble than you're worth. And to be blunt, they don't want to take the risk that you might fuck their wives." Javier's tone is some-where between annoyed and pitying. "If you were a superstar, you could get away with this kind of stuff. But you're not—not anymore. I know that's messed up, but that's the truth."

I go quiet as I process everything he's said. As harsh as it is to hear him lay it all out like this, he's right.

Pretty much ever since my college hockey years, all I've cared about was hockey and having fun. I played hard and trained hard to be the best I could be on the ice, but off the ice, I was all about partying and hooking up. I never really thought about taking things more seriously or the consequences of my behavior. I never had to. I was a hot shot for the first few years of my career, so no one cared that I was so reckless.

But now that I'm pushing thirty and well out of my hot shot years, I can't get away with that crap anymore.

I tug a hand through my hair, dizzy as I process the fact that I've been blacklisted by the NHL because I was too stupid to realize that I can't act like a party boy manwhore forever. And I've got no one to blame but myself.

"This isn't necessarily the end, Theo," Javier says after a moment.

"Really? Because it sure as hell feels like it," I mutter.

"I understand that this is devastating news. I really do. And look, I don't want to get your hopes up, but I don't want you to think your career is DOA. At least not yet. Spend these next few months rehabbing your knee and cleaning up your image. No more drunken nights out. Lay low. I don't want to see you pop up on social media unless someone films you helping old people cross the street or saving orphans from a burning building. And no more hookups—especially not with the wives of NHL coaches."

He gives me a scolding look that I can't blame him for.

"If you can rehab your knee and stop acting like a horny

frat boy—if you can show a more responsible and professional image, you'll have a shot at a comeback."

Hope slices through the dread in my gut. "You think so?"

"I can't guarantee that Denver will want you back, but—"

"I don't care," I say quickly. "I'll happily play for whatever team wants me."

"Good. Get to work then."

I shoot up from the chair to shake his hand. "I will."

I leave his office and head to the elevator, determined to un-fuck my image. If saying goodbye to partying and sleeping around is what I need to do to get my career back, I'll be a goddamn boy scout.

As I make my way through downtown Denver toward my car, I notice a few lingering gazes from passersby. I wonder if they recognize me because of my time on the ice... or because they saw me on social media drunkenly stumbling out of a club or making out in public with the nearest attractive woman...

I hunch my shoulders as I walk, feeling every stare, like a hot iron poking into my skin. Before I never used to care why people looked at me. I was just happy they noticed me. Any publicity was good publicity...or so I thought. But I don't want to be a laughing stock or some sideshow, especially if it leads to the end of my career.

I wince as I climb into my car, my knee throbbing from walking so much.

I check the time and note that the Bashers game is about to hit the third period. I let out a heavy sigh and wonder if I've got the stomach to watch my team play without me.

I pull my phone from my pocket and stare at the screen for several seconds.

"Fuck it," I mutter to myself. I pull up the game on my phone just in time to see the Bashers and the Warriors set up for the puck drop. We're up one to zero.

When I see the ref toss the puck onto the ice, the muscles in my hands and forearms twitch with the need to grip a hockey stick and slap the puck. My brain knows I'm not there, but my body doesn't seem to care. That's years and years of muscle memory built into my blood, my muscles, my bones. It's impossible to turn off.

I watch as my teammates dart across the ice, battling the opposing team for possession of the puck. I grit my teeth and my muscles tense once more as I observe Bashers' superstar Xander Williams smash into a player from the other team and swipe the puck from him, then speed toward the net. Another teammate catches up to him, and Xander passes the puck off once a Warriors player gets in his space.

He manages to maneuver around the guy and get open right in time for our other teammate to pass to him. He gets the puck, hits it, and a split second later he sinks it into the back of the Warriors' net. The entire arena erupts in cheers.

But I don't even smile. Yeah, I'm happy my team scored, but that's overshadowed by the dull pain radiating inside of me. I don't even realize until I feel a pressure in my chest that I've been holding my breath and gritting my teeth.

If I hadn't been a brainless dipshit solely focused on having a good time, I'd be there. I'd be darting across the ice, playing my heart out until my lungs and legs were on fire. I'd be celebrating with my teammates, instead of hiding in my car watching my team kick ass without me, like some washed-up has-been.

Maybe they're better off without me. They're clearly doing just fine on their own.

That pain burrows deeper into my chest. I close the browser window on my phone and toss it onto the passenger seat of my car. For a while I sit there and stare straight ahead as cars and pedestrians pass by, feeling a weird mix of numbness and regret.

But then Javier's words from earlier echo in my mind.

Rehab your knee...clean up your image...lay low

A flash of determination hits. I'm in a shitty situation for sure, but I'm not ready to give up just yet.

It's going to take a while to heal my knee *and* my image. But laying low? I can do that no problem. I just need my cousin's help.

I grab my phone, prop it onto the holder on my dashboard, and pull up Ingrid's phone number. As I drive off, I can't help but think of Maya too.

I lick my lips, savoring the phantom taste of her mouth and tongue. Her grabbing me and kissing me last night was hot as fuck. My brain pulls up her image, how sexy she looked in that tight little dress with her boobs practically spilling out of—

I launch the thought from my brain. Hooking up with Maya should be the last thing on my mind. Not that she'd even want to. She was repulsed by me the moment she realized it was me she had kissed. I'd bet good money she'd rather run me over with her car than come within ten feet of me ever again.

Get her off your mind. You're a Boy Scout from now on, remember?

I refocus on the moment, counting the rings as I wait for Ingrid to answer. When it rings a half-dozen times, I start to lose hope, but she finally picks up.

"Theo! Hey! How was physical therapy? Is your knee feeling any better?"

I bite the inside of my cheek, angry at myself for lying to my cousin in the first place. No question she'll be upset once I come clean about what's been going on with me.

But I'm desperate to save my career. And I need her help to do it.

"Actually Ingrid, things are kind of trash right now."

"What do you mean? Are you okay?"

I let out a breath before I dive in. "I'm fine, it's just...I lied to you last night, Ingrid. I'm sorry for that. I'm a fucking mess, and I owe you an explanation."

Chapter 4

Maya

"I can't believe I kissed Theo at your party last week." I take a long gulp of my mimosa until my nose burns.

"Ha, yeah. Weird." Ingrid clears her throat before downing the rest of her blackberry mimosa, then flags down a nearby server. "Another round, please," she says in a squeaky voice.

"Are you okay?"

She's nodding before I even finish speaking. "Yeah! I'm good! It's just..." She shakes her head and stares out the nearby bay window of the restaurant at La Jolla Shores Hotel, which overlooks the beach. For a long moment, she watches the crystal blue waves crashing along the shore before turning back to me, a tight smile on her face. "It's just, uh, weird....like you said, you walking up to Theo and, um, kissing him."

She clears her throat again before chugging from her water glass. When the server drops off a fresh round of mimosas for us, she downs half of the fizzy liquid in her champagne flute, then coughs.

"Ingrid, are you sure you're okay?"

"I'm sure." This time her smile looks less forced. "Hey, your earrings are gorgeous."

I gently touch the dainty half-circle brass earrings I'm wearing. "Thanks."

"You made them, didn't you?"

I nod. "Out of that antique brass we found at that random flea market."

Ingrid beams at me. "Gorgeous. You're gonna be a famous earring designer someday, I know it."

"Ha. Tell that to my brothers."

"Don't say that. I bet they'd be proud of you for starting your own business."

"They'd be more likely to lecture me for changing jobs for the millionth time. They both think it's kind of ridiculous that I'm working for you as your personal assistant since you're my best friend."

As embarrassing as it is to admit, it's true: I've had a million jobs and have yet to find a career that I enjoy, and a lot of my family writes me off as a massive flake because of it.

"When are you gonna let me showcase the pairs you made me on my Instagram?" Ingrid asks. "If you cranked out a bunch and showcased them online, I'm positive you'd make a killing."

I smile despite the punch of doubt that lands at the center of my chest.

Maybe when that thought doesn't completely terrify me.

Designing and making jewelry is something I truly love. My dream is to someday have my own line of earrings, but the thought of putting my work out there for people to judge and criticize freaks me out...and it would be yet

21

another career failure that my family would look down on me for.

"I'll think about it." I down more of my mimosa and glance at the beach. "Such a pretty view, right?" I say in an attempt to change the subject. Even though we're inside, I can still pick up on the faint salty ocean smell in the air.

Our server drops off a plate of fruit and pastries, and for a few minutes, we eat and chat.

Ingrid sighs. "I still can't believe my cousin showed up to my party."

"You and me both," I mumble as I finish the rest of my mimosa. My mind drifts back to a week ago when I walked up to Theo and kissed him.

Despite how much I dislike him and his cocky attitude, I still can't get over how hot he looked. Yeah, he's always been attractive, but time has been very, very kind to him. He's gone from boyishly good-looking to ruggedly hand-some. Instead of those floppy blond surfer waves I remember from my twenty-first birthday, his hair is cut in a fade style with short, clean sides and length on top. Faint crow's feet flank his mesmerizing whisper-blue eyes. Even as I silently swoon over them, I can't help but grind my teeth in irritation. He's gonna age like a fine wine with his killer bone structure and that glowing skin. Goddamn it.

That annoyance fades when I recall that healthy sheet of stubble he's now sporting along his chiseled jawline. I've never been a fan of a clean shave or thick beards, and Theo has the perfect amount of facial hair...

My mind flashes back to an image of Theo in that Gatsby-style gray suit he wore, how it looked like it was tailored to fit his tall, broad body. Even through the thick fabric of his jacket, I could tell that his shoulders and arms were jacked.

And that kiss…

Just the memory of *that kiss* has my clit pulsing. God, it was good. *So fucking good.* My mind flashes back to how Theo's tongue was teasing, soft, and firm all at once, how he hummed into my mouth, how he smelled like pine and pepper, how he tasted like whiskey and mint…

I gulp from my water glass, irritated with just how flustered I'm getting at Theo's physical appearance. Sure, he's an undeniable hottie, but he's also obnoxiously cocky and smug. Always has been and always will be. Yeah, kissing him was off-the-charts hot, but it was also a terrible mistake. I'll chalk that up to the fact that I was reeling from seeing Aaron kiss another woman right in front of me and wasn't thinking straight.

I start sipping my second mimosa and refocus on brunch with Ingrid. "Thank you again, Ingrid. You didn't have to go all out like this. We're just arrived in San Diego and we're supposed to be working."

"Maya, you know I don't have to do anything when it comes to you. I *wanted* to do all this for my best friend to cheer her up after you had to witness your ex practically cheating on you."

I smile at my best friend. "It's really okay. I'm over it, and I've learned my lesson. No more dating for me. I'll just stick to hook-ups like I normally do."

Ingrid looks like she wants to say something, but instead, she takes another long pull of her drink.

"Enough about Aaron. Let's go over what's on the schedule for the rest of today." I grab my phone and pull up my notes. "I took care of your dry cleaning this morning and sorted through those handbag samples. You've got a Zoom meeting with those YouTube influencers at three. Oh, and later today I'll pick up your dress for that boutique opening tomorrow night."

When I look up, I notice she's frowning.

"Did I forget something?"

She shakes her head. "No, you're doing a perfect job, Maya. Seriously. You've been my assistant for a week and you're knocking it out of the park." She stops to clear her throat. "But, um, I have a favor to ask you."

"Sure. You know I'll do anything for you, Ingrid."

She grimaces. "Please don't hate me."

I hold my breath, wondering what my best friend is about to ask me. The last time she uttered those words, she signed us up for bungee jumping.

She lets out a breath. "Theo called me on New Year's Day. And he's, um...well, he's kind of a train wreck."

I choke out a laugh. "Really? He seemed in a pretty great mood at your party."

Her shoulders fall slightly as she exhales, her expression on the edge of pained. For a second, I feel awful for being so dismissive. As much as I dislike Theo, he's still Ingrid's family.

"I know, but apparently it was all an act. He's hit rock bottom. Hard."

"What? How?"

I don't follow sports at all, but last I heard Theo was playing for the Denver Bashers and had earned quite a reputation for being a playboy, always partying and hooking up. And he's often all over social media because of it.

She shakes her head and explains that because of a knee injury, Theo's been dropped from his team. No other league in the team wants him either.

"Oh." I go quiet for a few seconds. Even though I can't stand the guy, I feel bad for him that his career is over.

"I'm sorry, Ingrid. That sucks he's going through that," I say softly.

"When he called me, he admitted that he brought it on himself." She hesitates. "I guess he, um, fooled around with the wife of his team's assistant coach. And he walked in on them and attacked Theo with a hockey stick." Ingrid clears her throat. "That's why his knee's messed up."

I sit there, my mouth hanging open in disbelief. That sounds like something out of a soap opera. Wow, Theo is a dog.

Ingrid sighs. "He admitted that his frat boy lifestyle finally caught up with him and that's part of the reason why no team wants him, even if he were to recover from his injury," she says. "I've never seen him like this. I'm so used to him joking around and being the life of the party. Now he sounds so sad, so defeated. It's so unnerving. I'm really worried about him."

I'm stunned. Theo didn't come off like he was upset or worried about anything when I saw him at Ingrid's New Year's Eve party. He was his cocky and smug self.

She pauses for a second, like she's working up the nerve to say more. "He asked to hide out for a while at my place in the mountains outside of Denver. Just so he could get away and clear his head for a while. And, um...my favor is this: could you maybe go and stay at my house with him for the next couple of months?"

I choke on my mimosa. "Um, what?"

She reaches across the table and grabs my hand in hers, the look in her eyes sad and desperate. "Maya babes, I know this is a huge favor. I feel like such an asshole even asking you this, to move all the way back to Denver when you've just moved all the way here to San Diego to work for me."

When I see her bottom lip start to wobble, I start to soften.

"I want to support Theo, I really do. Yeah, he's irresponsible, but he's my cousin and I love him. Beyond that cocky exterior, he's kind and thoughtful and insecure and vulnerable. I know you've never seen that side of him, but I swear it's true, Maya. At the core, he's a good guy. When we were kids, he'd save all the red Skittles in a plastic bag whenever he ate candy and would give them to me because he knew they were my favorite."

A wistful smile pulls at her lips. When I don't say anything, her smile fades.

"Okay yeah, that's really sweet," I say quickly.

"He's just a...liability with all the partying he does," Ingrid says. "And yeah, he swore to me up and down that being dropped from the league was a wake-up call, that he's done being so reckless, but I just want to be extra careful. Part of me is paranoid he'll throw a rager or invite a bunch of groupies to my place for a sex party."

She wrinkles her nose like the thought disgusts her. "But if you're there, he won't step out of line."

I take a moment to process everything Ingrid has said. "So let me get this straight: You want me to be your cousin's adult babysitter for the next few months?"

She winces and shakes her head. "I'm so, so sorry to ask you this. But the only way I can feel comfortable with Theo living at my house is if you're there with him."

When I don't say anything at first, Ingrid starts up again.

"I'll take care of all of your moving expenses back to Denver of course. And I'm doubling your pay."

My jaw unhinges. "Ingrid, that's way too much. The

salary you're paying me to be your personal assistant is high to begin with."

She shakes her head. "It's not. I'm asking you to go above and beyond as my personal assistant. I'm asking you to watch my cousin like a hawk. You deserve every penny."

I grip the edge of the table for a second, feeling dizzy as I struggle to process what my best friend is asking me.

"I know this is a lot to ask," Ingrid says after a quiet moment. "I understand completely if you don't want to do it."

I take in the pained and guilty look in my best friend's eyes. Ingrid is the sister I never had but always longed for. She's always had my back ever since that day in middle school when a group of popular girls made fun of my haircut. She marched right up to them and told them off, then checked on me to make sure I was okay. We've been inseparable since.

Even though she's the dictionary definition of a trust fund baby, she's never once let our difference in financial status make things weird between us. I'm fortunate to come from a family that's always been financially stable. I grew up upper middle class thanks to the dozen high-end restaurants my famous chef father runs. But Ingrid's family has fuck-you money due to their global luxury hotel and resort chain. When she's not helping out with her family's business, she spends her time traveling, partying, and cultivating her social media following. To outsiders, I know she comes off like a carefree party girl, but she's one of the most generous and kindest people I know. Whenever we go out anything from coffee to a Michelin-starred meal to a surprise trip, even when I insist and try to pay, she never lets me.

I think back to that time in college when I failed my

statistics final. I was holed up in my dorm room crying for an entire weekend, so Ingrid surprised me with a trip to the Bahamas to cheer me up. I think about how I overslept and missed my flight to visit my family for Christmas a few years ago, so Ingrid flew me home on her family's private jet.

I'm certain living with Theo will be a complete disaster, but I love Ingrid. She's my best friend and I'll do anything for her.

I reach back across the table and grab Ingrid's hand in mine. "I'll do it."

She jumps up from the table, squealing so loud that most of the nearby diners turn to gawk at us. She pulls me into a hug and plants a kiss on my cheek. "Oh, Maya. You're the best. Seriously. I'll owe you forever for this."

I squeeze my arms around her. "You don't owe me anything, Ingrid. You've always done so much for me."

When we break apart, I hold her by the shoulder. "I promise your home will be in good hands while I'm there."

Ingrid flashes a relieved smile at me. A second later it all starts to sink in. I'm about to share a house with a guy I can't stand.

He's also a guy that you shared the hottest kiss of your life with.

I push that thought to the back of my mind. That kiss was a one-off. It will never, ever happen again.

No more thinking about that kiss. From this moment on, I'm channeling all my energy into keeping Theo Thompson in line.

Chapter 5

Theo

I drop my suitcases at the entryway of Ingrid's place, shut the door behind me, and kick off my boots.

A gust of warm air laced with cinnamon scent greets me. Ingrid's place always smells like this in the winter. I smile at how cozy it feels, especially since the temperature outside is single digits and it's snowing.

I glance up and see a bottle of sparkling grape juice with a red bow tied around it and a card sitting on the kitchen island. My cousin is so thoughtful. I really don't deserve it.

As I walk over to the kitchen, I think back on our conversation a week ago. Ingrid was so understanding when I explained my situation to her. She didn't even go off on me when I told her just how badly I'd fucked myself over with my reckless behavior. She just listened quietly and said how sorry she was that I was going through all that.

I remember how nervous I was to ask her to stay at her place. I can't forget the long pause she took before she answered...and that slight hesitation in her tone when she told me yes.

Not that I can blame her. Growing up I was always a wild child, always throwing parties at my parents' house and leaving the place trashed. I'm ashamed to say I kept up that habit as an adult and it's led to my current shitty situation: on the brink of losing my dream career with no one to blame but myself.

A heavy sigh rattles my chest as I open the card.

Hey, hockey star! Welcome home! I know you're laying off the hard stuff, so you should give this a try ☺

Ingrid

I let out a chuckle and pop the bottle in the fridge. Such an Ingrid thing to do. She's always been so thoughtful and kind.

I shoot her a quick text.

> Hey, thanks again for letting me stay at your place. And the warm welcome. Promise I'll be a dream guest. When you come back, you won't even know I've been staying here ;)

She replies a few minutes later as I'm hauling my suitcases to the master bedroom.

> Ingrid: Of course! Happy to have you ☺

> Ingrid: One *tiny* change in plans that I need to tell you about.

I squint at my phone screen as three gray dots appear and disappear over and over again for a solid minute.

Just then I hear the front door unlatch. What the hell? No one else is supposed to be here.

But then I think that maybe this is what Ingrid was talking about in her text. Maybe she's coming back for a bit?

Phone in hand, I leave the bedroom, head down the hall, and stop dead in my tracks when I see Maya standing in the entryway

"Hey," I say, shocked. "What are you..." I spot a trio of suitcases next to her along with a small fish bowl with a black betta fish in it on the floor. What the...

Snowflakes dot her nearly waist-length wavy black-brown hair. She shakes her head slightly and the snow falls around her. For a second, I'm hypnotized. She looks like an angel.

She crosses her arms and frowns at me. "Ingrid hasn't told you yet?"

Her sharp tone yanks me out of my trance. I clear my throat and refocus. My phone buzzes in my hand. When I read my cousin's text, my jaw drops.

> Ingrid: Maya's going to stay at the house with you.

Maya starts to say something, but I'm too shocked and confused to hear it.

"You're staying here too?" I say to Maya.

"Yup," she says through a heavy sigh.

This is nuts. "Um, why?"

"Because your cousin is worried that you'll destroy her gorgeous home in the mountains with one of your epic drunken ragers. I'm here to make sure that doesn't happen."

My mouth hangs open at what she's said. "Wait, are you serious?"

Maya purses those gorgeous bee-stung lips, like she's annoyed with me already. "Dead serious, Theo."

What the hell? I can't believe this. I call Ingrid.

"I know this is a bit of a shock," my cousin says instead of "hello."

"Ingrid, what's going on?" I say, stunned. "You sent your best friend to babysit me?"

There's a pause on her end. "Theo, listen. I'm behind you one hundred percent. I believe you have what it takes to clean up your act and your image to save your career. Maya's just there as backup."

"Backup?" I almost laugh at how ridiculous this is.

"She's there to make sure that you don't fail."

"She's here to police my every move, you mean."

"Come on, Theo. Think of it like she's there to help you."

I glance at Maya, who's glaring at me. I know for a fact that Maya would rather smother me in my sleep with a pillow than help me.

"You sure about that?" I say to Ingrid.

She sighs. "Theo, I love you to bits. I'm here for you no matter what, and I'm happy to have you stay at my place. But let's be straight with each other, okay? You have a history of partying like a wild man and leaving a trail of destruction in your wake. I don't want my house to be a casualty of that."

My cousin's sweetly spoken words cut deep. And I deserve it. Because she's right. With my track record, I should have expected Ingrid to do something like this. I can't be mad that she's treating me like an irresponsible teenager when that's how I've been acting almost my whole life.

Awareness finally hits, and right along with it comes a hefty dose of shame. I'm such a fuck-up that even my good-natured cousin doubts that I'll be able to change my ways.

"I get it," I say to Ingrid. "Sorry for getting upset just now. You're letting me stay in your home. You have every right to do whatever makes you feel comfortable."

"Thanks for understanding," she says.

We tell each other goodbye and I hang up, the urge to shrink into myself hitting hard. I'm a twenty-eight-year-old man-child who has to be chaperoned by my cousin's best friend. God, I'm pathetic.

I shove that thought aside. Enough of this self-loathing loser act, especially not in front of Maya, who probably already thinks that about me. Yeah, it sucks to know that my cousin and her friend believe that I'm incapable of acting like a responsible adult. But it's not like they're the only ones who think that about me. My coach, my teammates, my agent, hockey fans...literally everyone thinks I'm a reckless, irresponsible loser. There's only one way to change that: prove them all wrong.

When I glance up, Maya's glare is dialed back to a harsh frown. She hangs up her coat on the nearby hook.

I grin. "Welcome home, roomie. And fish."

Her glare is back with a vengeance at my teasing words. But honestly, it's worth it because now seeing how cute she looks when she's angry has distracted me from feeling all hurt and embarrassed.

"Let's get something straight," Maya says. "I'm here to do a job for my best friend. And that's to make sure you behave yourself while you're living in her home. Nothing more, nothing less."

"Damn, that's too bad. I was hoping we could have pillow fights and braid each other's hair."

That tell-tale red flush spreads across her full cheeks. Christ, she's hot when she's pissed.

She grabs her bag and pulls out a notepad. "I made a list of house rules for you."

"You what?"

"You heard me," she says while flipping through the pages. "Rule number one: no alcohol."

"Are you kidding?"

"Nope. Rule two—"

"Whoa, wait." I hold up a hand. "I can't even have, like, one beer with dinner?"

She aims a laser stare at me. "Moderating your alcohol intake isn't exactly your strong suit, Theo."

I open my mouth to object, but she's right. "Okay, fair point."

"Plus, you're gonna be rehabbing your knee, right? I figured staying away from all alcohol would be a good move for you in that case."

"Fine. What's rule two?"

"No parties."

"That's fair."

"Rule three: no bringing people over for hook-ups."

I bite back a smile. "Wow. We're going for full-on Puritan vibes, huh?"

Maya tilts her head at me, her glare positively lethal. "If you don't like the rules or you break them, you're gone. Understand?"

I exhale sharply. "Understood."

"Good." She shoves her notebook back into her bag and grabs her suitcases.

"What's the rule about kissing?" I tease.

She stills at my smart-ass question, then looks at me. "No kissing in the house."

"Oh, come on. Not even a peck on the cheek? When I've been to Europe that was like saying hello."

She rolls her eyes.

"I'm just saying that if you have the urge to grab me and kiss me again, you have my permission to do that."

"Shut up, Theo."

She grabs the fish bowl and sets it on the side table next to the entryway. "This is my fish, Mr. Pudding."

"Cute."

She glowers at me.

"What? I'm being serious. That's a really cute name."

The fury in her gaze dials back the slightest bit. "You don't have to worry about him. I'll take care of him while I'm here."

"Sounds good. Guess I should send back those three cats I just adopted from the animal shelter."

"Hilarious," she bites.

I try and fail to hold back a laugh as she starts to walk past me in the direction of the hallway.

"Oh, come on." I gently touch my hand to her arm. She stills instantly, her gaze fixed on where I'm touching her before she looks up at me.

I probably shouldn't have touched her. Actually, I *know* I shouldn't have touched her. She can't stand me and would clearly rather be anywhere other than in this house sharing a living space with me.

But I can't bring myself to take my hand away, not when I can feel the heat from her skin burn through the fabric of her sweater. Not when we're standing this close together—the closest we've been since we kissed on New Year's Eve.

Not when it feels this good to be near Maya.

I take in the dazed look in her eyes as she stares at me, how it's shock and something else. Something I can't quite put my finger on.

A second later my brain kicks in.

Get your hand off of her, you creep.

I pull my arm away and take a step back.

"Sorry, um, I just...I mean, I'm sorry for teasing you."

35

"It's fine."

"I can bring your bags to your room."

"No need," she says, her tone sharp, but lacking the bite she had earlier. And maybe it's pathetic or weird or whatever, but it makes me think that maybe Maya didn't totally hate me touching her.

Chapter 6

Maya

"So how goes babysitting the hockey hottie? Anymore surprise makeouts?"

I roll my eyes while FaceTiming with Tori. "God, no. Don't even bring that up."

She giggles, her cinnamon-hued eyes bright on the screen. Tori works at Sweet Cheeks, the ice cream shop that Becca owns. Tori and I have become good friends ever since Becca and my brother Gage have been together. She's sweet, hilarious, and lets me crash at her place whenever I'm in town and we go out for a girls' night so I don't have to stay with my mom or brothers.

"Okay, okay. I'm sorry," Tori says. "I just can't get over the fact that you're living with Theo Thompson. I mean, what are the odds?"

"I've asked myself that same question a million times." I grab my mug of coffee from the kitchen counter. "How are things at Sweet Cheeks?"

"Busy as ever. We've got lines two blocks long out the door in January. It's wild."

I smile. "That's awesome. You and Becca deserve all the success."

I still can't believe how Becca and my brother Gage met. A year ago she drunk-DMed his TikTok account asking him to help her film sexy videos to boost her ice cream shop, which was struggling at the time.

"Tyler's been by a few times to help us out too. So nice of him to do that."

I don't miss the hitch in Tori's voice and the sudden brightness in her eyes. She bites back a smile. Her crush on him is so obvious.

"Yeah, Tyler's a saint," I joke. "Be careful, Tori, okay? I love my brother, but don't let yourself get too attached. When it comes to dating and relationships, he loses interest. Fast."

"I'm not attached to him," she says defensively. "I just think it's nice that he's helping out."

I hold back on saying more. Tori's crush on Tyler is a touchy subject, and I don't want to upset her.

"I'm so happy business is booming for you guys," I say, changing the subject.

"Can you believe it's all due to your hot brother's TikTok account?" Tori teases.

"Oh my god, stop talking about how hot my brother is. Please." I make a gagging noise. It's no secret that Gage has a hugely successful TikTok where he prepares gourmet dishes while shirtless. And he always writes suggestive captions, which has made him a bonafide TikTok sex symbol.

As much as I love my big brother and am proud of his success, that doesn't mean I want to see or picture him doing sexy stuff.

"I'm his sister," I say to Tori. "I don't want to hear about how sexy he is. That's beyond gross."

"Okay, you're right." She chuckles. "Oh, and thanks so much again for the earrings you gave me for Christmas. They're so pretty, I love them."

"Of course, I'm so glad you liked them."

"My mom wants a pair for herself. Can you make some for her? I'll pay you."

I open up my suitcase and pull out the kit where I've been storing the earrings I've been designing and crafting in my spare time. "You don't have to pay me."

"Yes, I do. The earrings you make are one of a kind and so beautiful. You should really start selling them."

I sigh. I've had this conversation with Tori as many times as I've had it with Ingrid and my cousins Austin and Millie. Every time, it goes the same way. They try to convince me to sell my hand-made earrings, I tell them I'll think about it even though I have zero intention of ever doing that. Rinse, repeat.

"Maybe someday."

Tori goes quiet at my go-to answer that she's heard a million times. "I really hope you do."

The disappointment in her voice catches me off guard.

"Sorry, I just...the idea of selling my jewelry, of putting it out in the world for everyone to judge just feels so daunting. I'm not sure if I'm ready for that right now."

Tori's expression softens. She nods like she understands. "I get it. Sorry to push you like that. You're just really talented, and your pieces deserve to be out there."

Her words warm me from the inside out. "Thanks, Tori. Are you finally ready for the virtual tour of Ingrid's place?"

"Yes!" She grins wide and nods her head so enthusiastically that her fiery, copper-hued hair falls out of its messy bun. "When can I come over so I can see it in person?"

"Whenever you want. I'm here all day, every day making sure that Theo doesn't burn the place down. It's a full-time job."

Tori gives me a look. "Come on. How hard can it be to get paid while living in your rich best friend's house with her insanely hot hockey player cousin who happens to kiss like a demon?"

I shake my head, but Tori's right. From the sound of it, this is a pretty cushy job. That doesn't mean I'm going to slack off though. Ingrid's house is her pride and joy, and I'm not going to let her cousin ruin it.

"Where is Theo, by the way? Will I get to see a close-up of him?" Tori waggles her eyebrows.

"He went for a hike, I think."

"But it's snowing. It's coming down hard here in the city, it must be ten times worse in the mountains where you are."

I shrug. "He wants to get back in shape, I guess. This is the kitchen." I turn the phone slowly around the room.

"Whoa. Are those countertops marble?"

"Yup. Practice using a coaster before you come over. This kind of marble is soft and you can't even set a glass on it for a minute without a coaster or else you'll damage it."

"Noted. Oh my gosh, is that a balcony?"

"It's a deck and it's massive. Seriously Tori, check out this view." I scurry across the open concept space and aim the phone so that she can see the all-glass wall at the far side of the living room. I open the French doors and say, "Ta-da!" as I pivot my phone to the snow-covered trees and mountains in the distance.

"Whoa," Tori murmurs. "If you ever get sick of your job, tell Ingrid I'll do it for free. Her place looks incredible—holy crap, is that a guest house on the property?"

I chuckle. "Yup. It's such a cute setup. Living room and kitchen with a loft bedroom."

Ingrid's place here in the mountains looks like something out of *Architectural Digest*. It's literally my dream home with its modern cozy cabin aesthetic and gorgeous views.

I show Tori the living room and take her down the hall.

"Wait till you see the master bedroom, it's insane." I open the door and yelp at the sight of Theo, who's standing there totally naked.

"Oh my god!" I scream. Tori makes a choking noise.

His sky-blue eyes are wide for a split second before a more natural expression takes over. A smug grin pulls at his lips. "Well, that's one way to say good morning."

He makes zero attempt to cover himself while I stand and stare at him in shock.

I try my absolute hardest to keep my gaze above his neck, I really do, but against every silent command to keep my eyes up, turn around, and walk out of the bedroom, I look down.

Holy. FUCK.

It's no surprise that Theo is in shape. He's a professional athlete, so I knew his body would be impressive.

But he's *jacked*. He's got the body of a literal god. I think of the marble Roman statues I saw during my semester abroad in Italy. Theo's physique rivals the perfection of those works of art.

My gaze travels down his cut pecs and abs. When I count eight ab muscles, I make a noise that sounds like a cross between a gasp and a laugh. He's cut all over—arms, shoulders, forearms, quads, calves...

God, what is wrong with me? Am I really this shallow that a leanly muscled body would turn me into a cavewoman? My gaze lands on the package between his ripped thighs.

Well hello there, you absolute stud.

Evidently, I am *that* shallow.

Theo's low, rumbling chuckle jerks me out of my trance. He grins at me, like he's enjoying every second of me ogling his flawless body.

He winks at the phone in my hand. "Hey. I'm Theo. Nice to meet you..."

"T-T-Tori," she stammers before making a crazed giggly noise. "Good to meet you, Theo. You're quite...impressive. Just like...wow!"

When her eyes dip down between his legs, I finally come to my senses. I spin around and dart out of the bedroom.

"I'll call you back, Tori." I hang up and scurry away.

"Whoa hey, Maya. Hold on a sec," Theo calls from behind me.

I contemplate running out the door and burying myself in a snow drift to avoid the sheer awkwardness of this moment, but I don't. I stop walking as embarrassment cooks me from the inside out. I just violated Theo's privacy and objectified him—right to his face. I may not like the guy, but I have no right to treat him like a piece of meat. I owe him an apology.

I close my eyes and take a breath. "You better have clothes on, Theo."

That low chuckle echoes in the hallway around me. "A

towel is the best I can do at the moment. You kind of caught me off guard."

I swallow back a groan, spin around to face him, and keep my eyes on his. "I'm sorry. I, uh, I thought you were still out hiking. I must not have heard you come back in when I was getting ready in my room earlier."

I take in how his smile doesn't waver. Neither does his eye contact. He looks completely relaxed while standing in front of me, wearing just a towel.

"It's fine."

I press my eyes shut and shake my head. "No, it's not. I shouldn't have gone into your room like that. I was just trying to show my friend Tori a tour of Ingrid's place and I thought that you weren't here and..." I cover my face with my hands for a moment before looking at him again. "I'm so, so sorry."

Theo's expression softens. He no longer looks smug and it's throwing me off. "Hey. It's okay."

"Really?"

"Really."

"How are you so cool with this? I would have been livid if you had walked in on me naked."

I expect Theo to make a smart-ass joke about just how much he'd enjoy that, but instead, he flashes a smile that looks more tender than I've ever seen. It's so beautiful, so arresting that I have to remind myself to breathe. I'm not used to Theo showing a genuinely sweet smile. He's breathtaking when he smiles that like.

"I've played hockey almost my whole life. My second home is a locker room. I'm used to people seeing me naked."

"Oh. I guess that makes sense."

I start to feel my body loosen as the embarrassment begins to fade. For a second we're quiet as we look at each other. I take in his gaze, how it's somehow teasing and sincere all at once.

And that's when I realize how different the air between us feels. For once we're not arguing or taking jabs at one another. We're being decent to each other. And it feels...it feels really freaking good.

Something about that throws me off. Does this mean Theo and I could actually get along?

The corner of his mouth hooks up in a half-smile, not a trace of smugness. More like amusement. My skin starts to tingle at just how sexy that is.

"I think this is our first conversation that wasn't an argument. Point for us," Theo teases.

"I guess you're right." Heat flashes across my skin. "I like it."

A grin plays on his lips. "You like what, Maya?"

His voice is low and soft with an edge of growl to it. I really, *really* like that.

"Getting along with you," I say. "Talking to you without arguing. It's nice."

His half-smile goes full and there's a flash in his eyes. "I really like it too."

Another stretch of silence passes between us. This time the air feels charged...but in a good way. Like there's a current of electricity flowing between us. It's exciting. Enlivening, even.

Theo's gaze turns expectant the longer he looks at me. He opens his mouth to say something, but then his phone rings from his room.

He twists his head around to look down the hall before looking back at me. "I should get that."

"Of course."

He walks off and I stand there for a full minute, my brain struggling to process two things.

One: That was the most pleasant conversation Theo and I have ever had—and it kicked off with me barging in on him naked.

And two: I'm undeniably attracted to Theo.

Chapter 7

Maya

I lie in bed, tossing and turning, unable to get the image of naked Theo out of my brain.

It's been almost twelve hours since I've seen him in his birthday suit and I can't for the life of me get him off my mind. I tried everything. I avoided him the entire rest of the day, making sure to eat my meals in my bedroom and avoid the common spaces of the house. I did a ninety-minute yoga session in my room and thought of Theo the whole time. I tried meditation before bed, but every time I tried to clear my mind and focus on my breath, images of Theo's ridiculously gorgeous body would flash in my mind. Those abs, those shoulders, those quads...all those hard lines running across his body...his peaches and cream skin...his impressive cock...

I turn over and shove my head into my pillow, softly groaning to myself.

I shouldn't be thinking any of these naughty thoughts about Theo. Up until this morning, I couldn't stand him...

As soon as the thought materializes in my brain, I roll my eyes.

What the hell does liking someone have anything to do with finding them attractive?

A faint ache pulses between my legs.

Seriously, body? This is how you're going to act? Like a horny animal?

I close my eyes and take a deep breath. For a second I wonder how the hell I got here, how seeing Theo naked has completely changed how I feel about him. But when I think about it, I know it's not just a physical thing. I've been aware of Theo's attractiveness ever since the night I met him, but that didn't stop me from loathing him.

I admit to myself that it was the way he handled me barging in on him that started to turn things around. He was so kind about it. He treated it like it was no big deal. And I could tell while we talked it out that he was going out of his way to make sure that I was comfortable moving forward.

That's why I can't get him out of my mind. Because I'm starting to realize that Theo is more than the cocky douchebag I've pegged him as. I've seen that he can be sweet and considerate too—and that, combined with his nuclear hotness, is attractive as fuck.

The ache between my legs intensifies. My clit is throbbing. I bite my lip as my heartbeat kicks up. There's no way I'm going to be able to fall asleep when I'm this turned on.

I check the clock on my nightstand. Just past midnight. I heard Theo pad to his room down the hall well before ten o'clock this evening. I'd bet anything he's sleeping right now.

I let out a slow, steady breath and climb out of bed. As quietly as I can, I tip-toe to my bedroom door and crack it open. I peek my head out and look in the direction of Theo's room. I can't see any light coming from underneath his door, which means he's sleeping.

Which means that if I'm quiet and careful enough, I can take care of this pesky ache between my thighs.

I shut the door and silently make my way back to bed. I don't bother to crawl back under the covers. I'm too hot, too worked up. With a shaky hand, I reach for the drawer of my nightstand and pull out one of the toys I packed with me. I almost didn't even bother to bring them but decided to on a whim. Thanks, past me, for being so prepared.

I grip the silicone vibrator in my hand and flip it on the lowest setting. Typically I start at a higher speed, but I want to be as quiet as possible. Yeah, Ingrid's place is massive and Theo is down the hall and fast asleep, so the likelihood that he would even hear the soft buzz of my favorite vibrator is slim to none, but I don't want to risk it.

When I press the toy against my clit, my eyes instantly roll to the back of my head. The thin cotton material of my panties may as well not even be there for as intensely as I feel the sensation.

The ache inside of me deepens, winding tighter with each passing second. My skin has gone from hot to the touch to on fire. With my free hand, I grab a pillow and shove a corner of it into my mouth, muffling my moans.

Holy...whoa...

I've never, ever gotten this turned on, this fast while using my vibrator on its lowest setting. I guess I have to credit Theo for that. His lethal combination of hotness, sweetness, and humor has me turned on to the max. The vibrator is just a handy side tool.

The pressure between my legs builds and builds until I feel that tell-tale heat...that hurts-so-good heat.

I'm getting so close, so quickly...but I know what would send me straight over to the edge.

Closing my eyes, I replay the moment I walked in on Theo but let my filthy imagination change a few things...

I close my eyes and picture his face the moment I walk into his bedroom. Instead of looking shocked, he's wearing a smug smile on his face. He stands in all his gorgeous naked glory, his sky-blue eyes looking me up and down.

"Took you long enough," he growls through a knowing half-smile.

"What do you mean?" I ask.

That smug smirk stays in place as he walks up to me. With both hands, he grips my waist, pulling me flush against him. The heat of his naked body warms my skin despite the barrier of my clothing. I instantly feel his hardness against my thighs.

"Do you know how long I've wanted this, Maya? How long I've been fantasizing about you walking in here and looking at me like that?"

My breath is shaky as I imagine Theo running his fingers through my hair with one hand and gripping my waist with the other.

"How long?"

"Way, way too long."

Theo doesn't kiss me. Instead, he drops to his knees and yanks down my leggings. And then he flicks his tongue over the crotch of my panties.

Against the bed, my knees buckle. I press the vibrator harder against my aching, throbbing clit. Even though I'm in total control of this fantasy, fantasy Theo's boldness floors me. I have no idea what he's actually like in bed...but something tells me he'd be like this. Confident. In control. Focused on my pleasure.

It's not long before I've soaked through my panties—both in my imagination and in reality.

49

Fantasy Theo yanks down my panties and goes to town on my clit with his tongue.

"Fuck, Maya. Do you know how good you taste?"

Eyes pressed shut, I shake my head against the pillow, like I'm answering him—like this is actually playing out in real time.

"So fucking good," Theo groans before running his tongue up and down my soaking wet slit. It's not even a minute of this filthy fantasy playing out before I explode. Heat and pressure converge between my legs, and I come so hard, I'm thrashing against the bed while shoving the pillow against my face.

Thank god Theo's asleep because even with the barrier of this plush down pillow, my moans are loud.

When I start to come down and catch my breath, I toss away the pillow and flip off my vibrator. I throw that to the side of the bed, my head dizzy as I process what I've just done.

I just masturbated to Theo Thompson. While he sleeps down the hall from me.

I wait for the shame to set in, for the instant regret to follow. But to my utter shock, they never come.

Instead, I feel...giddy. And satisfied. And very, very naughty.

That was the hardest and fastest I've ever made myself come—and it was all because of Theo.

A guy who I can barely stand.

But as I crawl under the covers, I silently admit to myself that's no longer true.

I no longer despise Theo Thompson. I think I'm starting to like him.

And that's the last thing I think about before I fall asleep.

Chapter 8

Theo

I blink as I stare into the darkness of my bedroom.

Okay, I definitely wasn't hearing things. That was a buzzing noise.

I sit up in bed and strain to see if I can hear it better. It's dead quiet for several seconds...and then it starts up again. It sounds like it's coming from the other side of the house, maybe down the hall. Shit, is it coming from the kitchen? Maybe I forgot to turn something off. Or maybe Maya did. Or maybe one of the appliances is broken.

I hop out of bed and head for the door. When I open it, I stop dead in my tracks. There's a soft moaning noise right alongside the buzzing sound.

I frown, confused as to what the hell that could be...but then a second later I notice the light spilling from the bottom of Maya's closed bedroom door. That's where the sound is coming from...

Oh damn, is she...playing with herself?

I keep my feet planted in my open doorway but stick my head out slightly and strain to listen. Yup, that's the unmistakable sound of a vibrator. And yup, that's the sound of Maya moaning.

For a second, I just stand there. I'm not gonna lie. It's hot as fuck hearing her pleasure herself. My dick strains in my boxers as my imagination takes hold. I can picture her laying on her bed, that cascade of dark hair all over her pillows like spilled ink, eyes closed, chest heaving as she presses a vibrator to her pussy...

A moment later awareness hits. God, I'm a fucking creep. I'm standing here eavesdropping on what's supposed to be a private moment.

I step back and shut the door as quietly as I can, then walk back to bed. My dick is at full mast, poking up through my bedsheets. Jesus, I belong on some sort of watch list. What kind of maniac gets turned on by invading someone's privacy like I just did?

But then it dawns on me. Maya hasn't spoken to me all day...not since she barged in on me when I was naked. Yeah, we had that talk afterward to clear the air, but I could tell she was still pretty flustered at what happened.

When I think about the moment she walked into my bedroom and saw me naked, I can't help but smile. I was surprised to see her, but I was pretty amused too. For someone who supposedly hates my guts, she didn't seem to hate looking at me.

I think back to how the shocked look on her face morphed into something else as she looked me up and down before zeroing in on my cock...it didn't take long for me to decipher that new expression on her face.

Desire.

Maya liked seeing me naked. I'd bet anything she was turned on in that moment.

And maybe that's why she's in her bedroom right now, using a vibrator on herself...because she's turned on. By me.

My skin is hot for a different reason now. Yeah, I probably sound like a cocky bastard when I admit just how good it felt to see Maya look at me that way—like she was undeniably pleased to see my naked body. But it's the truth.

It's no secret that I think she's insanely hot. I always have, even though she's hated my guts since the second she met me.

If I'm being brutally honest, that's the whole reason why this feels so good. There's just something really fucking satisfying when someone who openly loathes you admits that they actually like something about you—even if it's something shallow like the way you look.

And hey, shallow or not, I'll take the compliment.

That shame from earlier has dissipated, leaving behind intrigue and my now rock-hard dick.

I hold my breath and zero in on the buzzing-moaning sound still coming from Maya's room.

Okay, so maybe I can't say for certain that's the reason she's in her bedroom working herself over...but my cock certainly thinks it could be.

Before I can think too hard about it, I'm fisting the base of my dick. I hold back a grunt as my mind drifts back to earlier this morning when she walked in on me. I give myself a rough stroke as the image settles in my brain. Instead of that surprised look, she's smiling at me. And when her gaze follows the length of my body and settles between my legs, there's not a hint of embarrassment or shame in her expression.

She licks her lips before looking up at me, her stare hungry. I groan softly to myself as I start to stroke my cock slowly. Yeah, this is perverted as fuck, reimagining our run-in like some sex fantasy. But I don't care. It feels too fucking good.

Eyes closed, I give my cock a rough tug while imagining Maya walking up to me. She palms my dick in her hand, her gaze locked with mine the whole time. Pleasure slingshots through my entire body with just that single move from her beautiful hand.

"That's a hell of a way to say hi," I say. My hands are on her waist, gripping tight as she licks her lips.

"I can't help it. You look so good, Theo. Do you know how badly I want you?"

She runs her hand up and down the length of my shaft, gently at first. But it's only a few seconds before her grip turns firmer and her strokes pick up speed.

I press my eyes shut and my head falls back. "Fuck, Maya..."

She runs her tongue along my bottom lip before she nips me with her teeth.

My eyes fly open, shocked at the bold move. I'm grinning though.

"Do you like that? When I'm a little rough?" she asks as she works me over.

"Fuck yeah, I like it," I groan. "God, Maya..."

I force my hand to slow down. If I keep up this pace, I'm going to blow, and want to draw this out a bit.

In my mind, I gently wrap my hand around Maya's wrist, stilling her. She frowns slightly like she's confused.

"What's wrong?" she asks.

"Nothing." I spin her around and set her on the edge of my bed before kneeling between her legs. "It's my turn now."

Slowly, I slide off her yoga pants along with her panties. She bites her perfectly pink, perfectly plump

54

bottom lip before she grins at me. I dust the insides of her thighs with soft kisses, relishing her soft moans and the way her muscles twitch every time I press my mouth to her skin.

When I lap my tongue on her clit, I look up and watch as that gorgeous smile disappears. Her jaw falls open and she leans back on the bed.

"Theo, oh my god...your mouth...your tongue..."

Just the thought of going down on Maya has me aching to unload. I work my dick harder and faster. I can't help it. Hearing her moan gave me a good idea of what she sounds like when she's turned on. And now I can't get that sound out of my mind. I want to hear her get loud and wild. I want to hear her moan again and again.

Which is exactly what she's doing in my fantasy. She's writhing against my tongue, those mile-long legs wrapped around my head like a vise. Minutes later she's falling apart while screaming and moaning my name.

As I imagine that very scenario playing out, I work my cock harder and faster. What started as pressure in my lower abdomen now feels like liquid heat in my balls and the base of my spine. I'm hard as steel and right on the edge.

I picture Maya as she starts to come down post-orgasm: hair messy, eyes cloudy, a pleasure-drunk smile on her face.

She drops to her knees, those doe eyes glued to me. "I need you in my mouth, Theo. Now."

She guides my cock into her mouth and takes me all the way to the back of her throat, her soft, wet tongue gliding along the underside of my dick.

I tug my dick like I'm crazed, like I've lost all self-control. And then I come. A growl starts to rip from the base of my throat, but I quickly grit my teeth and swallow it down. When I finish, I'm shaking. Holy fucking shit. That was the hardest I've come in...Christ, I can't even remember.

I blink until my eyes are finally adjusted to the darkness and glance down at the mess on my stomach. I yank a few tissues from the box on my nightstand and clean myself up before rolling over in bed.

It's dead quiet now. No matter how hard I strain, I can't hear any more buzzing or moaning. Hopefully, that means Maya is fast asleep and didn't hear anything.

I lie there in bed, in disbelief. Did I really just do that?

"You know you did," I mumble to myself.

Fatigue kicks in and soon I'm so tired I can barely keep my eyes open. But even as I fall asleep, I can't help but think of Maya and her sweet, soft moans.

Chapter 9

Maya

W hen I walk into the empty kitchen the next morning, I go through my usual morning routine of feeding Mr. Pudding and brewing coffee.

As I pour myself a cup, I glance down the hallway to Theo's room. When I think about what I did last night, my entire body flushes. I crossed an unspoken line by making Theo the star of my self-pleasure fantasy. But he doesn't have to know that.

I shudder at the thought of anyone finding out about what I did. I'll be taking that to my grave.

I'm scrolling through my phone and halfway through my coffee when Theo pads out of his bedroom, rubbing a fist to his eye.

"Morning," he says through a sleepy half-smile as he makes a beeline to the coffee machine.

"Good morning," I reply, trying my hardest to keep from gawking at him since he's wearing nothing but flannel pajama bottoms that hang low on his hips.

I hazard a glance at his beautiful bare chest as he digs

through the cupboards for a mug. The muscles in his stomach and chest and arms ripple while he reaches and grabs. I can't help but stare in awe. How the hell can a human being look this flawless first thing in the morning?

I glance down at the oversized oatmeal cardigan I'm wearing over a thin sleeping shirt and sweatpants before my gaze slingshots back to Theo's gorgeous form. I'm so frumpy in comparison.

It's not till he makes eye contact with me while he sips from his coffee mug that I realize I'm staring at him.

"Something on my chest?" he teases as he brushes nothing off his sculpted left pec.

He laughs, which makes my face feel like it's engulfed in flames. I avert my gaze to a random spot on the kitchen island, where I'm standing.

"Couldn't be bothered to wear a shirt, huh?" I dump more oat milk in my mug and try to keep my tone as neutral and uninterested as possible, but I'm certain Theo can tell by the hot flush igniting my skin that I'm embarrassed at how he caught me staring.

I'm treated to a smirk when I look back up at him. He glances down at his bare chest and shrugs. "Wouldn't want to deprive you of such a stunning view." He holds his arms at his sides, like he's presenting himself.

I can't help but smile as I roll my eyes. "I prefer that view," I tease, nodding my head at the snow-covered mountains in the distance through the massive living room ceiling-to-floor windows.

Theo clutches his chest and jokingly stumbles back a step. "Ouch."

"Seriously though, how can you stand to be shirtless right now? Even with the heat on I can still feel the chill from outside. It's way below freezing."

"I'm hot-blooded. I swear I was a polar bear in another life. It's probably why I'm a hockey player."

I laugh. He chuckles right along with me. This feels good, to laugh and chat with Theo. It feels like we're friends, which is a nice change from our usual exchanges of me snapping at him whenever he riles me up.

I top off my mug with more coffee and oat milk before offering it to Theo. He shakes his head.

"I slept pretty well last night so I'm good with one cup. But how can you drink that?" He makes a face at the carton of oat milk. "That stuff tastes so chalky."

I look him straight in the eye as I sip. "I love it."

He laughs.

"So you had a good hibernation last night then?" I ask.

Theo's smile twitches the slightest bit. He clears his throat and looks down at his mug, which he's now cradling in both of his hands. "Yeah. It was a good sleep. Uh, you?"

"Yeah, I slept great." I quietly take in the way he's now conducting a staring contest with the floor. Strange. He's always been the kind of guy to maintain easy, confident eye contact, even when I'm yelling at him. Why the sudden change?

"That's good," he says before clearing his throat again. "That you slept well, I mean."

A second later I notice a pink flush creep down his neck and chest. When he finally makes eye contact with me, the look in his eyes is shy and something else...embarrassed? No, that's not it. It's more like he's embarrassed for me for some reason.

For a long moment, I'm confused until it finally hits me: he heard me last night.

A tidal wave of shame washes over me. "Oh my god..." I mutter. "You heard me, didn't you?"

He opens his mouth but hesitates. His lips twitch like he's trying not to wince. "I swear, I didn't mean to. It was just really quiet and I heard a buzzing noise."

The shame wave levels my insides. I cover my face with my hands and groan.

"Maya, it's okay. Really. I get it. We all have, um, urges."

Theo's comforting tone makes me wish the ground would swallow me up right here, right now.

I drop my hands to my sides and groan even louder this time. He gawks at me with wide eyes, like I'm a wild animal and he's not quite sure how I'm going to react.

"It's completely natural." He starts to say some more reassuring things, but I hold up my hand.

"Please stop talking." I tug a hand through my hair. Suddenly I'm no longer cold. The utter humiliation of this moment is roasting me from the inside out.

His brow furrows like he's confused. "There's no need to be embarrassed, Maya. It's a totally normal thing to do."

I stare at him.

He shrugs. "It happens. I swear, it's no big deal. I've overheard a couple of my teammates jerking off sometimes when we play away games and we have to share a hotel room—"

"Oh my god, shut up!"

Theo pulls his lips into his mouth and quickly nods at me.

I shake my hands at my sides, the nonsensical movement the only way I can think to expend the nervous energy coursing through me.

"I never, ever want to speak of this ever again," I blurt.

Theo frowns like he's confused. "Maya, there's nothing for you to be embarrassed about."

I let out a laugh of pure disbelief. "Theo, you overheard

me masturbating last night. That's one of the most mortifying things that could ever happen to someone."

His gaze on me is mystified as he shakes his head, like he can't quite make sense of why I'm so embarrassed.

"You have nothing to be mortified about," Theo says. "Hearing you last night was hot as fuck."

The shame tsunami inside of me skids to a halt. "What?"

The expression on Theo's face as he gazes at me is a strange mix of intensity and intrigue. He opens his mouth to speak, but then the doorbell rings.

I spin around to the front door. Who the hell could that be? It's barely nine in the morning on a Sunday.

I spot movement in the glass side panels flanking either side of the front door. I recognize Tori's auburn hair instantly. She leans over and smiles at me. And that's when I notice she's not alone. I spot both of my brothers, Becca, my cousin Austin, and his husband Declan.

"Were you expecting someone?" Theo asks from behind me.

I let out a sigh. "Nope." I walk over and let them in.

"Surprise!" Tori announces before pulling me into a hug. I smile despite the awkward timing of my family's surprise visit.

"What are you guys doing here?" I ask as I hug all of them.

"We thought we'd surprise you with some goodies," Tori says. She gestures to Becca and Austin, who are holding two massive paper bags of what I assume are Tupperware containers of food.

"Oh...thanks..."

Tori's smile starts to drop. "Is this a bad time? It's just that you said yesterday it was cool for us to stop by whenever, so I gathered everyone who was free. I thought it would be fun."

I instantly feel bad. This was such a thoughtful thing for Tori to organize. It's not her fault that they happened to arrive when I was in the middle of navigating a weird-as-hell conversation with Theo.

I glance over at Theo, who's still standing in the kitchen and waving at my family with a nervous smile on his face.

I think back to a minute ago when the single sentence he uttered threw me for a loop.

Hearing you last night was hot as fuck.

When he makes eye contact with me, I recognize that flash in his eyes. Without a doubt, he's thinking of what he said too.

I swallow back the flip in my stomach and focus back on Tori. I smile at her. "This is perfect timing. I'm so happy to see you guys. And thrilled that you brought food because I'm starving and don't feel like cooking."

She grins and stops to give me another hug. "That's from Millie. She says she's sorry she can't make it, but baby Evelyn is teething and had her up half the night."

I gesture to the kitchen. "Guys, this is Theo, Ingrid's cousin. Don't mind his shirtless state, he doesn't own any tops."

My family chuckles as they descend on Theo and bombard him with hugs and hellos. He excuses himself quickly and runs to his bedroom, emerging seconds later tugging a hoodie over his head. I take a slow, steadying breath before I hazard another glance at him. He's charming my loved ones with that devastatingly gorgeous smile and friendly chit-chat. When he catches eyes with me, he holds my gaze for an extra second before focusing back on my family.

And that's when I realize my skin is still on fire, but not because I'm embarrassed...

Hearing you last night was hot as fuck.

I swear, I will never, ever forget the low growl of Theo's voice when he spoke those words...

I shake my head. I can't think about that right now, not when my family is here.

But his words linger in the back of my mind the whole time.

Chapter 10

Theo

"Dude, that sucks about your knee," Maya's brother Tyler says to me as we all sit around the dining table and finish up breakfast.

"Yeah, it does." I try to smile.

He nudges my shoulder with his. "Hey, I remember that goal you scored early in the season against Toronto. The puck flew so fast into the net. If you blinked, you missed it. That was badass, man."

"He's right," Maya's other brother Gage adds. "That was the highlight of that game." Her cousin Austin and his husband Declan nod along.

"You'll be at it again soon," Tyler says. "You're an asset to the Bashers. They're probably counting down the days till you're back."

I hope my smile doesn't look as fake as it feels when I look at them all. "Thanks. Means a lot. But I'm nothing special. There's a million more talented guys in this sport."

Tyler smirks at me. "You seem to do pretty well for yourself, ladies man."

My stomach drops right along with my smile. I clear my throat. "Right..."

I can tell Tyler expects me to say more, but I can't. I'm too embarrassed. Because this is yet another example of just how much I've managed to fuck myself over. Here's another fan who can only focus on my sex life instead of my skill on the ice.

When I look over, I see Declan and Austin exchange a look. I notice Gage is frowning at his brother. My stomach twists. They all know my pathetic reputation. It's written on their faces.

Just great.

I hunch over in my chair, disheartened and angry at myself yet again. "I'm not really into that anymore," I say.

Tyler pauses. "Oh."

Everyone is quiet for a long moment.

"Trying to clean up your image?" Tyler chuckles.

Gage elbows him, but I tell him it's okay. As uncomfortable as this conversation is, I'm a grown man. I should be able to answer for all the messy and irresponsible shit I've done.

"Something like that." My cheeks go hot.

"Good for you," Tyler says in a chipper tone. "You know, if you really wanted to go all out, you should do something like rescue puppies and kittens. That's, like, Mr. Rogers-level of wholesome. People would be all over that... oof!"

Gage elbows Tyler again. As the two brothers quietly grumble at each other, I catch eyes with Maya, who's sitting on the opposite side of the table as me. I notice her gaze on me is focused, like she's trying to decipher something.

"Enough with your unsolicited life advice, Tyler," she says.

Becca and Tori nod along.

"When can we have a tour of the place?" Becca asks.

"When we clear the table and load the dishwasher," Maya says. Tyler, Austin, and Declan groan.

She rolls her eyes. "You guys are such whiners. Come on, the faster we get it done, the quicker you'll be able to see the heated deck Ingrid has."

That seems to be the motivation everyone needs because the kitchen and dining table are cleared in minutes. Maya leads everyone to the deck and I hang back to push in the chairs and wipe down the dining table. I glance over at Maya, who's now on the deck and pointing out the property to her family. They're looking at the small frozen pond and the small guest house in the back.

I think about how I brought up overhearing her last night. I scrub a hand over my cheek and bite back a groan just thinking about it. What the hell was I thinking telling her that?

Honestly, I wasn't going to. I planned to never, ever tell her that I heard her last night. But then she made that cute joke about me hibernating and I couldn't help but think of last night, specifically how well I slept after cranking one out to the sound of her...cranking one out.

I press my eyes shut, feeling the fire on my cheeks once more. I must have the world's worst poker face judging by how quickly Maya was able to figure out what I was trying to hide.

Guilt throttles me at how mortified she was when she realized I had overheard her touching herself. Embarrassment follows close behind when I remember admitting to her how hot it was...

Eyes still closed, I pinch the bridge of my nose and let out a breath. Fuck, I'm a dumbass. I actually thought that would make her feel better. Behind the darkness of my eyelids, I can picture perfectly Maya's shocked expression when I told her that. She looked horrified.

Can I blame her? Hell no. I just proved what an unbelievable perv I am.

The door to the deck opens and they all file back inside and crowd around the fireplace to warm up. I join them on the sectional.

Austin pulls Maya into a side hug. "Pretty cool gig you've got, cuz. Wanna trade? I've gotta teach thirty middle schoolers the Pythagorean Theorem tomorrow morning and I'd much rather hang out in this cozy place with Theo."

I flash a thumbs up at Austin as Maya laughs. "No way. Remember how I was always epically bad at math? Your students would be so screwed."

"So is this a new business venture for you? Housesitting?" Gage asks.

Maya shrugs. "Not sure."

I notice how Maya doesn't look at her brother when she answers him. Her shoulders stiffen the slightest bit too.

"Once this gig is up, you think you'll go back to San Diego with Ingrid?" Tyler asks.

Maya chucks a heavy log into the fire. "That's the plan."

Gage and Tyler exchange a look. Tyler's brow lifts and he looks like he's about to say something, but Gage shakes his head. Tyler raises an eyebrow at his brother and sighs.

"I made an appointment for you to get winter tires on your car," Gage says to Maya.

She looks surprised. "Why?"

"Because I knew you wouldn't have time since you moved back so quickly. Drop it off next Tuesday first thing in the morning at Linus Auto. Gary will take care of you."

She aims a tight smile. "Thanks."

Gage tilts his head at her. "Don't be mad. I'm your older brother. It's my job to look out for you."

Becca rests a hand on his arm. He looks at her and his expression softens instantly.

"I get that, Gage. I really do," Maya says. "And I appreciate it. But I'm twenty-seven years old. I can take care of myself."

"Could have fooled me," Tyler mutters under his breath.

"What was that?" Maya says sharply.

I notice both Tori and Becca's eyes go wide as they look between Maya and Tyler.

"Look, all I'm saying is that maybe you should have a little more focus when it comes to your career," Tyler says.

"Here's the thing, big brother: I didn't ask for you to give me career advice. Besides, you've had a slew of random jobs before you started working for Dad's business. Don't act like you're some white-collar hero."

I let a laugh slip at Maya's quip right as Gage speaks up to mediate his sister and brother.

"We're just trying to help you, Maya," Tyler says. "You're right, I was aimless too when I was younger. But now I'm trying to get serious about my career. You should too."

The siblings start up with their bickering, but Austin cuts in.

"Okay, okay." He holds up a hand. "Guys, I know you care about your sister and you mean well, but she's right. She can take care of herself. She's managed to make it this far into her life on her own. She doesn't need your unsolicited advice."

Maya aims a grateful look at her cousin as she loops her

arm around his and side-hugs him. Tyler grumbles but nods his understanding.

"You're right. We're sorry, Maya," Gage says to her.

She nods.

Tyler clears his throat. "Speaking of Dad, I'm pretty sure he and Mom are seeing each other."

He raises an eyebrow and looks like he's trying not to smirk as he makes pointed eye contact with his brother and sister. I take in their different reactions. Gage, who has the sternest resting face I've ever seen, actually seems kinda happy. He's not smiling, but the look in his eyes is bright.

I notice how Maya's angelic face is the exact opposite. She almost looks irritated.

Huh. Not sure the story behind that.

Austin turns to me. "Their parents have been divorced since they were kids. They seem to be reconnecting now."

"Ah. Interesting," I say.

"Especially when you know that their dad is famous TV chef Andre Thomas Grant," Austin says.

It takes a second for that name to register. The famous chef and restaurant owner.

"Seriously? That's your dad?" I say to Maya.

"Yup. The one and only."

"Damn, that's pretty cool."

"Yeah, kinda," Gage says. "He wasn't around much when we were kids, but he's trying to make up for it now."

"With Mom, especially," Tyler says. When he wags his eyebrows, Gage tosses a pillow at him.

"Try being mature. Just for one day, see how it feels," Gage says.

Tyler chuckles as Gage rolls his eyes. Maya shakes her head at her brothers before looking at me. "It's kinda weird, right? Hearing that your divorced parents are dating again and maybe getting back together?"

"I think it's kind of romantic, reconnecting after all those years," Becca says, a sweet smile tugging at her lips. Gage cracks a grin and swipes her hand in his and kisses the back of her knuckles. Her pale skin turns rosy as she beams at him.

"Yeah. Good for Dad if he can win Mom back," Tyler says through a groan as he reaches his hands up and stretches. I notice Tori sneak a peek at the lower part of his stomach, which is exposed due to his shirt riding up.

"We'll see how it all works out," Maya says, crossing her arms. I can't help but wonder why she seems so annoyed about her parents' reconciliation while her brothers are supportive. But I let the question die on my tongue. It's none of my business.

Becca offers to make everyone hot chocolate, and for the rest of the morning, we hang out and chat. Noon rolls around and everyone gets up to leave.

When Maya shuts and locks the front door, she turns to me. "Sorry about that," she says, the look in her eyes shy.

"Sorry about what?"

"My family dropping by unannounced. I know that's kind of annoying."

"It wasn't. They were nice. And your brother Gage and his girlfriend Becca are really good cooks. They can drop by whenever they want when they bring gourmet food like that with them."

Maya laughs, but then her expression turns hesitant. "Sorry my brother Tyler made that comment to you about your...personal life. He can be a real douche sometimes."

"It's alright. That's what people know me best for anyway. I can't be surprised when they say stuff like that."

She looks like she wants to say more, but instead, she just nods.

She starts to turn toward the hallway, but she stops. "Hey, um...what you said earlier...when you said that hearing me...do *that* last night was hot as fuck. Did you mean it?"

For a second I'm quiet. I'm shocked she brought it up.

"Of course I meant it."

"Okay..." She glances off to the side, like she's taking a second to collect herself.

"Is that okay?" I ask after a moment.

She shrugs.

"What does that mean?"

I ask.

"It means..." She doesn't break eye contact with me as she lets out a heavy breath. "It means that I'm surprised."

I snort out a laugh. She responds with a lethal frown.

"That's funny to you?" she asks sharply.

"No, it's just...Maya, you're insanely sexy. Don't you know that? Of course I'd think it's hot to hear you touch yourself. Anyone would feel the same way."

There's not an ounce of sarcasm, smugness, or cheeki-ness in my tone. I'm speaking in the most pointed, blunt voice ever. Because this is the most obvious fact I could ever state, and it blows me away how surprised Maya seems to be to hear it.

Her full cheeks go rosy and her doe eyes are wide as she takes in what I've said.

"I'm sorry if I made you feel embarrassed or self-conscious," I say after a moment. "I should have said that sooner. But I don't want you to feel ashamed about what you did."

Her eyes are wide and inquisitive as she looks at me, but

Sarah Smith

like before she says nothing. She just nods her understanding. "No guy I've ever been with has ever said that to me before."

Now it's my turn to feel shocked. What the hell kind of losers has Maya been with?

Something that feels a lot like anger bubbles up in my chest. Yeah, I know that Maya doesn't like me, but that doesn't matter right now. She doesn't deserve to be put down or made to feel like she's not good enough—not sexy or beautiful enough.

I let out a laugh of pure disbelief. "Well, Maya. Then every guy you've been with is a dipshit. You're hot as fuck. And that's not me trying to rile you up. That's me being honest. Any guy who made you feel anything less than the stunner you are didn't deserve you."

And then I walk past her and into my room, hoping that my words were enough to make her feel better.

Chapter 11

Maya

I hold my breath as Theo walks past me and goes into his bedroom.

My heart shouldn't be hammering in my chest. My skin shouldn't be hot to the touch. And my clit definitely shouldn't be pulsing right now.

But that's exactly what's happening. Because as much as Theo drives me nuts, my body is ridiculously turned on by him.

I quietly make my way to the guest room, shut the door behind me, and plop on my bed. I swipe my phone from my nightstand and do something I never thought I'd do in a million years: I stalk Theo's social media accounts.

When I pull up his Instagram, my eyes nearly pop out of my head. His most recent post is him standing in the snow wearing nothing but a pair of snow boots, his bare back and ass facing the camera, his arms in the air.

I sputter out a laugh when I read the caption.

Wishing you all a booty-ful morning ;)

And like the perv I am, I spend a dozen seconds

gawking at his muscular ass. I can't help it. That is one flaw-less backside.

I notice that the naked snow pic was taken right around Christmas. He hasn't posted since. I do a quick skim of his posts before then. He seemed to post regularly, every few days. There are loads of mid-action shots of him on the ice along with candids of him smiling and chatting while in his hockey uniform. I take in how hulking he looks all decked out in pads and skates. Theo is a tall and built guy without all that gear on, but when he's got it all on, he looks like a freaking unit.

I take in the dozen or so semi-nude pics of himself he's included in his Instagram grid. I smile to myself. Theo's Instagram page is pure sports and smut, and I dig it. And judging by the countless glowing comments on all of his posts, so do his fans and followers.

When I head over to TikTok and search him, my smile starts to fade. Almost every video that shows up in his search results is of Theo drunkenly stumbling out of a club or bar, always with a gorgeous woman—or two or three—on his arm.

I watch video after video of him alternating between drunken rambling and making out with whatever woman he's with. I make note that in each video, he's never with the same woman.

Heat flashes across my cheeks for the second time today, but for a completely different reason now.

Because now I realize that Theo's flattering words from earlier likely didn't mean as much as I thought they did.

Now I'm reminded that Theo is a playboy. I've got the video evidence right here on my phone. I'd bet anything that his comments about how hot he thought I sounded aren't anything to read into. He's a ladies' man. When he's not in self-imposed celibacy to save his career, he's with a different woman every night. I'd bet he pays those ladies similar compliments. As aggravating and cocky as he is, he's also a charmer. He could flirt the skirt off of any woman with zero effort. Of course, he'd be able to charm me with minimal effort—and of course, it would mean next to nothing to him to do that.

I toss my phone to the side, feeling so foolish. I'm an idiot for feeling special, for letting Theo's words charm me. I should have known better than to let myself read too much into what he said to me. He heard me masturbating and he thought it was hot. That's it. For a guy like Theo who's used to being with loads of beautiful women, that's probably as mundane as eating an apple or going for a walk.

I sigh, annoyed at how embarrassed and disappointed I feel.

Just then my phone buzzes with a text from Ingrid.

> Hey! Just checking in to make sure that you haven't murdered my cousin lol

I quickly type a response.

> Me: No worries, he's still alive

> Ingrid: Haha phew! I assumed he'd have done something to piss you off by now

I stare down at my phone, surprised at how things have changed. In a handful of days, I went from loathing Theo to feeling smitten with him.

Well, that stops right now. That was a fleeting crush I had, likely because I've seen him naked. He's undeniably sexy, but that's it. What I felt for him was purely physical attraction. Nothing more, nothing less. I've seen just how dispensable the women in his life are, and I can feel that physical attraction dimming as the seconds pass.

I reply to Ingrid.

> Me: He's definitely pissed me off, but that's nothing new. Don't worry, your place is in perfect condition!

Ingrid: You are THE BEST and I love you

Ingrid: You know, when I told my mom that you and Theo were staying together, she said she thought things between you two would get romantic in no time. Isn't that crazy? Never mind the fact that you can't stand him

A faint sinking feeling lands in my gut. I ignore it and text her back.

> I love your mom, but no way, I can guarantee that Theo and I will never, ever get together

Chapter 12

Theo

"Things just aren't the same without you, man," my teammate Xander says as he slides a beer bottle to me from across the rickety table at the dive bar we're at.

"No alcohol for me. Just water."

He looks at me like I've just told him I'm planning to drink battery acid for the rest of my life.

I point to my knee. "I've got PT in the morning. I've gotta hydrate."

Xander shrugs. "Suit yourself." He double-fists my beer along with his own.

"Coach Porter is way pissier after the stunt you pulled. Blomdahl showed up late to practice the other day and he made him do fifty laps around the ring. He was drenched in sweat," my other teammate Dylan says.

"It sucks, man. He's running us all ragged," Xander says.

I flash a smile before taking a long sip of ice water, hoping the ice-cold liquid eases the sting working its way down my throat and chest. "Told you that you'd miss me when I'm gone. And come on, you should be able to handle it, you young buck."

Xander laughs. At twenty-two, he's the superstar of the team. He was a first-round draft pick and consistently runs circles around everyone else. He's smug and cocky but he can play like hell.

"Seriously though, why'd you have to go and sleep with Estella?" Xander asks. "I mean, our assistant coach's wife? What were you thinking? Thank fuck Marquez isn't around anymore. He'd kick all our asses at practice too."

Shame heats my face. I'm embarrassed just thinking about what I did. It happened only weeks ago, but it's wild just how differently I feel about it now. I'd take it back if I could.

My teammate Isaac plops down with a handful of what looks like tequila shots. "I don't think Theo was doing much thinking, guys. At least not with his brain."

He crumples a napkin and tosses it at my junk, then cackles. The rest of our table joins in, roaring with laughter. I laugh along, despite that stinging sensation in my gut intensifying.

This isn't the first time my teammates have given me shit. We give each other shit constantly actually. But that was before I was kicked off the team—that was when I was still one of them, when I was still part of the group, playing the sport that means so much to me.

"How you faring now? Still thinking exclusively with your dick?" Isaac asks.

I roll my eyes and flip him off, which earns me a laugh from the table. "What do you think?"

"I think that I'd bet good money that you're still acting like a total man whore." He claps me on the shoulder. "That's what I'd be doing if I were in your shoes."

"Pretty sure your wife would hang you by your balls if you tried to pull that," I say.

He chuckles. "Yeah, she would." He grins down at the gold band on his ring finger. "God, I love her."

One of the servers drops off another round of shots at our table. Xander slides one to me, but I tell him no.

He tilts his head at me. "Dude, come on. One shot isn't going to kill you."

"Fine," I grumble. I down the tequila and wince. "Jesus, what the hell is this? Dog piss?"

Isaac frowns at me. "Look around. This place is worse than a dive bar. You think we're getting top-shelf tequila here?"

I glance around the dimly lit space of this basement bar on the edge of downtown Denver. It's half-full on this week-night, and even that's an impressive showing given the state of this place. Fake wood paneling lines the walls and the black-brown carpet is sticky, likely due to decades' worth of alcohol being spilled on it. Vomit too, probably. And piss. I count three flat screen TVs mounted above the bar, two of which don't work.

When I lean back in my wooden chair it makes a cracking noise. I tense up, fully expecting it to crumble under my weight.

"Why do we keep coming here?" I ask, taking a long pull from my water glass to erase the piss taste in my mouth.

"Because the drinks are cheap," Dylan says.

I scoff. "You're professional hockey players. You can afford to drink at a decent place."

He shrugs. "We've been coming here since we were rookies. Force of habit."

The rest of the guys nod along.

"The owner's cool too," Isaac says.

"You mean the old guy who looks like a deranged Santa that has never said more than two words to us even though we've all been coming here for the past handful of years?" Dylan asks.

"Yup," Isaac says. "He leaves us alone instead of every other place we've hit up, where the staff bombards us with annoying comments about how we played."

We all murmur in agreement. It's always irritating when we try to go out and unwind and people come up to us offering their two cents on our skills as players.

Isaac elbows me and smirks. "Seriously, though. Still going buck wild?"

"Nope," I say as I bat my empty glass between my hands.

The entire table starts to laugh until I frown at all of them.

"Oh. You're serious?" Dylan says.

I tell them what my agent told me: how my only chance at getting picked up again is to clean up my image.

When I take in the hesitant stares of my teammates, I glare at them. "Wow. Thanks for the vote of confidence, guys."

"No, hey, it's not like that," Dylan quickly says. "That's a, uh, noble goal, man."

I catch him frowning at everyone else at the table. They all clear their throats and offer jumbled encouragements.

"Good for you, man," Isaac says.

"Yeah, uh, way to be," Dylan adds.

I feel myself deflate at just how obvious it is that my former teammates don't think I can act like a decent person.

"Wow. Thanks," I mumble.

"We're serious," Isaac quickly says. They all start to offer encouraging comments, but I hold up a hand.

"I don't want to talk about this anymore." I turn to Dylan. "How's it feel to know you're gonna be a dad of twins in a few months?"

"I'm scared shitless." He downs another shot without even wincing.

"Aww come on, you'll be okay. You've been a stepdad for three years now," I say.

"Yeah, but that's different. I met Annabelle when she was a toddler, not a newborn. And she is a literal angel. I've got twins on the way. They're gonna annihilate me."

He gazes ahead at nothing in particular with a thousand-yard stare.

Isaac claps him on the knee. "Don't sweat it. Three kids are a piece of cake."

Dylan glowers at him. "Fuck off. You of all people know damn well it's not."

Isaac laughs. "I mean, it kind of is. Okay yeah, it feels like fucking chaos at first, trying to keep three babies alive all at once. But you get used to it. If I can handle being a dad of twins, anyone can. Even you."

Dylan looks barely comforted. He's still got that dazed look in his brown eyes. He ruffles his dark hair with a hand.

"The upside is that they're really cute," Isaac says. "It's kinda cool to see smaller, more adorable versions of yourself running around too. My twins are like my mini-mes. They've got my hair."

He laughs as he runs his hand over his short-buzzed blond hair. Dylan finally cracks a smile.

"You wish, baldy," he says.

Xander scrubs a hand over his beard. "Okay, all this talk about kids is freaking me out."

"That's because you're a twenty-two-year-old manchild

who can't remember to put on his skates properly most days."

Xander socks Isaac in the shoulder for his insult. Isaac laughs as he shoves him back.

"Someday you'll grow up and be like us," Isaac says to him.

Xander frowns while furiously shaking his head. "No way in hell."

Isaac and Dylan tell Xander all about the joys of sleepless nights, daycare drop-offs, tantrums, and poopy diapers.

Xander cups his hands over his ears. "Christ, that's enough."

I laugh. Xander shakes his head at me. "Why don't you throw some of this Theo's way? He's the one who wants to look mature and grown-up. Kids are the fastest way to do that."

Once again the entire table is roaring and I'm sitting there, shocked at their reaction. Is the thought of me as a parent really that laughable?

"Aww come on, dude. We're just fucking with you." Isaac shoves my shoulder.

I chuckle like I get it, but it takes a second for the sting to fade. Okay yeah, I'm nowhere near ready to have kids right now...but I always thought that maybe someday I might. But given the way my teammates cackled at the thought of me with kids, maybe I shouldn't even think about it.

Xander leaves to get another round. When he returns, he's back with three college-age women.

I turn away to chat with Dylan and Isaac, but then I feel a tap on my shoulder. I turn and see one of the women aiming a coy smile at me.

"Hey. You play hockey too, right?" The pretty blonde

runs her fingers along my arm, clearly interested. Before my career was in freefall, I would have flirted back. But right now all it does is make me want to pull away.

But it's more than just wanting my career back. The thought of hooking up with someone I barely know doesn't even sound like fun anymore.

Maya's beautiful face flashes in my mind. Yeah, sometimes she can barely stand me, but we're starting to get along. And we managed to navigate the awkwardness of me admitting that I overheard her touching herself without her murdering me.

Even though I know I shouldn't, I think back to that moment, how hot it was...

I can't deny the effect that being around Maya is having on me. For starters, she's smoking hot...and she can kiss like a demon. And yeah, we bicker, but I honestly like that. I fucking love it when a woman gives me shit. It's a weird turn-on, but whatever. I like what I like.

Just then my mind flashes a filthy image: Maya in my face, yelling at me, right before grabbing me hard by the jaw and kissing me.

Without a doubt, I'd rather jerk off to that fantasy or the memory of Maya's sexy moans than hook up with a stranger.

I clear my throat and slowly slide my arm out from under this blonde's candy apple-red nails. I look her in the eye and offer a polite smile. "I don't play hockey anymore."

Before she answers I stand up and drop some cash on the table. I tell my teammates I'm calling it a night. Isaac and Dylan get up to join me, leaving Xander alone with the trio of ladies. Through a smug smile, he tells us all goodnight.

"Never thought I'd see the day you walked away from

free alcohol *and* a table of beautiful women," Isaac says as we climb the stairs to the exit.

"You just did. Get used to it," I say.

We enter the street and round the corner. We're not even to the end of the block when some dude aims a camera at us.

"Yo, Theo Thompson! Is that you leaving a bar without a lady friend? Holy shit, has hell frozen over?"

I purse my lips and stay quiet, even though I'd love to cuss out this annoying paparazzi. I don't want to end up trending on social media for acting like a hothead. That would interfere with my plan of reforming my image.

"Just having a quiet night with friends," I say as the three of us walk ahead.

"Theo Thompson acting like a quiet little choir boy? Oh man, I never thought I'd see the day," the paparazzi says. "Guess you're a changed man then?"

"Yup," I say curtly while staring straight ahead. I notice Isaac and Dylan giving me sympathetic looks, as if to silently tell me I'm doing a good job of not going off on this guy.

"Ah, I see, trying to act like a good boy so you can play for your team again, right?" the guy taunts.

Isaac stops and glares at him. "Dude, don't be a dick."

"Whoa, hey. No need to get testy. I was just asking some questions," the guy says with a smirk.

We continue walking but he keeps following us. "What's your backup plan if the new good boy act doesn't pan out? Opening up an orphanage? Maybe an animal rescue?"

When the paparazzi guy cackles, it singes my last nerve. Maybe it's because everyone from my friends and team- mates to this stranger thinks it's a complete joke that I could be good at anything other than hockey, partying, and fucking.

I stop walking and turn to face the guy. His brow hits his hairline and his eyes go wide as he looks at me.

"I'm doing volunteer work now."

"R-Really?" he says.

"Yup." Out of the corner of my eye, I see Dylan and Isaac exchange a look.

"Oh. That's...unexpected." The paparazzi guy stands there awkwardly with his camera aimed at me for another few seconds before walking off.

"You were joking, right?" Dylan says to me.

I turn to him and Isaac. A wave of raw determination pummels my insides. It finally registers: maybe it's time to show people that I can be different. That I can be better than what I was.

"I'm dead serious. I wanna start a hockey camp for kids," I say to my former teammates who are both staring at me like I've sprouted a third head. "And I'm gonna need your help to do it."

Chapter 13

Maya

"Hey. I have a favor to ask you," Theo says when he walks in the front door.

I look up from scrolling on my phone while sitting on the couch, wrapped in a fuzzy blanket. "No 'hello?'"

I take in his uncertain facial expression as he tugs a hand through his sandy blond hair.

"Oh, uh, sorry," he mumbles. "Hello."

"I was kidding. What's going on with you? Is everything okay?"

He hesitates. "Yeah, fine. Actually, that's a lie. It's not fine. I'm going to ask you something and I really, really need you to say yes."

I scoff. "I'm not agreeing to that. What happened tonight? I thought you were just going out for a catch-up with your teammates. You look all panicked and flustered."

He rips off his parka and hangs it in the nearby coat closet before walking over to the couch where I'm sitting. He lowers himself onto the arm. "Okay, listen. I have this idea. You're gonna think it's ridiculous. But I need you on board."

He rests his palms on his knees and takes a breath. It catches me off guard. I'm not used to seeing Theo like this. He's normally so smug and cocky and smooth. Right now he looks...nervous.

"I want to start a hockey camp for kids," he finally says.

"Oh..." I don't say anything for several seconds. "Wait, you're serious?"

"Dead serious." I take in how the hope in his gaze fades.

"That's great," I say quickly. "Sorry, I just wasn't expecting..."

When I notice a flash of uncertainty in his blue eyes, I stop myself. I sound like a jerk. Theo is the last person on the planet that I'd ever think would do something like this, but I shouldn't tell him that. That's a shitty and hurtful thing to say.

"Seriously, Theo. That's wonderful. Good for you for wanting to work with kids." I smile at him, but his worried frown remains.

"I want to host it here, at Ingrid's place. On the frozen pond in the back of the property, by the guest house."

He gestures to the massive floor-to-ceiling window on the far side of the living room. The guest house is barely visible in the blue-black sky since it's so late at night. A few seconds of staring and I can make out the snow-covered roof. I glance over at the pond, where the reflection of the full moon shines bright on the frozen surface.

"Oh..."

"And I need you to help me convince Ingrid to let me do it here," he says.

I hesitate. "I don't know. You know how much your

cousin loves her place. I'm not sure if she'd be okay with having a bunch of little kids around—"

"And I need you to help me run the program," he blurts.

I'm speechless. I wasn't expecting him to say that either.

"Theo, I don't know the first thing about coaching hockey."

"I know," he says, holding up a hand, like he knows he's made a ridiculous request. "Look, I know this is a huge request, but..." He pauses like he's taking a moment to collect whatever thoughts are racing in his head. "Ingrid told me that you used to work at a daycare so you have a lot of experience with kids."

I let out an exasperated laugh. "That was almost ten years ago, in high school. And I only worked there for, like, four months."

"That's still four more months of experience than I have. You're practically an expert compared to me," he says, his hurried tone verging on desperate.

"Then why did you come up with this idea in the first place when you don't even know what you're doing?"

His broad shoulders slump and he gazes off to the side, out the massive floor-to-ceiling window on the far side of the living room. When he looks back at me, I'm jolted by the expression on his face. He looks so sad and defeated.

"Maya, people think I'm a joke. They think I'm nothing more than a hockey player who parties and fucks a lot. It's kind of hurtful."

I'm taken aback at the blunt way he describes himself. He seems so vulnerable and stripped down right now. It's so different from the cocky charmer I'm used to seeing.

I think about his social media posts that I saw, how his overall vibe is smug, fun-loving, party boy pro athlete. I wonder how much of that is truly who he is...and how much of Theo is this different side he's showing me now.

"I know that's my fault. I was an irresponsible dipshit for a long time. I only cared about hockey and having a good time." He clears his throat, the look in his eyes shy, like he's embarrassed. "I was pretty reckless and it never occurred to me that I shouldn't be because I never had to take anything other than hockey seriously in my life. And, um, well, now I'm paying the price for that, and I've got no one to blame but myself. I can't get away with the crap I used to. But honestly, I don't want to. I want to be better. I want to show people that I can be more than the worst of what they think of me."

He goes quiet for a moment. "I've always thought it would be fun to work with kids. It's just...no one's ever asked me to. They've always thought I wasn't responsible enough, wasn't good enough."

Something about the way he's talking to me hits deep. That cocky jokester façade is gone. He's being so raw and honest right now. And honestly? I can relate to how he feels. I know what it's like to have people write me off as flaky and vapid. For the past several years I've jumped from job to job, city to city, without any real plans or goals, just floating around, waiting for something to stick. And people think I'm a joke because of it. They think that I'll never amount to anything, that I'll never be successful or have a meaningful career. And I fucking hate it.

That surge of empathy I feel for Theo slowly morphs into determination.

"Okay. I'm in."

Theo's brow jerks up in disbelief. "You are?"

I nod. "I don't know what it's like to be in your position. But I know how it feels to have people write you off as someone to not take seriously." My gaze falls to my lap as I go quiet. "It really sucks. And it makes you want to prove everyone wrong."

I glance up and see Theo looking at me, sincerity shining in his blue eyes. "You too, huh?"

I nod. "I'm the free spirit of the family. Always moving and traveling. I never keep a job or an apartment for very long. Never mind that I've always managed to support myself. Almost everyone kind of writes me off as a flake because I choose to live my life differently. My brothers constantly worry about me."

Theo nods. "I kinda picked up on that when your family came over for breakfast the other day."

"I know they mean well, but it feels a little insulting in a way. Like my own brothers don't trust that I can take care of myself. They don't take me seriously. No one other than Ingrid and my close friends do."

I silently admit to myself that this is ultimately why I'm scared shitless to start my own earring business. I'll inevitably mess something up or lose interest or something will go wrong. And my entire family will be there to roll their eyes at me or lecture me or tell me, "Told you so. Now go get a real job."

Theo raises an eyebrow at me. "You're serious as hell, Maya. You're running a tight ship here at Ingrid's. I know not to step out of line."

I chuckle. "Thanks."

A quiet moment passes between us. The look in Theo's eyes turns determined. "We can do this, Maya. We can prove everyone wrong."

I'm more determined than ever. "I'll call Ingrid right now."

He grins. "You will?"

"Yeah. I'll do my best to convince her, but I can't make any promises. This is her place and what she says goes."

A hopeful smile tugs at Theo's gorgeous plump lips. "Of course, I understand. I just...thank you, Maya."

I let a small smile free. "Sure."

Theo gets up and heads to his bedroom. I pick up my phone, pull up Ingrid's number, and take a breath. Here goes nothing.

* * *

"I think that's a brilliant idea!" Ingrid practically squeals on the other line.

"...You do?" I'm shocked. I thought she'd be a hard no at having a bunch of kids running around her place.

"Yes! Oh my gosh, Maya babes, this is so wonderful. This means that Theo is taking this opportunity to rehab his image seriously."

"Yeah, I mean, that's what it seems like."

"And the fact that you two would work together on this is pretty freaking amazing."

"Is it?"

"Of course it is! You two are like oil and water. You can't stand him, so if even you believe he can pull this off, then he's clearly on the right track. You have my full support."

"Wow. Thanks, Ingrid."

"Just please don't let the kids destroy my house. Or the guest house." She gasps. "Don't let them in the guest house, okay? I still haven't put away the decorations from Kiley's bachelorette party last month."

"Oh crap..." I trail off, remembering how we left her guest house looking like a scene straight out of *Magic Mike*.

"Promise the kids won't go in there. And I promise your place will be intact."

"Maya, you're seriously amazing. Just a couple weeks of my cousin being around you and look what a good influence you've been on him. He's volunteering with kids. Never in a million years did I ever think he'd do that."

Pride swells in my chest even though I have no right to feel that way. This was one hundred percent Theo's idea. I had nothing to do with it.

When I tell Ingrid those exact words, she makes a scoffing noise.

"Whether you realize it or not, you're having an impact on Theo," she says before saying she has to go.

"I've got a Zoom meeting with a company in Hong Kong. I'll talk to you later, okay? And keep me posted on the kids' hockey program! I wanna see how it all goes."

I promise her that I will and we hang up. And then I head to Theo's room to tell him the good news. Before I even knock, the door swings open.

"What'd she say?" he says, breathless with anticipation.

I grin. "She's all for it."

He lets out a "woo hoo!" before scooping me up and swinging me around. I can't help but laugh and squeal. My hands fall to his shoulders to steady myself and I pause. Whoa...that's some solid muscle right there.

When he stills and gazes at me. "Thank you for making this happen. I owe you."

The low growl of his voice catches me off guard. That's when I realize how tightly he's holding me...and that his arms are braced around my ass.

Our gazes are locked as I hold my breath. A hard swallow moves down the length of his thick, throat. For a second all I can focus on is the feel of his hard, firm body against mine, how good it feels...

"We should start planning," he says.

I snap out of whatever dreamy daze I was just in. "Right."

I start to wiggle and he sets me down, then follows me out to the living room. I pull up my laptop and for the rest of the evening, we hammer out all the details...and all the while I ignore that borderline sexy moment that just passed between us. We're housemates *and* coworkers now, nothing more.

Chapter 14

Theo

"Don't be nervous."

Maya's comment catches me off guard as zip my coat up.

"I'm not nervous," I mutter.

I grab my skates and throw the bag of equipment over my shoulder, then head down toward the pond.

"You've checked your phone about a million times this morning," she says while walking behind me. "Don't worry, they'll show up."

I huff out a breath, focusing on the sound of the snow crunching under our boots as we walk toward the frozen small pond at the end of Ingrid's property.

"Hey," she says softly before gently grabbing my wrist and stopping me in my tracks.

She pulls me to face her. I take in the way her deep brown eyes shine with sincerity.

"I mean it. You've played hundreds of games in front of thousands of hockey fans shouting at you. This is playtime with a half-dozen kids. It'll be easy and fun." Maya offers a small, sweet smile that quells the churn of nerves in my stomach.

Together we walk the rest of the way to the pond, unload the bag, and get all the equipment set up.

My instinct when I'm feeling nervous or uncertain is to joke, but I don't want to do that right now, not when Maya is being so kind and supportive.

I look over to where she's setting up tiny orange cones along the edge of the frozen pond a handful of feet away from me.

"I guess it is kind of weird that playing in front of a packed stadium doesn't unnerve me, but the thought of screwing up in front of these kids does." I let out a nervous laugh.

Maya looks up from her spot and offers yet another kind and reassuring smile that sets my nerves at ease...and does something strange to the center of my chest.

"It's not weird," she says. "It's what you're used to."

I move to set up the tiny goal that I brought down earlier in the morning at the edge of the pond. "I just want this to go well. How much of an asshole would I look like after begging my teammates to bring their kids to this weekend hockey camp and their kids end up hating it? Or what if something goes wrong? I've got a lot riding on this."

When I look up, Maya is staring at me with a thoughtful expression.

"What?"

She shakes her head and looks down, a small smile on her face. "Nothing."

"No, tell me."

She pauses for a second. "It's just...I thought that you were going to say how worried you are about how this will affect your image. But you want this to be good for the kids."

"Yeah. I do." I tug at the stocking cap I'm wearing. Does admitting that make me sound like a dork? Probably. But it's how I feel.

She smiles at me. "I think it's really sweet how much you care about making this camp good for the kids."

Her sweet words send warmth through me, despite the cold temperature.

She checks her phone. "Kids are due for drop-off in a few minutes. We should head back to the house."

We walk up the path together.

"If you had gone to a camp like this when you were a little kid, would you have cared if the coach was prepared?" she asks. "I bet all you would have cared about is having fun with your friends."

I smile at Maya's question. "I wouldn't have wanted to go to hockey camp when I was a little kid."

"Really?"

I nod. "I didn't start playing hockey until middle school."

"I guess I just figured all pro athletes played their sport since they were barely able to walk. Shows how much I know." She chuckles.

"Definitely wasn't the case for me. Though I'd been ice skating since I was pretty little."

"Did you skate with Ingrid a lot growing up?"

"Yeah. That's why we ended up being so close. None of her other siblings ever wanted to go ice skating with her and I was always up for it. Plus we're only a year apart in age, so we were close to begin with."

"I took ice skating lessons with Ingrid for a year when we were kids," Maya says. "We both got told off almost every lesson for being lazy with our spins. And talking while we were supposed to be listening to the instructor."

I chuckle at the thought of Ingrid and Maya getting in trouble at that age.

"Did you play other winter sports then?" she asks.

"Kinda." I smile at the snow-covered ground. "You'd laugh if I told you what I was into at that age."

"What? Investment banking?"

I snort out a laugh. "Horrible guess."

When I look over at Maya, she narrows her gaze like she's studying me. "Ice fishing."

"Nope."

"Curling?"

"Wrong again."

She pauses. "I've gotta be close."

"You'll never guess it."

Two more wrong guesses later, Maya lets out an exasperated laugh. We reach the back deck of Ingrid's place and walk up the stairs.

"Okay, I give up." She stops when we reach the deck. "What weird and random winter sport were you into as a kid?"

"Dog sledding."

She gawks at me. "No way."

"I swear. My favorite thing to do was go on dog sled rides with our grandpa. One of his brothers ran a dog sledding tour in Aspen, and our grandpa helped out with it. Of all the businesses he ran, that was his favorite one, so he spent a lot of time there."

I tell Maya that I used to spend most weekends and winter breaks with my grandpa.

"I'd help the workers feed the dogs and groom them, clean their kennels, and go for sled rides. It was awesome."

Just thinking about those memories makes me smile.

"Okay, the image of you as a little kid playing with a bunch of huskies is pretty freaking adorable."

Maybe it's ridiculous, but hearing Maya, who used to hate my guts, call me adorable makes me feel pretty damn good.

"I mean, I was a pretty cute kid. I can show you pictures."

She laughs. "So have you been able to get back on the sled lately?"

A pang of sadness hits me. I shake my head. "My grandpa passed away from a heart attack when I was still pretty young. His brother eventually sold the business a couple of years later and I haven't been dog sledding since."

Maya's face falls. "I'm so sorry."

"It's okay. That was a long time ago."

She touches my arm. Despite the layers of winter clothing between us, I swear I can feel the warmth of her hand, and...it honestly feels really good. Comforting. Like she truly cares about me in this moment.

"I'm sorry you lost your grandpa when you were so young."

I take in the sadness and sincerity in Maya's eyes, how she's standing here with me, feeling for me—feeling for my loss, even though it was more than twenty years ago.

And something about that, the fact that she's taking the time to acknowledge my loss, lands deep.

"Thanks, Maya."

We walk through the glass doors into Ingrid's house.

"Would you ever want to go dog sledding again? Or would it be too hard with your grandpa gone?" Maya asks as she unzips her coat. Her tone is soft, like she's hesitant to ask me.

That emotion swirling inside of me deepens. It's like

she's trying her hardest to handle my feelings with so much care.

For a second, I just stand there and soak it in. I'm not used to people talking to me like this—like they care about my feelings. Most days it's coaches yelling at me or joking around with my teammates or flirting with women I barely know.

But this conversation with Maya hits differently in the best way. She's asking about my life like she truly wants to get to know me.

She frowns slightly as she looks at me and shakes her head. "Sorry, that was probably really weird for me to ask you that."

"It's not at all. It means a lot that you'd care to ask me."

She looks relieved. That intense feeling inside of me eases. And then I realize why: I made her feel better, and it feels good to know that I could comfort her in some small way.

"I'd love to go dog sledding again sometime," I say, feeling light and happy as I say it. "I just haven't made the time. I got started with hockey and that kind of took over my life. But I should probably look into going dog-sledding again. That would be nice."

A small smile tugs at her lips. "You should."

As we stand there and look at each other, the air between us feels different. Charged, but in a good way. Like we crossed some sort of threshold by talking about something so personal and important to me.

Just then the doorbell rings. Maya turns to the door before looking back at me and smiling.

"Looks like the kids are here. You ready, Coach Theo?"

"I'm ready."

* * *

I take in the chaotic scene in front of me: five elementary-school-aged kids are decked out in winter wear and ice skates, racing around the frozen pond like they each have a death wish.

Exactly one minute ago, I led the group of kids out here and started going over the drills I wanted them to try out, but as soon as they got their skates on, the kids took off.

My heart races as I watch two of them nearly collide while flying across the pond at lightning speed. Another pair is playing tag and giggling as they bump into another kid who's standing in the middle of the pond staring up at the sky.

The nerves I managed to ward off earlier in the morning are back in full force, like a rogue wave annihilating a shoreline. Fuck. We're not even five minutes into the day and I'm on the verge of losing every single one of these kids to some catastrophic accident.

One kid attempts to jump two of the orange cones but trips and falls face-first into the nearby snow bank. I start to rush over to check on him, but Maya beats me over there and pulls him out of the snow bank. When I see the kid giggling, I let out a breath of relief. I need to get this under control now.

"Stop!" All the kids freeze at my monster shout. Five pairs of eyes look at me, clearly frightened. Shit. I was way too harsh with that.

I clear my throat and force a smile that, judging from the still freaked-out faces of all the kids, looks more deranged than friendly.

"Who's ready for some hockey drills?" I say in the most awkward fake cheery tone I've ever attempted.

Dead silence. Even Maya is looking at me with a confused expression.

"I've got some cool activities planned today for guys," I say. "First, we'll do laps around the pond, then I'll teach you how to shoot a goal, and then we'll..."

One of the kids—the one who fell head-first into the snowbank—raises his hand.

"Uh..." It takes a second for me to remember his name. "Yeah, Parker?"

He sniffles before wiping his nose with the back of his mitten. "But...I wanna dive in the snow some more."

"You do?" I ask, dumbfounded.

He nods.

"Okay, um, maybe we can save that for—"

"I wanna do spins," says Annabelle, my teammate Dylan's stepdaughter. She's wearing a hot pink glittery stocking cap and matching gloves. "Mommy and Dylan said I could do all the spins I wanted if I came here today."

"Oh. Well, that's..."

"Mommy says that hockey is a cash cow and that once Daddy retires from playing, he's screwed. Is that true?"

I stand there with my mouth open at the random-ass question the kid standing next to Parker just asked.

"I don't know if that's—"

Just then Maya comes up and stands next to me. "How about we kick things off with a fun skate? You guys keep skating around the pond however you want. Just be careful to give each other enough space so you don't bump into each other and get hurt. Does that sound good?"

All the kids tell her yeah.

"And then after that, we'll have snacks and rest time and Theo will show you some cool hockey tricks. Do you wanna see his super cool trick shot?"

The kids offer a resounding "yeah!"

She smiles and flashes a thumbs-up before telling them to go ahead with fun skate. They go back to playing and laughing and screeching.

All I can do is just stand there and look at her in complete awe. In less than a minute she completely turned this disaster around. And she did it in a way that was appealing and fun-sounding to the kids. No way could I have managed that.

I think back to the brunch with her family all those days ago, how her brother Tyler made those comments about her acting unfocused and aimless in her job history. He's got the wrong idea about her because there was nothing aimless and unfocused about how she took control of this situation.

I let out a breath and turn to Maya. "I guess it was a good idea for you to bring me on after all," she teases.

"That's an understatement. You saved my ass."

She shrugs. "Sometimes it's best to lean into the chaos."

I glance over at the kids, who are skating and screaming and laughing and playing. "You're right about that." I shove my gloved hands into my pockets and laugh. "God, what was I thinking? Did I honestly think that a group of five- and six-year-olds would be able to run through structured hockey drills for four hours?"

I shake my head. Maya pats my shoulder. "They'll get there eventually. They just need to get some of their energy out first, eat some food, then they'll be good to go."

Three hours later, after skating and playing and the kids have had a snack along with rest time and a bathroom break, they're calmer. We're back down at the pond and the kids are standing around me, watching as I pick up a puck with my hockey stick and tap it a dozen times in the air before shooting it across the pond and into the net I set up.

When all the kids let out a collective, "Whoa..." I laugh.

Half the kids shout that they want to learn how to do it. Maya and I grab the gear bags we brought down and dump out a bunch of sticks and pucks. For the rest of the hour we have left, I'm able to work with each of the kids and show them how to balance the pucks and tap them on their sticks while Maya takes photos and videos to send to their parents.

Maya announces that it's 1 p.m., meaning it's the end of day one of hockey camp.

"Everyone, let's pack up and get ready for your moms and dads to come get you," she says.

When most of the kids go "aww" with disappointment, I feel a tug of joy in my chest.

"But I wanna play for longer," Annabelle says.

I smile down at her and lightly pat her shoulder. "We'll play some more tomorrow."

She perks up at what I've said. Parker fist-pumps the air. The rest are smiling at the thought of coming back. Damn. I think that means they liked spending their day here with me and Maya. Despite how I completely fucked up the first part of the day, they still had a good time. And they're even looking forward to coming back.

As I let the shock of that realization work through me, I help the kids pack up their things and lead them back up to the house. Maya brews up some hot cocoa for everyone to drink while they wait for their parents to pick them up. A few of them notice Mr. Pudding the betta fish, and I show them how to feed him. When the last kid leaves, I shut the front door, spin around, and fall back-first into the door. Maya laughs.

"Holy shit." I huff out a breath. "We did it."

She walks over and high-fives me. "We pulled it off. Day one of hockey camp is in the books. And judging by how the kids responded, they enjoyed it and are excited to come back tomorrow."

I push off the door and glance around, smiling to myself. "I can't believe it."

Just then the text alert on Maya's phone goes off. She beams at her screen before showing it to me. I quickly read the texts.

> Parker said he had the best time and can't wait to come back tomorrow!

Another text pops up, this one from Dylan. Maya and I read it together.

> Annabelle can't wait for tomorrow. Can't thank you enough for setting up such a fun weekend camp, man. This is a godsend, she hates every other activity we've signed her up for.

My phone buzzes with a text, this time from my teammate Isaac's wife.

> Sloane and Emerson won't stop talking about how much fun they had. They're excited to show me the cool trick Coach Theo showed them lol. And they've said about five times that Coach Maya makes the best hot cocoa.

I'm grinning so wide my cheeks hurt. I look at Maya, who's beaming.

I feel a weird pull in my chest. It's not just because I'm stunned at how beautiful she looks when she's happy. It's more than that. It's the fact that working together with her was a blast today and I can't wait to do it again tomorrow, and every other weekend for the next two months that we scheduled for this hockey camp.

It's how much I like being around her. It's how, despite how much she couldn't stand me before, she agreed to help me with this camp.

Like she cares about me.

The longer that thought bounces around in my head, the more that pull in my chest intensifies.

I clear my throat as I look at her. "Hey, um, thanks again for saving the day today. It would have been a disaster without you."

For a moment she looks surprised. Maybe it's because of how soft and low my voice is. But I want her to know that I mean it.

A rosy flush paints her beautiful tan complexion. Her eyes are shy. "It was nothing."

"Maya, it was everything. Can you imagine what would have happened if you weren't here to take control of this morning? I would have had five kids screaming and crying through hockey drills. This camp wouldn't have lasted more than today because I'm certain their parents wouldn't let them come back."

She chuckles. "Okay, but you had them hypnotized with your stick tricks. I couldn't compete with that."

"My stick tricks pale in comparison to your hot cocoa."

This time when she laughs, I take a second to savor the sound, how light and joyful it is. We both go quiet for a moment as we look at each other. I notice that even though we've put away our phones, we're still standing close to each other. So close that I can count the light gold-brown freckles on the bridge of her nose. So close that I can breathe in that vanilla-rose scent she's wearing. Christ, it's intoxicating.

Maya bites her bottom lip. "I should call Ingrid. She's dying to know how day one of hockey camp went."

I nod, shaking myself out of my stupor. "Absolutely. I've gotta run to make my physical therapy appointment."

"Cool." Maya gives a soft smile, her gaze on me lingering and focused. A second later she walks toward her bedroom, but I can swear there was something in her look… like she could sense a shift between us too.

During the drive to physical therapy, all I can think about is that look.

Chapter 15

Maya

I watch as Theo leads the kids in a skating conga line around the perimeter of the pond. I can't help but laugh. It's so cute and sweet and funny to watch him be so goofy and playful around the kids.

He shimmies his hips to the beat of the Kidz Bop version of Cardi B's "I Like It Like That" blaring at full blast from his phone. He rounds the curve of the pond, careful to keep a slower pace so the kids can keep up with him.

"Okay guys, arms up high! Like you're touching the sky!" he says. Five pairs of tiny arms reach up.

I snap a photo and send it to the group text I have with all the parents of the kids that attend the camp.

> We're doing a musical conga line as part of this morning's fun skate!

They send back glowing compliments and heart emojis.

> So cute!

> Awww!!!

Wow, Theo is so great with the kids!

The longer I watch Theo play with the kids, the weaker my limbs feel. It's the second weekend of hockey camp and Theo is thriving as the kids' coach. And every time I see him in his element, whether it's leading them in a fun and silly playtime or patiently teaching them some cool hockey move, I'm on the verge of swooning. There's just something so freaking attractive about a guy who's good with kids—and I don't even know if I want kids.

For a second, I think about how confusing that is. But I guess it makes sense. When a guy can be patient and doting with kids, it shows that they can be sweet and sensitive. And that's hot as hell.

Plus, he's *literally* hot as hell.

My gaze glides down the length of his body. He's wearing a parka, beanie, scarf, and gloves since it's the middle of winter, but all the fabric does little to hide how tall, broad, and muscular he is.

And I've got the image of his sculpted form in all its naked glory seared in my memory from that one time I walked in on him...

I shake my head and feel ashamed that I've allowed such a dirty thought to enter my mind. There are kids around, for crying out loud. And I shouldn't be having these thoughts about Theo of all people. Even now when I think about it, I can hardly believe it. I mean, it's Theo—the guy who I couldn't stand weeks ago. The guy who I've loathed since the day I met him years ago because he's cocky and never misses an opportunity to give me a hard time.

But I'd be lying if I said I still feel that way about him. Yeah, we still bicker...but it's more like fun-loving teasing.

Now that we're living and working together, I actually like him and consider him a friend.

I think back to the first day of hockey camp when Theo was flustered after the kids admitted they wanted to play around instead of doing hockey drills. He looked to me for guidance—he let me take the lead. He took me seriously. And god, did that feel good.

I've lost track of the number of times people have doubted me and wrote me off as a flake who had no idea what I was doing. Not Theo. On that day—and every day that we've worked together at this hockey camp—he's let me take the lead on so many things. He asks for my opinion when it comes to planning activities and coming up with back-up plans. He doesn't assume I'll drop the ball or flake out or lose interest. He has confidence in my work ethic and my abilities. And that's given me a level of confidence I've never had before.

That warmth in my chest intensifies. He is amazing.

The song ends, pulling me out of my thoughts.

"Who's ready for a snack?" Theo says.

"Me!" the kids shout in unison. I lead them back up to the house, and Theo and I help them out of their winter outwear. While Theo gets them seated in the living room, I get to work plating up peanut butter and jelly sandwiches and hot apple cider.

While the kids chat and eat, Theo and I stand at the kitchen island and drink mugs of tea.

"You were pretty adorable out there," I say to him.

He chuckles and quirks a thick sandy blond eyebrow. "Adorable, huh?"

I laugh. "I just mean that you were really great with the kids. Music conga line skate has become a favorite activity."

"It was your idea. I owe it all to you." He grins at me. There go my limbs feeling weak again.

Just then one of the kids stands up and looks over at us.

"You want another sandwich square, Parker?" I ask.

"Yes, please!"

Theo walks over and drops off another square for him. He asks what kind of hockey tricks they feel like working on after snack time, and Annabelle is the first to answer.

"I wanna do a spin holding two hockey sticks!" she says.

"Yeah, that sounds fun!" Parker says.

A couple of other kids complain that they don't know how to do a spin.

"It's okay, I can show you," I say.

Theo squints at me. "Really? I thought you were terrible at those," he teases.

I tilt my head at him. "I know when to mess around and when to get serious."

"Well, damn. Show me up then, Coach Maya," he says with a smirk.

"Coach Theo. You shouldn't say that word. It's naughty," Sloane says in a low, scolding voice.

I bite back a chuckle as I watch Theo fight a smile. "You're right, Sloane. I'm sorry. I won't say it again," he says in a sweet but serious tone. "How about when we finish up, we'll head back down and Coach Maya can show us her spins?"

All the kids excitedly agree, which makes me happy. Maybe it's silly, but it feels really good to have a group of kids look up to me who are so eager to learn.

Twenty minutes later we're back at the pond, and I'm helping a few kids spin on their ice skates.

"Wow, look at you all go! Amazing job!" I cheer them on. I look up and catch Theo watching me.

"So cute," he mouths to me, and I chuckle. I look over at the kids around me and he's right, it's pretty darn cute to see a handful of children spinning in their ice skates.

Camp ends that day in the adorable chaos of five little kids rotating like spin tops while holding and dropping hockey sticks.

"Incredible, guys! Stellar stick skills for sure," Theo cheers.

Sloane's twin sister wobbles on her skates, loses grip of her stick, and it goes flying, nearly hitting Theo in the leg, but he jumps to the side just in time.

I double over in laughter.

Theo chuckles. "Whoa. You almost took me out there, Emerson. Did you learn that move from your dad? You should think about taking up hockey."

Theo and I cheer them on until the end of the camp, then lead them back up to the house to get them ready for pickup. A weather alert pops up on my phone, forecasting rain tomorrow.

I frown at my screen and show Theo. "Shoot. We might have to cancel camp tomorrow if the weather's gonna be crummy."

A chorus of sad noises follow. I look up and realize that all the kids heard me.

"But I don't wanna miss hockey camp," Emerson whines.

"Yeah, me either," Annabelle says.

"I know guys, but if it's raining, it won't be safe to skate on the pond," I say. I silently curse myself for talking about the weather in front of them and upsetting them.

"How about we do an inside camp day?" Theo says.

"I don't know if that's such a good idea," I say. "There's not much for them to do inside the house."

111

He flashes a knowing smile that borders on smug. "Not here. Somewhere else."

* * *

"Wow, this is so cool, Coach Theo!" Parker says.

"And it's all ours? No one else can skate here today?" Annabelle says.

I glance around the empty hockey rink that Theo managed to reserve for today's hockey camp. I still can't believe he pulled it off, but he was able to pull some strings with his hockey buddies and reserved it for us for the next few hours.

"Yup. It's all ours," Theo says as he skates around the kids.

They're all grinning and giddy, their cheeks rosy from the crisp air in the rink.

He pulls his phone out of his pocket. "Now who wants to do music conga line?"

Everyone cheers, "Yes!" Their adorable high-pitched voices echo in the rink. Theo turns on the Kidz Bop playlist saved to his phone and leads the kids around the rink. I follow behind like usual, grinning to myself at how awestruck the kids are to have an entire ice skating rink to themselves. They look like cute little ants skating around the massive space.

When the first song ends, a familiar-sounding pop song comes on and the kids start cheering when the singer croons about holding hands.

"Let's all hold hands!" Parker says. Adorably all the kids grab hands. I snap a few photos to send to their parents.

"Coach Maya and Coach Theo, you're not holding hands," Emerson says.

"Yeah, you have to hold hands too," her twin sister says. "We all are."

In a smooth move, Theo spins around, skates backward, and locks eyes with me. The corner of his mouth hooks up in a half-smile. "She has a point."

He quirks his eyebrow at me and I can't help but grin in response. Theo is dangerously charming right now and if I'm not careful, I'll melt into a puddle on the ice.

"Okay," I say before skating ahead and joining him at the front of the conga line. When he grabs my hand in his and grins at me, the urge to swoon hits hard.

"Don't act like you're not loving this," Theo teases as we skate along the curve of the rink.

I roll my eyes. "Don't flatter yourself. I'm doing it for the kids." I try to keep my tone as uninterested as possible, but I can't help the grin tempting my lips.

"Keep telling yourself that. I know the truth, Maya," he says, his voice a low growl.

When he winks at me, my knees buckle. Damn. Things are getting pretty damn flirty between us...and I really, really like it.

He squeezes my hand in his and I swear my skin starts to tingle. Heat flashes across my skin. I breathe in the cool air to steady myself. This is ridiculous. I'm acting like a shy middle schooler who's silently freaking out that the cute boy in class is holding her hand.

But I can't deny how good this feels—how good it feels to hold Theo's hand.

A quiet minute passes between us.

"Who would have thought that the two of us would be holding hands?" he asks, his tone teasing.

"Definitely not me."

The corner of his mouth hooks up. "I would have thought it was more likely for you to slap me."

My head falls back as I laugh. "Me too." When I look at Theo, I make sure to hold his gaze for an extra second. "But look at us now."

Heat flashes behind that soft blue gaze as he stares at me. He runs his tongue along his bottom lip, never breaking eye contact with me. "Look at you," he rasps.

Despite the chill in the rink, I can feel the heat coursing between us. I wasn't dreaming it...things between Theo and me are definitely shifting.

One of the kids screeches and we both turn around, but then we realize they're laughing. We chuckle as we look at each other.

"False alarm," Theo says. He blinks and his gaze on me turns focused. There's a flash of intensity. A hard swallow moves along the length of his throat, which is covered in golden stubble.

"Maya, I—"

"Yo! Coach Theo!"

Theo and I twist our heads to look across the rink and see a dozen guys in hockey uniforms skate onto the ice.

Theo lets go of my hand and skates toward them, grinning. "What are you guys doing here?"

"We wanted to see you in action," a tall guy with buzzed blond hair says.

"Daddy!" Sloane and Emerson break from the conga line and make a beeline for a huge dude with the same blue eyes as theirs. He crouches down and scoops them both in his arms.

"You girls were skating so well! Good job, my loves!"

I smile at the way Theo's teammate fawns over his

daughters. The three remaining kids skate up to their dads and hug them.

"Mind if we join hockey camp?" one of the players asks Theo.

He smiles at me. "Only if it's okay with Coach Maya."

I grin. "Of course it's okay."

Theo introduces me to everyone. The kids all start talking at once, asking their dads and the other players to teach them cool tricks and to skate fast.

"Dylan, will you teach me how to shove people into the boards?" Annabelle asks.

A dark-haired guy who I'm guessing is Dylan shakes his head at her. "No way. Your mom would kill me."

The guys on the team chuckle. For the next hour, the kids have a blast playing with the team. I take photos and chat and play with the kids. Every once in a while Theo and I lock eyes and exchange knowing smiles. The whole time I can't stop wondering what he was about to say to me before his teammates surprised us...

No more obsessing about that. I need to focus on the kids.

"Okay guys, snack break!" I holler.

I lead them over to one of the team boxes. They all sit down on the bench and wait as I hand out muffins and juice boxes.

"Did you bring any extra?" A deep voice says behind me. I spin around and see a ridiculously handsome guy with wavy chestnut hair. One of Theo's teammates.

I shrug and smile. "Sorry. Only packed enough for the hockey camp kiddos."

He makes a mock sad face that has me laughing. "Break my heart, why don't you," he says.

I roll my eyes good-naturedly before turning back to check on the kids.

"So you and Theo are running this hockey camp, huh?" the guy asks.

"Yup. We've been up and running for a few weeks now," I say as I hand out orange slices to the kids. When I see that there's a single extra orange wedge, I spin around and hand it to him.

"You lucked out," I say.

"You angel. Thanks." He holds up the wedge. "You know, if my coach brought such good snacks to practice, I wouldn't be late all the time."

I laugh. "So orange wedges are your weakness then?"

I notice he holds eye contact with me for an extra second. "You could say that. I'm Xander, by the way."

He sticks his hand out and I shake it.

"Maya."

"Lovely to meet you, Maya." Xander flashes that pretty boy smile. Yup. Definitely getting flirty vibes.

He skates off and I hear a couple of the kids giggling.

"Coach Maya, I think he likes you," Annabelle says through a mischievous smile.

"I think he just wanted a snack."

The kids giggle some more. When they finish their snacks, they hit the ice once more to skate and play with Theo's teammates. I grab the garbage from snack time and walk it to the nearest trash can, which is by the bathrooms. As I round the corner, I hear Theo's voice.

"Nah man, we're just friends," he says.

"You sure?" Xander says. "Because I don't wanna step on your toes. You two are working together on this hockey camp, which is really cool by the way. I don't want to ask her out if that would piss you off."

I take a step back, trying my hardest to be quiet despite how shocked I am. They're talking about me...Xander is asking Theo if it's okay to ask me out...

"I'm sure, dude. Maya's nothing more than a friend," Theo says.

"It's just that I saw you two skating and you were holding hands. I guess I thought that maybe you were a thing."

Theo lets out an easy chuckle. "We were only doing that because the kids wanted us to. There's nothing between us, I swear."

A weird sinking feeling lands in my stomach. I guess I was wrong about things between Theo and me. Evidently, all that hand-holding and flirting back and forth meant nothing to him.

My skin heats once more, but this time it's because I'm embarrassed. I can't believe I let myself get so smitten with Theo.

I hear them walk off. For a minute, I stand there and take a moment to collect myself. I have no right to feel this way, to feel so...hurt. And disappointed. It's not like Theo and I are anything. We just live together. And work together. That's it. There's nothing more between us. Yeah, we're getting along now...and yeah, things have been flirty between us lately. That's probably why I was letting my feelings get the best of me. Maybe I was so excited not to be arguing with Theo for once that I confused that for legitimate romantic feelings.

The longer the realization sinks in, the more foolish I feel. Wow. I was acting like a smitten middle schooler.

I let out a breath and swallow back the embarrassment. I guess it was all in my head.

Chapter 16

Theo

It's hell keeping this smile on my face while I talk to Xander. But I can't do what I really want to do, which is glare at him and threaten to kick his fucking ass if he so much as thinks about asking out Maya.

I'd look like a psycho.

And really, I have no right to feel that way. Maya and I aren't a thing. Not even close. Yeah, we've been getting along really well lately. And flirting a bit. Working together has been awesome too. We're a pretty damn good team running this camp together.

But I'd be lying to myself if I didn't admit that what I'm feeling for Maya is more than that.

The truth is that I really, really like Maya. I'm attracted to her for sure, but this is more than just physical. She's been so kind and supportive ever since I told her that I wanted to start this hockey camp. When everyone else laughed at me, she actually believed I could do it and went out of her way to help me make it happen.

But it's more than that too.

It's the fact that when I held her hand while we were skating together earlier, I could swear I felt my skin tingle—that's never happened before. I could swear that when I looked at her, I could sense a change in the way that she looked at me...like she could feel a shift happening between us too.

And if my teammates hadn't barged in and interrupted us at that exact moment, I was going to talk to her about it.

Maya, I can feel something between us, do you feel it too?

"It's just that I saw you two skating and you were holding hands. I guess I thought that maybe you two were a thing," Xander says, yanking me back to the moment.

My jaw aches at how hard I'm holding this smile. Minutes ago, I would have bet my left nut that Maya was into me. But then I looked over and saw her laughing and talking to Xander during snack time with the kids. That's when I felt that punch to the gut sensation. She was flirting with him, which meant that she wasn't into me. I just dreamed it all up.

"We were only doing that because the kids wanted us to," I tell Xander after forcing out a chuckle. "There's nothing between us, I swear."

Xander practically beams as he claps me on the shoulder and walks off. I walk behind him back out to the rink, fighting that surge of jealousy that's settled like a needle in my side.

Xander is going to ask Maya out, I have no doubt. I clench my jaw at the thought. And then a second later, I catch myself.

Maya isn't my girl. I have absolutely zero right to feel any of this. I just got caught up in the moment after spending all this time with her.

That's what I tell myself over and over for the rest of the day.

* * *

"That was a cool surprise you pulled off." Maya beams at me as we walk into Ingrid's place.

I try to smile as I take off my coat. "It was nothing."

"Wow, Theo Thompson being modest? Never thought I'd see the day." She playfully nudges me with her elbow. "Seriously though, this is the one time you have a right to be full of yourself. The kids were so sad that we'd have to cancel camp because of the rain, but you turned it around. They had a blast at the rink today because of you. Did you see how much they were smiling and laughing? You made that happen, Theo."

I take in the sincerity flashing in those beautiful brown eyes. "That means a lot. Thanks. And thank you for everything you did today—everything you've done to get this camp off the ground. I couldn't have pulled it off without you," I say.

Her full, tan cheeks flush as she smiles. "It's my pleasure. It's a blast working with you."

Christ, that smile.

Just then her phone buzzes. When she pulls it out of her pockets and looks at it, she frowns.

"Everything okay?" I ask.

It takes her a second to answer. "Yeah." She shoves her phone back into her pocket and walks to the kitchen and grabs a glass of water.

"You sure?" I ask as I walk over and stand on the opposite side of the kitchen island where she is.

She looks at me and bites her lip. I have to command my

knees not to buckle because Jesus, it's hot when she does that.

"It's just...that's your teammate Xander texting me. He invited me to watch the Bashers game tomorrow night and hang out afterward."

"Oh." I'm taken aback at how hesitant she sounds. When I saw the two of them talking and laughing earlier, she seemed pretty into him.

"You gonna go?" I ask, annoyed at the strain in my voice. I sound so bothered and I have no right to be. I turn and start loading the dishwasher to burn off this anxious energy coursing through me.

"I don't know. Maybe. Would that, um, bother you?"

I take a second to fiddle with the silverware in the dishwasher before I turn back around to her. "Of course it wouldn't bother me," I say.

Her brow wrinkles like she doesn't quite believe me. I catch my reflection in the nearby kitchen window and notice how angry my frown looks.

I clear my throat and take a second to relax my face before turning back to the dishwasher and rearranging the plates in the rack.

"You sure?" she asks. "You're acting kind of weird."

"I'm fine." I glare at the row of dishes and shove them around again.

Her phone dings with a text.

"Oh wow," she murmurs.

I stand up. "What is it?"

She stares at her phone. "Xander said he can get me club lounge seats for tomorrow's game." She looks up at me. "I know nothing about sports and I've never been to the arena, but I'm guessing they're nicer than regular seats?"

I swallow back the jealousy that bubbles up my chest.

Sarah Smith

"Club lounge seats, huh?" I have to spend a solid five seconds relaxing my jaw before I'm able to get out those four words.

I've seen Xander pull this move before. He'll surprise whatever woman he's interested in with club lounge seats to woo her. He'll have a bottle of champagne on ice waiting for her, and then after the game he'll take her out for a drink or dinner. And then it's off to his place to finish out the night...

Bile burns in my gut at the thought of him doing all of that with Maya. Yeah, no fucking way is that happening.

I slam the dishwasher door shut. "I'll come with you."

She laughs at first, then wrinkles her brow when I don't say anything. "Wait, you're serious?"

"You said yourself never been to a game and you've never been to the arena. Wouldn't want you to get lost. That place is huge. Parking can be a nightmare, too."

She blinks at me, looking utterly confused. "Um, okay..."

A weird relief washes over me. This time when I smile, my face muscles are more relaxed. I walk up to her and pat her on the shoulder. "We'll have a great time."

I stroll out of the kitchen and down the hall to my bedroom, feeling lighter. I'm essentially cock-blocking Xander and Maya. Is it petty and immature? Yup. Do I care? Nope.

* * *

Maya glances around the club lounge. "This is way nicer than I expected."

I chuckle as I settle into the plush leather seat next to her.

"What did you expect? Concrete benches?" I tease.

She smiles at me. "I guess. I just didn't know watching sports could be so luxurious."

Behind us is a full-service bar and kitchen with bartenders, cooks, and wait staff to cater to the club lounge ticket holders. This section definitely sticks out among the standard seats that make up the majority of the arena. That's why the club lounge ticket holders pay so much to sit here. They want the perks of a killer view, cushy seating, and top-tier food and drinks while they watch the game.

"Not all of us sports fans are heathens," I joke. She playfully shoves my shoulder.

We watch as the ref drops the puck at center ice, kicking off the first period of the game. Bashers players scramble for control of the puck against the Nashville Wolves.

I breathe in the crisp, cool air of the arena. The crowd roars when the Bashers attempt an early shot at the visiting team's goal, but it's a miss. A collective, "ugh" echoes through the stands.

As I take a few seconds to soak it in, there's a faint spark of nerves in my gut. I take a second to breathe through it. I wait for a second, stronger wave of nerves and tension to resurface, but it never comes.

On the drive here, my stomach was in knots. I thought the moment I stepped into this arena my nerves would go haywire. I was about to walk back into the place I've played at so many times and watch the team I was kicked off of. But that panicked, haywire feeling never came. Just a slow simmer of nerves. And at first, I wasn't sure why. But now I know.

It's because as much as I wish I were on the ice with my team, it's not the only important thing in my life anymore. I've got hockey camp now. And yeah, never in a million years did I ever think that I'd be coaching a group of elementary schoolers, but it's fulfilling in a way that hockey never was. Maya and I have a group of little kids who look at us like we hang the moon just because we play with them every weekend. Something about that is so wholesome and heartening. And as much as I love hockey and wish I could still be playing, I've discovered that there are other things I'm good at.

A server stops by and asks to take our drink order. Maya orders a gin and tonic.

"Would you like regular tonic water, cucumber, or grapefruit?"

She flashes a flustered smile that has my heart racing. She shrugs. "Dealer's choice. Tell the bartender to surprise me."

I smile at how cute she is experiencing this for the first time.

When the server turns to me, I catch the recognition in his eyes instantly. "Oh wow, Mr. Thompson, so thrilled you're joining us tonight."

I flash a polite smile. "Thanks. Could I just get a bottle of water, please? And you don't have to call me Mr. Thompson. That's my dad's name."

He laughs. "Yeah, anything you want, just let me know." He clears his throat. "Um, maybe this is out of line to ask, but..." He hesitates for a second. "Could I record a quick video of you saying hi to my little brother Jameson? He's your biggest fan. He broke his leg sledding last week and he's so bummed that he can't play on his hockey team for the next six weeks. It would make his year to hear from you."

I'm heartened by his request. "Yeah, absolutely."

He pulls his phone out of his pocket and aims it at me.

"Okay, whenever you're ready, Mr. Thomp—I mean, Theo." He lets out a flustered laugh.

I grin at the camera. "Hey, Jameson. Your big brother told me about your broken leg. What a bummer. I just wanted to say hang in there. Those six weeks will fly by and you'll be better before you know it."

He stops recording and puts his phone away. "Thanks so much for that. That was really cool of you."

"It was my pleasure. I hope your brother feels better soon."

I shake his hand and he tells me his name's Kyle.

"Thanks for being so cool about that," he says. "I know that must be annoying, getting bothered for pics and videos and autographs."

"It's not. It's honestly really great." I think back to the last time I was approached by anyone. It was that obnoxious paparazzi guy from weeks ago who hounded me as I was leaving that bar with my teammates. Shit like that is annoying of course, but this is different. This is a kid who genuinely loves the team and the sport and for some reason thinks I'm important enough to care about.

Just thinking about that makes my chest go warm.

Kyle says he'll be back with our drinks, and we turn back to the game. I catch Maya looking over at me.

"That was sweet, what you did," she says with a smile.

I shrug and glance down at my lap. "It was nothing."

She pats my arm. "Don't downplay what you did, Theo. Obviously, it meant the world to Kyle and his brother."

Kyle returns with our drinks. When I hand him a bunch of cash for a tip, his face lights up. He thanks me, but I tell him it's no problem.

"You're a real sweetheart when you want to be," Maya teases. For a long moment, I just gawk at how absolutely gorgeous she is when she smiles. I almost forgot that I'm here because I was jealous at the thought of another man trying to woo her.

That's still true; I still feel that way. But for this chunk of time that it's been just Maya and me, it's been nice. Actually, better than nice. I wouldn't want to be here watching this game with anyone else.

Just then the crowd around us starts shouting, "Fight! Fight! Fight!"

I look up and see a black Wolves jersey zoom across the ice, crashing straight into Isaac. He manages to stay on his feet as the Wolves player tosses his gloves on the ground and shoves him. Isaac barely moves a foot across the ice before he takes a swing at the Wolves player, connecting with the side of his face. The impact sends the Wolves player into the nearby boards. The crowd lets out a blood-thirsty roar. Fans slap the boards, pumped to witness a fight. It's then that I get a clear view of the other player. Del Richards, center for Nashville. A fucking asshole who is best known for starting fights over the littlest shit.

Maya winces as she watches the two of them go at it. She glances around the arena, a mystified frown on her face. "Jesus. I feel like I'm in the Colosseum and they're cheering on the gladiators."

"I guess this part is kinda intense," I say as I watch another Wolves player join the fight.

I hold my breath, worried for Isaac, but thankfully I see a maroon jersey come into view and tackle the second Wolves player. When I see it's Dylan, the worry is gone. He's scrappy as a Tasmanian devil when it comes to fights and will be a good backup for Isaac.

Not even thirty seconds pass before players from both teams move to pull their respective teammates back. Then the refs come and put Del in the penalty box for starting the fight. Another ref gives what looks like a stern talking-to to Isaac, who's hunched forward and huffing as he catches his breath but nods along with his scolding.

A mix of cheers and faint boo's sounds from the crowd. I glance over at Maya, who's sporting a dazed expression as she observes the chaotic scene, her hand resting on her chest.

I lean over to her. "You okay?"

She slow-blinks and nods. "Yeah. That was a little barbaric, watching them fight like that."

I tug a hand through my hair, just now realizing how fast my heart was beating. "I guess you're right."

"Do fights break out often?"

"Sometimes we can go a few games with no fights. And sometimes we have a game where three fights break out. It just depends on the mood of the players, the vibe of the crowd, if the refs' calls are fair or not."

She twists her head to look at me. "You sound so chill. Like fighting is as mundane as going grocery shopping."

"In hockey, it kind of is. And other times it can be a chaotic blood bath. It just depends on the day."

She's smiling like she's amused and mystified all at once. "You talk like it's no big deal."

"It's different when you're in the fight. Adrenaline is pumping through you and you're not really thinking about how it looks, mostly just, 'how do I make it out of this intact while kicking the other guy's ass as much as possible.'"

She bursts out laughing.

"But yeah, watching it from the stands is stressful, I see that now," I admit.

She sips her drink and watches a few minutes of the

game before turning to me. "Is this hard, being here and watching your team when you can't play?"

"Yeah, it's a little weird. But it's good that I'm here. I'm learning that I can go through something difficult and make it out okay."

She smiles like she's comforted to hear my answer. The first period ends and I get up to use the restroom. On my way out and back to my seat, I hear someone call my name.

"Theo Thompson? No way!"

I spin around and see Rod Lukasik, a sports reporter from the local city paper. I aim a practiced smile at him as he walks up to me, his signature palm-sized notepad in hand and a ballpoint pen tucked behind his ear.

"How the hell are ya?" he asks with a laugh.

"Good, you?"

"My editor got sick with food poisoning, and I got his club lounge seat, so I'm doing pretty damn good." He flashes a tooth grin and pats his belly. "Hell of a nice break from the press box. The food here is..." He kisses the tips of his fingers. "My poor waistline though. Bye-bye, six-pack I never had."

His shiny bald head falls back as he cackles.

"The food is pretty tasty, that's for sure," I say.

Rod straightens back up and grabs his phone from his pocket. "Say, you wouldn't mind if I got a quote from you for the story I'm writing tonight, would you?"

I hesitate. I'm supposed to be keeping a low profile after being kicked off the team. No one explicitly told me that I couldn't come to Bashers games as a spectator, but I could imagine how that could rub my agent and the entire Bashers coaching staff the wrong way if they found out I was here.

That's what happens when you let your jealousy get the better of you.

Yeah, the whole reason I'm at the arena tonight is because I didn't want Maya to be alone with Xander. But what's done is done. I'm here now. And I don't miss that pointed look in Rod's eyes. I know it when I see it—it's the look of a reporter who's angling for some juicy gossip to publish in their article. Something that's sure to make the rounds on social media. And seeing as I've been the subject of my fair share of sports and social media gossip, maybe I should take this as an opportunity to show them I'm not that irresponsible douchebag anymore. I'm a different person now. A better one.

I smile at him. "Ask away."

Rod is practically giddy as he presses "record" on his phone. He narrows his gaze at me. "So, Theo. How's it feel to be back at the arena where you've played most of your career as a spectator now that you've been kicked off your team for your playboy ways?"

I don't miss that gleam in his eyes. He'd love for me to go off on him or to lose my cool so he'll have some viral-worthy sound bite.

That's not gonna happen though.

I keep my smile in place. "It feels amazing honestly. It's thrilling to be on this side of things as a fan."

Rod's fuzzy brows crash together and his smile drops. "Oh...But I imagine it's gotta feel a bit like a knife to the heart, right? I mean, that's your team. You played for them for years and then one day out of the blue they dropped you."

I shake my head. "I respect the decision that my coaches and the team's leadership made. They know best. And no matter where I am or what I'm doing, I'll always be a Bashers fan to the core."

Rod stands there with his mouth open but says nothing.

"Good chatting with you, Rod. Now if you'll excuse me, I'd like to watch the rest of the game."

I don't wait for him to respond before I walk off and head for my seat. I sit back down next to Maya and watch the rest of the game, feeling like I won even though I'm not even on the ice.

Chapter 17

Maya

I take a sip of my drink and glance over at Theo. His eyes are glued to the game, captivated by the action on the ice.

I turn back to the game, feeling the tiniest bit silly. Last night he acted so weird when he insisted he come with me, and for a while, I thought it was because he was jealous that Xander invited me.

But now I realize I was totally off. It probably had more to do with him being nervous about watching his team play without him. But clearly, he's cool with it.

A weird embarrassed feeling hits me. After overhearing Theo's and Xander's conversation yesterday at the arena, I should know better than to think that Theo would be jealous of anything I do. He made it clear that he doesn't see me as anything more than a friend.

I let that feeling fade and focus on this moment. I'm here having a great time with Theo. I should be happy that we're able to hang out as friends after all that time I spent loathing him.

The game wraps up with the Bashers winning one to

zero. While Theo and I finish our drinks, my phone beeps with a text alert.

> Xander: Hey, gorgeous. You still in the club lounge?

> Me: Yup! Thanks again, it was really cool to watch the game from here.

> Xander: No problem ;) I'm going to get cleaned up, do you want to grab a drink with me with I'm done?

I glance up at Theo. "Do you mind if I grab a drink with Xander when he finishes up here?"

His eyebrows furrow, turning the easy expression on his face stern. "I'll come with you."

"Oh. You don't have to."

"I'm your ride. It makes sense for me to come along since I'm going to take you home."

I'm surprised at how insistent he's being. "It's really fine. I'm sure Xander won't mind giving me a ride back to Ingrid's place."

Theo's shaking his head even before I finish my sentence. And that's when I notice: the flash in his eyes, the bulge in his jaw as he bites down, how he's pursing his lips like he's tasting something bitter.

He's jealous. He doesn't like the thought of me hanging out with Xander alone.

I let that thought tumble around in my head as I take a long sip of my drink. I guess I wasn't totally off after all.

132

An hour later, Xander, Theo, and I are sitting in a ratty vinyl booth at a random bar a few blocks down from the arena. I'm seated between them picking at a basket of fries, trying to ignore Theo as he death-glares Xander while he smiles and chats with me.

"So. How was the game from the club lounge?" Xander asks. He half-smiles as he pushes back his damp chestnut hair that's fallen over his forehead.

"It was great. I didn't realize hockey arenas could have such luxurious seats," I say.

Xander laughs. His hazel eyes flick to Theo. I notice Xander's smile falters a bit.

Xander clears his throat. "You sure you don't want a beer, man?"

"Nope," Theo mumbles.

"Come on, live a little. Just one beer."

"Nope," Theo repeats, only this time his tone is harder.

Xander holds up a hand like he's backing off. "Gotta say, I was kinda surprised to see you at the game with Maya."

"Sorry, I should have asked if it was okay for him to come too," I say quickly.

Theo makes a grumbling noise.

Xander doesn't even acknowledge it as he flashes another boyishly handsome smile at me. "No apologies necessary. I'm glad you came. Even if you brought this loser with you."

He chuckles, clearly joking. Theo's frown doesn't budge. I give him a playful nudge on the arm.

"He's joking, Theo," I say gently.

"I know. I just didn't think it was funny," he mutters before taking another long swig of water.

Out of the corner of my eye, I see Xander roll his eyes. I roll my shoulders back in an attempt to loosen the tightness in my shoulders. God, sitting between two guys who don't seem to like each other is unpleasant. And stressful.

The irritation I've been pushing aside resurfaces. What the hell is Theo's problem? Why is he acting all jealous and moody when he told Xander yesterday that it was totally fine for him to ask me out?

I hold back from going off on him. Now's not the right time to bring it up, not when we're in public and not in front of Xander. I can only imagine how uncomfortable this is for him to deal with Theo acting like this.

Xander leans closer to me before touching the earring dangling from my left ear. "These are nice."

"Thanks."

"Where'd you get them?" he asks.

"I made them."

"Really?" Xander raises his brow like he's impressed. "I didn't know you were a talented jewelry designer."

I shrug. "I'm okay."

"What're you talking about? These are killer," Xander says. "I mean, I don't know shit about jewelry, but they look really fancy and nice."

"He's right. They're amazing, Maya." I'm caught off guard by Theo's sweet tone. When I look at him, he's not frowning anymore. There's an earnestness in his eyes that catches me off guard.

His gaze drifts to the gold square hoops I'm wearing before his stare connects with mine once more.

"How long have you been designing earrings?" Theo asks.

"Awhile. I've designed my own jewelry since I was a kid," I say.

"Damn, really?" Xander asks.

I nod. "It's the one interest I've kept for most of my life. I've started and quit dozens of hobbies."

"It's good you stuck with it," Theo says. "You're ridiculously talented. Don't talk yourself down, okay?"

I swallow as I nod at what he's said. "Thanks," I say quietly.

The conviction in his tone makes me dizzy. This is so freaking awkward. And weird. One minute I'm pissed at him for acting like a territorial douche and the next my entire body is flushing at how he gushes over me.

His gaze drifts to my earrings once more. "You made a pair like that for Ingrid, right?"

"Yeah. I've made her lots of earrings. She says she loves them, she's so sweet." I let out a shy laughing sound.

Theo holds my gaze and quirks an eyebrow. "She's got good taste."

"You ever think about selling them? I bet you'd make some good money," Xander says.

I smile politely even though this is the millionth time I've been asked this question.

I give my standard answer. "Maybe someday. We'll see."

Xander downs the rest of his beer, sets the empty glass on the table, and looks at me. "Wanna hit up another place? Or maybe you could come over to my place for a nightcap." His half-smile turns wicked.

"We have to get going," Theo says before I can even answer.

I whip my head at him, annoyed that he has the audacity to speak for me.

"It's getting late. Gotta feed Mr. Pudding, remember? He hasn't eaten since this afternoon." He slides out of the booth and pulls on his coat.

My annoyance tempers at his valid point.

"Who's Mr. Pudding?" Xander asks.

"My fish. I forgot to feed him earlier," I say.

"Ah." He smiles, but I can tell he's disappointed that we're cutting the night short. "You'll have to let me take you out for a proper meal tomorrow night," Xander says, that panty-dropping smile on display once more.

"I'd like that."

We slide out of the booth. The three of us walk out of the bar and stand off to the side of the entrance.

"I'll text you tomorrow," Xander says.

"Perfect."

He leans in and kisses me on the cheek before turning to Theo and clapping him on the shoulder. "Good to see you, man," he says, his tone on the edge of curt.

Xander walks off, leaving Theo and I standing in awkward silence together. It's so obvious that Theo is jealous. I just wish he would admit it. Then maybe we could clear the air and go from there instead of navigating this weird cloud of tension and awkwardness.

His brows are furrowed and his jaw is bulging again from biting down hard. He clears his throat. "We should go. Mr. Pudding needs food."

"Yeah."

It's more tense, awkward silence on the walk to the car and the drive back to the cabin.

Chapter 18

Theo

When we walk back into the cabin, my jaw is aching and I feel the beginnings of a tension headache.

But that's what I deserve. I spent the entire drive gritting my teeth because I knew if I opened my mouth, the first thing I'd say to Maya is that I don't want her going on another date with Xander, and I'd come off like even more of a psycho than I already have.

I make a beeline for the kitchen as I relax my jaw and down a glass of cold water. Maya walks up to the refrigerator, grabs a bottle of water, and opens it.

When I finally work up the nerve to look at her, she's staring at me, her eyes focused. Like she's studying me, like she's working out what she wants to say to me.

"So tonight was fun," she says.

I almost laugh. "Yeah. Tons of fun."

She sighs. "Okay, Theo. What's going on with you? You were fine at the game, but as soon as Xander came out with us, you turned into a broody jerk. What gives?"

I rinse out my glass. "Nothing."

She crosses her arms and tilts her head at me, like she's silently calling "bullshit."

"It's late and I'm tired. Sorry," I finally say.

That unimpressed expression doesn't budge. "It's pretty clear that you don't like Xander, Theo."

I shrug. "He's fine. I just have to be in a certain mood to hang out with him."

She rolls her eyes. "Look, whatever your deal is with him, can you put it aside for a minute so we can talk?"

I roll my shoulders despite how tight they are. "Fine."

"I just don't want it to be weird if I go out with him."

"*If* you go out with him?" It's not till I finish speaking that I pick up on the hitch in my voice.

She leans back slightly. "That sounded weirdly aggressive."

"I didn't mean to come off like that." I rub the back of my neck in a piss-poor attempt to expend this sudden surge of energy I feel. "You're gonna go out with him then?"

She nods.

"Okay," I mutter.

She frowns. "Okay, what?"

"I just mean that I'm not sure he's your type."

"And how would you know what my type is?" she asks, her tone pointed. Fuck. I'm screwing this up.

"Okay, maybe that was a bad way to phrase it, but Maya, he's not the kind of guy you should date."

She scoffs and crosses her arms. "And what gives you the right to dictate the kind of guy I should date?"

Frustration rockets through me. I shake my head. "Nothing. You date who you want to date, okay? I'm just saying that Xander is the kind of guy who fucks anything that moves. So if that's what you're into, go right ahead. I was just trying to look out for you."

"Wow," she mutters. "That's a pretty judgmental thing for someone like you to say."

"Someone like me?" I lean forward.

She steps toward me, closing the space between us. Now we're barely a foot apart. "Yeah. You. Because last I heard you were quite the ladies' man yourself. Pretty hypocritical of you to bash your teammate for the very behavior you engage in," she bites.

"Not anymore," I bite back. "That's why I'm here in this cabin, agreeing to be babysat by you, remember? I'm done acting like that. And I'm just trying to do you a favor. Xander is a good guy overall, but no way in hell would I ever let any woman in my life within fifty feet of him."

She leans back and lets out a frustrated laughing noise that sounds more like a growl.

"Oh my god, you sound like one of my brothers."

"Maybe they have a point. They're just trying to look out for you. Like I'm trying to look out for you. Because I'm your friend and because..."

I trail off when her gaze on me turns focused. And something else. Something I can't put my finger on.

"And because what?" she says, her tone less sharp but just as firm.

"Because..."

The words I'm aching to say burn the tip of my tongue. The words I actually want to say, but I'm not brave enough to. Not when she's standing there, looking like she wants to dump that bottle of water in my face because I'm acting like a possessive asshole.

Because I like you, Maya. I really, really like you. And the thought of you going on a date with another guy makes me want to rip apart this marble countertop with my bare hands. That's how much it pisses me off to think about you with another man. That's how much I want you.

But I hold back. Instead of all that, I say, "I just don't like the thought of you two together."

She purses her lips, like she's disappointed. Like she could tell I had more to say but lost my nerve.

She exhales and stomps off to her bedroom. And I stay standing there, regretting everything I said and didn't say.

Chapter 19

Maya

I take one last look at my reflection in the full-length mirror in my bedroom. My boobs are spilling out of this black lace top. If I lean over too quickly, they'll fall out for sure. Perfect.

I grab my purse, walk out of my bedroom, and head for the front door.

Yeah, this is petty. And immature. I don't care.

When I think about what Theo said to me yesterday, when he acted like a jealous psycho after I mentioned wanting to go out with Xander, anger surges through me like a flame.

Where the hell does he get off telling me who I can and can't date? Especially after that conversation I overheard between him and Xander at the arena the other day. I heard him say that he sees me as nothing more than a friend. Why the hell was he acting like the thought of me going out with Xander would send him over the edge? He had zero right. Even though I hate it when my older brothers pull that over-protective bullshit on me, at least it kind of makes sense. I'm

141

their little sister. They just want me to be safe. But Theo? We're just friends.

I'm just trying to look out for you, Maya. Xander is a good guy overall, but no way in hell would I ever let any woman in my life within fifty feet of him.

Just thinking about the condescending way he spoke to me last night has me in a fury. He treated me like I was some helpless, defenseless damsel, like I can't navigate my own dating life without him intervening to save me.

I shake my head, annoyed. Whatever. I'm done being mad at Theo for his ridiculous and completely unreasonable jealousy. It's time to show him I don't need his advice.

When I walk into the main part of the house, Theo is standing at the kitchen island clad in sweats and a t-shirt, eating an apple and frowning at his phone. When he looks up, his eyes bulge out of his head. His jaw plummets to the floor, and a chunk of apple falls out of his mouth.

I mentally high-five myself. Just the reaction I was hoping for.

"Whoa..." he murmurs, his gaze fixed on my chest.

"I'm going out," I say without even looking at him as I head to the coat closet and fetch my coat. "With Xander."

Behind me, I hear a choking noise. I bite back a smile.

"Dressed like that?" His voice hitches up and I laugh. He's about to blow a gasket.

"Yeah. Do you have a problem with that?" I cross my arms, pushing my boobs up even more. Theo's peaches-and-cream complexion turns red as he glares at my tits.

"Nope. No problem," he mumbles as he glowers at his phone.

"You sure? Because you seem a little testy," I taunt.

His gaze cuts to my face. "I'm fine," he bites.

I purse my lips to keep from grinning. Yeah, it's a cheap

shot to wear the most revealing top I own on a date that Theo doesn't want me to go on. But I don't care. I want to make it clear as fucking day to him that he doesn't get to dictate what I do or who I date.

I walk over to where he's standing in the kitchen. I'm so close that he stumbles back from me. "Do you think this top is too revealing?"

His jaw bulges, he's biting down so hard. He huffs out a breath. "Nope. You're actually pretty dressed up for a date with Xander. He prefers the women he goes out with to wear as little as possible. Naked is best, honestly."

Anger flashes through me. He wants to play dirty?

I grin at him. "Good. I like being naked."

A choking sound rips from his throat and his gaze is a crystal blue bonfire. Satisfied, I turn to walk away, but he catches me by the wrist and pulls me back to face him. In a flash, my ass is against the edge of the countertop and Theo is caging me in, his hands gripping the counter on either side of me. Our faces are barely two inches apart.

"What the hell are you trying to pull here, Maya?" he growls.

I bat my eyelashes and smile sweetly at him. "Whatever do you mean, Theo? I'm just standing here waiting for Xander to pick me up."

"Bullshit. You're doing this to fuck with me."

Like a brat, I tap the tip of his nose with my index finger. "Bingo!"

He blinks furiously for a second and shakes his head, like he's confused, but his stance over me remains.

"You're damn right I'm fucking with you, Theo. The next time you think you can comment on or control who I date, think again." I lean my face closer to him. "Think of me wearing this outfit while I'm on a date with whoever the hell I want. And know that it's none of your business."

His arms fall to his sides and he steps back. I start to walk off, but Theo grabs me by the waist and pulls me against him. Before I can think or say anything, we're nose to nose, his mouth hovering over mine.

"And when you're on your date, think of this," he rasps.

A split second later his mouth is on mine, and I'm in shock. Theo is kissing the absolute fuck out of me.

As much as I should push him away and curse him out, I don't. His mouth, his lips, his tongue...they all feel so fucking good.

If I thought our first kiss on New Year's Eve was good, this one blows it out of the water. This kiss is dynamite. This kiss is urgent, desperate. It's passion and fire and lust. His lips and tongue are firm and teasing, like he's savoring me. Like he's using his mouth to prove a point—that he can kiss the fuck out of me even in a moment when I can't stand him.

Because yeah, Theo pissed me off with that possessive act he pulled just now. But that's a distant memory in the wake of this earth-shattering kiss. I'd take a million knock-down, drag-out arguments with Theo Thompson if it meant that each one would end with a mind-bending kiss like this.

My knees wobble. My inner thigh muscles twitch.

When I feel that faint, tell-tale pulse between my legs, I moan into Theo's mouth.

"You like this, don't you?" he rasps.

"Yes," I whine. It falls from my mouth instantly, like a reflex.

I move my mouth in tandem with his, barely able to keep up, he's so rabid and desperate with his rhythm. God, Theo Thompson can fucking *kiss*. He's got the mouth and tongue of a demon. And as he laps his tongue against mine, I can't help but let my imagination run wild. Zero doubt that Theo's demon tongue would play my clit like a fiddle.

Almost like he can read my mind, I feel his hand start to slide from my waist to my hip. He gives me a gentle squeeze before tracing his finger along the waistband of my jeans.

I let out a desperate whimper against Theo's lips in anticipation of his fingers moving lower, right where I want them...

But then he leans back, breaking our kiss. He hovers his lips over mine, his hot, wet breath dusting over my mouth.

"Tell me how bad you want this, Maya. Tell me how much you want me to touch you."

He pins with me a cloudy, feral gaze.

That ache between my legs is a full-on pulse now. My thighs are twitching with the need to feel his fingers work my pussy.

"Please touch me...please..." I pant.

The corner of his mouth hooks up in a devilish smile that makes my knees buckle.

He unbuttons my jeans, yanks down the zipper, and slides his hand inside.

My eyes roll to the back of my head as I feel his palm, hot and firm and soft all at once. My clit jumps even though he's not even touching it yet.

I claw at his chest before snaking my hands through his thick, wavy, blond hair. When I tug my fingers through it, he growls into my mouth.

"Fuck, you're so wet. For me."

I nod and let out a whiny, "Yes," not caring one bit about how desperate and needy I sound. The only thing my body wants right now is for Theo to make me come.

He works the pads of his fingers gently over my clit. I

inhale sharply, and my legs start to shake as the pleasure in my core builds.

Theo leans back just enough to lock eyes with me. "You wanna ride my hand, Maya?"

I nod.

"Say it." His tone is low and guttural and demanding and god, do I like it.

"I wanna ride your hand."

"You wanna come?"

"Yes."

He swirls faster. The pleasure grows hotter within me.

"How bad?"

"So bad."

He traces his tongue along my bottom lip and I gasp. That's such an unexpected move. So erotic and teasing...

He shifts so he's palming my pussy. He gives a gentle squeeze that sends a jolt of pleasure rockcting through me. My eyes roll back.

"Ride my hand, Maya."

I grip a hand around his wrist while I do exactly what he says. It's not long, barely a minute before I feel that flash of heat and intensity.

My head falls against his shoulder, and I feel him shift and lean closer. His hot breath ghosts over the side of my neck. His lips land on my skin in a soft, gentle kiss.

"God, you're soaked," he murmurs.

He slides his hand farther down my panties and then I feel his fingers inside of me. I gasp when his thick fingers work my g-spot.

"Right there?" he grunts.

I nod quickly as I grind against his palm. My orgasm lingers right on the horizon. I start to shake as the pressure and heat build and build...

"Come hard, Maya. For me. Right now."

Theo's rasped command is the trigger for my climax. Soon I'm thrashing and shouting as I explode. He sinks his teeth into the side of my neck, which makes me come even harder. Wow. I didn't think I liked being bitten, but this is fucking hot.

I don't know how long it takes for me to start to come down, but by the time I do, I'm panting. My lungs are hollow and raw, like I've just sprinted a race.

I have to blink several times before those white bursts that filled my line of vision when I came start to dissipate.

He stumbles back and my hands drop from his body. He gazes at me, his eyes cloudy with arousal, chest heaving as he catches his breath.

He's the mirror image of me: panting, mouth hanging open, skin flushed, clothes rumpled.

My entire body is aching for more as I stare at him in disbelief. That really happened. I just rode Theo's hand until I came.

My gaze dips lower and I spot the bulge in his sweatpants. My mouth waters and the urge to fall to my knees and take him in my mouth throttles me.

But before I can, I notice his gaze shifts from pleasure-drunk to pointed in two seconds flat. He pins me with that razor-sharp stare as he slashes his tongue along his bottom lip.

"Have fun on your date, Maya."

Oh, right. I'm supposed to go on a date. With Xander.

Theo walks away to his bedroom and shuts the door behind him, leaving me a strange mix of confused, turned on, and pissed off.

* * *

147

As I sit across from Xander at a booth in this ski-lodge-themed bar and grill, I try my best to nod as I struggle to pay attention to whatever he's talking about. But I only catch bits and pieces of what he's saying. Something about jet skiing in Jamaica...or was he talking about the movie he just saw?

"Man, it was wild. That wave came outta nowhere." He laughs before sipping more of his beer.

"Yeah. Just...wow." I force a smile even as my shoulders sag. I let out a silent breath, fully aware that there's zero chance I'll be able to focus on anything other than the earth-shattering orgasm Theo delivered to my body an hour ago.

No question that was hands-down the single hottest moment of my life. I shift in my seat, still vibrating in the aftermath of that unholy moment in the kitchen. I can barely focus on a single word that comes out of Xander's mouth.

Have fun on your date, Maya

Theo's taunting words from earlier this evening echo in my mind, which pisses me off even more. He knew it would be impossible for me to think about anything other than the way he worked me over in the kitchen. He's all I can think about. And it's completely ruined this date with Xander.

Not that I thought things with Xander would turn into a love connection. But at the very least I thought it would be a fun and flirty time. No way that's happening with Theo the only thing my brain can think about.

Fucking Theo

"What was that?" Xander asks, about to sip from his water glass. And that's when I realize I said that out loud.

I clear my throat. "Nothing, sorry. Just, um..."

I guzzle more water and silently command myself to get it together. I've been on a date with Xander for almost an hour and can't remember a single thing he's said because I've got Theo on the brain.

Xander grins, showing off a cute pair of dimples. "You sure you're good?" he asks. "You look a little distracted."

I try to smile despite the flash of guilt rocketing through me. Theo has thoroughly fucked with my head. "Sorry. Just thinking about some stuff for hockey camp."

He nods at the lie I've thrown out. "I get it. Work can be distracting for sure. Try not to think about it though."

And just like that I'm transported back to an hour ago, to the moment I was experiencing the most intense orgasm of my life...and that was just with Theo's hand...

A familiar heat flashes all over my skin. And that familiar throb makes a reappearance. I cross my legs and squeeze hard to keep the ache at bay. It's no use though. That's how much my body likes Theo. That's how badly I need to come again.

I can't sit here and ignore the ache within me. I need to do something about it.

My legs are trembling when I shoot up from the booth.

"Sorry, I just need to run to the restroom," I say, my voice squeaky.

"Yeah, of course," Xander says right as I scurry to the bathroom at the back of the bar.

When I make it to the single-occupancy women's restroom, I let out a breath of relief. Thank god this isn't some multi-stall setup. I can't have unsuspecting bar patrons walk in on what I'm about to do.

I quickly lock the door, spin around, and fall against the wall. That throb in my clit is so strong, so intense, I'm on the verge of collapsing.

I unbutton my jeans, yank them down, and slide my hand into my panties.

Sarah Smith

I groan as I slide my fingers over my soaking wet slit. It doesn't feel as good as Theo's thick, massive, powerful fingers, but they'll have to do.

I look down and see that I'm so wet, I've left a wet spot in the crotch of my jeans. Thank god they're black.

My heart races as I work my fingertips up and down myself, slowly at first. But it's not long before I swirl the pads of my fingers over my swollen, aching clit. It's good, but nowhere near as good as Theo's hand...

God, I'm depraved. I'm on a date with another man, and I'm about to bring myself to orgasm at the thought of someone else.

Theo

Just his name in my mind is enough to make my knees weak. I'm so pissed at him, yet the things he's doing to my body...the way he turns me on...

I close my eyes and let myself relieve that kiss in the kitchen. His lips...his tongue...the firmness of his body...how he looked at me with fire in his eyes, like there was nothing and no one in this world that he wanted more...

That unmistakable hardness pressed against me as he kissed me...

That ache between my legs turns to fire. I swirl my fingers faster and faster. My jaw drops as I let out a whimpered moan and I immediately cover my mouth with my free hand. How mortifying would this be if someone overheard me?

Behind the darkness of my eyelids, I imagine Theo's hand instead of mine, those massive thick fingers working me until I'm shaking and breathless and begging for release.

I picture that annoyingly handsome smirk as he looms over me. He leans his mouth to my ear.

"You failed so fucking hard at trying not to think of me, didn't you, baby?" he growls. The cocky bastard.

I nod anyway because imaginary Theo is right.

He scrapes his teeth softly against the shell of my ear. "Good. I wanted you to."

I slide my fingers inside of myself and press my palm against my clit. The heat in my pussy turns to delicious, delicious fire. I'm on the verge of bursting.

"I'm the only one on your mind, Maya. I'm the only one who makes you feel this good. I'm the only one who can make you come this fast, this hard."

This imagined dirty talk pushes me over the edge. I explode, grateful for the support of the door behind me as I shake and tremble. Pleasure pulses through me like unstoppable shockwaves. Even though I'm covering my mouth with my free hand, a few breathy yelps escape.

When I start to come down, I'm shaking. Every muscle in my body feels like I've worked it to the max. I drop my hands at my sides as I struggle to catch my breath.

Holy...whoa. That's the hardest I've ever come by myself in my life. And it happened in a public restroom while I fantasized about a guy I can't stand.

As I process what I just did, heat flashes across my body yet again, but this time all I feel is shame. Xander doesn't deserve for me to do this behind his back.

I stumble on wobbly legs to the sink and splash cold water on my cheeks. I can barely look at myself in the mirror, I'm so ashamed.

I dry myself with a paper towel, take a breath, then walk back out to the bar and do what I should have done the minute Xander came to pick me up.

Chapter 20

Theo

My arms are throbbing as I push the barbell up from my chest and rack it. Sweat drips down my face as I catch my breath. I sit up on the workout bench and rest my elbows on my knees. My brain is still bogged down with that bullshit I pulled earlier tonight.

What the fuck was I thinking? Did I really think an extra tough workout session would magically erase what I did? That it would stop me from feeling like a massive dipshit?

I roll my eyes at myself before guzzling water from my bottle. And then for the millionth time tonight, I replay what happened between Maya and me before she left for her date with Xander.

When I think about how I kissed her and worked her over with my fingers, my dick starts to stiffen and my balls ache. The way she grabbed and clawed at my chest...the way she whined and begged for me to touch her...the way she thrashed as she came...

She was pissed at me, that was clear as fucking glass. But she was also one thousand percent into it.

But when I threw down the gauntlet, she called my bluff. Hard.

Have fun on your date, Maya

Those words I uttered in the heat of the moment right before I walked off had the opposite effect of what I intended.

For one moment—one fleeting, horny moment—I honestly thought Maya would ditch Xander and choose me. I was half-hard and clearly in some boner daze because I actually thought she'd follow me to my bedroom and have her way with me.

I let out a bitter chuckle. God, I'm a dumbass. I was out of my mind to think that. Because she didn't follow me. Not even a minute after I walked off, the doorbell rang, I heard hers and Xander's muffled voices, and then the soft thud of the front door closing shut. She was gone, off on a date with Xander—the guy she actually wants.

I shake my head at myself. What did I think was going to happen? I saw the way Maya was dressed for her date, like a fucking smoke show, her perfect tits spilling out of the top she was wearing. I saw how pissed she was at me for acting all jealous and territorial last night after the game and when we got home and argued about her going out on a date with Xander. She's right, I had zero right to act that way. Of course she was going to leave me in the dust.

And I was left at the house looking like an asshole *and* an idiot with my dick in my hand—literally. Despite how embarrassed I was, I still had a painful erection to deal with. So like the hard-up loser I am, I went to my bedroom and cranked one out, then immediately headed for Ingrid's workout room to burn off the shame and regret coursing through me.

I stand up from the bench and grab the heaviest kettle-bell I can find. I pump out swing after swing until my lungs are on fire and my arms feel like they're on the verge of falling off just to distract myself from how badly I fucked this all up.

Why couldn't I have just been honest with her and told her how I really feel about her? Why did I have to let my pride and insecurity get in the way?

I set the kettlebell on the rubber mat floor of the home gym, my injured knee on fire. I hunch over, hands on my legs, and gasp for breath. My physical therapist is going to rip me a new asshole when we meet for our next session. This was supposed to be a rest day, but no way could I just sit around after what I did. I'm buzzing with regret and adrenaline, and I need to burn it off.

And no doubt that when Maya comes home tonight from her date, she's going to let me have it.

If she comes home at all.

Acid curdles in my stomach. Just the thought of her spending the night with Xander has me on the verge of puking. Or punching a hole in the wall.

I swallow back the urge. "Get it under control," I mutter to myself.

For the millionth time, I repeat the silent scolding to myself.

She's not your girl. You don't get to feel this way about her

Just then my phone rings. When I see it's Ingrid, I contemplate ignoring it. I don't have the energy for a catch-up chat. But then I remind myself that it's because of my sweet cousin's generosity that I can even stay here. I owe her the courtesy of replying to her texts and calls.

I power through the pang of guilt in my gut and answer her call.

"Hey, Theo! How's everything going? Is hockey camp going well?"

That kick in my gut intensifies. Ingrid is calling to check up on me and I was going to ignore her. I'm a bastard.

"To everyone's surprise, including my own, it's going well." I tell her about the kids who attend and how excited they are to come to camp every weekend.

"That's freaking awesome! Way to go! And hey, how's your knee? You're resting it okay, right?"

"Yeah," I lie. "Trying to."

I ask her how things are going in San Diego and she tells me she's been staying busy with all the hotel and social media events she's been planning and hosting.

"Oh, and I have a favor to ask," Ingrid says. "Can you run to the guest house and do a quick check of the lights and the faucets? Just to make sure everything's running okay? I'm paranoid about the circuit breaker blowing and the pipes freezing since no one's been staying there."

"No problem, I'll go down there right now and check." I guzzle more water.

"You're the best, Theo," she says sweetly. "Oh and warning: ignore all the sex toys and pictures of dicks when you're in there, okay?"

I cough up a mouthful of water. I'm hacking for a solid twenty seconds before I can get it together enough to speak. "Um, what?"

She sighs. "I hosted my friend's bachelorette party a couple days before New Year's and I didn't have time to put away the decorations and gag gifts before I left for San Diego."

I make a disgusted noise.

"Oh grow up, Theo. There's nothing wrong with a group of grown women celebrating with adult toys and penis—"

"Holy shit, Ingrid. I could go the rest of my life without hearing my cousin say the words 'sex toys' and 'penis.' Please, for the love of god, never say that again."

She cackles. "Okay, okay, I'll stop."

"You couldn't clean up your guest house before you left for San Diego?" I ask.

"You know how much I hate cleaning. So how are things with you and Maya?"

"What do you mean?" I mutter.

"I was just curious how you've been getting along. You're not exactly besties," she teases. "But I thought that since you're doing the hockey camp together you two might have buried the hatchet."

I think back to before today, before I fucked things up between Maya and me by acting like a jealous dickhead.

"Things are fine," I say curtly.

Ingrid chuckles. "Oh, I bet. Let me know how it goes when you check on the guest house, okay?"

I tell her I will, she thanks me, and we hang up. I grab my coat from the closet, throw on my boots, and head to the guest house. When I open the front door and flip on the lights, my eyes are wide. Holy shit, this place is...I don't even have the words.

My cousin's spacious loft guest house looks like it was the staging area for a male strip club act. There's a giant penis poster tacked on the far wall with a half dozen smaller, bookmark-sized penises taped around it haphazardly. Like they were playing some 'pin the penis on the penis' game. Penis-shaped balloons crowd the space. Some are clustered along the ceiling while others dot the floor. And there are vibrators everywhere. On the coffee table, the kitchen counter, and the couch. I make my way up the stairs and see more of the same in the loft bedroom: a bunch of half-deflated penis balloons and dildos strewn about like confetti.

When I see what's on the bed, my mouth falls open: there's a giant male blow-up doll decked out in plaid boxers and an oversized black t-shirt with the words, "A hard man is good to find" on the front.

I press my eyes shut and shake my head. I could have gone the rest of my life without knowing what an absolute freak my cousin is.

I huff out a breath, then I make myself check all the faucets and lights in the place. I text Ingrid the good news.

> Me: Everything in the guest house is all good

> Ingrid: Yay! Thanks so much!

> Ingrid: And if you're looking to blame someone for all the sex toys and penis stuff, blame Maya lol. She hosted the bachelorette party with me. It was her idea to make it sex toy-themed

Ingrid sends a trio of laughing emojis. I roll my eyes and head back to the house. When I go to open the door, it's locked. I exhale sharply and dig into my coat pocket for the key, shivering as the frigid winter air whips around me, turning the sweat coating my skin to ice.

But I can't find the key in any of my pockets. And that's

when I realize: I never grabbed the key to Ingrid's house. My brain was such a muddled mess from thinking about Maya and my fuck-up from earlier to tonight that I forgot to grab it.

"Fuck!" I boom out at the darkness around me. For a few seconds, I just stand there, in utter disbelief that I just locked myself out of the house. I let the momentary anger at my stupid mistake roll off my back before I try and think of what to do. I could call Maya and ask her to come back to the house and unlock the door with her keys...

That would most definitely lead to an argument. Or at the very least a talking-to about what a dumbass I am for forgetting my key. I'm not in the mood to be told off by her right now. But I'm not exactly in a situation where I can avoid it.

I let out a sigh and type out a quick text to Maya.

> Hey. Locked myself out of the house. Currently in the guest house. Could you text me when you get home and just leave the back door unlocked for me? Thx.

Shivering, I walk back to the guest house and plop on the couch, annoyed at myself for how I fucked up two things in one night.

I yank off my coat, the now-dry film of sweat pulling across my skin. On top of feeling like a dumbass, I also feel disgusting.

I fall back against the couch and let out a groan. My head lolls to the side and the bathroom comes into view. I've got nothing else to do. May as well shower.

When I finish, I flip off the water, grab the white fluffy towel hanging on the nearby rack, and dry off. I wrap the towel around my waist and let out a satisfied sigh. Well, that's one good thing to come out of this disaster evening. At least I'm clean.

I go to get dressed and freeze when I realize the only clothes I have are soaked in sweat. No way I'm putting them back on. I groan at my impressive lack of forethought when it hits me: I could wear the clothes on the blow-up doll.

I hurry upstairs, yank that godawful shirt off the blow-up doll along with the boxers, and throw them on. Beggars can't be choosers.

I'm halfway down the stairs when I hear the front door to the guest house swing open and see Maya standing in the doorway, an annoyed frown on her face. She slams the door shut and glares at me.

Even though she looks like she wants to murder me right now, I'm relieved. She's not with Xander anymore.

"Hey," I say, shocked. "You didn't have to come out here. I said just to unlock the door at the h—"

"I forgot my keys," she booms out.

"What?"

Her lips purse as she looks at me expectantly. "I forgot my keys to the house," she snaps.

Five seconds of tense silence pass. "Oh. Uh...well...that sucks," I finally say. I run a hand through my damp hair.

"Yeah. It does suck, Theo. Because if you hadn't distracted me with that bullshit in the kitchen before I left, I would have had a nice date with Xander instead of asking him to take me home early, and I wouldn't have forgotten my keys and we wouldn't be stuck in the guest house together."

I stumble back a step at what she's said.

Bullshit in the kitchen.

It certainly didn't feel like she thought it was bullshit, not by the way she moaned and pleaded, not by the way she grabbed at my body, not by how hard she came on my hand...

I focus on Maya's face, how her eyes are fire. She looks like she wants to run me over...and maybe maul me and...devour me...

Heat flashes across my skin. "What do you mean bullshit—"

"Never mind that," she snaps as she yanks her phone out of her purse. "Let's just focus on calling a locksmith and getting someone out here to unlock the house as soon as possible." She squints at me. "What the hell are you wearing?"

I tug at the hem of the shirt, feeling weirdly called out. I explain what happened—how Ingrid called me in the middle of my workout to check on the guest house, and when I realized I had locked myself out of the house, I figured I'd take a shower to pass the time.

"I didn't want to wear my sweaty clothes. So..." I shrug. "I had to improvise with some of the bachelorette party decorations you left lying around."

The corner of Maya's mouth twitches and for a split second I feel a burst of pride that I'm about to get her to smile in this moment where she's pissed at me. But she clears her throat. Her mouth remains a stern line.

"Whatever," she mutters before looking at her phone, presumably to look up locksmiths.

For the next few minutes, the two of us call places on our phones while standing in the living room. Neither of us gets far though. All of the locksmiths in our area are closed since it's late into the night.

"Damn it," Maya mutters. "Not a single place is open."

"I'm not having any luck either," I say.

She sighs, her delicate shoulders sagging with the movement. She kicks off her boots and sheds her parka. "I guess we're stuck here till morning. Great," she says, clearly irritated.

But then she blinks and her entire expression shifts to worry. "Crap, what about Mr. Pudding? I haven't fed him since before I left. He needs to eat one more time tonight."

"I fed him like an hour ago. He'll be okay."

"Thanks," she says in a gentle voice.

Her expression is soft, but then she blinks and she's frowning again.

"If you're trying to get me to like you, it's not gonna work," she mutters.

I just stand there and look at her. What the fuck? It feels like she's reminding herself to act all annoyed and angry at me after that moment of liking me for remembering to feed her fish.

A flash of boldness ignites within me. "I gotta tell you, Maya, I don't buy this whole act."

"What act?"

"Fine if you're pissed at me for what went down in the kitchen earlier. You're right, I was jealous seeing you go out on a date with Xander. I was pissed that you looked hot as fuck and were leaving to meet another man."

Her lips part, her expression shocked and dazed. "What?"

I tug a hand through my hair, worked up and frustrated and annoyed at myself for letting things escalate instead of just telling Maya how I felt—how I *feel*.

That changes right now.

"I don't want you to be with anyone else other than me," I growl, heart pounding, my breath shallow. My entire body is one giant knot at the risk I've taken saying all of this out loud. But enough hiding my feelings.

Enough pretending like I don't care about Maya when I do.

She stares at me, her eyes as wide as her open mouth, like she can't believe what I just said.

"Are you kidding me, Theo? I heard what you said to Xander the other day at the ice rink. When you told him you and I were just friends, that there was nothing romantic between us, that you were totally fine with him asking me out. And now you change your mind?" She aims an incredulous look at me. "I'm just supposed to stand here and be cool with that? With the fact that you're capable of flipping your feelings at the drop of a hat? Or is this part of your jealous caveman act? You don't actually want me, you just don't like the thought of any other guy with me either."

I tug a hand through my hair. Fuck, I'm screwing this up so bad.

"No, that's not...Maya, I lied, okay? I lied to Xander when he asked me about you because I didn't know if you liked me back and I wanted to save face."

She frowns like she's not quite sure she believes me.

"But now, I don't give a shit about saving face or looking cool or any of that. So I'm gonna lay it all out there. I've liked you this whole time, Maya. And the thought of you being with someone else makes me wanna puke."

A long moment of silence passes. And then she lets out a laugh that doesn't sound happy at all. Just exasperated and annoyed. And that's when I know I fucked this all up.

Chapter 21

Maya

I stand there and look at Theo, in utter disbelief. Is he serious right now?

He thinks he can just pull a reverse Uno-card—he thinks he can take back everything he said and did and *that* will make me fall for him?

Irritation and anger collide inside of me. Yeah, I've got feelings for Theo. And yeah, I'll even admit that it's satisfying to finally hear him admit how he feels about me. But how can I trust what he says when it seems like his feelings are changing at the drop of a hat?

When I blink my eyelids are heavy. I'm exhausted and exasperated after this mind-fuck of a day.

I spin around and head up the staircase to the loft.

"Where are you going?" Theo asks.

"To bed. It's late and I'm too exhausted to keep talking about this. We're putting a pin in this discussion for the rest of tonight."

My legs feel like cement as I trudge up the steps. It's like my body is finally feeling the effects of the emotional rollercoaster these past few days have been.

163

I'm unzipping my jeans and crawling into bed when I see Theo make his way to the other side.

"What the hell are you doing?" I yelp.

He frowns at me. "What does it look like I'm doing? You said you're going to bed, so I'm going to bed too."

My jaw hangs open for a solid three seconds. He can't be this ballsy...or stupid.

"Theo, you've lost your mind if you think that we're going to sleep in the same bed together."

He tilts his head at me like I'm ridiculous for having a problem with this.

"Maya, there's only one bed in this place."

I blink at him. "And?"

His eyebrows crash together. "And I'd like to get a good night's sleep too. I'm exhausted."

I let out a laugh of pure disbelief. "Then go sleep on the couch."

This time he's the one laughing. He shakes his head. "No way can I fit on that weird sectional thing. I'm a foot taller than that longest part of it."

I stand there and stare at him. "You're seriously suggesting that we sleep in the same bed together?"

"Yeah." I almost laugh at his deadpan delivery. He's acting like this is the most logical thing in the whole world for the two of us to share a bed.

I shake my head. "No way in hell."

This time when he frowns at me, he looks irritated. "Then you go sleep on the couch."

I let out another crazed laugh. "Why should I? I made it to the bed first. It's mine."

Theo plops on the bed, ignoring me. I stand there and glare at him.

"We'll share it. We're both adults, right?" he says,

stretching his arms up and groaning slightly. "Besides, this bed is huge."

I stand there, stunned. Theo and I are mid-argument about our feelings for one another and we're about to sleep in the same bed. What in the ever-loving hell is going on?

When he opens his eyes and sees that I'm still standing over him, he looks confused. "Why aren't you in bed?"

"Theo, we're in the middle of a discussion about our feelings—for each other."

"And you just said we're putting a pin in it for the rest of tonight so we can get some sleep. I agree with you. Let's go to bed."

"Not together!" I shriek.

He sits up, tugs off that ridiculous shirt, and tosses it aside, leaving me speechless once more, but this time it's for an entirely different reason. Because Theo's body is utter perfection. Like, "carved from marble, can see every beautiful line and muscle" perfection. And yeah, I've seen him shirtless before...naked, actually...but it doesn't matter, I could see him naked a million times, and I'd turn to putty every single time.

What's his deal? He knows I'm attracted to him.

And then it starts to click...

He looks over at me, blinks, and I see it. That flash of mischief in his eyes. He's crawling into bed half-naked because he knows I like him. He knows I find him attractive. And he thinks he'll be able to break me, to get me to admit that I like him too. All he needs to do is show some skin.

"Come on, Maya we're adults. We can be mature about this." I don't miss that teasing lilt in his voice.

I bite my tongue. Maturity? Really? The guy who acted like a Neanderthal earlier today, who is now

165

offering up his body as a bargaining chip in this weird standoff we've got going on, is going to lecture me on maturity?

Something about his audacity to pull a move like this sets off a wave of determination inside of me.

Two can play this filthy game.

I unzip my jeans and slide them off to reveal my panties. I look Theo straight in the eye as I discard my lace top and toss it aside, leaving me completely topless.

His face resembles one of those cartoons when their eyes pop out of their sockets. He doesn't even flinch at the sound of my top knocking over the half-dozen vibrators and dildos sitting on the nightstand.

"Maya." My named is a strangled choking sound on his tongue. "What are you, um, doing?" He clears his throat a half-dozen times while trying to get out those five words.

"What does it look like I'm doing?" I say as I nonchalantly crawl under the covers, making sure to stay on my side. "I'm getting ready for bed." I twist my neck to look at him. "This is what I wear to sleep. Panties only. You can be *mature* about that, can't you?"

Yeah, this is a cheap-as-hell shot, unleashing my naked boobs just inches from him. Yeah, it's gonna make his dick hard. Yeah, he'll probably be flustered as hell and have to scurry off to take care of himself in the bathroom. But I don't care. I'll at least have won this battle, and after feeling like I've been jerked around the past few days, it'll feel *so* satisfying.

I throw the bedsheets off of me and fuss like I'm trying to get comfortable. Out of the corner of my eye, I see Theo's gaze is still plastered to my tits.

"Jesus..." he mutters.

I pull the covers back over me and close my eyes.

"Hopefully seeing me sleeping half-naked like this doesn't bother you," I taunt.

He lets out a scoff-laugh noise. "You think seeing your gorgeous, perfect tits is going to bother me?"

Annoyed, I open my eyes and whip my head to him. His face is flushed red and he looks downright stunned.

"Maya, lying next to you while you're topless is the least bothersome thing in the world."

Half of me is flattered that this guy I've been harboring romantic feelings for is so unabashedly attracted to me. But the other half of me is annoyed because I want to win this one time over him.

"I talk in my sleep sometimes," I blurt. "Hope that doesn't bother you either."

Theo furrows his brow like he's completely thrown at what I've said. But a second later the corner of his mouth quirks up the slightest bit. He knows exactly what I'm doing.

He shrugs. "That's cool. I snore like a freight train."

I clench my jaw, still irritated but also...intrigued. Like this ridiculous game of one-upmanship is thrilling me. Or maybe it's the fact that we're half-naked and lying a foot away from each other in bed.

"I'm a kicker when I hit the deep part of my sleep cycle," I say. "Better watch out. I could do some damage to your precious athlete body."

His half-smile turns full, like he's up for this challenge. "I'm a bed hog. There's a one hundred percent chance I'm gonna starfish on this bed and you'll go flying."

I bite my tongue to keep from laughing. We're almost nose-to-nose now. We've inched our faces closer and closer with each admission.

My heart is racing. My skin is white hot. And I'm wet.

Like, soaking wet. I guess I can't be too surprised given that my body already knows just how wet Theo can get me. Even as we play this ridiculous and sexy game I've made up on the fly, it's getting me insanely hot.

I take a second to swallow and work up the nerve to say what I'm about to say. I know for sure it's going to kill Theo.

"I can't get a proper night's sleep without having an orgasm first. Preferably with a toy." I'm looking him dead in the eye when I say it. I clock the exact moment my words register in his brain: his pupils dilate, turning into two inky black pools of lust.

His grin drops. He looks like he's had the wind knocked out of him.

I turn away for a split second and grab the closest vibrator I can find. I bite my lip when I see it's a massive glittery purple one.

With my gaze glued to Theo's, I hold my breath, waiting to see what his response will be. Will he retreat? Or will he call my bluff?

A hard swallow moves down his neck, which is fiery red. He looks like he's about to pass out.

Seconds pass as I wait for him to make his next move. And that's when I realize, I don't actually want him to leave. I want this naughty, messed-up game to play out fully.

My clit pulses. Faintly at first, but as the seconds pass, it throbs harder and harder.

I want to see just how far the two of us are willing to push this.

"Do it," he rasps.

I let out a shaky breath as I push the comforter off of me once more. My gaze stays glued to his as I flip on the vibrator and press it to my aching clit.

My mouth falls open as I inhale sharply. All that playful

teasing and buildup in the last few minutes has proven to be effective foreplay because I'm on the verge of coming already.

But I don't want to. No, no, no. I want this game to keep going.

I pull the vibrator away, close my eyes, and lean my head back against the pillows.

"Maya..." Theo sounds like he's being choked and he's enjoying it.

"Yeah?" I say through a breath.

"You know I'm not leaving this bed, right? A fucking herd of bison could stampede in here right now and I'd stay fucking put for just the chance of seeing you fuck yourself with that vibrator."

His growled words send me to a new dimension, one where my clit is pulsing, aching, on the verge of orgasm, and I'm not even touching myself.

Licking my lips, I smile to myself and twist to look at him. "I figured you'd probably stick around. You seemed to enjoy watching me come the first time."

He blinks and his eyes take on that familiar sheen of arousal. He reaches his hand over to my face and gently brushes away a lock of my hair. "I thought you were trying to get rid of me," he says.

"I changed my mind." I return the vibrator to my clit. My eyes roll back and my breath starts to pick up. My clit aches and pulses, begging for release, but I pull away again.

"You edge yourself when you use a vibrator?" Theo asks, his hot breath dusting across the shell of my ear and my cheek.

Eyes closed, I nod my head. "Yes."

I feel the warmth of his hand as he gently grips my hip. "Did you edge yourself that night? When I heard you use your vibrator at the house?" I still for a split second, open my eyes, and look at him.

"You're still embarrassed," he says, like he can read my mind.

I nod.

"You realize that hearing you do that was the hottest thing I've ever heard in my life," he says, like he's trying to reassure me. "I mean, up until this moment, when I get to actually *see* you use a vibrator on yourself."

I grin at him, the last of my embarrassment fading. "You're being serious?"

"Dead serious, Maya."

Theo dusts a kiss on my shoulder and I inhale sharply. There's just something about the sweetness of that move combined with the pleasure and pressure building in my pussy that turns me on even more.

I turn up the speed of the vibrator and look Theo square in the eye. "I edge myself. It's my favorite."

His chest heaves as he mutters a curse while gazing at me.

"You weren't the only one touching yourself that night, Maya," he says after a second.

"What?" My question is a breathy yelp.

"When I heard you using your vibrator, it turned me on. Obviously." He chuckles, glancing down at his lap. His rock-hard dick is evident through the fabric of his boxers. "I had to do something about it."

The pleasure inside of me intensifies. My entire body flashes hot at the thought of Theo touching himself while thinking about me.

"Do you have any idea how fucking hot this is to watch you *and* hear you?" Theo asks.

I open my eyes and glance down at the impressive bulge

between his legs. "Pretty hot," I rasp. He lets out a throaty chuckle.

I look up at his face, relishing the way his hungry gaze devours my body. I notice he pauses at my boobs.

"You're a boob guy, aren't you?"

"I'm an everything guy," he says, which makes me laugh. "Actually, I'm a Maya guy, one thousand percent. Everything about you gets me hot."

His words send tingles and warmth all over my body. My legs twitch, a tell-tale sign that I'm almost there.

"Theo, I'm close," I whine, the pleasure inside of me building hotter and tighter and faster.

"That's good, baby. So good."

I gasp at the deep rasp of Theo's voice, how his lips graze the shell of my ear. He runs his fingertips along my arm, sending a million goosebumps across my skin.

"You're gonna come hard with that vibrator, Maya. Real fucking hard. But not as hard as you will on my tongue, which is up next. And then you're going to take my dick like a good girl."

Good girl.

Holy shit, that's hot. Never in my life has any guy I've been with called me that. And honestly, if you had asked me before this moment in bed with Theo if I'd like a guy to call me "good girl" I would have wrinkled my nose and said hell no.

But right now, in the moment, it's hot as hell. I couldn't even tell you why, honestly. There's just something so... dirty, so filthy about the way that Theo says it that gets me off.

"You're gonna fucking lose your mind on my tongue and on my cock, Maya. It's gonna feel so fucking good."

With Theo's rasped words, I break.

Sarah Smith

It's not gentle, this orgasm. It's rough—exactly the way I like to come. I'm writhing against the bed, legs and arms shaking, eyes rolling back, panting, yelping, moaning.

"That's it, baby. Get yourself ready for me."

Somehow, some way, I come even harder. My muscles tense tighter, my limbs thrash harder, and that explosion inside of me burns hotter. *That's* how much Theo's mouth and words push me over the edge.

When I finally start to come down, I toss the vibrator across the bed and blink furiously. All I can make out at first are white bursts in my line of vision. It's a solid ten seconds before I begin to see clearly again. My chest heaves as I breathe, struggling to catch my breath. When I twist my head to the side, I'm met with a smiling Theo, those whisper-blue eyes on fire. He runs his tongue along his bottom lip, and it's like a tease and a dare all rolled into one.

"My turn, Maya."

Chapter 22

Theo

I take in the image in front of me and try not to blow my load in these boxers I'm wearing. Because next to Maya grinding on my hand, this is the hottest thing I've ever seen in my life.

I sit up and take a slow, steady breath as I look at her, sprawled out next to me in bed. Her skin is flushed, her pretty pink nipples are hard, her eyes are dazed, and she's biting back the sexiest, smuggest grin I've ever seen her make.

Christ, she's beautiful.

I blink, grateful that when I open my eyes she's still there, that this isn't a dream.

This is actually happening. Maya and I are in bed together. She played with herself using a vibrator while lying next to me. She had an orgasm and let me watch. And now she's looking at me, expectant and eager.

Pleasure and pressure rocket through my dick. I'm so fucking hard it hurts. If she so much as grazes me with the tips of her fingers, I'm going to come. That's why I need to focus on her.

I move farther down on the bed so I'm by her legs. When I look up at her, she's biting her bottom lip. Her saucer-like brown eyes are focused even through the post-orgasm daze she's sporting.

"This is really happening," she says, her tone mystified.

I nod before lightly running a hand up her leg. I stop at her thigh, lean down, and press a kiss to her skin. I moan at how hot her body feels against my lips. She lets out a whimpering noise that sends another jolt of pressure to my dick.

I look up at her. "Is this still okay with you, Maya?" As much as I want this—want *her*—I only want it if she wants it too.

She blinks and her stare goes softer. Tender, even.

"More than okay." She reaches down and thumbs my bottom lip. I can't help but grin. "You run your mouth a lot. I'd like to see you put it to better use."

My mouth waters at the way she teases me, the way she's looking at me.

I smirk. "Gladly."

With my hands on her thighs, I slowly, gently push her legs apart. And then I kiss the inside of both legs before gently scraping my teeth along her impossibly soft skin.

When I groan against her thigh, her muscles tense under my mouth. Above me, her breath hitches.

"Wow," she says through a broken breath. Like she hasn't been teased like this before. Interesting.

I take my time, kissing up her inner thighs until I'm at her pussy. For a second I just look at it and take it in. So slick, so pink, so fucking pretty.

I lick my thumb and gently run it up her slit. Her head falls back and she whimpers yet again.

A shiver runs through my body. "Maya, that whimper is going to be the end of me."

"What do you—OH MY GOD!"

I smile to myself as I softly, gently run my tongue along her swollen clit. As I make slow circles, it's not long before she tugs a hand through my hair. I moan. I fucking love getting my hair pulled when I'm eating pussy. There's just something so carnal about it. Like it feels so good that she can barely handle it.

"Oh my god...holy...Theo, your mouth..."

Maya lets out a desperate whiny noise, and her legs tremble on either side of my head.

"How are you this good?" she babbles.

I won't lie—it feels really fucking good to know that I turn her on this much.

Gently, I slide my middle finger into her pussy. She squeezes tight around me.

"More," she rasps, grinding harder and faster against my face. I slide in another finger, and another when she demands it.

Her whole body starts to shake. I flick my tongue faster and faster.

"Theo, I'm so close..."

She squeezes tightly around my fingers, but I can tell she needs even more. Out of the corner of my eye, I spot something. And I then I get an idea.

I lean up and reach over to the nightstand

Maya props up on her elbows and looks down at me. "Why'd you stop..."

She goes quiet when I hold up the dildo. Then she bites her lip and nods excitedly. I lower it to her pussy and run it up and down her sopping wet slit, gently pressing it against her clit.

She closes her eyes and her head falls back. She lets out a moan. I slowly, gently glide it inside of her.

Sarah Smith

"That feels so good, Theo..." she pants.

For a second I just sit there and admire how fucking gorgeous Maya is in this moment, her body open and exposed, turned on, lost to pleasure.

My balls ache for release, but there's not a chance in hell. Not until she's gotten hers.

I hold the dildo steady inside of her, lower my face back down to her swollen clit, and gently lap my tongue.

Maya lets out a breathy yelp as she yanks her hands through my hair and grinds her pussy against my face. I groan at how fucking hot it is to feel her lose herself against my tongue.

It's barely a minute before she breaks. She thrashes against me, her screams ricocheting off the walls. I grip my free hand around her thigh and work my tongue at that steady pace while holding the dildo inside of her.

When she starts to come down, I pull away. Slowly, I pull it out of her before pressing a kiss to her thigh.

I lean up, brace my hands on my knees, and grin down at her. She has the most adorably mystified look on her face, like she's in shock at what just happened.

She looks at me, her mouth a perfect "o" shape. I can't help but laugh.

Soon she's smiling. "Oh, you think this is funny?"

"I think you're cute as fuck."

Her cheeks turn rosy right as her smile turns shy. "I'm just blown away honestly."

I raise an eyebrow at her. "Why?"

She opens her mouth, then closes it, like she reconsidered what she was about to say. I trace my index finger up the inside of her leg, relishing the way she shivers. She shakes her head, which makes me even more curious.

"Tell me."

"This is going to sound terrible."

"I doubt it."

"Theo." She tilts her head at me. She looks like she's seriously conflicted, which is more intriguing than anything.

"Whatever it is you're gonna say, promise I won't get upset," I say, my tone light.

"You might get offended."

I shrug.

She narrows her gaze at me. "You're surprisingly laid-back about this."

I tilt my head at her. "Maya, if I'm not mistaken, I just gave you a pretty good orgasm."

She bites back a smile. "Fucking incredible orgasm. Two actually, if you count the one from earlier."

"Right. Almost forgot about that," I say before winking at her. She laughs.

"My ego is riding pretty high right now because of that. Unless you're about to insult my dick size, you could say anything and I won't be mad."

Grinning, she rolls her eyes before zeroing in on the undeniable bulge between my legs. "There's nothing to criticize when it comes to that."

I don't miss the hungry way she looks at me down there. Yup. Ego is perfectly intact.

"I was just surprised that a pro athlete like you would be so good at oral sex."

"Why?" I let out a chuckle, I'm so confused.

She shrugs. "I guess there's just an expectation that some pro athletes would be lackluster in bed because they're full of themselves. And you can be pretty full of yourself sometimes."

I chuckle.

"But you're not lackluster. At all," she says.

177

What I'm certain is a smug, shit-eating grin pulls at my mouth. I lean down so that I'm hovering over Maya and look her dead in the eye. "Glad I could prove you wrong on the oral sex theory." I press my lips against hers and lead her in a slow kiss that has both of us breathless by the time we break apart.

I kiss the side of her neck. I slide a hand between her legs and gently circle her clit. I lower my face to her perfect tits and swirl my tongue around her candy-pink nipples.

"Christ, you taste amazing, Maya. Every part of you does."

She lets out a shuddery breath. And then she glides an arm down the front of my body and grips me through the fabric of these boxers.

I groan against her boobs as she slides her fingers down the waistband and works my shaft up and down her hand.

My dick and balls ache. Fuck, just her hand feels like heaven.

"I need you to fuck me, Theo."

Maya's breathy request stops me dead in my tracks. I still. "I, uh, don't have a condom."

She smiles. "No problem."

She rolls over to the nightstand, opens the drawer, and digs through whatever's in there. When she holds up a foil square, a wide smile on her face, I'm chuckling.

"Party favors from the bachelorette bash," she says. "Good thing Ingrid thought to buy so many extra—"

I wince and hold up a hand. "I don't want to hear about my cousin's condom stash. Let's just pretend it was magically there."

Maya laughs. "Fair enough." She crawls back over, holding the condom between her teeth as she yanks down my boxers. She grabs the condom, but instead of ripping it open, she tosses it to the side and leans her head down.

She licks her lips, flashing a devilish grin at me before lowering her mouth to my cock.

It only takes a single swirl of her tongue over the head of my cock for my knees to buckle. Thank fuck I'm already sitting on the bed. If I were standing, I'd be a puddle on the floor.

That mouth...holy fucking shit, that mouth...

Maya leans back, gently dropping me from her mouth before chucking.

"So you like my mouth then?" she teases.

I must have said that out loud. Heh.

My cheeks flush and I tug a hand through my hair, slightly embarrassed. "You could say that." I bite back a grin.

She leans up and kisses me. "Don't be embarrassed. It's hot to see you turned on."

She drops back to her knees and takes me in her mouth once more. My dick pulses, aching at what Maya's heavenly tongue and mouth are doing to me.

"Maya, baby, good god. We're gonna insure that mouth. For a billion fucking dollars. Jesus Christ..."

She moans around the head of my cock. Closing my eyes, I tilt my head back and take a slow, silent breath to steady myself. Still though, the intensity builds. I grip my hands along the edge of the bed and flex the muscles in my legs, just to distract myself.

But then Maya grips my balls and works them gently in her hand. A strangled noise rips from my throat.

"Fuck, baby..."

When she starts to lick my balls while jerking my dick

with her hand, my eyes fly open. I let out a grunt so feral, I'm certain I sound like a caveman.

Pleasure slingshots through my cock and balls, all the way up my chest. A string of curse words pours from my mouth.

I run my fingers through that beautiful mass of inky black hair and gently pull her off.

When I look at her, I take in the naughty gleam in her eyes, that knowing grin. I trace my thumb along her smiling lips, then pull her mouth to mine.

"I thought you said you wanted me to fuck you," I growl against her lips between kisses.

"I do. I just couldn't help it. I needed you in my mouth for a while."

I smile against her mouth. "Baby, believe me. Now that I know what that mouth can do, that won't be the last time you suck my dick. But right now, I need to be inside of you."

I swipe the condom from the bed, rip it open with my teeth, and sheath myself. Maya moves to straddle me, gripping my shoulders before she lowers herself onto me. When she does, we both let out dual groans.

She rests her forehead against mine. "Holy fuck," she rasps.

"You took the words right out of my mouth."

She starts to thrust, but I grab her by the hips and hold her still.

"Whoa, wait a sec." I press my eyes shut.

"What's wrong?"

I take in the concern in her expression.

I grin. "Nothing. You just feel fucking incredible and I need a minute."

Recognition flashes in her eyes and she unleashes a

naughty smile. I savor the feel of her tight pussy gripping me. So hot and wet…

She starts to glide up and down on my cock. I tell her to wait, but she shakes her head. "I like that being inside of me has you on the verge of coming." She gasps. "Do you know how hot that is? To know that I turn you on that much…"

Her rasped words spur me on. Suddenly I see it as a challenge against my own body to last longer than it thinks it can.

I grip her chin with my hand and bring her mouth to mine. "You're damn fucking right you turn me on," I grunt between kisses.

The corner of her mouth quirks up in a pleasure-drunk half-smile. "You've got such a filthy mouth."

"You love this filthy mouth."

She smiles. "I do." A breath shudders out of her. "God, you're so big."

"Look at how well you're taking me, baby."

She moans as she works herself on top of me. I cup her face with my hand. "Look at you ride my dick like a good girl. So fucking good," I grunt.

Her eyes roll back as she grips my shoulders. I run my tongue along the side of her neck, savoring the sweet taste of her skin.

"That's it, baby. Harder. Ride me harder."

As she bounces up and down, she digs her nails into my shoulders before dragging them down my back.

I growl at the sting. So fucking carnal and sexy. Plus the added bonus of pulling my attention from just how good Maya feels that it's helping me last a little bit longer.

"That…keep doing that," I groan.

She scratches me harder and I'm practically growling.

"You like that?" she says through a stuttered breath. "You like it when I'm rough with you?"

"I really, really like it." I lean forward and take one of Maya's perfect nipples in my mouth and dear fucking god, I could die a happy man right now, her riding me with her flawless tits in my face and mouth.

She moans my name and slips a hand between her legs, circling her clit. I growl against her skin, taking in the visual in front of me: Maya looking like a goddess, hair wild and beautiful, tits bouncing, skin rosy, working her clit with those beautiful fingers, moaning and panting like she's lost in the throes of pleasure.

She moans my name, and instantly I'm even harder, even closer to coming. I could hear Maya moan my name forever and not get tired of it.

With my hands on her hips, I help her thrust faster. No way am I getting mine first. I need her to come before I lose it.

Urgency flashes in her eyes. "I'm so close."

I take that as my cue to unleash, to let myself get even filthier to help her reach climax.

"I can feel it. I can feel how close you are, baby. Your pussy is so tight, so wet. You're gonna explode on my cock like a good girl, aren't you?"

Lightning strikes in those big brown eyes when I drop that "good girl." She grins, licks her lips, and grips my shoulder even harder with her free hand. Her hand on her clit moves faster.

I could tell she liked it when I called her that earlier. Now it's clear as day. Maya fucking loves being my good girl.

She starts to nod right as her whole body trembles. Her eyes turn cloudy and her body starts to shake. And then I feel it: her pussy clenches around me. Her legs tremble.

As she comes, she lets out a yelp that makes my ears ring and I fucking love it. I fucking love knowing that I can turn Maya rabid and feral in bed. This gorgeous, strong, feisty woman comes completely undone just for me.

I lean my head down and bite her shoulder lightly. She lets out a, "Yes!"

And then I feel it—the build-up of pressure in my lower abdomen, the heat, the way all the muscles in my lower half tense...

When I come, my entire body shakes. Every muscle tenses and a caveman sound rips from my throat. White bursts flood my line of vision.

Holy fuck.

I dig my fingers into Maya's beautifully curved hips. She shudders and collapses into me, burrowing her face in my shoulder. I slink my arms around her, hugging her tight to me.

For what feels like minutes, we stay like that: her cradled in my lap, me hugging her to my chest.

When we finally pull apart, she leans back and aims a half-lidded, satisfied gaze at me.

"Did we really just do that?" she asks through a giddy smile.

I chuckle and cup her face in my hands. "Afraid so."

I stare at her, in awe of what we just did. And happy as hell. And satisfied. As I look at Maya, something in my chest squeezes. I swallow back the sensation. Damn. That feeling hasn't happened in...I can't even remember when. And honestly, I don't even know what that feeling is. It just feels intense. And kind of raw and unsettling.

I shove it aside. It's probably the sex, how good it was. I

can't remember the last time sex felt like *this*. Earth-shattering, soul-shaking, and a million other adjectives that I can't think of because one, I'm not that smart. And two, my brain is useless after the mind-blowing sex I just had with Maya.

Before I can think about anything else, she captures my mouth in a kiss that turns filthy in seconds. With her palm on my chest, she pushes me down flat on the bed and hovers over me.

She bites back a grin. "How long is your refractory period?"

Chapter 23

Maya

Turns out Theo has a non-existent refractory period. Like, a handful of minutes.

I fall back-first onto the bed, after yet another mind-bending orgasm. What is this, round four? Five? I've lost count.

"Wow...wow..." The words fall from my mouth in a shuddery breath. And then I start to giggle.

"Damn, was I that bad?" Theo teases as he hops off the bed and discards the condom in a nearby trash can.

I raise my eyebrow at him. "You know exactly how good you are."

A smug grin tugs at his lips. He climbs back into bed and lies beside me. "I need to be reminded. Tell me again how amazing I am."

I roll my eyes and laugh, then gesture to my legs. "God, you're the worst. Obviously you can see how wrecked I am. And it's all because of you." All of the muscles in my legs twitch and tremble.

That smug grin on Theo's face turns full-on. "I'm hoping I've shattered that stereotype you've held of pro athletes being selfish in bed." He cups a hand over my cheek.

"It's been officially annihilated."

Theo's hand falls to my waist. He scoots me closer to him and kisses me. Soon our tongues and hands get filthy. And then my stomach interrupts with a growl.

He pulls away, looking amused.

"Sorry." I chuckle. "I guess I forgot that I haven't eaten much. You distracted me."

Theo moves to grab his phone off the nightstand. "What are you hungry for?"

I pause. "We're kind of in the middle of something."

He shakes his head despite the naughty look in his eyes. "Nope. You need actual food first."

I let out a joking groan. "Fine. Breakfast food. Though I'm not sure how easy that'll be to find since it's the middle of the night."

Theo and I have been going at it the whole night. I still can't believe it. I'm not usually a sex-all-night person, but with Theo, it's all I want. It's like my body can't get enough of him.

I laugh at the mock-serious face he flashes as he swipes his finger across his phone. "Ah, damn. Every place that delivers around here is closed. Does Ingrid have much food here?"

I shrug. "Not sure."

When he hops out of bed, I get an up-close view of that flawless sculpted ass as he bends over and pulls his boxers on. I'm mesmerized by the slow-rippled of his back and shoulder muscles. When he spins around and looks at me, he chuckles.

"Enjoying the view?" he teases.

"Maybe a little." I move to get up, but he shakes his head.

"No way. You stay in bed." He leans down and presses a kiss to each of my calves. "Those legs need a rest."

He disappears down the stairs, leaving me breathless and swooning. Holy crap, that was cute and sweet...and really freaking romantic.

As I pull the covers over me, I think about just how wild this is. Theo Thompson, a guy who I couldn't stand for the better part of the last six years, has just given me the best sex of my life. *And* he's sweet and romantic and doting in bed.

My brain takes an extra second to process it all. It's hard for me to reconcile *this* Theo with the cocky, obnoxious Theo who would work me up for no reason...with the ladies' man hockey pro who has a reputation for bedding a new woman every night and partying until the wee hours of the morning.

He's not that guy anymore. You see how he's changed this past month. You're living with him

Despite that fact, doubt lingers. Yeah, I've seen a different side of Theo this past month...but that's only a month compared to an entire lifetime of living like a playboy pro athlete. Which one is the real Theo?

The sounds of pots and pans echo from downstairs. I shove the thought from my mind. I shouldn't be trying to dissect his character. Right now he's making me breakfast in the middle of the night while I rest in bed.

My chest aches at the sweetness of the gesture. And when he appears in the loft ten minutes later with a plate of waffles, I'm grinning so wide my cheeks are aching.

"Breakfast in bed," he announces. I sit up and he sets

the tray gently on my lap. "All I could find were some penis-shaped waffles in the freezer. Hope that's okay."

I smile so wide my cheeks ache. I kiss him. "It's perfect. Thank you."

When he settles next to me, he hands me a giant bottle of water.

"You need to hydrate," he says.

I chuckle before drinking some. "Is this you in coach mode? 'Remember to eat. Always hydrate.'"

I expect a joking answer, but then I notice his gaze on me turns watchful. He tucks a chunk of my hair behind my ear. "I can't help it. I like taking care of you. In and out of bed."

Thank goodness I'm sitting. Otherwise, I'd have collapsed onto the floor and melted into a puddle of goo because that's the sweetest, most romantic thing anyone has ever said to me.

But immediately after that comes a jolt of something unfamiliar. It lands at the center of my chest. I don't know what exactly it is, but it has me feeling the slightest bit panicked.

This is what couples do—thoughtful gestures like breakfast in bed, sweet kisses, incredible sex...

But I'm not interested in being a couple.

I think about my parents' marriage, how it ended in divorce, how I don't have any memories of my mom and dad happily together. All I remember is the two of them arguing and my dad being gone all the time for work.

And then I remember rummaging through a bunch of old boxes in our basement as a teenager and stumbling upon my parents' wedding album. I remember studying every photo, in awe of how happy and in love they looked. That was the only time I ever saw them like that. I remember the punch in my stomach when I realized that this album was proof that they used to be happy...but then it all went wrong. My dad became a workaholic and left my mom home with us to raise on her own. That's when the resentment and the pain set in...

I remember that tinge of sadness in my mom's eyes that I saw so many times growing up. Even though she tried to act happy in front of my brothers and me, I could tell she was sad and lonely. I could tell it hurt her that my dad wasn't around to help her raise us.

I swore right then and there I wouldn't let myself go down that same path. I was never going to get married and legally bind myself to someone who would abandon me and hurt me in the worst way.

I refocus on this moment with Theo, how good it feels to be with him right now, when everything is exciting and sexy and not at all serious.

I'm not the slightest bit interested in turning something fun, like whatever this is with Theo, into something that will turn sad and bitter and heartbreaking.

I eat the yummy breakfast he's cooked for me and let my thoughts unfold in the quiet.

Theo's history makes me think that he's not interested in anything serious either...but I don't want him to get the wrong idea about me and what I can handle.

When I set my fork down, he swipes it and takes a few bites of waffle. For a second, I soak in the moment, the two of us in bed, totally naked, sharing a meal. This moment screams "couple."

I down some water and then clear my throat.

"We should, um, talk." I hate how squeaky my voice sounds.

To my surprise, Theo looks more amused than worried at my tone.

He sets down the fork, finishes chewing, and then swallows. "Let's do it."

"I didn't expect things to go this way between us," I say.

"Neither did I," he says without missing a beat. I take in that playful look in his eye, how he looks like he's trying not to smile. "Pretty fun turn of events though, right?"

"It's just, um...look, you've been really sweet making me breakfast. I love it. But I don't want you to get the wrong idea."

"About what?"

"I'm not interested in anything serious. Like a relationship."

Theo blinks like what I've told him is as unsurprising as the sky is blue or that snow is cold.

"That's okay. I'm not into that either." When he flashes an easy smile, I let out a breath of relief.

"Okay good. I just didn't want you to think I thought of us as a couple now. I'm not a relationship kind of person. I mean, I love that you did this." I gesture to the tray of food. "I just don't want you to think I expect romantic, couple-y stuff like this. Especially since I'm not really good at romantic gestures." I make a weak laughing noise.

"You naked is all the romance I need," he says.

"I'm serious, Theo. If you want something serious, I can't give that to you."

He shakes his head. "It's okay, Maya. Really. We can keep doing what we're doing without any expectations or putting a label on it."

"Really?"

He nods before taking the tray from my lap and setting

it on the nightstand. He pulls me onto his lap and I straddle him. I savor the feel of his muscled quads, his warm skin.

He cups my face in his hands and pulls me close to his mouth, his lips barely skimming mine.

"It's just sex, Maya," he rasps before leading me in the slowest, hottest kiss I can ever remember having.

My brain short circuits at the way his tongue teases and laps at mine, the way he groans into my mouth.

Soon our rhythm picks up. I'm clawing at his bare chest with one hand and tugging my fingers through his hair with my other.

"This is okay with you, then?" I get out between kisses. "Everything is the same between us. We just have sex too."

He smiles against my mouth.

"I just don't want any confusion or hurt feelings..." I rasp with my eyes closed as he runs his mouth along the side of my neck.

He dips his head down to my breasts and teases my nipple with his tongue.

"I'm one thousand percent okay with this," he says before swirling his tongue around my other nipple.

My breath catches as I feel that familiar ache between my legs. I grip his shoulders as he works me over with his mouth until I'm shuddering and swearing.

In an impressively swift move, he flips me over so I'm on my back and he's hovering over me. My cloudy-with-arousal brain takes in how his breathing didn't even pick up with that strength move.

Theo reaches for the nightstand drawer and pulls out a condom. He sheaths himself, then teases the tip of his dick at my sopping wet slit.

"Tell me how you want it, Maya. Fast? Slow? Hard? Sweet?"

"Fast. And hard. Please."

Something sparks in those blue eyes. His mouth assumes a dangerously hot half-smile before he slides in. My head falls back as I moan. How can he feel this good every time?

He does exactly what I ask, and takes me hard and fast. The whole bed is shaking.

That tell-tale pressure inside of me winds tighter and tighter. When I see him clench his jaw, I can tell it's amazing for him too.

Liquid heat seeps from between my legs all the way up my abdomen to my chest. My eyes roll to the back of my head. Every sound I make is desperate and pleading.

"Play with that pretty little clit for me, baby," Theo demands in a steady, husky voice despite the Superman pace he manages. "I can tell you're close."

I do what he says and circle my clit with the pads of my fingers.

"Good girl," he rasps.

The pleasure and the pressure inside of me intensify. I take in the glassy look in Theo's eyes. He's close too.

Wild that in just the last few hours we've gotten to know each other's bodies so well, we can pick up on our physical tells already.

I squeeze around his dick and he shudders. He grips my hip and grunts. "Fuck, baby. Not yet. You first. Always."

I didn't think heart flutters were an actual thing, but apparently they are because that's exactly what happens. My heart literally flutters at how adamant Theo is about prioritizing my pleasure.

And that does something to my body because a second later, I explode. Just like every other time I've been with him, I'm reduced to thrashing and cursing and screaming. I can't help it. He's just that good. Pleasure courses through me like a lightning bolt, leaving me trembling on the bed.

Theo finishes with a hard thrust and a shudder, then buries his face in the side of my neck. When he groans against my skin, I shiver.

He leans up and grins at me before pressing a kiss to my lips. Then he rolls off, discards the condom, and crawls back into bed.

He cuddles me into his chest before pulling the covers over us. My eyelids are heavy as I blink, aching for sleep. But that does nothing to dull that heart-fluttering sensation. It lingers even as I fall asleep.

Chapter 24

Maya

"Okay everyone, who's ready for s'mores?"

My question is met with all of the kids shouting "Me!" They all skate to the edge of the pond where I'm standing and drop their hockey sticks. They follow me back toward Ingrid's house and chat loudly with each other as I help them shed their winter gear.

I catch eyes with Theo, who's setting up the s'mores at the kitchen table. The corner of his mouth quirks up in a knowing half-smile. A shiver runs through me at the same time as my skin flushes hot.

I bite back a smile and try my best to focus on making sure that all the kids' scarves and gloves are in a neat pile on the bench by the sliding glass door.

"Okay guys, I know you're dying for some s'mores," Theo says excitedly. "But I'd get in big trouble with your parents if I only let you eat sugar. So you have to have some fruit too."

Theo grabs a big glass bowl of sliced fruits from the fridge and sets it in the middle of the table alongside the toasted marshmallows, graham crackers, and chocolate squares. Most of the kids groan while a few dig into the strawberries, grapes, orange slices, and grapefruit wedges.

"Aww come on, guys. Fruit's good," Theo coaxes before grabbing a strawberry slice, tossing it into the air, and catching it in his mouth. The kids giggle.

He looks over at me and blesses me with a sexy grin. I can't help but grin like a goober right back at him.

It's been almost a week since Theo and I first hooked up and I still can't believe it. I'm in a friends-slash-roommates-slash-coworkers-with-benefits setup with Theo Thompson, the pro hockey player ladies' man who I couldn't stand for years.

When I look back over at him, he's finishing helping plate up the snacks for the kids. He catches eyes with me and nods his head at the kitchen island. I meet him there. For a second we stand and watch the kids as they chow down and chatter with one another.

"If only I had half their energy," he says as he offers me a small bowl of fruit.

I grab a strawberry slice. "Don't even start. You keep up with these kids like it's nothing with your pro athlete stamina."

He winks at me. "I've got pretty good stamina."

He swipes a grapefruit slice and runs his tongue along the membrane. The naughty move reminds me of how he woke me up this morning: his tongue teasing my clit until I was screaming through an orgasm.

My cheeks heat. I lean my head closer to him. "Keep it PG, Coach Theo," I say, my voice low so the kids can't hear. "Or else I'll have to put you in time out."

He quirks an eyebrow. "Sounds hot."

I give his shoulder a light shove before checking on the kids.

"It's my turn to feed Mr. Pudding," Emerson says. "Can I, Coach Maya? Please?"

I tell her of course and she darts off to the table by the foyer to feed him. I'm in the middle of refilling the kids' drinks when my phone buzzes with a text from my cousin Austin. It's a group text with my brothers, Austin, his twin sister Millie, and his husband Declan.

> Now that we're all in the same city for once, it's about time we get Karaoke Cousin Night going again, don't you think?

I smile. Karaoke Cousin Night was a thing we all did ever since we were kids growing up on the same block together. My brothers along with Austin, Millie, and I would go over to each other's houses once a week and sing karaoke while our moms gossiped and played cards. As we grew older and moved away for school or jobs, we couldn't do it as often, but whenever we're all in Denver, we make it a point to get together.

> Millie: God, yes. I need an evening with adults
>
> Gage: I'm in
>
> Tyler: Me too
>
> Gage: I'm bringing Becca btw
>
> Austin: Duh, of course she's invited. She's family
>
> Millie: Gage, will you pretty please ask Becca to bring some ice cream for me? I'm dying for more unicorn swirl
>
> Gage: Sure

Declan: Who can host? I know Austin and I usually offer, but we're redoing the floors and our place is a disaster zone

Millie: I'd offer up my place but Evelyn goes to bed at like 7, and you know how loud karaoke gets

Gage: Becca and I can host if you don't mind squeezing into a cramped space, our apartment is kinda small

I glance around Ingrid's place. It's more than enough room. I just need to clear it with Theo. I walk over to him.

"Hey, I have a favor to ask you."

He smiles. "Anything."

I give him a quick explanation of Karaoke Cousin Night. "Would you mind if I had them over here to do it? My family's going to goad you into singing karaoke too."

"Of course they can. This is your place too. But I have to warn you: I have a godawful singing voice."

"No one is worse than my cousin's husband. Declan sounds like a mountain lion in heat when he sings. It's never once stopped him from participating though."

Theo laughs. "Okay, I'm in."

I text my family.

Me: If you don't mind trekking to the mountains, we can have it here

Everyone replies that they love that idea.

Tyler: Will Theo be there??

Me: LOL yeah. He lives here too, remember?

Tyler: Oh hell yeah! Theo Thompson is gonna be at our family karaoke night!

Austin and Declan send laughing emojis

> Gage: Are you done fanboying?
>
> Tyler: Shut up, buzzkill

I roll my eyes before tucking my phone back in my pocket and checking on the kids. Theo and I walk them back down to the pond to finish out the day. He peers over at me, a knowing smile playing on his lips.

"What's that look for?"

"Just planning the song I'm gonna sing. It'll blow your mind. Can't wait to see what your family thinks."

Excitement blooms in my chest followed by a jarring realization: I can't remember the last time a guy I was with acted this eager to spend time with my family. The few times I brought a guy home to meet my family, they were always hesitant and nervous.

Theo and I aren't even dating, and he's so...happy to hang out with my brothers and cousins.

I try not to think too hard about it. Theo and I are just friends with benefits. Nothing more. He's joining karaoke with my family because he's free that night and he'll be around anyway. It means nothing more than that.

Theo aims a smirk that's both teasing and hot. "I've got a set of pipes on me. Wait till you hear me."

Chapter 25

Theo

Seven pairs of eyes fix on me as I sing the opening lyrics of "Welcome To The Jungle." When I attempt the falsetto part, my voice cracks, just like I knew it would. I hold back a laugh and keep singing as every single member of Maya's family, who are sitting in the living room of Ingrid's cabin, winces at me.

When I try again to hit the falsetto, instead of my voice cracking, I make a sound that's both piercing and grating. I sound like a dying animal.

Everyone covers their ears. This time I can't help it. I burst out laughing and drop the karaoke microphone. The whole room joins me until we're all laughing so hard and so loud, we can no longer hear the music track.

Tyler crawls over to the karaoke machine and pauses it, clutching his free hand over his stomach. "Holy shit, man. What the hell was that?"

When Gage stops laughing, he clears his throat. "Yeah, um...wow. I don't really have any words."

Becca elbows him even though she's giggling too. She

takes a breath and looks at me. "That was a really good try, Theo."

I hold back a laugh. Becca's so pure and sweet, I can't help but smile at her and thank her sincerely.

"Becca's being kind," Maya says, letting out a final laugh before she wipes at her eyes. "Theo, that was horrific. I'm pretty sure you cracked Mr. Pudding's fish bowl."

"Seriously," Declan says, his expression dazed. He sips his beer. "Oh my god, man. Someone go check on the fish."

I laugh even harder. Millie, Maya's other cousin who I just met tonight, pats me on the back. "You get the 'A for effort' award, Theo. Hands down, that was the most enthusiastic performance I've ever seen in the history of Karaoke Cousin Night. And there's been a lot of bangers."

She aims a smirk at Declan, who rolls his eyes despite the smile on his face. He runs a hand through his fiery red hair. "I have no idea what you're talking about. I always give sophisticated performances."

"Sophisticated, huh? Is that the word we're gonna go with?" Austin hooks his arm around his husband's neck, pulling him closer. He ruffles Declan's hair. Declan laughs and playfully shoves him.

"I don't know if sophisticated is the word I'd use," Millie says. "More like deranged. And deafening."

Declan frowns like he's hurt. Austin kisses his cheek.

Millie holds up a hand like she's trying to prove a point. "I'm just saying that attempting to sing Whitney Houston's rendition of 'I Will Always Love You,' is one of the toughest things you could do. That song is freaking hard to sing. Especially with your, um, range, Declan."

Becca cups both hands over her mouth to stifle a laugh. Gage grins adoringly at his girlfriend before biting his lip, presumably to stop himself from laughing too.

"And yet that was your go-to karaoke song for years," Maya says to Declan. "You sang it. Over and over and over. And over." She groans behind the rim of her glass of wine. I can't help it, I let out a laugh.

Declan crosses his arms like he's put out but clearly joking along with his in-laws.

"You've got the projection of Whitney. Just not the pitch," Austin tells him.

Declan shrugs. "Well, now I can say with confidence that I'm not the worst singer of the bunch." He chuckles before pointing at me. "Thanks for that, Theo."

I flash a thumbs-up. "Anytime."

We all laugh as we sip our drinks. Tyler gets the karaoke machine started up again, and Austin hands the mic to Millie, who sings a Dua Lipa song.

I turn to Maya, who's sitting next to me on the couch. "Millie is a billion times better than me. And Austin. Your whole family is. You're all pretty good carrying a tune."

Maya flashes that gorgeous smile that has me instantly mesmerized. "We're Filipino. Karaoke is in our blood."

She winks at me and it takes everything in me not to grab her and kiss her right here, right now. I have to remind myself that we're in front of her family right now and it would be pretty gross for us to go at it.

It's been just over a week since we started hooking up and I've never been so happy. When we're not busy with hockey camp we spend most of our free time fucking like animals on every available surface of this place.

I shake my head at that realization. I sound so...smitten. Shit, have I ever used that word to describe how I've felt before?

I sneak a glance at Maya as she chats with her brother. She turns and smiles at me and it feels like fireworks going off in my chest. That's never happened to me before.

I tug a hand through my hair in an attempt to ground myself. Have I ever felt this...giddy? Ever?

I know the answer to that question right away. Nope. Not even close.

This thing with Maya feels different. It's thrilling and fun and comfortable too. Like, I've never felt so at ease, so at home with a person.

A weird squeeze happens in my chest. It throws me off completely.

Maybe the reason this feels so different is probably because this thing with Maya *is* different. We're living together *and* hooking up. I've done the friends-with-benefits thing plenty of times, but never like this—never with someone that I've lived with. Maybe that's why it feels so much more intense.

Maya scoots closer to me on the couch we're sitting on. When she looks at me, she quirks an eyebrow and runs her tongue along that beautifully plump bottom lip. Just that little movement has my dick aching. All those thoughts about my feelings and what they mean halt in my mind as I flash back to this morning when I was leaning against the arm of this couch while she took my dick in that perfect mouth...

I clear my throat and squirm in my seat. Maya covers her mouth, stifling a chuckle.

"Oh, you think that's funny?" I say quietly so only she can hear me. Thankfully Millie's belting out the last part of the song and everyone seems to be fixated on that.

Maya wrinkles her nose, a teasing smile playing on her lips. "Maybe," she mouths.

That ache in my dick is back. "Later," I mouth back.

The song ends and we all clap.

"Amazing, Millie," I tell her. "About ten thousand times better than that crime scene of a song I attempted."

Her head falls back as she laughs before she thanks me.

"Snack break?" Becca asks. Everyone says yes. She and Gage get up and head to the kitchen, returning a few minutes later with a fresh bottle of wine and a tray of home-made flatbread with what looks like mozzarella, herbs, and fresh tomatoes.

When Becca offers to top off my glass, I tell her no, thanks.

"I've got PT in the morning, so only one glass for me." I guzzle down some water.

"How's the knee?" Tyler asks me.

I bend it back and forth. "Almost good as new. PT is killer, but it's working."

"You think you'll be able to play again?" he asks.

"Here's hoping."

I haven't heard from my agent since I moved into Ingrid's place so I could lay low and recover from my injury. Javier didn't reach out to me last week when Rod Lukasik published his article about the Bashers' win. Rod included my quotes in his story, but I guess what I said wasn't impor-tant enough for anyone to care about.

I shouldn't be so surprised. Did I really think a couple of well-worded lines in an article would completely change people's opinions about me? That it would magically get me my spot on the team back?

I think about never being able to play again. It stings for sure, but the thought isn't as gutting as it was when Javier delivered the news to me in his office. It would hurt not to be able to play hockey with my team ever again, but I'll get through it. Like I'm getting through it now by coaching camp with Maya. I found something else that makes me happy other than hockey, and it's a good feeling.

I catch Maya's gaze lingering on me before she takes a bite of her flatbread slice. Her expression changes instantly.

"Whoa. That's incredible," she says around a mouthful of flatbread. She offers me a bite. My reaction is the same.

"Damn, that's good," I say through a bite, savoring the flavors.

Gage hands me the tray of flatbread. I grab a slice and scarf it down.

"Any chance you can make about a hundred more of those flatbreads?" Austin asks after finishing his plate. I look at the tray, which is sitting on the coffee table. It's empty.

"You got it," Gage says, chuckling.

"I'm serious." Austin sits up and exchanges a look with Declan. They're both smiling.

"We have something to tell you all," Austin says. "We're hosting an anniversary party."

"At Seb'on," Declan says. "We'd love for you all to come."

Everyone responds with smiles and congratulations.

Maya jumps up from the couch and scurries over to Declan and Austin and hugs them. "Of course we'll come. We'd be honored."

Everyone takes turns hugging Declan and Austin. I walk over and shake their hands. I'd be down to hug them, but I've only met them a couple of times and I don't want them to think I'm joining as part of their family when I'm just Maya's housemate.

"Congrats, you guys," I say. I go in for a handshake, but Declan pulls me in for a hug. So does Austin.

"No handshakes, dude. You're practically family now.

After that horrendous karaoke performance, you're bonded to us," Austin says.

Everyone laughs, including me. Maybe it's weird, but hearing him say that feels comforting.

"You're invited to the anniversary party," Austin says to me. I thank him and say I'll be there.

"You know I'm always down for a party," Tyler says. "Even though it's kinda weird you two are throwing one after only being married a couple years. But hey, any excuse to get drunk and celebrate."

I notice the sharp look Gage gives his brother. I'm ninety-nine percent sure Tyler was joking—he seems like the kind of guy who makes a joke out of everything. I can relate to that.

"Okay sure, it's probably kind of silly that we're having an anniversary party already," Austin says, his tone good-natured. He doesn't look offended at what Tyler's said.

He aims a warm look at Declan, who grabs his hand.

"We just figured why the hell not?" Declan says. "For a while, we didn't always know if we'd be able to get married."

Austin nods once, his smile turning sad for a moment. "We just want to take every opportunity to celebrate the fact that we can be together."

And then it dawns on me. They're talking about the fact that as gay men they weren't always guaranteed the right to legally marry.

"Good for you guys," I say, feeling a surge of conviction and emotion well up inside of me. "I'm honored to celebrate with you. Thanks for letting me be part of it."

When I turn my head, I catch Maya staring daggers at Tyler, who now looks embarrassed.

Gage tells Austin and Declan that he'd love to cater their party. Becca offers to make a fancy ice cream cake for dessert. The rest of the night everyone talks about Austin and Declan's anniversary party. They reveal that Maya, Gage, and Tyler's dad offered up his restaurant as the venue for free as his gift to them.

The night winds down and everyone starts to leave. All that water I've been guzzling finally catches up to me and I head to the restroom. As I open the door to walk out, I stop when I hear Maya's firm voice.

"I don't care that you meant it as a joke, Tyler. It was still a shitty thing to say," she says.

Tyler huffs out a breath. "I get it. I told them I was sorry."

I stay behind the bathroom door. This is a charged conversation and I don't want to interrupt.

"Imagine what it would be like if you couldn't legally marry the person you love because a bunch of bigots were in charge of the world. And then, one day everything changes and you can. Hell yeah, you'd want to celebrate that," Maya says. "If Austin and Declan want to throw themselves an anniversary party every year, they deserve to do that. And we should be right there with them celebrating."

There's a long pause before Tyler speaks. "You're right." His voice is softer now, remorseful. "What I said wasn't cool. I should apologize to them again."

Another long pause.

"Thanks for helping me see what an asshole move that was," Tyler says. "Never thought you, Ms. I'm Never Getting Married, would be the one going on about how great marriage is."

Maya starts to speak, but her brother stops her.

"I'm kidding, Maya. I swear, I'm not that dense. I know what you mean. It's not about how great marriage is. It's about the fact that everyone has the right to get married if they want."

"Look at you learning lessons, big brother."

"Told you I'm more than just ridiculously good-looking."

Maya makes a scoff-laughing noise, and I hear them walk off.

For the rest of the night, all I can think about is what Tyler said about Maya.

Ms. I'm Never Getting Married.

I know I've got zero right to wonder about this. I've never really thought about getting married honestly. It's not because I'm anti-marriage. I think I'd like to get married someday. It's more like I just never thought about it.

But now I am.

A weird unsettled feeling hits me. I think about Maya and acknowledge the fact that it's bothering me not knowing why she's written off marriage completely.

Even though she and I are hooking up, I know we're not serious. We aren't even technically a couple. Whatever her stance is on marriage, it's none of my business.

But that doesn't halt my curiosity. I wanna know why she never wants to get married.

Chapter 26

Maya

"I wish you would have told me it's black tie," Theo hollers from the master bedroom.

"I did tell you. Twice," I holler back from the hallway bathroom while applying my lipstick.

"Really?" His chuckle echoes down the hall before he mutters a curse.

"Everything okay?" I ask.

"These shoes are uncomfortable as fuck. And Christ, this tie. Every time I try to tie it, I almost choke myself."

His chuckle echoes down the hall. I observe my reflection in the mirror, how I'm struggling to hold back a smile so I don't smear the deep red stain on my lips.

I set my lipstick on the counter, then walk to his bedroom. "Let me help—whoa..."

I lose my breath the moment I get a look at Theo. I take in the impeccable tailoring of his black suit, how it looks like it was fitted to his body. Even with his black tie hanging loose around his neck, he looks incredible. Like a male model getting ready to strut down the runway. When I make it to his face, I nearly choke. He's smoothed back his sandy blond waves and did a clean shave of his face. He is mind-achingly handsome.

He flashes a dazzling grin and holds his hands up at his side. "I clean up pretty good, huh?"

"Good? Try incredible. You look like James Bond."

"You say that like you're pissed." He chuckles.

"No, it's just..." I walk up to him and rest my palms on his chest. I tilt my head up and peck my lips on his. I'm aching to lay a proper kiss on him, but I can't risk messing up my makeup and making us late for Declan and Austin's party.

"No human being has any right to look that hot in a suit," I growl softly.

That familiar fire flashes in Theo's eyes. He runs a tongue along his bottom lip and grips my waist. He pulls me tight against him before thumbing the belt of my robe.

He lowers his mouth to my neck. "How much time do we have?" he asks against my skin. The soft vibrations send shivers across my body. I close my eyes and hum in an attempt to keep myself from ripping that gorgeous suit off Theo's body and having my way with him right here on the floor.

"The party starts at seven," I say through a shaky whisper. "It'll take us at least forty minutes to drive down..."

"So that gives us ten whole minutes." He runs his tongue along the side of my neck and kisses me hard. My knees give out, but he's gripping me so securely that I stay standing, propped against him.

It's only been a couple weeks of us hooking up and already he's memorized what makes me literally weak in the knees...both in and out of bed.

There's no second-guessing or shy moves when it comes to Theo. He navigates my body with confidence, always knowing where and how to touch me. And kiss me. And fuck me.

I think back to the first time we were together in the guest house. How he watched me get myself off. He must have been cataloging everything that turned me on because every single time we've been together, he's never, ever missed.

He may be cocky and obnoxious, but god, does he know his way around a woman's body.

My eyes roll back as he gently scrapes his teeth along the drop of my shoulder. It takes all the strength inside of me to lean back and step out of his touch.

"We'll have to finish this later," I tell him, tugging the knot of my robe tighter. "I still need to get dressed."

Theo groans. I can see the struggle play out on his handsome face. He eyes me with a hungry look. "The second we get home though, I want you naked and in my bed."

Heat flashes straight to my lower abdomen, and my clit pulses. "Yes, please."

I reach up and help him tie his tie.

"How do you know how to do this?" he asks.

"I have two older brothers and a dad who runs fancy restaurants. I've seen them tie ties millions of times. I could do it in my sleep."

When I finish, I turn to leave, but he catches me by the wrist and pulls me in for a filthy kiss. When we break apart, my lipstick is smeared all over his mouth.

"Crap." I move to wipe his face, but he shakes his head and instead grins proudly.

I can't help but chuckle.

"Get cleaned up. I'll throw on my dress, and we'll head out," I say as I scurry out of his bedroom to my room.

I slip into an emerald green chiffon, floor-length dress,

throw on a gold bracelet and my favorite pair of earrings, and slide into my heels.

When I walk out into the living room, I see Theo leaning against the back of the couch scrolling on his phone.

"Ready," I say.

When he glances up at me, his eyes look like they're on the verge of popping out of his head. His jaw unhinges and he drops his phone.

"Fuck, you look hot," he mutters. Then he blinks and shakes his head, like he's coming out of a trance. A hungry grin tugs at his lips.

He walks toward me. Actually, walks isn't the right word. "Prowls" is better. Like I'm the only thing in the room he sees and he has to have me right now.

He grabs me by the waist and pulls me against him.

"That dress..." His hungry gaze falls down the length of my body, landing on my boobs.

"It's your cousin's. Ingrid said I could borrow it," I tease, holding back a laugh as he grimaces.

"I'm gonna pretend I didn't know that."

I laugh.

"All the more reason to rip it off you when we get back home tonight."

He eyes my boobs once more, which look impressively ample in the strapless, sweetheart neckline of this dress.

I trace my finger along his impossibly square jawline. "Can't wait. Now let's go before we're late."

* * *

Forty minutes later we're at my dad's restaurant Seb'on in the upscale Cherry Hill neighborhood of Denver.

"This restaurant is incredible," Theo says as we walk into the dimly lit space outfitted with sleek modern décor.

"My dad put a ton of work into it." I shed my faux fur coat—another item I borrowed from Ingrid's closet—and hand it to the hostess. Theo hands his top coat to her as well and together we walk into the main part of the restaurant and spot my family milling around the space, chatting and laughing.

"You're here!" Austin rushes over to hug us both.

"Happy anniversary, cuz." I hand him a gold gift bag.

"You didn't have to get us a gift," Austin says. He hands the bag to Declan, who joins us. They're both wearing charcoal gray suits and look so dapper.

"It's a bottle of your guys' favorite champagne that you haven't been able to track down for months," I say.

"What?!" Austin and Declan say at the same time.

I chuckle at the pure joy on their faces. "Theo helped me find it." I turn to look at him and go weak at the adorably bashful look on his face.

He shoves his hands in his suit pockets. "One of my old teammates is from France. He helped me get it. It was nothing, really. If you guys want, he said he can get you a case of it. Just let me know."

Declan yanks him into a hug so hard that Theo makes an "oof!" sound. The second he releases him, Austin does the same.

"Definitely put us down for a case. This was our honeymoon champagne. We've been craving it nonstop since we went to France for our honeymoon," Declan says.

"We'll love you forever for this, Theo." Austin claps his chest. "So this is a gift from the two of you then?"

Theo doesn't pick up on the lilt in my cousin's voice or the curiosity in his expression as he looks between us.

"Yup," Theo proudly says without missing a beat.

"Huh." Austin aims a knowing smile at me, as if to non-verbally say, "Interesting..."

I try to keep my face as neutral as possible, but it's no use. Austin is not only my cousin but one of my closest friends. He's always been able to tell just by my expression when something is up.

While Theo and Declan talk, Austin raises an eyebrow at me.

"So you two...?" he whispers.

I scrunch my lips and nod once. He unleashes the cheesiest grin.

"Don't. I don't want to get into it in front of our whole family," I tell him in a low voice.

He holds up a hand. "Understood. But the second we get a moment to ourselves, you're telling me everything."

I exhale. "I always do."

Declan points toward the glossy black onyx bar at the far end of the restaurant. "Bar is over there. Be sure to try the signature cocktail, it's delicious."

"There's a mocktail option for you, Theo," Austin says.

Theo smiles. "You didn't have to do that."

"It's no trouble, really," Austin says. He turns to me. "Your dad and Gage have outdone themselves on the menu. The appetizers that the waiters are passing around are..." He kisses the tips of his fingers.

"Be sure to tell them that when you get the chance. It's necessary to feed their massive chef egos," I tease.

Declan glances at my earrings. "Gorgeous. You made those, right? Austin said you make jewelry."

"Yeah, just earrings though," I say.

Theo frowns. "What do you mean 'just'? Maya, those are incredible."

My heart thuds in my chest. He sounds so proud of me.

"We've all been trying to get her to start an online earring business," Austin says.

"Why haven't you?" Declan asks.

I feel my face start to heat. I shrug. "It's a lot of work. And there are a ton of jewelry lines out there. I probably wouldn't do that well."

"Don't say that," Theo says. "Tons of people would love them, I bet. And if they didn't, I'd buy them all."

My heart literally skips in my chest. How is he this perfect?

"That is ridiculously sweet, Theo," Austin says. Declan nods in agreement.

I bite back a smile as I look at Theo.

Just then some relatives pull Declan and Austin into a nearby conversation. A waiter passes by with a tray of shrimp toast. Theo and I grab some.

"Oh my god," I moan at the burst of flavors on my tongue. Fatty, salty, rich, and herby.

"Whoa..." Theo says before flagging down the server and grabbing a few more.

He hands me one. I chuckle as he stuffs his face.

"What?" he says with his mouth full as he smiles.

We grab some sesame chicken bites when a different server walks by. Another server offers us some champagne and Theo swipes two flutes. He hands one to me.

"To Declan and Austin," he says, clinking his glass to mine. "And your dad and brother's amazing cooking skills. Good god, this food is incredible."

I laugh. "Cheers."

We take a sip together before I start pointing out family to him.

"Just so you know, everyone's gonna come up to you and

hug you. That's the default greeting in my family. Sorry in advance."

Theo laughs. "It's all good. I'm good with hugs."

Just then Millie and her husband Peter walk in with baby Evelyn in a carrier. I wave them over and we hug. I crouch down and say hi to baby Evelyn. I give her chubby cheeks a gentle squeeze.

"Oh my gosh, look at this chunky monkey," I coo.

Millie and Peter laugh.

"She's outgrown all her onesies already," Peter says.

We fawn over Evelyn's cuteness for a few minutes until Tyler walks in with our mom.

"Mom, look at you. Gorgeous!" I hug her and we do our usual air kiss that we always do when we're both wearing makeup.

"Oh, thank you, *anak*. It's been a while since I've gotten dressed up."

I take in her flawless makeup and how she's opted for a crimson lipstick. I can't remember the last time she picked a color that bold, and it looks amazing on her. She even took the time to curl her shoulder-length black hair.

"That dress is so pretty," I tell her.

"Oh, this old thing?" She blushes while glancing down at her cocoa-hued lace cocktail dress. "I haven't worn it in forever."

"You look amazing in it," I say with a smile.

"Seriously, Auntie. You really do," Millie says. Mom thanks her and hugs her before insisting she carry baby Evelyn.

After a few minutes, she hands her back to Millie and turns back to us.

"I can see where Maya gets her beauty from," Theo says to her.

Mom's cheeks are now ruby red as she smiles at him. "I'm sorry, have we met?"

"I haven't had the pleasure." He holds out his hand to shake Mom's. "I'm Theo Thompson. Ingrid's cousin."

Mom beams. "Oh, that's right! You're staying with Maya, aren't you?"

"Yes, ma'am."

Mom waves a hand. "My goodness, no calling me that. I feel so old."

"No way. I'd have mistaken you for Maya's older sister if she didn't tell me you were her mom."

Mom giggles like a teenager with a crush at Theo's suave line while I chuckle behind my champagne glass.

"I should have recognized you as Ingrid's cousin," Mom says. "You two have the same beautiful blue eyes and blond hair."

Theo chuckles. "It runs in the family."

He grabs a glass of champagne and hands it to Mom. He offers to hold her purse when she grabs a prawn canapé.

She aims a smitten look at him. "Such a gentleman." She turns to me. "*Anak*, you haven't updated me on how things are going with that camp you two are doing together."

"It's good. Busy and exhausting," I say.

"Kids will do that to you." She laughs, then turns back to Theo. "That's so charitable of you to spend your free time volunteering with kids. That must be so special for them to have a professional athlete like yourself teaching them so many wonderful things."

This time Theo's the one blushing.

"It's been a lot of fun. I feel really lucky to be able to do it," he says shyly.

"Well, you should be proud of yourselves. Both of you." She beams at both of us before scooping my hand in hers.

"*Anak*, it's so nice having you back in town for longer than your usual short stays. Keep this camp going for as long as possible if only to keep my daughter around, will you?" she says to Theo.

"I'll do my best," he says.

Mom's tone is joking, but I know she means it. She wants me to stay home as long as possible. She tells me that every time I'm home for a visit and it normally drives me nuts. But this time? I don't feel an inkling of annoyance. This time when she says I should think about staying in Denver longer, it sounds fun. And exciting. And something else I can't quite nail down right now.

It takes a moment, but I finally put a word to that feeling: settled.

The thought of sticking around—the thought of living in Ingrid's cabin with Theo and running the hockey camp together doesn't make me want to bolt like I expected it to. It makes me feel rooted and comfortable, like I belong here. And that's not something I've felt in years.

Just then Mom's clutch vibrates.

"My phone," she announces.

Theo kindly grabs her empty flute so she can grab her purse. I notice the name "Andre" light up on her screen. She grins at her phone screen, like she's giddy at whatever he's written her.

She looks at us. "Excuse me for a moment."

She walks off to the back of the restaurant, where the kitchen is. The door swings open and I see my dad in his signature crisp white chef's jacket. He greets her with a wide smile that reaches his eyes. He leans down to pull her into a hug, and I instantly look away. I guzzle the rest of my champagne and try not to think about the flirty exchange between my parents—and the fact that my mom is currently smitten with the guy who broke her heart more than twenty years ago.

I shove aside the feeling and distract myself by chowing down on a delicious chicken satay skewer. My parents' personal life isn't my business.

"Is there any hard alcohol?" Tyler asks while loosening his tie.

"I think I heard your cousin say there's vodka and gin," Theo says.

Tyler makes a face. "Gross. Oh well." And then he beelines for the bar and downs a shot of what looks like vodka.

I roll my eyes. "My brother is such a frat boy."

"A hot frat boy, but yeah, definitely a frat boy."

I spin around at the sound of Tori's voice and see her standing next to me, looking gorgeous in a gold cocktail dress. I pull her into a hug.

"What did I tell you about commenting on my brother's attractiveness?" I say to her.

She shrugs, her glossy bee-stung lips smirking. "Can't help it. Your brothers are hotties. So are you."

I let out a groan-laugh. For the next few minutes, we all chat until baby Evelyn starts to fuss. Millie and Peter frantically dig through their diaper bag.

"Where's her pacifier?" Millie asks.

"I thought you packed it," Peter says.

"I thought *you* did."

"Crap. Maybe it fell out in the car. I'll go check."

Millie coddles baby Evelyn as she cries.

"Sorry guys," she says, her cheeks flushed, clearly overwhelmed. "I know a crying baby isn't the most fun sound in the world."

Theo and I both tell her it's okay.

"Here, let me look again in the diaper bag." Millie moves to hand me Evelyn so she can dig into the bag. I tell her to hold on so I can set aside the plate and glass I'm holding, but then Theo swoops in.

"I can hold her." He gently takes her in his massive hands. Evelyn's big brown eyes go wide and she instantly stops crying as she stares at Theo, who's cradling her with his hands under her arms, her chunky legs dangling in front of him.

Millie stares in shock at Theo. "Oh my god. You're the baby whisperer."

He lets out a nervous laugh. "I don't know about that. I think she's just surprised and the shock is holding off her crying for a bit."

"Whatever it is, I'll happily take it." Millie chuckles. "I could use something a little harder than champagne. You mind holding her for a sec?"

She walks off before Theo can even answer her.

I move closer to him. "Sorry. I think Millie is just tired and happy not to be holding a crying baby for a few minutes."

Theo smiles at me. "It's okay. I'm good holding her for a bit."

Evelyn's unblinking stare hasn't budged in the ninety seconds that he's held her.

"Are you sure you're comfortable?" I ask, taking in how he's holding her in front of him, his arms bent.

"Oh, yeah. This is a great arm workout," he says. Tori laughs. He flashes a confident smile and I can't help but laugh too.

Millie hollers for Tori to come over to the bar. She grins and points at a trio of cocktail glasses.

"Wow, did she order that all for herself?" I ask.

Tori chuckles. "Probably."

She walks off and I catch a handful of my aunties and cousins gazing adoringly at Theo. Can't say that I blame him. He looks equal parts adorable and sexy holding a baby while decked out in a suit.

"You're making half of my family swoon by the way you're holding my cousin's baby," I say to him.

He frowns. "No way." When he looks around the room, his brow lifts. "Okay, maybe you're onto something."

The longer he stands there holding Evelyn, the more I start to swoon too. Seeing this burly hockey player cradle a baby is definitely having an effect on me.

And then my brain does something weird—something it's never done before. I reimagine this moment with Theo holding a different baby—*our* baby.

The image only lasts a second in my brain before it disappears.

My heart races and my skin goes hot. What the hell? I've never, ever imagined having a baby before. Not with anyone I've ever been with.

I glance at Theo once more. He makes a silly face at Evelyn, who starts to smile. Underneath the nerves crackling inside of me, I feel...warmth. And comfort.

What the...is this what people mean when they say their ovaries are bursting?

Just then Peter returns with a pacifier in his hand. "Found it!" he announces, his dark brown hair mussed. I notice a few tiny beads of sweat along his brow. Poor guy must have flipped his car inside out hunting for that pacifier.

He frowns like he's confused when he sees Theo holding Evelyn.

"Millie went to get a drink," Theo says.

"Oh. Thanks for watching Evelyn," Peter says.

"No problem." Theo hands a content Evelyn back to her dad. She happily takes the pacifier right as Millie returns, cocktail in each hand. Tori follows behind holding a glass too.

"Can I add you to my list of possible babysitters?" she jokes to Theo.

For the next few minutes, they chat and laugh. All the while I stand there and steal glances at Theo, struggling to figure out why the hell my brain just imagined a future and a family with him.

Chapter 27

Theo

"You okay?"

Maya nods at my question, despite the deer-in-headlights expression on her face. She's been quiet the last few minutes while we've been chatting with her cousin Millie and Millie's husband.

My gut tells me she's not okay. This isn't like her, to stand around and go quiet in front of her family. I know I've only hung out with her family a couple of times, but it was clear how comfortable she is around them, whether she was joking or laughing or bickering or calling her brothers out on their overprotective act.

But something's off with her right now.

Millie and Tori get pulled into a nearby conversation with some other relatives and Peter leaves to change Evelyn.

"Hey, you wanna get some air?" I ask Maya.

Again she nods without saying a word. I notice the panicked look in her burnt umber eyes has dialed back a notch before I lead her out the side entrance of the restaurant, which opens to the outdoor seating area. All the tables and chairs are covered in nylon tarps with a dusting of snow on them. I take her to the far end and lean against the wooden railing, then pull off my suit jacket and drape it over her shoulders.

I scoop her hand in mine. "You sure you're okay?"

She blinks before looking down at our joined hands. She takes a second to glance at my suit jacket on her. "Yeah, I'm…"

"Maya." Her name is a soft growl on my tongue. "It's me. You don't have to hide anything. Tell me what's up."

A flustered smile pulls at her lips. "Sorry, I guess I was a little bit thrown off back there."

"By what?"

I watch as the hesitation plays out in those hypnotic deep brown eyes. And then she lets out a breath. "This is gonna sound weird."

"Try me."

"Seeing you hold baby Evelyn was ridiculously sexy. You looked like a hot dad."

I pause for a second, stunned. "Okay yeah, I wasn't expecting you to say that."

She pulls her lips into her mouth and her gaze falls to the pavement, like she's embarrassed by what she's said.

"Sorry, I didn't mean that what you said was bad. I was just surprised," I say quickly. "I like that you think I look like a hot dad."

She looks back up at me. "You do?"

I nod. I let my hands fall to her waist and grip her tight. "I've been called a lot of things. Hottie. Hunk. Handsome. Hot dad is a first."

Her head falls back as she laughs. "Like your ego needs to be even bigger."

I shrug. "You said it, not me."

She gives me a playful smack on the shoulder before

cupping my face with her hand. "Look, I know that this... thing between us is casual."

Casual

Just hearing that word feels like someone sticking a needle in my side. It shouldn't feel like that...I know this setup between us is just sex. But to hear her say it feels off. Wrong, actually.

"And I guess I was a little scared that if I admitted to you that seeing you cuddle a baby made you even hotter in my eyes, you'd take it like I want something more serious with you now."

"Do you want this to be serious, Maya?" The words fall out of my mouth before I can even think about what I've said. I wasn't even planning on saying that. But it just happened, like a reflex. I said it because it felt right.

And then I realize: I like the idea of getting serious with Maya. I like spending every single day with her. I like the thought of my feelings for her growing and intensifying.

She leans back, clearly surprised at what I've said. "Do you?"

My heart thuds in my chest as I open my mouth. No words come out though. I'm too nervous to put my feelings on the line and get shot down by the woman I'm falling for more and more each day.

So I stay quiet and hold eye contact with Maya. I watch as her gaze goes from confused to focused...like she can tell exactly what I'm thinking.

She doesn't pull away, like I'm scared she would. She rests her palms on my chest. Like she's sure—like she's certain she wants to be right here, like she'd rather be standing here in the cold with me than anywhere else.

My heart thuds as I let the words materialize in my head.

I know I'm the last person in the world anyone would want to get serious with. I've slept around like it was an Olympic sport and my only serious relationship was in high school. But I've never felt this way with anyone before you. Screw casual. I want to get serious with you, Maya.

I open my mouth and start to speak, but then the squeak of the door on the far side of the building swinging open interrupts me. A burst of laughter follows.

We both whip our heads around and see Maya's mom holding hands with a tall guy I'm guessing is Maya's dad. Since we're at the far end of the outdoor seating area and they're facing away from us, they don't see us standing a dozen feet away.

"Sneaking out the side door of your restaurant, Andre? Really?" her mom says in a teasing tone.

"I couldn't help myself. I needed to get you alone for a minute."

She playfully pats his chest and grins at him. And then he leans down and pecks her on the lips.

I feel myself tense up. Yeah, they're not my parents, but it still feels weird to watch them kiss when clearly they were wanting a moment to themselves.

I glance over at Maya, who's looking at them, her expression something between weirded out and shocked.

I hold my breath and try to stay quiet, despite the urge to run off. This may be awkward as fuck for me to witness, but it's gotta be ten times worse for Maya given the fact that these are her parents we're watching.

"We'd better head back inside before people start wondering where we ran off to," Maya's mom says.

Her dad huffs out a disappointed sigh through his sly smile. "You're probably right. Call me tomorrow, will you?"

She grins up at him. "Okay." She steps back and

smooths her palm over the front of her dress. "I'll go in first, then you wait a minute and you follow."

Andre winks at her. She goes back inside. He stands there smiling to himself and for a second, the weirdness I'm feeling starts to fade away. Because I can relate to him right now, feeling giddy as hell after stealing a kiss from the woman he's nuts about.

He heads back inside, leaving Maya and me alone outside once again.

I glance at her and take in her dazed expression. She's staring straight ahead at where her parents were, her mouth in a perfect "o" shape.

I'm tempted to ask her if she's okay, but I already know the answer to that.

The thing is, I have no idea what to even say. That moment earlier, when I was about to tell her that I want things between us to go from casual to serious, is long gone. Right now she's processing the weird and jarring moment of seeing her divorced parents sneak off together. This isn't the right time to try and take our hook-up status to the next level.

Maya huffs out a breath, then laughs. But it's not a happy-sounding laugh. More like she's confused and in disbelief.

"What the hell was that?" she says.

"Um, I think that was your parents sneaking out so they could kiss."

She whips her head to look at me and frowns. Okay, that was definitely the wrong thing to say.

She slumps against the railing and gazes off to the side, clearly lost in her thoughts. Instead of saying another stupid thing, I stand there with my hands in my pockets and stay quiet.

Then she suddenly turns to look at me. "That was weird, seeing my mom and dad do...that."

"Yeah, um, I can imagine."

She sighs, her shoulders falling forward with the movement. "Never in a million years did I think she'd ever give my dad a second chance." Maya speaks to the pavement, her tone bewildered.

"What do you mean?"

She straightens back up. "My parents got divorced when I was seven. My dad was a workaholic. Too busy traveling the world and building his restaurant empire. My mom was pretty much a single mom my whole life, even when she was married."

"Wow. That sounds tough."

Maya nods. "It was. After they split up, my brothers and I would see our dad whenever he was back in town. But it was never consistent, just whenever he could fit us into his busy schedule. So we were always with my mom. And I didn't really understand it when I was little, but as I got older I realized how lonely that must have been for her. To have her husband traveling all over the world, setting up glamorous restaurants, and mingling with celebrities while she stayed home and raised his kids. He pretty much ditched her during the hardest part of their marriage. That must have felt like a slap in the face."

I take a second to process what she's said. I have no idea what it's like to be left at home while my partner is gone nearly all the time, but I'm certain it would piss me off. And hurt my feelings.

"That's really upsetting, Maya. I'm sorry your dad treated your mom like that."

"Me too," she says softly. "I don't ever remember them happily together, even when they were married. All I remember is them fighting. They were always arguing about my dad being gone and leaving my mom alone with us. And when they got divorced, I just got so used to seeing her on her own. She didn't pine after him. She just seemed so independent for the longest time. And honestly? I was proud of her for that. That she wasn't heartbroken over a guy who would treat her like an afterthought."

"I know I just met your mom tonight, but she seems like a really wonderful lady," I say. "She comes off so confident and genuine and kind-hearted. And pretty damn incredible that she raised three kids practically on her own."

A small smile appears on Maya's face. It feels like fireworks going off in my chest at getting her to smile when she's so upset.

"Don't get me wrong, I love my dad," she says. "He finally seemed to realize just how badly he messed up with us kids, apologized to us, and has been a more active presence in our lives recently. He goes out of his way to spend time with us. Yeah, that doesn't make up for what he did in the past, but I'm happy he's in our lives again." She pauses for a moment. "It just doesn't feel right for him to weasel his way back into my mom's love life and try and put the moves on her again. She deserves better than to wait twenty years for him to realize what a catch she is."

I nod and reach for her hand, softly gripping it in mine.

She looks down at our joined hands. "She married someone who left her to raise their kids while he traveled the world, only to want her back twenty years later after she did all the hard work on her own," she mutters, almost to herself. "Marriage is so pointless. Never in a million years."

Her words hit me loud and clear. It feels like a vault locking over the nerve I was building to bring up our conversation from earlier before her parents interrupted us.

This is why Maya never wants to get married, because of her parents' messy relationship.

This is why she was so shocked when I brought up the topic of the two of us getting serious.

This is why she's only interested in hooking up, in keeping things casual.

Maya doesn't do serious relationships. She's been pretty damn adamant about that from the start. And now I know why.

The side door swings open and Gage steps out in a white chef's jacket, glancing around until he spots us.

"There you are," he says. "Austin and Declan are about to do their toast. They'll kill you if you miss it."

Maya tells him we're on our way in. Gage darts back inside the restaurant and I move to follow, but Maya catches me by the wrist.

"Hey. Sorry you had to see that weird moment with my parents. Especially them kissing." She winces.

"I'll survive."

She chuckles before her expression sobers the slightest bit. "And, um, sorry I unloaded their marital history on you like that. I guess I just got a little caught up in my emotions."

"Hey." I cup her face in my hands. I take a second to savor the impossibly soft feel of her skin. "You don't have to apologize, Maya. I'm here for you through it all. When you wanna talk or unload or vent or rave about something. If you wanna read from the dictionary, I'll happily listen with a smile on my face—"

She leans up, grabs my face, and kisses me so hard, I forget where we are and what we're doing. When she pulls away, she gazes at me, the look in her eyes intense and soft.

"You're amazing, you know that?" she says.

"So are you."

"You were in the middle of saying something right when my parents barged out here. What were you going to say?"

I swallow back the sting of disappointment and smile, hoping I don't look as deflated as I feel. "Nothing. We should head back inside. I don't want to be on your cousins' shit list."

She laughs and I follow her into the restaurant.

Chapter 28

Maya

Theo gawks in the direction of the main dining area of my dad's restaurant where my brother Tyler is currently breakdancing.

Right after Declan and Austin's touching toast, our older relatives headed home, leaving the rest of us cousins to do what we do best after most family gatherings: turn it into a karaoke dance party.

He gawks at Tyler doing the worm on the makeshift dance floor that he and Gage created by shoving aside all the tables and chairs in the main dining room of the restaurant.

"Wow. I didn't know your brother was so…limber," he says, his eyebrows knit with what looks like concern and confusion.

I burst out laughing. "This is Tyler's party trick. He looks like a frat boy, but he'll cut a rug like an '80s break-dancer until the wee hours of the morning."

Millie walks up to us with a snoozing Evelyn cradled against her chest and tells us goodbye. We hug her and

Peter. Theo insists on helping them carry their diaper bag and baby carrier to the car.

I silently swoon as I watch him walk off with them. And then, for the millionth time this night, I think about our moment in the outdoor seating area of the restaurant, when I thought we were going to take our relationship from casual to serious.

"Do you want this to be serious, Maya?"

Never in a million years would I have thought that the word "serious" would have come out of the mouth of playboy Theo Thompson. But it did.

And the way he said it. His tone was eager. And urgent. It matched the look in his eyes as he stared at me. It all caught me completely off guard.

"Do you?"

I cringe as I think back on how the words sputtered out of my mouth. My tone bordered on incredulous. Because could a guy who has never had a relationship as an adult really commit to something serious? He's spent his entire adult life hooking up. Am I supposed to believe that he could give that all up for me?

My chest aches at just the thought, at how uncertain I feel even thinking about it.

Maybe we could have actually talked about it had my parents not stumbled out there like two horny teenagers sneaking around, interrupting us.

I press my eyes shut and shake my head, willing away the visual. Yeah, I know it's childish for me to cringe at seeing them kiss. But come on. No one wants to see their parents make out in front of them.

But that's not even the worst part. Just thinking of my mom taking back my dad after the way he treated her makes my blood boil.

I huff out a breath, my thoughts a mess. I focus back on the dance party unfolding in front of me. Tyler tries to get Gage to join him on the dance floor but no surprise that Gage isn't up for it.

"Fine, fine. You don't wanna dance, I get it," Tyler says in his signature taunting tone. "How about a push-up contest?"

Gage purses his lips like he's seriously considering it. I'm certain he'll take Tyler up on it. Given how much they both work out together and how competitive they can get, this is the perfect opportunity for them to throw down.

Gage nods once. "I'm in."

Everyone cheers. Gage sheds his chef's jacket and Tyler shrugs off his suit jacket right as Theo walks back in.

"Theo! You have to join the push-up contest!" Tori hollers. "I wanna see if these two can hang with a pro athlete."

Theo's cheeks flush pink and a shy smile tugs at his face. My knees go weak yet again. Good lord, my body is shameless. Anything this man does—smile, touch my hand, lick his lips, kiss me, grab me—and my body is aching for more.

Theo agrees to join and everyone cheers once more. He takes a few seconds to shed his suit jacket and roll up the sleeves of his dress shirt, and I swear, saliva pools in my mouth. *Holy forearms.* I've seen them plenty and no question they're muscle-y and sexy...but to see him pull that panty-dropping move of rolling up his sleeves in real time? Pure hotness...

The three of them get set up on the floor.

"Ready, set, go!" Tori yells.

The crowd counts along as the three of them pump out push-ups at an impressive speed.

"Damn. Look at your man go."

I turn to see Austin at my side, beer in hand, looking amused at the scene unfolding a handful of feet in front of us.

I roll my eyes. "He's not my man."

Austin scoffs. I elbow him.

He tilts his head at me before tugging his tie loose with his free hand. "Come on, Maya. I'm not blind. It's clear as day two you are sleeping together."

I wrinkle my nose at him, annoyed. "You don't have to be so crass about it."

Austin shakes his head and his thick black hair, which is starting to fall out of its slicked-back style, sways with the movement.

I look away until he says my name in that familiar tone.

"Maya, he really, really likes you. I can tell."

"Seeing as we're hooking up, that's kind of a given. I like him too."

I focus back on the push-up contest. Counting has slowed down now that Tyler, Theo, and Gage are slowing their pace. They're tired, but none of them have run out of steam as they knock out pushup after pushup.

Austin touches my arm. When I turn back to him, I take in the knowing look in his eyes. "Tell me," he says after a minute.

I let out a breath, wondering why I bother to hide anything from my cousin. He can read me like a book. I spill everything—how I couldn't stand Theo at first but slowly started to like him as I got to know him while living together. How working together and seeing him dote on the kids at the hockey camp made me like him even more. How we started as a casual hookup, nothing serious at all.

"But, um, the thing is..." I clear my throat. "I think I'm starting to catch feelings for him."

Austin flashes a warm smile at me. He pulls me into a side hug. "I can tell. You haven't brought a guy home to meet us since..." He frowns and looks off to the side, like he's concentrating extra hard. "God, was it your high school prom?"

I glance down at the floor, my stomach flipping at the realization. "I think you're right."

"Why are you so skittish about this?" Austin asks.

I steal another glance at Theo, who's grinning even though he's currently at sixty pushups. A second later Tyler drops to the floor and the crowd groans. Then it's down to just Theo and Gage. Their arms are shaking at this point as they struggle to push up every time they drop to the floor. Gage finally flops to the ground, leaving Theo to finish one final pushup before falling to the ground too. When he does, everyone cheers.

The three of them are panting as they smile and shake hands. Theo stands up, a bashful smile on his face as my family cheers for him.

My heart does that fluttering thing again. I hazard a glance at my cousin, but I stay quiet.

"Theo is amazing, Maya," Austin says. I look back at him. "He's kind and funny and easy to talk to. And he's a good sport. You saw the way he handled Millie's baby like a champ. Most people would be running for the hills if their friend-with-benefits' cousin handed off their baby to them."

I chuckle weakly at his wording. He's right.

"He seems down to join whatever we're doing," Austin says. "He fits in so well with our family. I mean, we're loud and we talk non-stop and we force hugs and food on him and still he sticks around. And as a bonus, he's ridiculously good-looking. He's a keeper for sure."

"Yeah, but he's also a pro hockey player who's built a reputation for being a ladies' man."

Austin doesn't even blink at what I've said. He nods his chin over at Theo, who's chatting with Becca and Tori while guzzling down a glass of water. Theo catches eyes with me and gives me a heart-stopping grin, like he's thrilled to see me even though he's been looking at me all day and night *and* can't wait to tear my clothes off. Goosebumps flash across my skin.

"You guys have been living together for what now, a month?" Austin asks.

"Yeah."

"And how many times has he hooked up with anyone else other than you?"

"Austin, there's a reason for that. He's trying to makeover his image so he can play for his team again. He wouldn't risk that to hook up with some rando. Besides, I'm only here temporarily. Even if we do decide to make things between us official, we wouldn't last. Once Theo figures out his next move and moves out of Ingrid's place, I'm heading back to San Diego to work as her personal assistant again. We'll be thousands of miles from each other."

Austin shakes his head like he's disappointed in me.

"It would never work, Austin. The only reason it works now is because we're stuck in the same house together." My tone is firm and insistent as I speak, but I can't help but feel off, like I'm trying to convince myself.

Austin looks at me like he's disappointed. "Maybe. Or maybe you're doing what you usually do and tossing up every excuse to sabotage yourself because you're scared. Because you're scared to take any sort of risk with your heart."

The pointed way my cousin speaks puts me on the

defensive instantly. I cross my arms and turn away, but he gently touches my shoulder.

"I'm sorry." I can tell by the look in his gold-brown eyes that he means it. "I didn't mean to sound so judgmental. Really. I can just tell that you're happy with him, Maya. Happier than I've seen you in a long time. I've never seen you smile this much with anyone." He hesitates. "Can you promise me something? Don't completely write off a future with Theo, at least not just yet. At least think about it."

I feel myself soften at my cousin's heartfelt words. I hug him. "Okay. I will."

"Now go congratulate your man," Austin says. "He keeps flashing heart eyes at you."

I chuckle and walk over to Theo. "That was an impressive showing."

When I squeeze his bicep, he winces.

"Shoot, sorry. Feeling sore?"

He nods and grins. "Worth it though."

He runs a hand through his sandy blond waves, which are mussed and falling in every angle from the impromptu push-up contest with my brothers. His face is flushed pink, his shirt is rumpled, and for a long second, all I can do is stand there and drink in the gorgeous visual of him, looking disheveled and dashing all at once.

"I feel like I won some sort of unspoken prize in your family," he says.

"You have. You showed up my muscle-head brothers, and for that, my family will respect you forever."

Theo laughs and downs more water. The music starts back up. The opening beat of PSY's "Gangnam Style" echoes in the dining space.

"Damn. Blast from the past," I say.

Theo holds out a hand. "We gotta dance."

He pulls me onto the makeshift dancefloor. I do a terrible job of replicating the dance moves I barely remember the few times I watched the music video a decade ago when this was a YouTube craze. Theo dances and grooves alongside me, looking just as terrible. I'm smiling and laughing so much my cheeks ache.

The whole time I imagine what a future with Theo would be like. Nerves crackle inside of me at the uncertainty, at the potential of just how much we could hurt each other...

But then he takes my hand. He holds me close. He gazes at me with affection in his eyes. I shove aside the whirlwind of doubts and focus on the moment.

"I haven't scared you off with my awful dance moves, have I?" he asks.

I smile at him. "Not even close."

Chapter 29

Theo

My stomach is crackling with nerves as I stand in the kitchen. I can barely swallow a sip of my morning coffee, I'm so nervous.

It's been a week since her cousin's anniversary party and things between us have been as fun and sexy as ever. When we're not at hockey camp and I'm not at physical therapy, we can't keep our hands off each other.

I think about how we almost talked about our relationship status that night...and how I lost the nerve to bring it back up to her after that comment she made about marriage being pointless...

Never in a million years.

I try to ignore that faint jolt of pain that shoots through my chest.

Before if someone I had dated uttered the word "marriage," I'd be running for the hills. But not with Maya.

It's not that I want to run out and marry her right this moment. More like the thought of being with her long-term and doing all the things we already do—living together, waking up every morning next to her, working together—doesn't freak me out. The opposite actually.

My stomach does this strange flip thing it's never done before. I catch myself smiling for no reason. The thought of sharing a life with her is thrilling.

And when I think about being apart from her—when I think about this setup ending someday—it feels like a punch to the gut. I dread even thinking about it. Because I'm starting to feel something deep for Maya.

That's why I'm standing here, quietly freaking out, wondering if this surprise I've planned for her will broadcast just how much my feelings for her have grown...and if that will send her running for the hills.

I set the mug on the counter and force myself to take another breath. I stare at the confirmation email that's displayed on my phone screen. Maybe this was a terrible idea.

I guess there's only one way to find out.

Just then I hear Maya padding down the hall. When I look up at her, the tension coursing through me eases. God, she looks so fucking cute with her messy hair and her big brown eyes puffy with sleep.

She walks over and kisses me. "Morning," she murmurs against my mouth.

"Morning."

I pour her a cup of coffee and work up the nerve to show her what's on my phone.

"Hey. Um, I have a surprise for you."

She grins wide. "A surprise?"

"Yeah." I clear my throat and fumble with my phone before showing it to her.

It's a few seconds before the recognition sets in. She looks up at me. "Theo, what is this?"

"I reserved a booth for you to sell your earrings at the Rocky Mountain Winter Festival."

I hold my breath as I watch her reaction. I remember going to this festival a bunch of times as a kid. It's huge, with tons of local small businesses in the Denver area participating.

At first, she says nothing. She stares at me like she's confused.

"You what?" she finally says. She blinks a few times like she's dazed.

My stomach drops. Crap. She's not excited like I hoped she'd be.

"I'm sorry," I say quickly. "I probably should have asked you before signing you up. But the way you talk about yourself as a designer made me think you wouldn't. You downplay yourself and your skills, but you shouldn't. You're amazing. You're so talented, Maya. Your earrings are beautiful you should put them out there for people to see. I promise you, people will love them and want to buy them."

She blinks once before the focus in her eyes returns. She bites her lip like she's thinking hard.

I grab her hand gently in mine. "I'm sorry I sprung it on you like this."

She shakes her head before the corners of her mouth curve up in a gentle smile. "Don't be sorry, Theo. This was so sweet. I just..." She glances off to the side and gazes out the huge floor-to-ceiling window that looks out at the snow-covered mountains. "You really believe in me, don't you?" she says, her voice quiet, like she can hardly believe it.

I cup my free hand over her cheek. "Of course I believe in you. You're incredible."

She smiles.

"I'm not the only one who believes in you, Maya. Ingrid

and your cousins see how talented you are too. That's why they're always telling you to showcase your designs. They see how good you are too."

"Yeah. I guess you're right." She glances back down at the confirmation message on my phone. "Thank you for believing in me enough to surprise me with this."

"Does that mean you'll do it? You'll showcase your earrings at the festival?"

She grins wide and nods. Relief and excitement course through me.

I let out a "whoop!" and kiss her.

When we pull apart, she cups her face in her hands. "I'm nervous. What if no one buys my stuff?"

"I told you. I'll buy all of it."

She chuckles and kisses me.

"No way, that's gonna happen," I say. "The people at the festival will go wild for your earrings."

She downs half the coffee in her mug and straightens up. She shakes her hands at her sides and shuffles her feet like she's restless and excited.

"I'm going to showcase my earrings at the Rocky Mountain Winter Festival. This is actually happening." She lets out a squeal and does a little jump. I laugh.

"You have to be there with me," she says. "I'll be so nervous if I have to stand there all alone..."

I reach out and pull her against me. "Nothing in the world could keep me away from you, Maya."

I don't miss that flash of emotion in her eyes as she gazes at me. She bites back a grin before grabbing my face in her hands and pulling me in for a kiss that leaves me dizzy.

"I need to work off my nerves. In the bedroom, preferably. Think you could help me out?" she growls against my lips.

A wide grin splits my face. And then I lean down, throw her over my shoulder, and head for my bedroom.

The whole way she's giggling. "Wow. Eager?"

"Think of this as a humanitarian mission. I'm eager to help you."

She bursts out laughing. "You're so kind."

I walk through my bedroom doorway and drop her on the bed. "I'm nothing if not a philanthropist. Now lose the clothes."

She's laughing as she strips off her top and sleeping shorts. She reaches up and grabs me by the waistband of my sweatpants, and pulls me on top of her. We make out like that for a while, until she starts to claw at my pants. I break our kiss and stand up, then yank them off.

She grins wide as her gaze fixes on my dick. When she licks her lips, my cock twitches. I drop to my knees and move my face between her legs, but she sits up and shakes her head.

"I wanna try something," she says with the slyest, sexiest smile I've seen.

My dick twitches again. "What did you have in mind?"

She stands up and grabs me by the arm, leading me to lie down on the bed. And then she crawls on top of me so her face is hovering over my dick and her ass is above my face.

She looks behind her shoulder and peers at me. "I wanna sit on your face and have your dick in my mouth at the same time."

Even more blood rockets to my cock, making me hard as concrete. I'm grinning as I hook my arms around her thighs and pull her pussy to my face. She yelps as I run my tongue up and down her sopping wet slit. I moan at how wet she is, how turned on she is.

Soon she slides my dick into her perfect mouth, slowly running that tongue along the length of me. I groan at how fucking incredible it feels to have her work me over with her mouth. As she bobs her head up and down, the pressure and heat build in my dick and balls. I focus all my energy on her so that I don't blow first, even though this feels incredible.

I move my tongue slowly at first, then I pick up speed, just how she likes it. Soon her legs are trembling and she's screaming with my cock in her mouth. I groan at how turned on I am hearing and feeling Maya have an orgasm. My entire body is hot, throbbing with pleasure, aching for release.

She starts to come down and works me faster in her mouth. A minute later, I explode, my entire body shaking. Holy shit, that was intense.

She rolls off of me and settles next to me on the bed. We're lying head-to-toe, so I peer down at her, smiling when I see that starry look in her eyes and how she's still panting.

I lean up and help her move so that she's lying next to me now. I wrap my arm around her and cuddle her into my chest.

I kiss the top of her head, closing my eyes as I take a deep breath of her vanilla-flower scent.

"So did it work? Did I help you get rid of your nerves?" I ask as I look at her.

She laughs and looks at me, a naughty glint in her eyes. "It definitely helped. But I'm gonna need another round with you to be sure."

I grin, feeling like the smuggest, luckiest guy in the world. I grab her and sit her on top of me. "Gladly."

Chapter 30

Maya

"**I** can't believe how many earrings I've sold. It's only been four hours and half of what I brought is nearly gone," I say as I scramble to change around the display of earrings I've set up at my booth.

Theo moves around the earrings on the display next to me. "Told you your jewelry would be a hit." He winks at me and my insides melt.

I'm still blown away that Theo surprised me with a booth at the Rocky Mountain Winter Festival, that he went through the trouble of arranging all this for me, and that he's been by my side this whole day. He woke up before dawn with me this morning to help me pack up my merchandise, load the car, drove me to the event center on the outskirts of Denver where the festival is being held, and has been giving me pep talks every time I got nervous and started freaking out.

Theo's been a literal dream guy for all the support he's shown me today.

I watch how careful he is as he rearranges the display, handling the earrings gently. It's crystal clear just how

245

much he cares about me—just how much seeing me live out my dream means to him.

My heart does a strange skidding move in my chest. I swallow it back and glance around at the lively festival taking place around us. I inhale, savoring the aroma of cinnamon cookies, pastries, kettle corn, cider, and other goodies from the food and beverage booths at the far end of the event center. White string lights and giant snowflake decorations dangle from the ceiling and most of the booths. Cheery mood music echoes inside. For a second I stop and smile to myself. I can't believe I'm here, selling my earrings like a proper business owner and designer. I need to enjoy the moment.

A man and woman who look to be in their thirties walk up to my booth. I immediately notice the woman. She looks familiar, but I'm not sure if it's because I've seen her before or she just looks like someone I know. She could pass for a young Naomi Campbell. She's wearing a vintage wool Chanel coat. Damn. That thing must have cost a pretty penny.

"Wow, these are so pretty," she says as she looks at a pair of dangly, rose gold chevron cut-out earrings.

"Thank you," I say.

"They're hand-crafted by this amazing woman," Theo adds gesturing to me. I grin at him.

The woman smiles. "Really? Very cool." She squints at the price tag. "Is this what you're charging?"

I smile and tell her yes despite feeling the slightest bit uncomfortable. So far no one who's bought my earrings has complained about the price, but I guess it was bound to happen.

"I know they're not the cheapest, but I procure the raw materials and treat them myself. There's no middle man so you're getting the best price, I promise," I say, hoping I sound professional and pleasant and not defensive.

She grins and waves a hand. "Oh totally. I just meant I couldn't believe how affordable they are. These are stunning."

I blush at her compliment. Theo flashes a proud grin and that heart-skidding sensation happens again.

She grabs the earrings and holds them up to her ear while studying her reflection in the mirror I set up next to the display.

"You can try them on if you'd like." I hand her a disinfectant wipe so she can clean the earpieces. She tries them on and looks in the mirror.

"Okay, I'm definitely getting these," she says.

The guy she's with is frowning at his phone and doesn't answer her right away. "Huh? Oh, sure. Yeah, great."

I hold back a laugh. Clearly, he doesn't care about women's jewelry.

She pulls a credit card from her purse and hands it to me. I do a double-take when I see it's a Black American Express card. Holy crap. This woman must be loaded. Why in the world would she want to buy my earrings? She could afford to shop at a high-end jeweler downtown, not at some random booth at this festival.

I push aside that thought and focus on running her card through the electronic reader attached to my phone. I send her a digital receipt before grabbing the earrings she selected and packing them in some tissue paper and a small paper bag.

I hand her the bag and she tells me thanks.

"Are you interested in selling your jewelry in shops?" she asks.

"Oh, um, yeah. Someday maybe. This is my first time selling my earrings actually."

She raises a perfectly threaded eyebrow. The corner of her mouth hooks up in an intrigued smile. "Interesting. How much stock do you have?"

I turn around and gesture to the two displays on the table. "You're looking at it." I chuckle.

She smiles. "I own a boutique in downtown Denver and I'm looking to add more jewelry to my inventory. Here's my card. When you bulk up your inventory, send me an email. I'd love to chat about possibly stocking you in my store."

She hands me a business card and walks off with the guy trailing behind her, his gaze still glued to his phone.

I look down at the card and my eyes go wide.

Sadie Skinner, owner of Lux Boutique

"Holy shit," I mutter.

"What? What's wrong?" Theo rushes to my side right as I let out a giddy laugh of pure disbelief.

I glance up in the direction of where she walked off, but she's gone.

My mouth hangs open as I point in her direction. "That was Sadie Skinner."

Theo frowns. "Who's Sadie Skinner?"

"The famous fashion model. She was huge when we were in high school. She was born and raised in Denver but spent her career modeling all over the world. But then she quit modeling and kind of disappeared," I say quickly. He looks at me blankly. "She wore that emerald-encrusted string bikini at the Victoria's Secret fashion show, like, ten years ago. It was all over the news and social media."

Recognition finally hits Theo's stare. "Hell yeah, I remember that. Wait, that was her?"

"Yup." I tug a hand through my hair to ground myself.

"I had no idea she owned Lux. That's the hottest boutique in Denver."

Theo's brow hits his hairline before he grins. "Holy shit, Maya. This is huge."

I let out a quiet squeal while nodding my head like I'm crazed. "Sadie Skinner wants to carry my jewelry in her shop. Oh my god..."

The excitement crests, which gives way to a wave of nerves. "That means I need to design and craft a whole new line of earrings. Crap, I don't even know where to start. I mean, they'd need to be really special to be in her store. And what if I send her my designs and she hates them? God, that would be so humiliating..."

Theo scoops my hand in his and flashes that gorgeous easy grin. "Maya. You're not allowed to freak out right now. All you're allowed to do is get excited. All that other stuff can wait till later. Right now just soak in the moment."

His calm, confident tone eases me. "You're right. Thank you."

I slink my arms around his neck and hug him. "None of this would have happened if you hadn't signed me up for the festival." I lean back and look him straight in the eye. "Thank you for believing in me, Theo."

He grins and kisses me. "Always."

Goosebumps flash across my skin and my heart thuds in my chest. This man. He is beyond amazing.

I give him a quick kiss before returning to the booth and helping more customers. The whole time I can't stop thinking about how lucky I am to be with Theo Thompson.

Chapter 31

Theo

"Alright, guys. Who's ready for fun skate?" I ask the kids.

They all cheer, "me!" I pull up the playlist on my phone, hit "play," and lead the kids out on the frozen pond.

I take the front like usual. One of the kids asks to hold Maya's hand as we skate around the pond. As I turn the corner, I catch eyes with her. She flashes that gorgeous smile, and something in my chest rattles.

I'd be lying if I said this thing with Maya was still casual. I know in my heart it isn't, that I'm starting to develop some serious feelings for her.

I think back to the other day when we were at the winter festival, what a hit her earrings were. She ended up selling out. And I still can't stop thinking about the pure joy on her face when Sadie Skinner approached her about carrying her earrings in her boutique. I could feel the pride swelling in my chest. My Maya, kicking ass, making her dream come true.

My Maya

That rattled feeling inside of me intensifies. I know I don't have any right to call her that. We're technically still casual, still friends with benefits...but I know deep down, that's not what I want anymore. I want something more. And I wonder if she feels the same.

I could ask her...

But then I remember what she said at Declan and Austin's anniversary party after seeing her parents sneak around. She's made it crystal clear she doesn't want anything serious. She doesn't ever want to get married either.

That intense feeling inside of me turns to pain. I clear my throat, take a breath, and try to ignore it. I can't be thinking about this right now, not when I should be focused on camp.

Annabelle skates up next to me. "Coach Theo, I'm gonna do a fun skate at my birthday party this weekend at the ice skating rink," she says.

"You are? That sounds really cool."

She grins, her front two teeth missing. She tells me that she's going to turn seven on Saturday.

"I'm gonna have pink cupcakes and pink lollipops, and my mom said I get to wear a tiara, and everyone from hockey camp is coming too," she says excitedly.

"Whoa! Sounds like it's gonna be a blast," I say.

"I'm so, so, so excited!"

"You know, Saturday is my birthday too."

Annabelle smiles wider. "It is?"

"Yup. We're birthday buddies." I high-five her.

"How old will you be?" she asks.

"Twenty-nine."

Annabelle's brown eyes are huge. "Whoa. That's old."

I hear Maya chuckle behind me. I laugh too.

251

"Yeah, I guess twenty-nine seems kind of old when you're six," I say.

"Almost seven," she says pointedly.

I hold up a hand. "Right. Almost seven. Sorry."

"What are you doing for your birthday, Coach Theo?" Sloane asks me.

I shrug. "Probably nothing."

All the kids stop skating and gawk at me.

"How come? Did you get in trouble?"

"Yeah, did you make your mom and dad mad and now they said you can't have a birthday party?'

"Yeah, were you naughty, Coach Theo?"

Maya laughs even harder.

"You can come to my party if you want," Annabelle says.

I smile at her. "That's really kind of you to offer, Annabelle. Thank you. But I don't want to mess up your cool party plans."

She tugs on my hand, the look on her face bright and eager. "My mom and stepdad said that I should always include everyone because that's the kind thing to do."

"Yeah, you should come, Coach Theo," Emerson says.

Parker nods along. "Yeah! Come to the party."

My resolve starts to soften as the kids all plead for me to go.

"Okay, okay. I'll go."

All the kids cheer.

"But only if Coach Maya is invited too," I say.

Annabelle says yes. Maya smiles at me.

We get the kids set up to do an easy obstacle course on the frozen pond. As they line up and go through it, Maya turns to me.

"Are you seriously not planning to do anything for your birthday?" she asks.

I shake my head. "Birthdays aren't a big deal to me anymore. But thanks to Annabelle, I get to have a birthday party with cupcakes and lollipops."

Maya laughs. "That's cute, but you need to do something to celebrate yourself."

"Maybe. We'll see."

Maya looks at me like she's brewing up something.

"You don't need to plan something for me, Maya."

"I'm not." She flashes a knowing smile that leaves me wondering what she's up to.

"Coach Theo, you look so pretty in your tiara!" Annabelle says when she sits next to me at the table set up outside of the ice rink.

I smile down at her. "Thanks, birthday girl. And thanks for letting me come to your party."

"Are you having fun?" she asks, her cheeks rosy from skating with her friends.

"A blast." I glance out at the ice, where my teammate Dylan is currently skating while dressed as some pink bunny mascot I don't recognize. A couple of kids skate up to him and hug him. One kid crashes right between his legs and he doubles over. I burst out laughing.

Annabelle notices and chuckles. "Dylan's so funny." She starts talking about her favorite cartoon, which is where that bunny character is from.

The rest of the parents start corralling their kids from the ice rink to the table for snacks and cupcakes.

Isaac, who's holding hands with his twin daughters

Sloane and Emerson, walks over to the table and helps them get seated.

I point out Dylan hunched over on a nearby bench, elbows on his knees, his bunny head hanging low. Isaac chuckles.

Annabelle points to the cupcake tower in front of us. "My mom made sure there's two cupcakes at the top. One for me and one for you." She grins wide.

"Thanks so much, Annabelle. You're so nice to share your birthday party with me."

I catch eyes with Maya, who's helping Parker get out of his ice skates.

"Did you see what Coach Maya got me?" Annabelle turns her face to the side, then the other side. Gold heart-shaped clip-on earrings dangle from her ears.

"Whoa! Those are pretty cool," I say.

"Coach Maya made them!" Annabelle says excitedly.

"She's really talented, isn't she?"

I think back to earlier this morning when I helped Maya pick them out for Annabelle. I've been racking my brain, trying to figure out the best way to bring up the topic of us getting serious without completely freaking her out...if she'd ever be willing to change her mind about our status.

I glance over at her as she chats with a couple of the parents.

"You and Coach Maya smile at each other a lot," Annabelle says.

I clear my throat. "Yeah. We do. You smile at your friends too, don't you?"

She nods. "But you look at her the way Dylan looks at Mommy." Her expression turns curious as she looks at me. "Do you *like* like Coach Maya?"

I ruffle my hair as I laugh. Damn, kids can be observant.

"Yeah. I do." I fiddle with the tiny plastic tiara that's about to fall from my melon head.

"Does Coach Maya know you like her? Like, have you told her that you *like* like her?"

I smile despite the uncertainty I feel. "I'm trying to work up the nerve to tell her."

"You should tell her. It's always best to be honest," Annabelle says.

I laugh. "Good point."

All the kids crowd around the table. Annabelle's mom sticks two candles in the top two cupcakes of the tower, lights them, and everyone sings Happy Birthday. When they finish, I help Annabelle up and out of her chair. Together we stand side by side and blow out the candles together.

As the kids chow down on their cupcakes, I spot Maya, who's standing by the small side table where the drinks are.

"Adorable," she mouths to me.

I laugh to myself before standing up to walk over to her. I bump into Isaac as he turns around.

"Damn, dude. Never thought I'd see you have such a wholesome birthday," he says pointing to the tiara on my head. I chuckle and take it off.

A couple more of my teammates, whose kids are attending Annabelle's birthday party, walk over to hand us plastic glasses of punch.

Dylan stands up from his spot, removes the bunny head he's wearing, and joins us, holding the giant pink head under his arm.

"A little different from your last birthday party, right?" Dylan jokes. He squints like he's thinking hard. "I'm pretty sure there was a strip club and body shots and a few ladies—"

A kid runs by and I elbow him, cutting him off. He frowns at me and I nod at the kid. "Don't talk like that right now," I tell him.

His brow eases. "Okay, yeah. You're right. I should know better, being around Annabelle." He sighs. "Seriously though, you've seemed to change your ways. It's cool to see."

The rest of the guys nod along.

"Yeah. Never thought you'd ever want to work with kids," Isaac says. "The girls love your camp."

"Annabelle comes home every day after camp raving about how fun it was," Dylan says. "You've clearly got a knack for it."

Pride swells in my chest. Maybe it's weird, but hearing my teammates compliment me for something that's not directly related to how I played during a game feels pretty damn great. Like I'm capable of being good at more than just playing hockey.

Isaac's kids call for him and he walks off along with my other teammates.

Dylan turns to me. "Coach Porter was talking about you the other day."

I hold my breath, shocked at what he's said. That could be good or bad. "Really?"

He nods. "I overheard him on the phone. I think he was talking to your PT. He sounded impressed at your recovery. And he said something about some article where you were quoted. Said he was impressed at how mature you sounded. And I think he's overheard us on the team talk about the hockey camp you're running and all the good stuff we've been saying about it—about you. I think he's impressed at how you've changed."

Hope bursts in my chest. "Dylan, I swear, if you're fucking with me—"

He holds up a hand. "I'm not. Look, I only heard bits and pieces of his conversation, but I know for sure he was talking about you and it sounded positive. I probably shouldn't even be telling you this, but I wanted to give you a head's up. You might be getting a call from your agent pretty soon. Just be ready."

One of the moms yells for Dylan to come take a photo with the kids and the cupcake tower.

He sighs. "Duty calls."

He puts the bunny head back on and walks off, while I take a second to think about what he just said. I know better than to get my hopes up, but I can't help it. If this happens— if I get back on the team, I'd piss myself with excitement.

Maya waves at me and I walk over, tempted to tell her the good news. But I hold back. Dylan wasn't even supposed to tell me. I should just keep this to myself.

"You look happy," Maya says when I make it to her.

"Can't help it. Cupcakes and tiaras are what bring me joy in life." I place the tiara back on my head.

She laughs. "You're such a good sport."

"When a kid invites you to share their birthday party with you, you dive in head first."

She laughs. "By the way, be ready to leave the house at eight o'clock tonight. I have a birthday surprise planned."

"I don't get any clues?"

"Bring a headlamp."

I quirk an eyebrow, intrigued. "I'll be ready."

Chapter 32

Maya

"Y ou're not making us explore a cave tonight, are you? Because I can get pretty claustrophobic in tight spaces," Theo says.

I chuckle and zip up my parka and feed Mr. Pudding. "Don't worry. Your birthday surprise involves zero caves."

We step out the front door bundled up to the max and walk to the end of the driveway. Never in my life have I planned a birthday surprise for a guy I've been with. But Theo isn't just some guy. He's incredible. These past couple of months together, I've felt the happiest I've ever been. He's the most thoughtful, sweetest, kindest guy I've ever met. He's made me feel so special and supported, and I wanted to do something that would make him feel that way too.

Theo shuffles as he stands next to me. He turns to look at me. "No more clues? Seriously?"

"Nope. Just be patient."

He huffs out a sigh through his smile and shoves his hands into his pockets. A second later there's a faint noise in the distance. Then another. And other.

"What was that?" He glances off into the darkness ahead of us.

I try my hardest not to smile. "What do you mean?"

"That yelping sound in the distance. Don't you hear it?"

I pretend to fuss with the pocket of my parka. "Hear what?"

"Maya."

That familiar shiver runs through me like it always does when he says my name in that soft growl.

I glance up at him and grin. I can't help it. I'm too giddy.

He aims a teasing smile at me. "What's going on?"

Before I can answer, that sound in the distance gets louder. The sound of barking dogs is clear now.

Theo whips his head back toward the darkened street in front of us, his mouth open in shock.

He turns back to me. "Holy shit, you didn't."

"I did."

Just then, two huskies come into view. They run side by side down the hill, revealing another two huskies, and another two, and another two.

I take in the sight of Theo standing next to me, mouth agape as he smiles, his sky-blue eyes wide with shock.

He makes an excited sound I don't think I've ever heard him make before a total of a dozen dogs pull a sled up to us. Behind them is a snowmobile.

A cheery older lady clad in an electric blue parka grins and waves at us from the sled. "Maya and Theo?" she asks.

"That's us," I say. I grab Theo by the hand and lead him to the sled.

The lady on the sled introduces herself as Judy, who's the woman I spoke to on the phone to arrange this. She gestures to her husband Walt on the snowmobile, who waves at us.

"I was told you've done this before," Judy says to Theo.

He chuckles. "Yeah, but not since I was a kid."

She waves a hand. "It's like riding a bike."

"Can we meet the dogs?" I ask.

"You sure can." Judy lets us pet the huskies, who greet us with excited noises, wagging tails, and licks.

Theo and I take a moment to pet each one. I watch as he gets down on his knees and nuzzles the dogs, laughing as they lick his face. Seeing him so happy sets off a warm and fuzzy feeling inside of me.

Judy gives us a rundown of how to ride in the sled.

"One person gets to sit and one person gets to stand at the back of the sled and steer," she says.

I elbow Theo gently. "That's all you."

He flashes the giddiest grin I've ever seen him make. Judy explains that she and Walt will drive the snowmobile ahead of the dog sled and lead us on a forty-five-minute ride through the mountains, complete with stops along the way.

I settle into the sled while Theo stands at the back.

"Are you kids ready?" she asks.

"Ready," we say in unison.

Walt brings the snowmobile up to Judy, she climbs on, and they ease ahead of us.

I gaze up at Theo. "Happy Birthday."

Emotion flashes in his eyes as he smiles down at me. He leans down and cups my face in his gloved hand. "Thank you for this."

He kisses me. When he pulls away, the sound of the snowmobile revving catches our attention. A half-second later we jerk forward as the dogs pull us ahead.

We zoom through the fresh layer of snow on the cold, the crisp winter air flipping around us.

"Oh my god! They're so fast!" I yelp.

Theo's laugh thunders behind me.

"They're huskies. They're born to sprint to the snow," he hollers.

"I can see that." I grip the sled, shrieking as they take turns sharply.

"You okay?" he asks.

"Yeah, all good. I feel like I'm in an ice luge."

For the next twenty minutes, we wind through the snow-covered forest. Every once in a while I twist around to see Theo's reaction. Every single time he's smiling, which makes me smile. By the time we make it to our first stop, which is a clearing in the forest next to a frozen pond, my face is aching from grinning so hard.

"Okay, you two. Here's a cool little spot to take a breather," Judy says. "Nice and romantic with the full moon." She winks at us and we both chuckle.

Theo hops off the sled and holds his hand out to me. "Wanna take a quick walk to the pond with me?" he asks.

"I'd love to."

Together we walk hand in hand the couple dozen feet to the edge of the pond.

"So how's your first time dog sledding?" he asks.

"It's bumpier than I thought it would be but so much fun. How didn't you go flying when you rode with your grandpa as a tiny little kid?"

Theo chuckles. "He would strap me into the sled."

"Oh. That's a really smart idea."

We stop just a few feet from the pond and take in the view.

"Wow. This is so pretty." I gaze up at the dazzling full moon in the indigo-black sky, how its reflection sparkles softly in the frozen water. The brightness of the moon paints the snow and the trees in a soft glow.

"I had no idea it was going to be a full moon tonight," I say. "Guess we got lucky."

"*I* got lucky."

I turn to Theo, who's gazing at me with what looks like adoration on his face. For a second, I forget to breathe.

A tender smile pulls at his mouth. "Maya, this is…" He huffs out a breath and shakes his head. "This is the most thoughtful gift anyone has ever gotten me. Thank you."

His low tone is full of emotion. It sends a flash of heat across my body, despite the chill in the air.

"You didn't have to do all this for me," he says.

I reach up and cup his face in my hands. "I know I didn't have to. I wanted to."

His blue eyes turn fiery. "You know, for someone who says she sucks at romantic gestures, you knocked it out of the park with this surprise."

His compliment has me soaring. "I guess I'm getting better at it."

I lean up and kiss him softly. He hums against my lips before parting my mouth open with his tongue. That heat inside of me burns hotter. Soon I'm clawing at his chest through his coat. A beat later I force myself to break the kiss.

"We should probably stop. We have an audience," I say before glancing over at Judy, Walt, and the dogs, who are yelping and kicking up snow.

Theo lets out a shaky breath and an equally shaky chuckle. He rests his forehead against mine. "Good point."

"We'll finish this at the house," I say. "For now, enjoy the ride. And get ready for surprise number two." I wink at him before pulling him back to the dog sled by the hand.

"Please tell me it involves you being naked at some point."

I turn around and smirk at him. "You'll just have to wait and see."

Chapter 33

Theo

When we make it back to the house, my cheeks ache because I can't stop smiling. This birthday surprise Maya planned for me was incredible. No one has ever done anything like this for me.

She goes to unlock the front door. "You're still smiling," she says as she turns around to glance at me.

I slide my arms around her waist and hug her from behind.

"Tonight was amazing." I nuzzle my face into her hair. "*You* are amazing."

She lets out a soft moan and I hug her tight against me. She twists her head around and I capture her mouth in a slow, teasing kiss.

After a few seconds, she pulls away. I take in that hungry look in her eyes. "Let's go inside," she rasps.

I follow her through the door and shut it behind me.

She spins around to face me. "Take off your coat and wait for me on the couch." Her smile has a naughty edge to it now.

My dick twitches in my pants. "Yes, ma'am."

Maya disappears down the hall and I head to the kitchen to guzzle a glass of water before going to sit on the couch.

Two minutes later she strolls out in this red lingerie thing that has my eyes bulging out of my head. I stare at her, unable to formulate words for a solid ten seconds.

She walks up to me, a sexy smile tugging at those luscious lips.

"You look fucking incredible," I finally manage to say.

She straddles me on the couch, resting her hands on my shoulders. That sugar flower perfume she wears fills my lungs as she leans her face to mine.

"Happy birthday part two," she whispers before kissing me.

She grinds against my hard dick and I groan into her mouth.

"Maya..." I growl between kisses. "You're gonna make me come in my pants."

She giggles. "Is that bad?" She teases me with an innocent stare.

"It would be very, very bad."

We keep kissing, our mouths and tongues getting filthier by the second.

"Does that mean you want me to stop?" she teases.

"Fuck no," I growl.

She grinds against me again, her breaths turning ragged and shallow. My cock is aching to be inside of her, but I want her as warmed up as possible.

All of a sudden she stills. She pulls away.

I look up at her. "What's wrong? Is everything okay?"

She starts to climb off of me and pull away. I take in her expression. She looks embarrassed for some reason.

As she stands between my legs, she cups her face with her hands. "Sorry, I uh...I just got my period."

"Oh."

She exhales like she's annoyed with herself. "Fantastic timing."

I reach up and grab her hand in mine. "Maya, that doesn't mean we have to stop."

She frowns like she's confused. "What?"

"It doesn't bother me."

For a second she just stares at me. "Seriously?"

"Seriously."

She bites her lip like she's not quite sure about what I've said.

"Sorry, I wasn't trying to pressure you." I shake my head, realizing what I've said kind of comes off like that. "It's just that I'm good to keep going if you want to. You being on your period doesn't make me want to do this any less. But if you don't want to, that's completely fine too."

Her expression eases. She starts to smile. "I didn't expect that. I'm not used to guys being okay with this. At least, the guys I've been with."

"Their loss."

She laughs at what I've said before looking down at our joined hands.

"Maybe we can do this in the shower?" she says.

I grin wide. "Lead the way."

A second later we're in the master bathroom. I rip off my shirt and pants. Maya chuckles at me.

"That was fast," she says.

"The promise of you naked in the shower is quite the incentive."

I shed my boxer briefs, turn on the water, and then grab her by the hips, pulling her closer to me.

I tug at the red lace panties she's wearing as she reaches behind her and unhooks her bra. The two delicate pieces of fabric fall to the floor. And then she steps into the shower. I follow behind.

Underneath the spray of hot water, I pull her close to me once more and kiss her. We stay like that for who knows how long. Keeping track of time is meaningless when I've got the most gorgeous woman in the world naked and wet in my arms. I run my hands all over her body. Her hips, her back, her ass.

I slide my hand between her legs and press gently. She groans into my mouth, digging her fingers into my shoulders.

I work my fingers slowly at first, in gentle circles, just like she likes it.

As our kiss amps up, I work my fingers faster. Maya yelps. She drags her mouth down my neck and shoulder, landing at my delt. When she bites me, I grunt.

"Harder," I growl.

She whimpers before sinking her teeth into me harder. Fuck, I love knowing that being with me makes her this rough, this feral.

My eyes roll to the back of my head. Pleasure shoots through my dick. She's not even touching me there and I'm so turned on.

She eases back and kisses the spot she just bit before biting it again. I smile. That's my girl. Feisty and soft all at once.

Her head falls back as she moans. I take in the look on her face, how those big brown eyes are dazed with pleasure. I work her in my hand with a steady pace, picking up speed when her breaths turn ragged and her moans get louder.

"Theo..." she rasps. "Theo..."

My chest aches at the sound of her voice, how she says my name like it's the only word she knows.

The longer I look at Maya, the more my chest aches. Except it's not exactly my chest…it feels a lot more like my heart…

This woman. This goddess who's sweet and feisty and caring and not afraid to go toe-to-toe with me.

"I'm gonna come," she says, her tone a desperate whisper.

I capture her mouth in mine. "That's my girl," I say against her lips as I swirl my fingers faster on her clit. "Come hard for me."

My girl

My own words echo in my brain. That ache in my heart intensifies.

My girl

She starts to shake against me as her orgasm takes hold. Her body thrashes and I hold her tight. She moans and screams. My name echoes against the shower walls. My heart feels like it's about to burst in my chest. That's when I know…

No matter how much I tell myself otherwise, this is no longer a hook-up, no longer casual.

I stare at Maya as she starts to come down, her body trembling, that glassy look in her eyes as she smiles at me. I try to swallow, but it's impossible. Not when my heart is lodged in my throat.

She smiles at me. "Your turn." She starts to reach for my dick, but I stop her.

"What's wrong?" she asks.

I shake my head, too rattled by the emotion surging through me to say anything at first.

A beat later I manage a smile. I kiss her. "Nothing's wrong. I just need to be inside of you."

I'm so turned on right now, I know it won't take long for me to come.

Something flashes in her eye as she stares at me and nods.

I push open the shower door, swipe my jeans from the floor, and pull out the condom in my pocket. I rip it open, slide it on, then grab Maya and kiss her.

When we break, she turns around and bends over, her palms flat against the shower wall.

I pause and take in the stunning visual of her perfect ass. I palm her plump cheeks in my hands before I grab her hips and slide into her warm, wet pussy. She arches her back up and hisses.

"God, Theo. You're so big."

"But you can take me, can't you?" I start to thrust slowly.

She nods. "Always."

I continue that slow thrust for a minute, savoring the warm, tight feel of her pussy.

"Look at you, baby. You're taking me so well. Good girl."

When she whimpers, goosebumps fly across my skin despite the hot water raining down on us.

"Harder, Theo. Please..."

Before I obey her command, I pause for a second. I have to. I can't take her begging like that when I'm inside of her and she feels this fucking good.

The heat and pressure building in my cock settles. And then I start up again.

My chest squeezes even harder. My brain is mush. All I

can focus on is how good she feels and how good I want to make her feel too.

I fuck her hard and deep, just like she asked me to. She's screaming and shaking. I can tell she's close. I reach a hand around and tease her clit.

"I'm gonna come again. Oh my god…"

"That's it, baby. Come on my cock. Come on my hand."

She shakes her head. "Not without you…how close are you?"

"Really fucking close." I grip her hip in my hand and thrust harder.

"Good because…because…fuck!"

I feel her pussy tighten around me as she climaxes. That's all it takes for me to lose it. I explode with a growl as I thrust hard and fast. All the muscles inside of me tense with the release. My entire body feels like it's on fire.

I fall forward, one hand propped on the shower wall, careful to keep from putting all of my weight on Maya. For several seconds we just stand there and catch our breath, water raining around us.

When I feel her start to move, I straighten up. She spins around, cups my face in her hands, and kisses me until I'm panting once more.

We break the kiss and rest our foreheads together. Eyes closed, I take a second to catch my breath.

"How am I still standing?" she asks, her tone faint, like she's mystified. "I can't even feel my legs."

Chuckling, I lean back to look at her. "Even if you fall, I've got you."

There's a flash of intensity in those beautiful brown eyes as she gazes at me. "I know."

In the quiet moment that follows we just look at each

other. That ache in my heart, in my chest returns. It deepens the longer I look at her.

That was different, right? That wasn't just a hot fuck in the shower for you either, right? You felt it, didn't you? Please tell me you felt it too...

The words rest on the tip of my tongue, aching for me to speak them.

"We should get cleaned up and head to bed." She smiles at me.

I hold back. I swallow, smile, and nod.

We get cleaned up, then rinse off. After we dry off, we head to my bed and I cradle her body into mine. She relaxes into me like she always does every night we've slept in the same bed together.

Tonight it's different though. It *feels* different. And I know why.

As Maya falls asleep, I silently acknowledge it. I'm falling in love with this woman.

Chapter 34

Maya

When I wake up, Theo's not in bed.

I lift my head and gaze around the room. He's nowhere to be found.

In my groggy state, I'm the slightest bit shocked. We've almost always woken up together ever since we started hooking up and to wake up without him feels...weird. Empty. Wrong.

Especially after last night.

I pad to the bathroom to pee and remember the look on Theo's face when I surprised him with the dog sled ride. My heart pumps in my chest just thinking about how giddy and happy he was. I've never seen him like that.

And then I think about how when we got home and my sexy surprise for him went wrong, he wasn't even fazed. How completely unbothered he was when I told him I got my period. At first, I was skeptical. But after what went down in the shower....

A faint pulse lands between my legs. He was definitely telling the truth when he said that my being on my period didn't make him want me any less.

I smile to myself, but it fades when I remind myself that's he not here right now.

Maybe the intensity of last night got to him?

I think back on that moment in the shower, right after having sex. Only sex doesn't seem like the right word.

Making love?

Just thinking that has me feeling ridiculous. But honestly, that feels closer to whatever it is that I'm feeling...

I wash my hands at the sink and replay that moment in my head. How being together last night felt different from every other time we've been together. When he touched and grabbed me, it felt urgent but soft and tender too. And the intensity in Theo's gaze when he looked at me...

How I stood there, waiting for him to say something, anything to acknowledge that feeling between us...

I shake my head as I dry my hands, annoyed with myself. This is exactly what I said I didn't want. What I initially told Theo I wanted was a hook-up. Friends with benefits. Nothing serious. And that's exactly what this is. So why am I getting all huffy when I wake up and he's not here? It's not like he's my boyfriend. It's not like he's under any obligation to wake up with me or let me know where he's gone off to.

Because you like him

"Duh. Of course I like him. I'm sleeping with him."

I roll my eyes. And now I'm talking to myself. Great.

Don't play coy. You planned a birthday surprise for him. When was the last time you did something so thoughtful for a guy you were sleeping with?

"Never." It falls out in a breath.

I could lie to myself. I could say that Theo and I are friends and I've planned a million surprises for my friends and family. And that would be true.

But I know better. I did that for Theo because I care about him. Because his happiness means something to me.

Because you're starting to fall for him. Hard. You know you are

My stomach feels like it's doing backflips. Because my annoying inner voice is right. In these past couple months of mind-blowing sex, working together, and getting to know each other, I've developed some serious feelings for Theo.

You could see yourself loving him

I go still at that silent admission. I glance up at the mirror and take stock of my reflection. My eyes are wide in reaction to what I've silently admitted to myself. I look like a deer in headlights.

"I'm falling in love with Theo," I whisper to myself. I stand there, waiting. For what? I have no idea. Not sure what I thought would happen when I said that out loud. But everything stays the same.

Except...my heart stops thudding at that back-breaking pace. I take a slow, steady breath. I'm...okay.

The longer I stand there and let it all sink in, the calmer I feel. Maybe a relationship could work out after all.

Just then the bedroom door opens and there's Theo, shirtless and holding a tray of breakfast food in his hands, like a fantasy come to life.

All the nerves swirling inside of me a second ago disappear. When my cheeks start to ache, that's when I realize I'm grinning like an idiot. Relief and joy crash inside of me.

He didn't disappear. He's been here all along, making me breakfast in bed.

Maybe I'm not the stone-cold commitment-phobe I thought I was. Maybe when I've got the literal man of my dreams to wake up next to, doting on me and caring for me, I can see myself being with him long-term.

"You're up," he says.

I bite my lip, still grinning. "Had to pee."

He glances down at the tray. "I wanted to surprise you with breakfast in bed."

My heart flips in my chest when I see the plate of waffles, berries, and cup of coffee.

I walk over to him and kiss him. "No one's ever made me breakfast in bed before. Except you." I sound so mystified when I say it, but it's true.

He flashes that smile I love so much—the one that starts with a half-smile, but a second later it turns full.

"Get back in bed so I can do this thing right," he says.

When I turn around, he slaps my bare ass with his free hand. I yelp before scurrying under the covers. He follows me and waits as I pull the comforter up to my waist. Then he sets the tray in my lap and crawls next to me.

I breathe in the heavenly aroma of coffee and sugar. When I take a sip, I hum. Then I pause.

"Wait, is this oat milk?" I ask.

"Yup." He swipes a raspberry from the small bowl on the tray.

"But we're out of oat milk."

He shrugs. "I slipped out this morning and ran to the grocery store."

"But you hate oat milk."

He looks at me, tenderness in those mesmerizing blue eyes. "Yeah, but you love it."

I go quiet as I stare at him. My heart thuds. This dream boat of a man woke up early to drive through snowy mountain roads to fetch me oat milk, something he can't stand.

Yet another tick in the column of "why I'm falling hard for Theo Thompson." He went out of his way *for me*.

I still, fork in hand, I'm so stunned by his thoughtfulness.

"You okay?" he asks before quickly kissing my neck and stealing another couple of berries from the bowl.

I nod, trying my hardest not to act like a lovestruck weirdo. I need to tell him how I feel...so I can see if he feels the same way.

He swipes the silverware from the tray and cuts up a waffle. He hands the fork to me, I spear a waffle chunk, and offer it to him.

He shakes his head before stealing another couple of berries. "No way. First, bite goes to you." He presses a kiss to my forehead.

For a second, I just look at him as he pops raspberries in his mouth and winks at me. Just when I thought my heart couldn't flutter any harder. I shove the waffle into my mouth, savoring the sweet goodness.

I can't just sit here while these feelings explode inside of me. I need to tell him how I feel about him.

I set down my fork and take a breath. "Theo, I lo—"

His phone blares from the nightstand, interrupting me. He frowns at it.

"Hang on, let me silence that." He reaches for his phone and swipes it up. But instead of silencing it, he stares intently at the screen.

"It's my agent." He looks at me.

"Oh..." Theo hasn't heard from his agent once in the two months that he's been staying at the cabin with me.

"I should probably answer it," he says while studying his phone.

"Um, yeah. Probably." I shove another hunk of waffle in my mouth.

He drags his index finger across his phone screen. "Hey, Javier. What's up?"

I try my hardest to focus on my plate of half-eaten waffles and not eavesdrop on Theo's phone conversation, but I fail miserably.

"Are you serious?" Theo says.

I turn slightly and see a bewildered smile on his face. Like he's getting some great news that he can't believe.

"You're serious, Javier? You're not fucking with me?"

A second later Theo jumps out of bed and fist-pumps the air.

"Holy shit...I can't believe it."

Theo stares ahead, grinning.

"I'm there. I'll be the first one to show up, I swear," he says after he's been quiet for a while. He rests his free hand on his hip and dips his head, eyes closed, but still smiling. Like he's soaking in whatever good news he's getting.

"Thank you, Javier. Seriously, thank you."

He hangs up and spins around to me. "That was my agent. I'm back on the team."

"What?" I move the tray aside and run over to him. "That's amazing, Theo!"

I jump up to hug him and he scoops me up. I wrap my legs around his waist and kiss him.

"Congra...tu...lations," I say between kisses.

He murmurs against my lips. For a minute we stay that way, kissing and giggling and grabbing each other. When he sets me down, he takes a breath, like he still can't quite believe what's happened.

He rests his hands on top of his head. "I guess laying low for a couple of months paid off."

He tells me that his contract with the Bashers has been

reinstated. He'll be able to play for them for the rest of the season.

"They've been keeping tabs on my rehab with my PT and I guess they're happy with my recovery. And the fact that I've stayed out of trouble. I can play again."

His eyes are bright and he's practically buzzing. Like he could suit up and play right now.

"I'm expected at the next team practice in two days." He shakes his head like he still can't believe it. A second later, he blinks and his gaze focuses. "Crap, I'm gonna have to quit hockey camp. I won't have time now that I'm back on the team."

I squeeze his hand. "That's okay. The kids will understand when you explain it to them. They'll probably be excited that they'll be able to watch you play hockey again."

A small smile tugs at his lips, but he still looks a little sad. "Maybe. Hopefully."

His gaze focuses as he looks at me. "And that means I'll have to move out of here. Now that I'm back on the team I guess I don't have to stay here anymore."

"Oh. Right."

Disappointment rockets through me. Now that Theo is back on his team and plans to move out of here, that probably means things between us will fizzle out...

I swallow through the sudden soreness in my throat and try to smile.

Theo steps toward me, the intensity amping up in his whisper-blue eyes. He slinks his arms around my waist and pulls me tight against him. "Unless you want to stay for a little while longer," he says in a soft, low voice.

A rush of excitement hits me. "I'd like that. I don't want to leave just yet."

The corner of his mouth hooks up. "Neither do I. This place feels like home with you, Maya."

My heart feels like it's going to burst in my chest. "I feel the same."

He presses a teasing kiss to my lips. When we break apart to catch our breath, I rest my forehead against him.

"Hey, um, I wanna ask you something," he says. "Maybe it's kind of a weird question, but..."

I lean back to look at him. "What is it?"

He takes a second to swallow. "Will you come to my first game back? It's Thursday."

He lets out a breathy laugh and tugs a hand through his hair like he's nervous to ask me this. "As excited as I am to be back, I'm nervous too. And having you there would help. A lot."

My heart is fluttering to the max. "You want me there?"

He nods. "Most of the guys on the team who are in relationships, their wives and girlfriends come and watch them play."

I'm quiet as I process what he's just said.

Girlfriend

"You want me to be your girlfriend?" I say, surprised.

He nods, but a second later he presses his eyes shut. "I know I'm probably coming off a little strong here. I know you said you're only interested in something casual, but I'm crazy about you Maya."

I can feel the thud of his heart as it hammers in his chest. I can tell just how nervous he is to say all this, to be open about his feelings for me.

He looks at me. "Sorry, that was weird of me to ask, wasn't it—"

I grab his face and kiss him. When we break apart, he looks dazed.

"I want to be your girlfriend, Theo. I want to come to your game."

He lets out a breath through his gorgeous smiling lips before kissing me again. "God, it feels amazing to hear you say that," he says between kisses.

Together we fall back into bed. As we get filthy underneath the sheets, my heart is bursting in my chest. I never thought I'd be this giddy, this eager to be in a relationship. But that's exactly how I feel right now. I'm Theo Thompson's girlfriend and I've never, ever been so happy.

I move so I'm on top of Theo. As I grind against his hard dick, I smile down at him and bite my lip.

"You're my boyfriend."

The way he grins, like he's never been so excited, turns me on even more. "And you're my girlfriend."

"I love the sound of that."

Love

I'm aching to tell Theo that I love him, but I hold back. This has been an exciting morning on its own with Theo finding out that he's back on his team and the two of us deciding to be relationship official. I don't want to overwhelm him by dropping the "l" bomb too.

I slide onto him and groan at how big he is. He lets out a curse as he digs his fingers into my hips.

As we writhe and kiss and grope each other in bed, I decide to tell him after his first game back. I smile against his lips, savoring the way he tastes, the way he touches me.

I'm vibrating with pleasure and anticipation. I can't wait to tell Theo I love him.

Chapter 35

Theo

My lungs are on fire as I sprint across the ice. I'm chasing after Luca Markov, the fastest forward on Seattle's team, who just got possession of the puck and is headed straight for our net.

Our goalie Blomdahl straightens up, ready to block his shot. And there's a good chance he will, considering Blomdahl has the reflexes of a goddamn cat. But I don't want him to even have to. I want to take that puck from Markov. I want to show my team, the other team, Coach Porter, the fans in the arena, and everyone watching tonight's game that I belong here. That even though I've been gone, I'm still a solid player who can hold my own on the ice.

Adrenaline rockets through my body as I speed ahead, closing in the space between Markov and me. He's just a dozen feet from Blomdahl now and sets up to take his shot, but I race forward and hit the puck away. Isaac appears and takes possession of the puck and skates off. The home crowd cheers.

I smile despite Markov shoulder checking me and cursing at me. As I race ahead, I inhale, relishing the cold air filling my lungs. I take in the deafening screams of the crowd. Damn, it feels good to be back.

Isaac aims for the Seattle net but the puck bounces off the post. We scramble with the Seattle defenders for a few seconds before Xander manages to grab the puck. Some giant Seattle rookie defender is on his ass, so I skate over into Xander's line of sight. I'm the only one near him who's open so he passes the puck off to me. Out of the corner of my eye, I see that defender barreling toward me so I hit the puck. A split second later, it lands at the back of the Seattle net.

The entire arena is on their feet, cheering and screaming. My teammates crowd around me, hollering and smacking me in celebration.

We break apart and head back to center ice. As I get ready for the puck drop, I catch eyes with Maya, who's sitting near the Basher's player box. She's grinning wide as she looks at me. Next to her are Tyler and Tori. Eyes glued to me, she mouths "Amazing." My stomach feels like it's flipping somersaults. As good as it felt to have my team and Bashers fans supporting me, seeing Maya cheer me on feels fucking incredible. The woman I love is watching me play, celebrating with me, supporting me. She's sharing one of the most important moments in my career with me. I feel like I could fucking fly.

I zero in on the white number eleven that's emblazoned on the red Bashers jersey she's wearing. My jersey. My number.

A fiery flash levels me on the inside. Like adrenaline but more raw, more powerful. There's something so primal about seeing the woman I'm crazy about wearing my number, my jersey. It's probably silly, but I don't care. I fucking love it.

The ref drops the puck and play resumes. When the game ends, we won, two to one.

While the rest of the team heads back to the box, I take a second to skate over to Maya. She hops up from her seat, beaming as she looks at me. Her eyes are sparkling. She's looking at me like she's in love with me, and god, it's doing a number on me. All I wanna do is take her back home to the cabin and have my way with her.

"You were incredible," she says.

"I was okay," I joke.

Still smiling, Maya rolls her eyes. Tyler walks up next to his sister.

"Dude, that was insane. What a comeback."

Tori nods excitedly in agreement.

"Thanks, guys," I say. "After I get cleaned up, you wanna hang out up in the team box? Most of the guys will be there."

Tyler's eyes go wide like he's a kid seeing Santa with a sack full of gifts on Christmas morning. "Are you serious?"

I chuckle. "Yeah. I just gotta debrief with the team and shower after the game, but I'll meet you up there. I'll give security your names."

Tyler and Tori thanks me. I turn back to Maya and do a slow scan of her in that jersey. "Hot."

She giggles. "I figured you'd like it."

"I fucking love it."

I wink and skate off with my team, buzzing with adrenaline and joy. I've got everything I could want. I'm back on the team and I'm with my dream girl.

I don't realize I'm still grinning till Dylan gives me shit while we're in the locker room.

"Happy to be back, huh?" he says.

I chuckle. "Definitely."

283

Chapter 36

Maya

"This is so fucking cool," Tyler says while doing a wide-eyed scan of the Bashers team lounge. We're lounging in plush leather chairs at a table in the corner.

He downs more of his Red Bull vodka. "I never thought I'd be having a drink in the Bashers' box after a game." He looks at me. "Hey, can I come with you to the next home game?"

"Only if you promise to stop taking so many photos."

Tyler frowns right as he's about to take another photo of the bar. "What do you mean?"

I shake my head and laugh. "Never mind."

"Thanks for letting us tag along," Tori says. "I haven't been to a hockey game since college. I forgot how wild and fun they are."

Tyler grins at her. "Gotta say, I didn't think you'd be so into hockey."

"Why? Because I'm a woman?" Tori teases.

Tyler chuckles and the two of them joke back and forth.

I take in the flirty tone and wonder if my famously oblivious brother can tell that Tori is into him.

He heads to the restroom and I look at her.

"What?" she asks.

"Nothing." I sip my drink.

She tilts her head at me. "If you're going to warn me for the millionth time to stay away from your player brother, you're wasting your breath. I know better, Maya."

I hold up a hand. "Okay, okay. Sorry. I didn't mean to come off like that."

Her expression eases. Her cinnamon eyes are soft again. "There's nothing wrong with talking and joking around together."

"You're right," I say. But I don't miss the flash of longing in Tori's eyes as she looks down at her water glass. I'd bet anything what she feels for Tyler is more than just some friendly flirting. I just wish that she didn't. My older brother has a pitiful track record when it comes to dating and relationships, and it would kill me to see him lead her on and break her heart.

Tyler comes back to the table and finishes the rest of his drink.

"Another?" I ask.

He says yes, please. I hop up and head to the bar to get another round while we wait for Theo to join us. While the bartender mixes our cocktails, I glance at my phone.

"Maya?"

I look up and see Tracy, Annabelle's mom, standing a few feet away. She rests a hand on her heavily pregnant stomach and smiles at me.

"Oh hey, Tracy!" I hug her. I haven't seen her since Annabelle's birthday party. We didn't chat a ton since she was so busy with party stuff, but she was really sweet and welcoming to me.

A pretty blonde woman walks up to Tracy, and she introduces me to her friend Kendra, who's the wife of another player on the Bashers.

"Maya is one of the coaches at the hockey camp Annabelle loves," Tracy says to Kendra. "Though now it's over since coach Theo is back on the team."

"Yeah, the kids were pretty sad when we broke the news to them that camp had to end," I say.

Tracy flashes a sympathetic smile. "She cried a lot that day. Dylan had to promise to take her to Disneyland *and* Disney World to get her feel better."

"Oh gosh, I'm sorry."

Tracy chuckles and waves a hand like it's no big deal. "It's alright. I've been putting off Disney for years, so it's about time we follow through."

We all laugh.

"I really can't thank you and Theo enough for putting on that hockey camp. Annabelle loved it. She usually loses interest in activities pretty quickly, so the fact that she loved camp so much was a big deal."

"I miss it. Theo does too," I say.

"Speaking of Theo," Tracy says with a glint in her eyes. "Are you two a thing? You guys looked pretty close at Annabelle's birthday party." She raises a perfectly sculpted eyebrow as she looks at me. Kendra rolls her eyes good-naturedly.

"You'll have to forgive, Tracy. She's obnoxiously nosy," Kendra jokes.

I smile. "It's okay. Yeah, we are actually."

Tracy lets out a soft squeal. Kendra rolls her eyes good-naturedly at her friend.

Tracy rests a hand on my arm. "I know I'm acting ridiculous right now, but I can't help it. Theo has been a confirmed bachelor for so long. Like, years and years. I'm just excited to see him settle down."

I tell them how his cousin is my best friend so we've known each other for years, but didn't get together until reconnecting the past couple of months.

Kendra and Tracy make dual "aww" sounds.

"That's so romantic!" Tracy says.

The bartender drops off our drinks. Tracy takes a sip of her cranberry juice before letting out a satisfied "mmm" sound and patting her stomach.

"Pregnancy cravings are wild. My whole life I couldn't stand cranberry juice. Now I'm drinking gallons of it every week."

I laugh.

Kendra turns to her. "When's your induction date again?"

"Exactly six weeks from tomorrow."

"Wow, that's coming up," I say.

"I would have liked to let myself go into labor naturally, but with Dylan's crazy work schedule I don't want to risk it," Tracy says. "How awful would it be if my water broke and he was playing an away game?"

Kendra nods. "I hear you. I was lucky that I gave birth in the summer when they weren't playing. My husband was around and could help me with feedings and changing diapers. That definitely wouldn't have been the case if I gave birth in the middle of the season."

Tracy pats my arm again, chuckling. "Word of advice from two women married to hockey players: get used to saving major life events for the off season."

They both laugh. I do too until I realize they're not joking.

"Oh. You're serious," I say.

Tracy's smile drops. She clears her throat, seeming to register my hesitation. "I just mean that the schedule is pretty rigid for pro hockey players. It's not a normal nine-to-five job, you know? So if you're in a relationship, you have to kind of work around them."

She shrugs and offers a sympathetic smile as Kendra nods along.

"Work around them?" I repeat.

Tracy nods and shrugs. "That's just kind of how it goes. It's not easy, but it's worth it."

"I would know," Kendra says with a sigh, though she's still smiling. "I put off getting my master's because I just can't do it right now. Not with having our kid and my husband traveling so much to play. Someone's gotta be the parent who stays home and holds down the fort, you know?"

"Right..." I murmur.

My mom flashes in my mind. A million memories follow, of her alone with us when my brothers and I were little while my dad was off traveling for months at a time, of her arguing with him on the phone, of her looking sad and exhausted as she took care of us by herself, day after day...

That's what life will be like with Theo. I know we've barely started a relationship, but if we get serious, this is a glimpse of what I'm in store for. Now that he's back on the team, he'll be traveling for away games. If we want to see each other regularly, I'll probably have to follow him around and put my own needs and goals on the backburner.

I think of Sadie Skinner and the earring designs I've been working on ever since she approached me at the Rocky

Mountain Winter Festival. If I'm following Theo around like some lovesick girlfriend, when will I have the time to establish my own career?

Probably never. If I choose to prioritize my career, that means I won't see him very often. He'll be traveling and training for a huge chunk of the NHL season, while I'll be in Denver trying to get my earring line off the ground. I'll probably be traveling too, depending on how things with work go. We'll hardly ever see each other. As much as I care about him...as much as I love him...that's not the kind of relationship I want. That's not the kind of life I want.

Dread pools in the pit of my stomach. My relationship with Theo is doomed, and it's barely even started.

Tracy pulls me into a side hug, jerking me out of my thoughts and back to the present moment.

"Okay, enough of us married ladies complaining. We don't mean to scare you off," she jokes.

I force a smile. I tell them it's all fine, despite the panic spiral churning inside of me.

I say it was great chatting with them and walk back to Tyler and Tori, who are still flirting and laughing. I set their drinks down and sit as they talk, thankful that they don't seem to notice how quiet I'm being.

A lump lodges in my throat and I sip water to try and soothe it. It doesn't work. I still feel like crying at the thought of what I'm about to lose.

Chapter 37

Theo

"Hey. Everything okay?" I lean over and ask Maya in a quiet voice as she sits next to me in the lounge.

She smiles and nods, but I can tell something's bothering her. She's been quiet ever since I got here a half-hour ago. Even when I hugged her and kissed her, something felt off. Like she wasn't into it.

I'm so confused. She seemed so happy up until now.

I let out a breath and try to focus back on the conversation. Tyler and Tori don't seem to notice anything's off judging by the fact that they're both chatting and laughing with each other. Damn, is the flirty vibe strong with these two. Maya says they're not a couple, but you could have fooled me.

Tyler keeps winking and smiling at Tori, and she keeps laughing at everything he says and touching his arm.

A few minutes later, the two of them stand up and announce they're taking off.

I shake Tyler's hand and hug Tori. Maya gets up and

hugs them bye. When they leave, we sit back down and I focus on her once more.

She stares at the tabletop, her glass of water, the floor, pretty much everywhere except me. My stomach twists. What happened?

I reach over and gently grab her hand in mine. When she finally looks at me, I see a flash of pain in those gorgeous deep brown eyes. My chest throbs.

"Maya. What's wrong?"

She opens her mouth but hesitates before quickly shutting it. And then she sighs. "Not here."

She stands up and I follow her as she walks out of the lounge down the darkened hallway near where a utility closet is.

When she stops near the stairwell exit, I reach over and grab her hand.

"Are you okay? I'm worried about you."

Her gaze softens. She presses her eyes shut. "Theo, I don't know if I can do this."

I stumble back a step. It feels like I've been punched in the stomach. Where the hell did that come from?

"What are you talking about?" I ask.

Her shoulders fall as she lets out another heavy sigh. "These past two months with you have been amazing. But I don't know if we're meant to last longer than that."

My mouth hangs open. "Maya, what are you saying?" I let out a laugh of pure disbelief. My head feels so heavy all of a sudden with the impact of what she's saying. Tonight has been perfect. Everything between us was perfect up until I walked into the lounge. What went wrong?

"I don't understand..." I trail off, mystified.

"Theo, I'm so, so happy that you're back on the team.

Watching you tonight on the ice was incredible. That's where you belong."

A sad smile tugs at her lips. I'm so confused.

"But now that you're back on the team, you'll be traveling for away games. You'll be playing and training constantly. We'll hardly see each other."

Shit. She thinks things between us are going to change now that I'm playing again.

"You can come with me," I say quickly, my brain scrambling to think of every reason why we can make this work. "Lots of players' wives and girlfriends come to the away games."

She crosses her arms and frowns. "I have my own life and my own career goals, Theo. You can't just expect me to follow you around and put myself on the back burner."

"What? Of course I don't expect you to do that. Maya, I'd never in a million years want you to put yourself second like that."

I go quiet, shocked that she'd think that. I was the one who encouraged her to pursue her earring business. Why would she think I'd want her to put that on hold?

"Theo, I heard your teammates' wives talk about how much they have to put aside in their own lives to be in a relationship with their husbands. It's no joke. They schedule their work, their education, and even the births of their children around hockey. That might work for them, but I'm not willing to do that."

My head is spinning as she speaks. I didn't even think about all that. She's right though. Our hockey schedules are non-negotiable. I never thought about how the significant others of the guys on my team felt about it though, how drastically it affects their lives too.

Still though, I'm not ready to give up on my relationship with Maya.

"Two months hiding away in a cabin in the mountains is one thing," she says, the look in her eyes pained. "But that was a fantasy. This is reality. And I don't think it can work for us. Either I have to give something up or you do. And I don't think either of us is ready to do that." She sounds so certain, like she won't ever change her mind.

Panic grabs hold of me. It feels like an invisible fist is crushing my lungs. With every second that passes, I'm getting closer and closer to losing her...

"We'll figure something out." I grab her by the waist and pull her close to me. When she stiffens under my touch, it feels like a punch to my stomach.

I try to ignore the pain and focus on doing whatever I need to get Maya to give me a chance—give *us* a chance.

She blinks as she looks at me, her burnt-umber eyes shiny with unshed tears. She sniffles. "It won't work, Theo. I can't follow you around for us to have a shot at making this work. And there's no way you can compromise with your hockey career."

It feels like my chest is folding in on itself. Even breathing hurts. Just the thought of losing Maya sends me into a spiral.

I grab her by the waist and pull her against me. I expect her to instantly step away, but she doesn't. It feels like the tiniest win in this moment when I feel like I'm about to lose her for good.

"Maya, please don't give up on us." I press my lips to her forehead and breathe in her sugary flower scent I love so much.

"I'm sorry, Theo. I can't." Her whisper is a knife in my heart.

I lean back and drop my hands from her. When I look down at her, her cheeks are shiny with tears. I don't know how long we stand there and stare at each other, but it feels like minutes. The whole time her words echo in my head. And then it dawns on me...

"You think I'm going to hurt you like your dad hurt your mom, don't you?"

Her eyes widen the slightest bit before she blinks. She wraps her arms around herself and takes a step back, like she's trying to protect herself. From me. Fuck, that hurts.

"Maya, do you honestly think I'd do that to you? Do you really think I'd just leave you and expect you to wait around for me? That I'd take you for granted like that?"

She's quiet. I'm shocked. It kills me to know she thinks I'd do that to her.

"I'm not saying it'll be easy, but I'm willing to fight for us," I say. "Can't you fight for us too? Can't you at least try?"

When she doesn't say anything, I know I have my answer.

Emotion surges through me. "I'd never do that to you, Maya. Ever."

She looks at me, pain in her eyes, like she's unconvinced by my promise.

"Maya, we're not your parents. We're different. Our relationship is different. We don't have to end up like them."

It takes every ounce of strength in my body not to reach out and touch her, hug her, pull her to me. But she clearly doesn't want that. So I just stand there and hope the pleading in my tone is enough to convince her.

But the longer she stands there, quietly refusing me, the clearer it becomes: we're over.

"I'm sorry," she whispers before walking off.

I take a step back and scrub a hand over my face, dazed by what's gone down in the past few minutes. I just lost the woman I love.

Chapter 38

Maya

"I can't believe you're leaving us, cuz! It feels like you just came back to Denver." Millie pulls me into a hug and kisses my cheek.

When she releases me I try to smile at her, but none of the muscles in my face seem to want to cooperate. I must look deranged based on the freaked-out look Millie gives me.

"I told you, I'll just be gone for a few weeks," I say. "I'll be back before you know it."

"You'll be back designing some killer earrings for a famous supermodel." She winks.

Again I try to smile, and it feels even worse this time.

"You okay?" she asks, frowning.

"Yeah, fine. Just tired. I was up late working."

Her expression softens and she pulls me in for hug number two. She steps back all of a sudden, wincing as she clutches one of her boobs.

"Are you okay?" I ask.

"Yeah, just gotta pump. My tits are engorged. I feel like

a dairy cow." She makes an annoyed noise as she walks off, and I chuckle. This is the first time I've laughed in days...

The urge to cry hits my chest and throat all at once. Ever since I broke up with Theo a week ago, I've been a wreck. After I ended things, I spent the night at my mom's house and cried myself to sleep. The following day, I headed back to the cabin while Theo was gone at a physical therapy session so I could grab all my stuff and move it out without running into him.

And then I called Ingrid and told her the news about Sadie Skinner and me finally taking my earring business seriously. She was thrilled for me, even though I explained this meant I'd have to go on hiatus as her personal assistant. She understood completely but asked me for a favor: to work for her for the next few weeks while she looked for a new assistant. I told her of course. So tomorrow I'm flying to meet her.

I didn't mention a word about what happened with Theo though. She still doesn't know that we were ever together. I feel awful keeping this secret from my best friend, but I don't have the energy to rehash it all, not when I'm barely keeping it together.

When I blink, my eyes are sore from crying every day since leaving Theo. I had to go buy eye drops this morning so my eyes wouldn't look so pink and swollen.

For the millionth time, I tell myself I did the right thing by ending it. We were never going to work out long-term anyway. It's for the best.

My chest aches anyway. My heart feels like it's been ripped to shreds.

I take a slow, steady breath before sipping from my water glass. I can't break down. Not now, not here when I'm

297

surrounded by my whole family. We're having a huge gathering at my mom's house so everyone can see me before I leave, even though I told them I'd be back in a few weeks. But that's my family. Any excuse to throw a party.

Laugher and chatter and music bounce around me as I stand at the kitchen island and pretend to pick at a plate of food I know I'm not going to eat.

Just then someone bumps into me, I open my eyes and turn around. When I see it's Tyler stealing *lumpia* from my plate, my annoyance overtakes the urge to cry.

"Whose *lumpia* am I gonna steal when you're away?" He wraps his arm around me while stuffing his face.

"I guess you'll have to learn to make your own plate of food for the next few weeks, you thirty-two-year-old man-child."

Behind me, I hear Austin laugh. He high-fives me as he grabs a napkin from the counter.

"Words to live by, Tyler," he says. "Listen to your baby sister."

Austin walks off, leaving Tyler rolling his eyes as he eats.

I jokingly take a bow, which makes Tyler laugh. He takes a long gulp of beer from the bottle in his hand before looking at me, the expression on his face noticeably more serious.

"Hey, um, I just wanna say that I'm sorry," he says, his voice quieter.

"For what?" I take a small bite of *lumpia*.

"For being an annoying, overbearing older brother." He sighs. "Look, I know you and I are really different. I'll probably never leave Denver. I like being close to home and family. And you're a free spirit to the max with all the traveling you've done. And that's honestly really cool. You've made a life for yourself traveling and living the way you want. That gig with Sadie Skinner? Pretty freaking sweet. Clearly, you're doing just fine." A small smile tugs at his lips as he looks at me. "It's just hard for me sometimes because I'm your big brother. I want to make sure you're okay, you know? Even though I show it in annoying ways like lecturing you about getting a real job."

He sets his half-empty beer bottle on the counter. "I guess I'm just trying to say that I'm sorry for making you feel like just because you live your life differently it's wrong. It's not."

I stare at my big brother, half heartened, half shocked. It takes a long moment for me to process what he's said.

"Wow, Tyler. I don't know what to say. Except maybe..." I frown at him and poke his arm. "Who the hell is this emotionally mature man and what have you done with my dipshit older brother?"

He grins and rolls his eyes. "Very funny."

I pull him into a hug. "Seriously though, that means a lot. Thanks."

"Always here for you, sis. Both Gage and me. You know that, right?" he says when we break apart.

"I know." I pat his arm. "Speaking of Gage, where is he?"

"Filling Mom's car with gas and airing up the tires so you're good to go when she takes you to the airport tomorrow."

I smile and shake my head. "Of course he is."

Tyler lingers at the island for a moment looking like he wants to say something.

"What?" I ask.

He hesitates. "I guess I just thought that Theo would be the one to take you to the airport."

A knowing look flashes in my big brother's eyes.

I fiddle with a napkin on the countertop. "And what made you think that?"

"Because that's what couples do. Give each other rides to the airport. That's half the reason to get into a relationship, I thought."

I don't laugh at his joke. "Well, you thought wrong."

"Come on, Maya. I know I'm an idiot, but I'm not blind. I've seen you and Theo together. You're crazy about each other. Why isn't he here?"

For the second time in five minutes, I'm stunned by the emotional astuteness of my frat boy brother.

That tightness in my throat hits. I take a second to down the water in my glass just to buy myself an extra moment to collect myself.

"It just didn't work out."

"That's all you're gonna say?" he says after a long moment, an incredulous look on his face.

"What, you wanna know the intimate details—"

He holds up a hand. "Hell no!" He says it so loud that everyone snacking in the kitchen spins around and looks at him.

He clears his throat. "I don't want to know *that* stuff."

I roll my eyes and poke my fork at the food on my plate. "It was never going to last. Our lives are too different. He's back on his team and that means he'll be gone a lot, traveling and training. We'll hardly see each other. I don't want to be left to wait around for a partner who's always away."

Recognition flashes in my big brother's eyes. I bet what I said is reminding him of our parents.

"Best to just end it now before we get in too deep," I say quickly.

"Look, I know I'm the last person to give anyone advice on relationships, but you two seemed really happy together, Maya. Maybe you should give it a chance."

I open my mouth to tell him that I don't need any more of his unsolicited advice, but then I hear a collective gasp in the house. We turn and see our dad standing at the entrance, looking slightly freaked out at everyone staring at him, most of whom are his ex-in-laws.

The aunties and uncles in the house start whispering to each other. I'm just as shocked to see him. It's been years since he's been to this house, not since he and Mom got divorced.

I walk over to him and hug him. He smiles at me and gives me a tight squeeze. "Hey, honey. I won't stay for long, I just wanted to get in a goodbye hug before you leave tomorrow."

"Thanks, Dad."

A bunch of relatives come over to tell him hi. He starts to say that he only wanted to stop by and say goodbye to me, but they won't hear of it. Soon he's being walked into the kitchen and handed a plate of food and a can of beer.

Tyler greets him with a laugh. "Welcome back, Dad."

He offers a flustered chuckle in return, but he's a good sport and sits at the table with our mom's family and chats over food and drinks.

An hour later the gathering is still in full swing. Someone says we're running low on soda in the fridge, so I head to Mom's garage to grab another case. I step out, shut the door behind me, and flip the light on. And then I see my parents kissing in the corner of the garage.

I yelp in shock. They break apart instantly. For a few

seconds, I just stand there and look between them, my mouth agape.

"Oh my god," I finally say. "What are you doing?"

The two of them stammer and glance at each other between glances at me. Mom fidgets while Dad tugs at the hem of his sweater.

"Honey, well..."

"*Anak*, we were just..."

I hold up a hand, quieting them both. I take a moment to process just how weird and surreal this moment is. Their youngest child has just busted their secret garage makeout session.

"Your mother and I are working things out. Trying to, at least," Dad finally says.

Mom nods. I notice she doesn't look embarrassed anymore. Her expression is sure and she's standing tall as she looks at me.

When the ick feeling starts to fade at seeing my parents kiss, clarity sets in. They're getting back together. Maybe I should be happy for them, but I'm not. All I feel is frustration.

"Are you two serious?" I say, looking between them. Then I aim my gaze at my mom. "Are *you* serious? After everything Dad's done to you. You're gonna take him back?"

Mom purses her lips, like she's annoyed.

When I look at my dad, guilt hits. He looks like he's been sucker punched. What I said hurt him, but that doesn't override what he did in the past.

"Look, Dad. You know I love you, but you'll have to forgive me for not jumping for joy at seeing you two together. I haven't forgotten how things were when I was little, how you'd leave Mom on her own with us kids for months on end as you traveled the world building your restaurant empire. And now she's supposed to just take you back, like you didn't totally abandon her years ago?"

I let out a laugh that is zero percent joy, just frustration and anger.

His shoulders fall forward and his gaze falls to the dingy garage floor. "You're right, honey. I was a terrible partner to your mother back then."

"Maya, stop."

I'm caught off guard by my mom's firm tone. She frowns at me.

"Mom, I'm just trying to protect you."

She holds up a hand. "I don't need you to protect me, *anak*. I know what I'm doing. And you don't need to be speaking to me or your father in such a disrespectful way."

I stand there, soaking in her scolding. Shame flashes over me.

She walks toward me, stopping when she's just a few feet away. "I love how much you care about me, *anak*. But I don't need you interfering in my love life. I want to be with your dad again."

She glances over to where he's standing. That's when I notice the warmth in her eyes.

"Aren't you scared that he'll hurt you again? That it won't work out? You guys already split up once..."

This time I don't sound mad or accusatory. I'm honestly mystified. How could she give him another chance after the way he abandoned her and broke her heart?

I look over at my dad, who doesn't look mad at all at the way I've brought this all up. He's looking at me with love in his eyes—like he understands completely where I'm coming from.

And then my mom gives me a familiar smile I haven't seen for a while. That smile she used to give me when I was little and used to say the most ridiculous things, but she knew better.

"*Anak*. I'm not naïve. I know what I'm getting into with your father." They exchange a look before she turns back to me. And then she shocks me completely by shrugging and laughing. "Maybe I'm a fool for giving him another chance. I don't care. Things are different now after this many years. *We* are different this time. Maybe we'll hurt each other, maybe we won't. All I know is that I'd rather be open to the possibility of love than be so closed off and cynical that I miss out on it."

Her words rattle me so hard, I have to plant my feet on the cement floor. She pulls me into a hug.

"It makes me sad, how jaded you are about love and relationships, *anak*," she says, her tone soft this time. She squeezes me hard. "And it kills me to know you're probably this way because of what you saw happen between me and your father. But love isn't perfect, *anak*. It shouldn't have to be. We all make mistakes. We all hurt the people we love. We just have to learn to forgive each other and move on."

Her voice shakes as she speaks. When she breaks our hug, she keeps hold of my shoulders. "Maybe we can show you now that sometimes it's worth it to take a chance on love."

She kisses my cheek before turning back to my dad.

"Let's head inside, Andre. I think Maya needs a minute to herself."

He smiles and nods, then hugs me and kisses the top of my head. He starts to walk off, but I stop him.

"Dad, wait. I'm sorry for saying the things I said. That was out of line."

His tender smile doesn't budge. "It wasn't, honey. The

way you love and defend your mom makes me so proud. Never apologize for it."

He follows Mom back into the house, shutting the door behind him. And I stand there in the garage and think about what my mom just said.

Chapter 39

Theo

I'm a fucking mess tonight.

The arena is buzzing as we play the Nashville Wolves. The crowd is feral with how much they're shouting and banging on the boards.

I can't focus though. I'm on edge. I feel like a caged animal ready to fucking brawl. I've gotten into one profanity-laced argument with Del Richards not even ten minutes into the first period after he tripped me with his stick and the ref didn't bother to call a penalty.

I noticed Coach Porter watching me like a hawk through that whole exchange. Like he was waiting for me to fuck up this second chance he's given me to be on the team by getting into a petty fight.

Fights in hockey happen all the time. But I'm on thin ice as it is, and I should be focused on playing well and staying out of trouble.

Despite reminding myself all that, I still played like shit through the rest of the first period. It was so bad that the Wolves' star defender took the puck from me and shot it to their forward, leading to a goal for their team. So now we're down, one to zero.

This is only my second game back since returning to play for the Bashers, and already I'm faltering, showcasing all my flaws like a fucking peacock. I need to get my shit together.

Pain radiates through the center of my chest. When I breathe, no matter if it's deep or shallow, it kills. It's not the chill in the air. It's not because I'm exhausted from running my ass off. It's not because of the countless hits I'm taking from the other team.

It's the pain of losing Maya.

It's been just over a week since she broke up with me, and I can't stop thinking about her. How much I miss her. How I should have tried harder to convince her to give us a chance. How I should have told her I loved her...maybe that would have made a difference...

My throat aches as I swallow back the rock that's suddenly appeared in my throat. I think back to the game when she was in the stands, cheering me on, wearing my jersey. And now she's gone.

Another sharp pain rockets through me. I shake my head. I need to focus.

I run my ass off to catch up with Del. Did he up his training the last couple of months? I don't remember him being this fast before. Jesus.

Del is trailing his teammate Mac Guilles, who's got the puck and is headed for our net. I know that if he can't set up a good shot, he'll pass it to Del so he can try and score. I can't afford to lose him.

I speed up, ignoring the fire in my quads. Isaac appears from out of nowhere, covering Guilles, so he does what I thought he'd do and hits the puck back to Del. A split second after the puck lands against his stick, I check him.

Del lurches forward and the puck goes flying, losing steam a dozen feet in front of our net. Dylan is all over it and takes off across the ice. I turn to follow him, but then Del shoves me.

"What the fuck was that, asshole?" he barks.

"Fuck off," I mutter as I push him back.

He shoves me again and I stumble back on the ice.

"You wanna fucking go, Thompson? I'll happily kick your washed-up ass, you fucking has-been."

The adrenaline coursing through me suddenly feels like I've been injected with jet fuel.

It's not a shocker that Del would insult me like that. If he had said that to me at a prior game, I would have just ignored him and skated off.

But right now I'm broken. I lost Maya. The one thing I've got left is hockey, and he's shitting on it. He wants to show me that I don't belong, that I don't deserve to be here.

"What wrong, Thompson?" Del taunts with an evil smile. "Aww, the has-been is too scared to fight."

Fury shoots like hot lava through my veins. I toss my stick and gloves on the ice. Del does the same. The entire crowd hops to their feet, slapping the boards, screaming for us to fight as we circle each other.

My heart thrashes against my ribcage. It feels like it's on the verge of exploding out of my chest. I can't think straight, I'm too pissed, too hurt. Before I know it, my fist connects with Del's scruffy jaw.

He lets out a grunt that I can't even hear because the crowd is deafening. It's no secret that hockey fans go nuts for a good fight, and that's exactly what they're getting right now.

Del retaliates with a punch to my left temple. Pain blasts through the side of my head, clouding my vision with white bursts, but I keep hitting, keep punching. With his free hand, he rips at my jersey. I'm punching him with both fists now. Half the time I get his padding; half the time I get his face. Between grunts and breaths, I call him every cuss word I can think of. He does the same.

After what feels like minutes, the metallic taste of blood fills my mouth. He must have landed a hit to my mouth. It's hard to keep track in this frenzy of fists and profanity.

It's weird. As much as it hurts, it's a relief to feel the sting of these hits and punches. My body will be bruised and cut up after this, but it'll heal.

My heart won't though. That'll be ripped to shreds for a long fucking time.

Emotion surges through me as I land one last punch to the side of Del's jaw before we fall to the ice. Hockey rules generally allow a fight to go on until both players fall onto the ice. Once we're on the ground, the linesmen pull us apart.

Out of the corner of my swollen eye, I see red jerseys swarming me.

"Holy fuck, dude," Dylan says. "That was brutal."

"Yeah. Wow." Isaac lets out an uneasy laugh. "You were a beast."

I wipe the sweat and blood from my eyes. I can barely see out of my left one, it's already so swollen.

Just then one of the refs comes up to me and my teammates back away. I don't hear a single word he says because my heart is pounding a deafening beat in my ears. I just nod when he points to the penalty box.

As I make my way there, my entire body throbs. It feels like I dove into a trash compactor. I catch a few horrified looks from fans in the stands. A woman reaches down and covers her little son's eyes with her hand. Guilt throttles me. This isn't the kind of player I ever wanted to be—a loose cannon who gets violent at the drop of a hat.

I clock Coach Porter glowering at me, arms crossed, as I settle into the penalty box. My stomach drops. I hunch over and rest my elbows on my knees and cradle my throbbing head in my hands.

Hockey is the last thing that means anything to me—the last thing I've got. I'm about to lose that too. Fuck.

Chapter 40

Theo

I fly across the ice, every muscle in my body aching.

"Damn, man. You're kicking ass today," Isaac says as he catches up to me. "Yo, Dylan! You owe me twenty bucks! Theo here kept up no problem. Told you he wouldn't let that fight slow him down."

Isaac laughs and smacks my shoulder. I grunt, too exhausted to speak actual words. Well, that and the fact that my entire body feels like someone shoved a battering ram through it.

It's been a couple of days since our loss to the Wolves and I've been a tense wreck ever since. I expected Coach Porter to pull me aside after that game, rip me a new asshole, maybe even suspend me from the team. But he didn't say a word.

So I fully expect him to do that at some point today, probably after practice since we're nearly done.

I sprint through the last of the drills Coach is running us through. I'm the first to finish. I hunch over, gasping to catch my breath.

"Nice work," Coach Porter mutters as he frowns at something on his clipboard.

I straighten up, shocked. "Um, thanks."

"Solid work today, gentlemen. Hit the showers," Coach Porter hollers at us.

I start to make my way out, but he stops me.

"Except you, Thompson. We need to talk about your performance last game."

Dread singes the pit of my stomach. I swallow back the ball of nerves that's suddenly rocketed up my chest to my throat. I nod.

I'm quiet as I wait for him to set his clipboard aside and look at me. He crosses his arms and his eyebrows crash together, like he's annoyed and pissed and disappointed all at once.

"I've never seen you fight like that before. What happened?"

"He shoved me first," I say. On the inside, I roll my eyes at myself. I sound like a little kid.

"You've been shoved plenty of times before. You never reacted like that. What's going on with you, Thompson? Is this a new persona you've adopted?"

I shake my head as I panic on the inside. "No way, Coach. It was just an off night, I swear."

He purses his lips, studying me. I hold my breath, wondering if he's going to call me on my bullshit.

"It was a hell of a departure from the way you were your first game back. That was an impressive showing. You were laser-focused and energized. Your head was in the game, I could tell. I could also tell you were happy to be back on the ice."

"I was. I mean, I definitely am happy to be back," I say, hoping to convince him.

He goes quiet as he keeps his hard, unrelenting stare trained on me. "I'm just trying to figure out which player you are now. The one who loves the game and who plays his heart out, or the one who's a hothead that's gonna get into fights all the time."

"I'm not a hothead. I swear."

He sighs. Even though he's still in that tall power stance, his shoulders lower the slightest bit, like he's easing up.

"Look, I'm not naïve. I know fights are a part of the game. I got into my fair share back in the day when I played," he says. "You can fight, Thompson. Just don't make it a habit, okay?"

Relief washes through me. "I won't."

He nods once. "Good. Glad to have you back on the team," he says, that perma-frown still plastered on his face.

"Thanks," I say. "And thank you for giving me a second chance."

"I won't lie. It wasn't an easy decision. And if Marquez hadn't left for that job in Toronto, you wouldn't be here," he says matter-of-factly. "But he's gone, so it's a non-issue. And the fact that you showed you could stay out of trouble counted for a lot. But so did your recovery." He glances down at my bum knee. "You're playing like you didn't take a stick to the knee."

Shame heats my cheeks. I think back to that night when I was in bed with Assistant Coach Marquez's wife Estella. It feels like a million years ago even though it was only a few months. That guy who partied and hooked up doesn't even feel like me anymore.

Maya flashes in my mind. Two months with her showed me that *that's* the kind of life I'd rather live. I'd rather share a life with her, up in the mountains, away from everything and everyone else.

But then I remind myself that I'll never get to live that life with her again.

That blasted-through feeling in my chest resurfaces. I clear my throat and do my best to swallow back the pain.

"You alright, Thompson?" Coach's gruff tone centers me.

"Uh, yeah. Just trying to catch my breath. It was a tough practice."

"Keep up the good work. You're doing well, but I don't have a lot of patience for repeated mistakes. Don't make me regret taking you back."

I nod. "Absolutely. I won't."

I head to the locker room, go to my locker, and start stripping off my gear.

"You get a good ass-chewing from Coach?" Dylan asks.

"Something like that," I mutter as I yank off my jersey and pads.

"Sloane and Emerson talk constantly about how much they miss hockey camp," Isaac says.

I look at him and feel the muscles in my back and shoulders start to loosen despite how worked up I still feel. "Really?"

Isaac nods. "It was all they could talk about for weeks. They loved it."

I wish there were a way I could keep up with hockey camp while playing. I miss it too.

"Speaking of hockey camp, how's Maya?" Xander asks from across the room.

Just the mention of her name sends a blast of pain through me.

"No idea," I mumble as I toss my skates in my locker.

"Really? That's too bad."

Out of the corner of my eye, I see him shed his pads and grab a towel. One of our teammates asks who Maya is.

"She helped Theo with his hockey camp," Xander says. "She's also an absolute smoke show."

I whip my head up at Xander, who's not even looking at me.

"I took her out." Xander smirks before turning to me. "Hey, you think you could follow up with her? Ask her to text me back? I never got to seal the deal with her. I'm heartbroken, dude. That's never happened to me before," he jokes.

My ears ring as steam levels my insides. Before I even realize what I'm doing, I clear the space between Xander and me in half a second. I slam my arm against his chest, pinning him against his locker.

"Don't fucking talk about her like that," I bite through gritted teeth.

Xander struggles against me, his expression confused. "What that hell?"

The locker room falls silent around us. Xander shoves me off of him just as Isaac and Dylan run over. Isaac pulls me back, and Dylan steps in front of Xander.

"Jesus fuck," Xander yells. "What the hell do you care if I see her again?"

"Because she's not some fucking conquest, you asshole!"

Xander glares at me. "Why the fuck are you acting like some jealous..." He blinks. Recognition flashes in his eyes. "Oh, shit. You like her, don't you?"

Just then I realize what a psycho I must look like, flipping out on my teammate. I've just been let back on the team and I'm about to rip my teammate's throat out. Christ, I need to get a hold of myself.

"Fuck," I mutter as I tug a hand through my sweat-soaked hair.

"What's going on in here?" Coach Porter's voice booms from the locker room entrance.

We all turn to face him.

"Sorry, I—"

"Just having a debate about which bar serves the best Rocky Mountain oysters," Isaac says, interrupting me.

Coach frowns. "Seriously?"

Isaac nods.

"Yup," Dylan says. "We have very strong feelings about it."

Coach narrows his gaze as he scans the room. "Keep it down."

We all say we will. He walks off and I turn to Isaac and Dylan. I tell them thanks.

Isaac pats me on the shoulder. "It's all good." He turns to Xander, who's frowning at me. He looks slightly less pissed, so that's something at least.

"You and Maya are together, aren't you?" Xander asks.

"Not anymore."

I head back to my locker, grab a towel, and head for the shower. I turn it to the hottest I can handle and stand under the steam for what feels like forever. My skin burns, but that's exactly what I need right now. Anything to pull my focus from the pain thrumming inside of me.

I rinse off, dry off, and walk back to my locker. I halt when I see Xander standing there, glaring at me. Everyone else is gone, it's just me and him.

"What?" I blurt when he says nothing.

He lets out a heavy sigh, like he's irritated with me. "Why didn't you say you were with Maya?"

I turn around, grab my clothes, and get dressed. "What do you mean?"

"If you had said you liked her, Theo, I would have backed off. I wouldn't have even asked her out in the first place. Now I feel like an asshole."

I pause, blown away by what Xander's said. I'm not used to him acting this...mature. And considerate.

"It's so obvious now," he mutters from behind me. "I thought you came to that game I invited her to because you were fucking with me. But now I realize it was because you're into her."

I don't say a word. I'm too embarrassed. He's exactly right.

When I finish getting dressed I turn back around to Xander.

"I'm a horny bastard, Theo. I've got no shame about that. But I'm not an asshole," he says. "But that's exactly how I feel after finding out that you like her. Why didn't you say something when I asked about her?"

I hesitate. This moment feels weirdly raw and emotional. Xander is my teammate. We've never talked about stuff like this, never gone deep like this.

But that was before, when I was reckless. I'm different now. Better. Hopefully.

I let out a breath. "I didn't say anything because I was still working out my feelings for her. It, uh..." I scrub a hand over my face. "It took you going out with her to make me realize how much I liked her and cared about her."

For a few seconds, he looks at me. "Huh. I guess that kinda makes sense."

He shoves his hands in his jacket pocket and stares at his shoes. "So that's why she never called me after our date. She was with you."

He doesn't say it like he's pissed or hurt. More like he's just making an observation.

"Yeah. Look, I'm sorry for how I acted earlier. That was fucked up."

He shrugs. "I get it."

It takes all the strength I possess to say these next words. But I do it. Because it's the truth. And I need to accept it, even if it cuts me to the core.

"But Maya and I aren't together anymore. So if you're interested in her still, you're free to call or text her."

The words are bitter on my tongue. Just the thought of Maya with anyone else makes me want to punch a hole through the wall. But that's my problem, no one else's. That's for me and only me to grapple with.

My stomach churns as I force away the thought and grab my gym bag. I start to head out of the locker room, but Xander stops me.

"Dude, do you think I'm that big of a piece of shit? I'm not gonna call her. Not when it's clear as fucking day that you're in love with her."

I spin around to him, shocked.

He chuckles. "Don't act so surprised. I know I'm a dumbass. I know the only two things I'm good at in life are hockey and fucking. But I'm not completely hopeless. I can read people just as well as anyone else can. And it's written all over your face, man. You're in love with Maya."

I'm stunned at Xander's spot-on assessment of me.

"It doesn't matter," I finally say. "She ended it."

"Why?"

I almost laugh. Never in a million years did I think I'd be having a heart-to-heart about relationships with Xander, my fellow manwhore.

But I never thought I'd enjoy coaching a kids' hockey

camp. I never thought I'd fall in love with my cousin's best friend. Weird shit happens sometimes. You just gotta go with it.

"She couldn't picture a future with me because of my job. It's not easy being with a hockey player. We travel all the time. Our schedule is nuts. I don't blame her." I swallow hard. "It still hurts though."

"That sucks, man. I'm sorry you're going through it."

Xander's words are weirdly comforting. I think he actually means what he says.

"Thanks," I say. My heart still feels like it's been thrown in a shredder and my chest still throbs, but this conversation with Xander has helped a lot.

He walks over to me and smacks my shoulder. "Hang in there. You'll be okay." He walks off.

I stand there alone. "I don't know about that."

Chapter 41

Maya

"Can't you believe how warm it is?" Ingrid puts on a giant sunhat as we walk to the resort pool. "It's the dead of winter and seventy degrees. God, I love Arizona."

I force out a laugh. "I know, it's great."

I follow behind her. We sit at a couple of lounge chairs near the edge of the pool and gaze out at the desert landscape in the distance. It's a blanket of sandy-red rock dotted with green cacti and shrubs against purple mountains. It's our first day at Civana, a wellness resort just outside of Phoenix that invited Ingrid to stay for free in exchange for her posting about the resort on her social media.

She turns and smiles at me. "Thanks so much for being such a good sport about flying to Phoenix two days after you landed in San Diego."

"It's my job, remember?" I try and smile again, but my face muscles feel tense. Probably because I haven't cracked more than a couple of genuine smiles since I broke up with Theo.

It's the right thing to do

I've been repeating that silent mantra to myself constantly. It hasn't done much to comfort me though.

That familiar tightness hits my throat. I swallow it back and quickly pull up the notes on my phone to distract myself from the urge to cry.

"We've got dinner in two hours at the resort restaurant Terras. The chef wants to do a private tasting and asked that you take some photos so you can post them on TikTok and Instagram," I say. "Oh, and that sunglasses line emailed this morning asking if you'd take some photos with the pairs they sent while you're here at Civana. They're hoping for some majestic desert shots of you wearing their shades. That should be super easy, I can take those for you after breakfast tomorrow. After that, we've got a couples' hot stone massage at the spa before that sound bath class."

Through the sepia-tinted lenses of her sunglasses, I see Ingrid close her eyes as she relaxes into the chair. "You're seriously the best, Maya."

I glance over at her, my stomach in a knot. I still haven't told Ingrid about me and Theo. It's not that I think she'd be mad or anything. Just that I don't see the point since we're not even together anymore.

Just the thought of that feels like a knife in my heart. I press my eyes shut, willing the pain to fade.

"You okay?" Ingrid asks.

I open my eyes and see Ingrid frowning at me in concern. She pushes her sunglasses on top of her head.

I clear my throat. "Yeah, um, fine. Just not used to this warmth at the end of February."

"Don't tell me you miss the snow and cold?"

I think of Theo and how he joked about being hot-blooded and loving the cold.

"Maybe a little," I say quietly. "I'm a Denver girl, born and raised in the mountains. Can't help it."

"Speaking of Denver and the mountains." Ingrid reaches over and grabs my hand. "I owe you big time, Maya. For how you stayed with Theo and made sure he didn't destroy my place."

That ache inside of me intensifies at just the mention of his name.

"It was no problem. Really." I fuss with a button on the long cover-up I'm wearing.

"I'm serious." She gently tugs on my hand to get me to look at her. "You were an incredible influence on my cousin. While he was living with you, he coached a kids' hockey camp *and* he got back on his team. And most importantly, you didn't kill him. Seriously, I can't thank you enough."

I smile at her. "I was happy to do it."

She sips her drink. "Speaking of Theo, I FaceTimed him this morning, and holy crap, he looked terrible."

My chest tightens with worry. "Is he okay?"

Ingrid frowns at the sharpness of my tone. I sound like I'm freaking out.

"Yeah, he's fine," she says. "He just got into a fight at his last game."

"Are you sure though? Like, you're positive he's okay?"

Ingrid just looks at me. "Yeah. He's just a bit bruised and cut up. Occupational hazard."

My heart, which was racing a second ago, eases back to a steady beat.

I take a breath and rest my hand over my chest. "Thank goodness," I say before chugging from my water bottle.

Ingrid narrows her gaze at me, like she's studying me.

"Maya babes, are you alright?" she asks after a quiet moment.

I force a laugh that sounds more like a squeak. "Yup. All good."

"You're acting kinda weird."

"It's the sunshine, I swear," I say to my phone. "I'm not used to the warmth this early in the year." I silently curse myself for how squeaky my voice is.

A few seconds later Ingrid gasps.

"Oh my god..." She shoots up on her lounge chair. "Something happened between you and Theo, didn't it?"

I think about denying it. I think about looking my best friend in the eye and lying straight to her face, but I can't. I'm tired of hiding this from her.

I finally look at her and nod.

I take in Ingrid's wide, unblinking stare. "Tell me everything."

I bite my lip as I work up the nerves. "Theo and I...we, um...we had a bit of a thing."

I give her a summary of how living together helped us see each other differently, how we spent more time together, how we started to get along, how we started to actually like each other.

Ingrid doesn't blink once the entire time I speak.

"We became friends after a while. I mean, we still argued and bickered, but it was different. There was a flirty vibe that developed between us. And well...one night, we locked ourselves out of your cabin by mistake and ended up in the guest house," I say. "And there was only one bed..."

Somehow her eyes go even wider. "No..."

"It just sort of happened."

Her jaw falls to the ground. "Maya, are you serious?"

I nod again. "We were essentially friends with b—"

She makes a face like she just tasted something rotten

and holds up a hand. "Please god, no details. I can fill in the blanks on my own."

"Right. Sorry." I clear my throat. "Feelings started to develop between us," I say in a soft voice, too scared to say more. "Anyway, it's over now."

For a while, we're both quiet as I observe Ingrid and her thousand-yard stare.

"You and Theo? Were together?" she finally says.

"Yup."

Another long pause and more staring.

She glances off to the side, looking at nothing in particular. "Wow. My mom was right when she joked about you two getting together. Never in a million years would I have thought you two would be a couple."

"Same," I murmur.

"What happened?" she asks. "Why did it end?"

Snippets from our last conversation flash in my head. How he pleaded for me to give us a chance. The broken look on his face when I rejected him.

"He wanted a serious relationship. I didn't."

Ingrid's eyes go wide. "He did?"

I nod. "I just couldn't figure out how it would work. His job is nuts. When I told him that all the traveling and training he does would make it almost impossible for us to see each other regularly, he asked me to come with him. But I can't. I have my own dreams I want to pursue. I can't put that on hold for a relationship."

I tell her about running into Tracy and Kendra.

"They pretty much have had to tailor their whole lives —their marriages, their careers, when they have kids— around their husbands' jobs as hockey players. I don't want that."

Ingrid looks sad, but she nods anyway. For a while she's quiet, but then she speaks.

"The past few days make so much sense now."

"What do you mean?" I ask.

"Ever since you've been back, you seemed a bit off. Like, you were acting all happy and energetic, but it felt like it wasn't genuine. Like you were hurt and trying to hide it. And now I know why." She pauses. "I don't remember you being this sad over any guy you've dated before. Definitely upset. But sad?" Her blue eyes are tender as she looks at me. "You're heartbroken, Maya."

"I am," I say, my voice weak. "Being with Theo...it felt different."

She squeezes my hand. "So this thing with Theo is not like anything else you've experienced before?"

"It's completely different. He's amazing. He's not at all what I thought he was. Behind that cocky humor, he's all sweetness and heart. He's funny and kind and thoughtful. I fell hard for him."

When I glance up, Ingrid is looking at me expectantly.

"Do you think that maybe you're making a mistake by ending things with him before you even tried to make it work?" she asks gently. "It sounds like you really care about him."

"Ingrid, I can't. The only way for our relationship to work is for one of us to give up something. I won't ask him to give up his career after working so hard to get it back. And I won't give up my dream for him." I think of my mom and what she went through, how she sacrificed her happiness waiting around for my dad all those years.

When I look at her, I can tell she's disappointed. But she nods her understanding anyway.

I wipe my face with my free hand. Ingrid digs a packet

of tissues from her bag, moves to sit next to me on my chair, and hands me the pack.

I tell her a snotty, "Thanks" before dabbing at my cheeks.

She pulls me into a side hug and I wrap my arm around her. I hold my best friend tight, grateful for her support and understanding in this moment.

"If you're upset at me for breaking things off with Theo, I understand," I say to her. "I'd even understand if you didn't want to be friends anymore..."

She makes a "psssh" noise as she hugs me tight. "Stop it. I love you, Maya. Yeah, I wish things ended differently between you and Theo, but that doesn't have any effect on our friendship. You've been there for me a million times. I'll always be there for you."

"I love you, Ingrid. Thank you."

She rests her head on my shoulder, and I rest my head on hers. We stay like that for minutes, until the reminder on my phone goes off.

I sniffle and wipe my nose. "Your dinner meeting. You have to get ready." We stand up, put our stuff in our bags, and head back to our rooms. On our way, my phone buzzes with a text from Austin. When I read it, I stop walking.

Emergency trip to Phoenix. We need to talk

When I show the text to Ingrid, she looks surprised. "You should text him back."

Chapter 42

Maya

My cousin Austin squints at the menu at Terras, the restaurant in Civana.

"What the hell does plant-forward mean?" he asks.

"It means they serve mostly fruits, veggies, and grains." I sigh, annoyed.

He frowns and leans closer to the menu. "It's so dark in here."

"Mood lighting. It goes with the décor."

He peers around the space, which is outfitted with a river rock wall, earth-toned carpet, and retro dining chairs.

He nods at the small potted cactus in the corner of the restaurant. "Hey, you think if I asked them to chop that up and put it in a salad, they would?" He chuckles. I roll my eyes.

"The more important question is why in the world did you text me and say that you were having an emergency and needed to see me? I missed a private chef's tasting with Ingrid for this, you know."

He takes a drink of his white wine. "Have you ever had

to blow off your long weekend plans to go to the most boring teacher's conference in the world? If that's not an emergency, I don't know what is."

I let out an exasperated noise and focus my gaze on my cousin. "Seriously, Austin. What's going on with you? You don't even tell me that you're coming to Phoenix till your plane lands and say that you need to meet me for dinner ASAP. Why are you really here?"

He raises an eyebrow at me. "Because you need someone to try and talk some sense into you, Maya."

He crosses his arms and I instantly go on the defensive. I straighten up in my chair and cross my arms. He's got that disappointed teacher expression down pat.

"What's that supposed to mean?"

My cousin tilts his head at me. "I overheard you talking to Tyler at your going away party. About breaking things off with Theo."

I pause mid-slip. I set my glass of water down. "Thanks for ditching your conference to let me know that you eavesdropped on me"

A heavy sigh rockets from Austin. He pulls at the collar of his dress shirt, then tugs a hand through his perfectly combed ink-black hair. I lean back in my chair, surprised. My flawlessly styled cousin never, ever messes with his hairstyle unless he's really, really upset.

"I heard you tell Tyler why you ended things with Theo. And I came here to tell you that I think you're making a huge mistake."

"Excuse me?"

"We're family, but we're friends too. And I'm not the kind of friend who's just going to sit back and watch you get in the way of your own happiness."

"Austin, what are you talking about?"

"I've never seen you happier than when you were with Theo. I've never seen you smile that much. We all noticed it."

I'm quiet. I can't argue with him there. That's all true.

"But then you just call it quits?"

"It's not that simple, Austin."

He throws up his hand like he's frustrated. "Explain it to me then."

I huff out a breath. "Theo is amazing. And you're right, being with him made me happy. Really happy."

My throat aches. I pause to sip my water to keep from breaking.

"But being in a relationship with a pro hockey player isn't a walk in the park. I'd have to put a lot of my life on the back burner, Austin."

He frowns. "How do you figure that?"

I tell him about running into a couple of the Bashers players' wives and hearing them joke about how they've had to put their interests and goals on hold for their husbands.

"I'm not going to give up my dreams and goals for anyone," I say. "I'm not going to sit and wait around for a partner who's hardly ever there."

Austin looks at me for a long moment. His deep brown eyes study me, like he's taking in everything I've said. He's quiet as he looks off to the side and through the nearby window that overlooks the resort patio and pool. And then he turns back to me.

"God, Maya. You're hell-bent on sabotaging your own happiness aren't you?"

I frown at him, taken aback at how disappointed and irritated he sounds. "What are you talking about?"

"You think I don't know where this all stems from? I know your hesitation to be in a serious relationship comes from your parents. Seeing how your dad ditched your mom growing up made you skittish to ever let your guard down and get emotionally invested in anyone," he says. "And okay, yeah, I get. All of us do that to a point. We're all affected by our parents' relationships in some way. But you're a coward to use your parents' failed marriage as an excuse to dump the guy you're clearly in love with."

I lean back in my chair, stunned at my cousin's spot-on assessment.

The look in his eyes is still pointed, but the intensity is dialed back a bit. Like he feels bad for me.

"Don't pretend it's not true, Maya. I can tell you're in love with Theo."

My chest and my throat ache. "You're right. I am in love with him. But sometimes love isn't enough when two people's lives are too different."

"God, Maya. How do you even know that? You didn't even give yourselves a chance to be in a relationship."

I start to talk, but he keeps going.

"You don't get it, do you? You didn't even try." He tosses up his hands, exasperated. "Okay, maybe you're right. Maybe a long-term relationship between you and Theo would be a total disaster and you'd have a horrible breakup. Or maybe it would work out. Maybe you could have a dream life with your hot hockey player boyfriend and be happier than in your wildest dreams. That's a possibility too, you know. But you'll never know because you made up your mind that it wouldn't work out before you could even attempt to see how it would actually go."

I'm speechless, unable to say anything in response. Because Austin is right. I was so fixated on everything that would go wrong with Theo that I ignored everything that could go right between us. And so much between us was already so good...we loved living together and working together, and we were crazy about each other...

Our server starts to walk over to us, but he picks up that we're having a charged conversation because he takes one look at us, does a U-turn, and scurries away.

"I'm not gonna feed you a bunch of bullshit and say that long-term relationships are always easy. They're not. They aren't always hot sex and cuddling in bed," Austin says. "Sometimes you fight. Sometimes you compromise. Sometimes you drive each other crazy. Sometimes you both get stressed and busy and can't see each other as often as you want. That's life though. Shit happens and you figure out a way to work through it. Because if you're with the right person, it's worth it. It's worth it to endure all that struggle and all that hardship because you've found your partner. You've found the one person in the world who makes you happier than anything and anyone."

It feels like my heart is shattering as my cousin speaks. Everything he says makes sense.

Austin drains the rest of his water glass before refocusing on me. He looks hurt and frustrated and disappointed all at once.

"But you'll never know what that feels like, Maya. You'll never know the joy of building a life with the person you love most in the world. Because you'd rather let your fear call the shots. Because you want to be right more than you want to be happy."

He stands up, drops money on the table, and walks off.

I sit there, rattled. His words land like an invisible anvil on my head. Now that my cousin has laid it all out for me, everything is crystal clear. I've been a selfish jerk who let my fear and my cynicism ruin everything I had with Theo—and everything I *could* have had with him.

You want to be right more than you want to be happy

Austin's words echo in my head like an alarm. He's right. And I was wrong.

An unfamiliar surge of emotion rockets through me. It feels like adrenaline mixed with panic and regret. Clarity hits. I've been miserable without Theo. I've missed him every minute of every day I've been without him. I made the biggest mistake of my life by ending things with him.

I love him so, so much. And I don't want to be without him anymore.

The muscles in my arms and legs twitch with the need to sprint to him even though I'm a thousand miles away from him right now.

I jolt up from the table anyway, nearly knocking my chair over. I take off out of the restaurant in the direction of my room.

I need to get out of here. I need to go to Theo right now and apologize to him. I need to see if I can fix this.

I need to tell him I love him.

My lungs and my legs are on fire as I pump faster, my brain in overdrive as I think about everything I'm about to try and pull off. Nerves explode inside of me. I hope I'm not too late.

Chapter 43

Theo

Someone shoves me and I crash into the boards of the arena. I get the wind knocked out of me and choke through a breath.

"Oops," the familiar voice behind me taunts.

I grit my teeth. Del Richards. Of fucking course.

I knew he was going to be an asshole to me. We fought the last time our teams faced off, and I'm certain he's trying to get another rise out of me.

Coach Porter's warning not to fight too much echoes in my mind. This isn't worth it.

"Fuck you," I spit as I turn around. He shoves me, but instead of taking the bait and socking him, I maneuver around him. I'm not wasting my energy on this prick.

He catches up and shoves me again, this time harder, then darts off, taking the puck I just had with him.

Fans smack their hands against the boards, cheering and screaming. Adrenaline slams through me like a freight train. I speed ahead and catch up with Del as he skates toward my team's goal.

My quads are on fire as I close in on him. A Wolves

defender tries to block me, but I ram him, throwing him off balance. Del closes in on the net right as I catch up. He shoots the puck and I dive ahead, blocking the shot with my stick. The home crowd roars.

I hit the puck to Xander, who takes off with it across the ice. My lungs on fire, I skate ahead and watch as Xander fires the puck straight into the Wolves' net, scoring the first goal of the game.

The entire arena shakes as the fans scream and stomp. I run up to Xander and give him a celebratory smack on the shoulder.

He turns to me. "Smooth as fucking silk, man."

I take in the crowd as they go wild in the stands. I do a double-take when I see a group of kids sitting behind the Bashers' box. They're holding a massive sign that says, "Go, Coach Theo!"

When I wave at the kids from hockey camp, they jump and cheer. Man, it's good to see them.

"Aww Coach Theo," Isaac teases as he skates past me.

"Did you guys plan that?" I ask.

As he skates backward, he shrugs and smiles. "Maybe."

I can't help but grin wide like a goober. I jump right back into the game, laser-focused.

The first period winds down and I head back to the box. I guzzle water and see the kids from hockey camp waving at me again. I make my way over to the far end of the box to say hi. The second I'm over there, they all start talking at once.

"Coach Theo, that block was awesome!" Parker says.

"Yeah, that guy from the other team was so mad when you blocked his goal," Emerson says. "He slammed his stick on the ice!"

334

"Will you teach us how to do that block when you start hockey camp again? Will you?" Sloane says.

I smile. "Absolutely."

"And maybe Coach Maya can teach us how to do more spins too?" Annabelle asks.

I try to keep smiling. "Yeah. Maybe."

It feels like someone's got their fist around my heart and they're squeezing it tight. I have to take an extra second and breathe through the pain. Will it ever not shatter me to think about her?

Most days it's a dull ache in my chest I can work through. Today's game is the first time I've been distracted enough not to think about her every single minute. But one mention of her name and that pain is back, wrecking me all over again.

I swallow back the ache in my throat. The buzzer sounds, signaling the end of the first period. I tell the kids I have to head to the locker room with the rest of the team. They all crowd around for high-fives. I clap my hand against the partition, where they're pressing their tiny palms. They giggle and squeal, which makes me laugh. That feels nice after feeling like my heart has been through a blender.

I move to follow the rest of the team as they walk off. But all of a sudden they stop.

"What the hell..." Isaac says.

I hear Xander chuckle. "What's up with that?" he asks me, pointing up at the scoreboard.

"What are you talking about?" I look up.

And then I almost drop my stick. Because I can't believe the words I'm seeing flashing on the scoreboard.

Maya loves Theo

"What the..." I trail off, my heart in my throat. No way...

The crowd cheers. And then I hear a wave of high-pitched squeals cut through the noise.

"Coach Maya! You're here!"

I whip my head back to where the kids are sitting. And then I lose all the air in my lungs. Because there's Maya, standing next to them, wearing a shirt that says, "I <3 #11," my jersey number.

For a few seconds, I just stand there and stare. My hearing goes fuzzy. So does everything and everyone around me. Except for Maya. All I see is her.

I take in the sight of her beautiful face, how she's smiling at me, but her eyes...she looks nervous and heartbroken all at once as she looks at me.

Heartbroken

"Shit, man. What are you waiting for?" Xander shoves my shoulder. "Go talk to your girl."

I hesitate for a second, suddenly aware that my entire team and this whole arena full of fans are watching this go down. Nerves crackle at the pit of my stomach.

I glance over at Coach Porter, who's frowning in Maya's direction. Shit. I need to explain things before he thinks this is some dramatic bullshit from my personal life that's bleeding into my job.

"She's my...we are...I mean, we *were* together, but some stuff happened and...we were trying to navigate our long-term relationship and I...it's just...she broke up with me... but now I guess..." I huff out a breath, mortified at how I'm rambling. "It's complicated."

Coach Porter's steely poker face holds steady. I hold my breath and brace myself for him to go off on me.

But to my total shock, he doesn't. He just looks at me and says, "You were in a relationship? Like an actual relationship?" His voice hitches up, like he's surprised.

"I...Yeah. I was."

"Huh." He pauses for a moment. "Well, color me shocked, Thompson. I didn't think you had it in you to do something so grown-up." He juts his chin in Maya's direction. "You've got fifteen minutes to work it out. Good luck."

I'm stunned as he and the team walk to the locker room. I hurry over to Maya. She runs to the partition in front of me and presses her hands against it.

"Did I get you in trouble?" she asks, breathless.

I shake my head. "Nah." My gaze falls to her shirt. My heart is in my throat. "Nice shirt."

Her big brown eyes are glassy with tears. She flashes a shaky smile. "I love you, Theo. So much."

I nearly topple over. I close my eyes and let out a breath. My forehead falls against the partition, I'm bowled over at hearing her speak those words.

"You love me?"

She nods. "I know you must be so angry with me right now. You have every right to be. You were right. I ended things between us because I was scared. I was scared that we'd end up breaking each other's hearts. My whole life I've been a jaded cynic when it comes to love and relationships. I was convinced that if I ever let myself fall for someone, it would end up with my heart getting shredded."

As I gaze at Maya, I take in the pain and pleading in her eyes, the conviction in her tone.

"I gave up on us before we even started out as a couple. I didn't even try. And now I realize how messed up that was —what a huge mistake that was." Her lips tremble. She stops to swallow. "I miss you so much, Theo. I miss you every minute of every day. I've never been happier than when I was with you. And now the only thing I'm scared of is losing you forever."

337

She pauses to take a breath.

"I know being together won't be easy," she says. "But I don't care. I don't want easy. I want you."

Her words knock me on my ass. I lock my knees so they don't buckle. I close my eyes and soak in everything she's said.

I take in how Maya's looking at me like I'm the only person in this entire arena. How she's put her feelings, raw and unfiltered, out there for me.

Emotion crashes through me like a tidal wave. I start to feel shaky on my skates, so I plant my free hand on the glass, right up against her palm. I glance up at the scoreboard and read those three words over again.

Maya loves Theo

My entire body is buzzing, I'm so overwhelmed.

I nod to the scoreboard. "I thought you weren't into grand gestures. You could have just called me," I tease as I get my bearings back.

A soft smile tugs at her lips. "I changed my mind. I kind of like them now."

That tightness in my chest eases. That invisible fist around my heart is gone now.

"I love you, Maya. I want to be with you."

She looks shocked and relieved all at once. "You do?"

"Without a doubt. You're all I've ever wanted."

That gorgeous smile I've been aching to see appears. It feels like a Fourth of July fireworks show in my chest.

I push back from the partition and scramble toward the stands. When I look up, I see her running down to me. Around us fans cheer, but I don't hear it. All I can hear is my heart thudding in my ears.

She's in my arms a half-second later. I kiss her like it's the end of the world. When we break apart, I rest my forehead on hers and catch my breath. I savor the feel of her in my arms, the taste of her on my lips.

"That's one hell of a grand gesture you pulled off." I have to yell, everyone around us is cheering so loud. "I'm impressed."

Her melodic laugh is heaven to hear. She cups her hands over my cheeks.

"Being in love with you has that effect on me," she says. "I've got more up my sleeve too."

My chest feels like it's about to explode in the best way. "Is that so?"

She bites her lip, nodding. "Like, years and years' worth."

I grin and kiss her. "Good thing we've got forever together."

Epilogue

6 **months later**
   Maya

    "Seriously, Ingrid. I can't thank you enough for letting me use your cabin as a workspace."

I've got her on speaker as I pack the last few orders of the day in the guest bedroom.

"No thanks necessary. I'm hardly ever there now that I'm spending most of my time in San Diego."

A pang of guilt hits. "I still can't believe that you weren't mad when I quit as your PA to focus on my earring business."

Ingrid chuckles. "How could I be mad that my best friend was finally pursuing her dream?"

I glance around the bedroom, which is cluttered with boxes, shipping labels, packing materials, and dozens and dozens of earrings. Despite the chaos around me, I smile, thrilled at the business I'm building.

"I can't believe I'm actually doing it. I have my own earring line." I let out a squeaky laugh.

"Believe it. Maya Babes Earrings is gonna be an empire,

I can feel it. I mean, the day you launched your website, you sold out in three hours. Do you know how amazing that is? On top of that, your earrings are in Sadie Skinner's boutique. You're a superstar already."

I beam at how my best friend pumps me up. I finish sealing the last package and drop it into a tote bag on the floor. I count four bags total packed with orders for me to take to the post office first thing Monday morning.

Phone in hand, I head out to the kitchen for a glass of water, stopping by Mr. Pudding's bowl to feed him. "I still owe you for helping me think of the name for my business."

"You can pay me by setting aside a pair of those emerald chandelier earrings you just finished designing."

"You got it."

"How's Theo?"

As I take a sip, I spot Theo near the pond playing with the kids from hockey camp. He laughs while darting around as they chase him.

I smile. "He's great. Just finishing up camp for the day," I say.

Since the end of hockey season, Theo and I resumed hockey camp with the kids. It's summer, so we've shifted from cold weather activities to warm weather ones like hiking and swimming and outdoor games.

I ask Ingrid how decorating her new place in San Diego is coming along. While we chat, I get a text from Tyler.

Hey, is Tori dating anyone?

"That's weird," I mumble.

"What's weird?"

"My brother Tyler just texted me asking if Tori is dating anyone."

341

Ingrid gasps. "Wait! Do you think he's finally going to ask her out?"

A pit forms in my stomach. The last thing sweet Tori deserves is to get strung along by my player older brother.

"He'd better not. For Tori's sake, I mean."

I frown at his text before typing a response.

> No, she's not. Why do you ask?

I see the text bubble appear, then disappear. Then nothing.

"Maybe he's changed. Maybe he's mature and sweet and romantic now," Ingrid says.

"Ha. Fat chance."

Instead of waiting for his reply, I shoot of a quick warning text.

> If you're thinking about asking Tori out, don't. We both know you're not exactly boyfriend-of-the-year material. She's a sweetheart and doesn't deserve to be strung along and ghosted, okay?

I notice Tyler leaves my text on "read." I roll my eyes.

"God, I can't stand my brother sometimes," I mutter to Ingrid.

"Yeah, but he's hot."

I make a disgusted noise.

"Okay, okay, sorry." She laughs. "I know how much it grosses you out when people go on about your hot brothers."

"Yup. And if you do it again, I'm going to go on and on about how wildly sexy I think your cousin is—"

"Okay! Point taken," Ingrid quickly says.

Just then Theo walks in with the kids. I tell Ingrid I'll

just be a minute. They all rush over to say hi and give me hugs.

"We missed you, Coach Maya!" Annabelle says.

"Yeah! How come you didn't play tag with us?" Parker says.

"I had to work at my other job, but tomorrow at camp I'll spend the whole day with you guys."

They're all happy to hear that. Theo steps over and kisses me. When all the kids make "eww" noises, we laugh. I hand Theo the phone so he can say hi to Ingrid while I get the kids ready for pick-up. Five minutes later all the kids are gone. I walk over to Theo, who's chatting at the kitchen island. When he sees me, he grins. Tingles flash across my body. He reaches over and gently grabs my hand and pulls me against him.

Ingrid chats away while Theo mumbles, "Yup. Uh-huh," his eyes on me the whole time.

He leans down and presses a kiss to my neck. I inhale sharply, trying to stay as quiet as I can so Ingrid won't hear.

As he dusts slow kiss after slow kiss along the slope of my neck, I bite my lip. Between my legs I'm pulsing, aching. I close my eyes and tug my hand through his thick blond hair.

"Hello? Anyone there?" Ingrid bellows.

Theo leans back. I yelp.

"Yup. Still here," he says.

"Wait, were you two kissing?" Ingrid asks.

"Uh…" I stammer.

Theo winces before bursting out laughing. "Possibly."

"Gross. I'm hanging up now," Ingrid says.

I wrap my arms around Theo's waist and hug him. "Sorry, Ingrid."

"Yeah, sorry about that," he says through a laugh.

"Oh! One last thing. Did a package arrive today?" Ingrid asks.

We glance around until we spot a large yellow padded envelope on the island. I grab it and see that it's from Thompson Industries, Ingrid and Theo's family conglomerate.

"Wait, did you send this, Ingrid?" I ask.

"I sure did. Open it." I can tell she's smiling.

I tear it open and pull out a stack of documents. I show it to Theo and together we skim it.

When I realize what it is, my eyes bulge. "You didn't..."

I glance up at Theo, who's gawking at the paper. "Ingrid, are you serious?" he asks.

"So serious!" she squeals.

I make a sputtering sound, I'm so shocked. My mouth is agape as I look at Theo. I grab the phone from his hand.

"Ingrid, you're giving us your cabin? But...this is your home. We can't accept this."

"You can," she says. "I'm never there and I don't want to go through the trouble of selling it. Besides, even if I were to move back to Denver someday, I don't want to stay there, not after knowing all the things you two probably get up to there."

I let out a laugh while I take in Theo's dazed expression. Ingrid tells us she'll pack up her stuff the next time she visits.

"Ingrid, you're a legend. I don't even know how to begin to thank you for this," Theo says.

"If you have a daughter, I want you to name her after me," she teases.

"Middle name," he counters.

"Deal."

I laugh and shake my head, still in shock. I can't believe it. This cabin is officially our new home.

"This is my early engagement gift to you guys. It's only a matter of time before you two tie the knot, you're so disgustingly in love," she teases. "Theo, you'd better pull off an incredible proposal for my best friend."

He smiles at me, affection clear in his sky-blue eyes. "Promise I will."

"Good. Now I'm hanging up for real this time."

"Love you, Ingrid," Theo and I say in unison.

She says she loves us and hangs up. I set the phone down and glance around the open concept space. "I can't believe your cousin gave us her cabin. This is officially ours. Our first home together."

Theo shakes his head, dazed. "I can't either. This is wild."

He slinks his arms around my waist pulling me against him. I wrap my arms around his neck and press a soft kiss to his lips. My heart hammers in my chest and my skin goes hot.

When we break our kiss, I lock eyes with him. "I can't believe this is my life. Perfect job. Perfect boyfriend. Perfect home."

Theo flashes that gorgeous smile at me. "I can't either. How did I get so lucky to land you, Maya Grant?"

Emotion blooms in my chest. I cradle his face in my hands.

"I can't wait to marry you," he whispers. That sensation inside of me deepens and intensifies.

Marry

That word. A word that used to terrify me does the opposite now. We've talked about it a handful of times in the past six months and each time it's felt a little less scary. I feel myself getting more and more excited at the thought of marrying Theo.

"I can't wait to marry you too," I say against his lips. He scoops me up and sets me on the counter.

His hands fall to the hem of my top and he starts to pull it off. "First order of business though." He tosses aside my shirt, then strips off his own. "Christening the cabin as officially ours. And I think fucking on the island is the best way to do it."

My head falls back as I chuckle. "So romantic."

I move in for another kiss before he leans back and pins me with an intense gaze. "I wanna marry you here, Maya. At the cabin."

I still, floored at the emotion in his eyes and the conviction in his tone. "Really?"

He nods. "This is where I fell in love with you. I can't imagine doing it anywhere else."

My heart feels like it's on the verge of bursting. I'm blown away at the sweetness of his request.

I gaze at him, overwhelmed by this moment. Overwhelmed at the fact I get to spend the rest of my life with Theo Thompson.

I grab him and kiss him until we're both breathless. "Let's do it. Let's get married in the winter. Surrounded by snow," I say. "Just like the day we moved into this cabin."

When he smiles at me, I can see his whole heart in his eyes. "Sounds perfect."

Want a spicy bonus scene with Maya and Theo?

Maya surprises Theo with something very, very sexy after one of his hockey games...
Sign up for my newsletter to read it:
www.sarahsmithbooks.com

Tyler and Tori's book *No Freaking Way* is up next! You're gonna love this fake relationship, friends to lovers, secret crush romance! Get it here! And Subscribe to my newsletter, I'll be dropping some big book news soon!

Keep reading for an excerpt of *No Freaking Way*.

Excerpt from No Freaking Way

When I turn around, I expect to see Becca and Maya returning from the bathroom.

But I don't.

Instead, I see Tyler, looking like James freaking Bond in a suit, gawking at me with his jaw on the floor.

I gasp. "What are you doing here?"

I'm suddenly aware of just how ridiculous I look standing in front of him in just my underwear. My skin heats from embarrassment. I was in the middle of changing out of my bridesmaids dress when I thought I heard Becca and Maya coming back from the bathroom. I was going to rush out and help Becca with her dress because she's wearing a ball gown with a full skirt. I didn't think twice about being in my underwear because Becca, Maya, and I are the only ones in the boutique right now. We're close friends, we've gotten dressed and undressed in front of each other a million times.

But Becca and Maya aren't here. Tyler is.

Tyler, who I've been thinking about non-stop since last night.

I haven't been able to get our kiss out of my mind. I replayed it over and over in my head all last night and this morning. Yeah, it was a little awkward to kiss in front of an arena full of screaming hockey fans, but it was also freaking HOT.

Even though it only lasted a few seconds, it wrecked me. The feel of Tyler's soft lips, the taste of his tongue, how he teased my lips open and lapped the tip of my tongue with his, the way he was soft and firm as he kissed me...it all drove me wild. There was such confidence in that kiss, I could feel it. And I wanted more.

But I tried to play it cool because we're just friends and this is a fake relationship. I shouldn't be fantasizing about our kiss cam kiss.

Tyler moves his mouth as he gawks at me, but no words come out.

Ten seconds go by. He closes his eyes and shakes his head.

He stares at me. "You look fucking incredible."

A surprised laugh falls from my mouth. That self-consciousness starts to melt away.

I fold my hands in front of me. "I'm in my underwear," I mumble.

Tyler licks his lips and takes two steps forward. "Yeah. You are."

I bite my lip, taking in the hungry expression on his face. He's looking at me like he wants to devour me.

Goosebumps fly across my skin. My nipples harden underneath my bra. That pulse between my legs reappears.

"You're wearing a suit." I let out a breath. "You look really, really good." I glance down at his crotch. "Those pants fit a lot better than the ones in the picture Theo texted us."

The corner of his mouth hooks up. "You didn't like those pants?"

"No, I did. You look good in anything."

His tan skin turns rosy at my compliment. "You didn't reply to the group text so I figured you weren't impressed."

"Oh, I was impressed. Very impressed. I was so impressed I was speechless."

That half-smile turns shy and the blush on his cheeks intensifies, like he's flattered at what I've said. I feel a sudden burst of pride that my words mean so much to this beautiful man.

He moves toward me. "I don't want to talk about how I look anymore."

He stops when he's less than a foot from me.

"What are you doing here?" I ask.

"Gage wanted me to drop off some earrings to Becca," he says before scooping my hand in his.

For a second, he stills. His eyes turn shy as he looks at me. "Is this okay? That I'm here? Touching you like this?"

I grin. "Of course it's okay."

My heart races. I think about how we were in this exact same position the other night when we almost kissed: standing close together, my hand in his, our breaths ragged, looking at each other's mouths...

My entire body is buzzing, aching with need.

I think about how badly I wanted to kiss Tyler that night...how good it felt to finally kiss him last night...how badly I want to kiss him again...

And then I realize nothing is stopping us.

I grab his face in my hand and crash my mouth against his.

He moans as he kisses me back. We don't waste any time teasing. Our tongues are filthy and rabid.

Tyler's massive hands squeeze my waist before gently skimming up my torso.

"Fuck, Tori. Do you know how long I've wanted to kiss you like this?" he rasps.

"Since last night?" I say in a breathy voice.

He chuckles. "Way, way longer."

He captures my mouth in another kiss. This time, his mouth and tongue move a bit slower, more teasing. He slowly flicks the tip of his tongue against the tip of mine. My clit pulses.

Hotttttt.

Is that how he'd work his tongue between my legs?

I moan just thinking about it.

He walks us back into one of the empty dressing rooms. I lean back against the wall as he pulls the curtain shut behind us.

I reach over and grab him by the lapel of his suit jacket and pull him back for another kiss.

"We have to be quiet," I whisper as I push his jacket off his shoulders.

He steps back as he takes it off. "You're the one who's going to have to be quiet, Tori."

I'm confused until he drops to his knees. He rests his hands on my hips and gazes up at me, those rich brown eyes eager.

"I want to break our no-sex rule," he rasps in a low, breathy voice.

My stomach does a somersault. Heat flashes across my skin.

"But I only want to do it if you want to, Tori."

I bite my lip and nod, my skin buzzing and my clit pulsing in anticipation.

"I need to hear you say it," he growls softly. "I need to hear you say you want me."

I reach down, grip his jaw in my hand, and look him in the eyes. "I want to break the rules with you, Tyler. I want this. I want you. So bad."

A wicked smile tugs at his mouth. He licks his lips as his gaze rakes up and down my body. "You look good in anything too, you know. I just prefer you in nothing."

He runs his fingertips along the waistband of my panties. My legs start to shake and my breath catches. I have never been this turned on by anticipation. Ever.

But this is what the sight of Tyler Grant on his knees, licking his lips, gazing at my pussy, does to me.

I'm about to explode and all we've done so far is kiss.

He skims his palms up the side of my torso, up my back. He undoes my bra and pulls it slowly down my arms.

His eyes go glittery as he gazes up at me.

"Jesus..." he mutters while gawking at my boobs.

I bite back a smile, giddy that he likes what he sees.

Then he closes his eyes and presses his forehead against my body, just under my boobs. Like he can't believe what he's seeing and needs a second to gather himself.

"Fuck, Tori. Your tits..."

I cover my mouth and giggle.

"Of course you have the most perfect tits in the world," he murmurs against my stomach. "Everything else about you is perfect."

My heart skids in my chest and I lose all the breath in my lungs. How can he make this moment filthy, hot, and romantic all at once?

He leans his head up again and looks me square in the eye. "The things I want to do those perfect tits. But I don't have the time right now. So I'm going to focus on the most important part."

He gently grips the sides of my panties and slowly slides them down. And then he slowly, softly kisses my pussy lips apart.

Read the rest of No Freaking Way on Kindle Unlimited or in paperback!

Also by Sarah Smith

Grant Sibling Series

Dessert Flirt Repeat

Snow, Ice, and Spice

No Freaking Way

I Heart SF Romance Series

The Close-Up

In Love with Lewis Prescott

Unlikely Pairings Series (written as Sarah Skye)

Sips & Strokes

Vibes & Feels

Whiskers & Sunshine

Standalone Romances

Faker

Simmer Down

On Location

The Boy with the Bookstore

If You Never Come Back

Acknowledgments

Thank you all for reading Maya and Theo's love story! I've always wanted to write a hockey romance, but I was honestly so intimidated by the idea...hockey romances are so revered in the romance community! But once it came time for me to write Maya's book, I just knew her love interest would be a hockey player. And I'm so happy that I pushed through my nerves because I ended up loving this book so much. If you enjoyed it, please consider leaving a review on Amazon and Goodreads. Reviews make a huge difference when it comes to my little book reaching more readers and getting more visibility.

I want to thank Sonia Palermo, Sandy Lim, and Rebecca Chase for being the most wonderful friends and beta readers I could ever ask for.

A gigantic thanks to Elle Maxwell for designing the most beautiful cover.

Thank you to Alex for being the most supportive and loving husband I could ask for.

Thank you to Maizie for all the pets, cuddles, and zoomie sessions that kept me entertained while writing this book.

And the biggest thanks always goes to my amazing readers. Thank you for reading and loving my stories. I couldn't do this without you.

About the Author

Sarah Smith is a copywriter-turned-author who wants to make the world a lovelier place, one kissing story at a time. Her love of romance began when she was eight and she discovered her auntie's stash of romance novels. She's been hooked ever since. When she's not writing, you can find her hiking, eating chocolate, and perfecting her *lumpia* recipe.

    instagram.com/authorsarahs
    tiktok.com/@authorsarahs
    bookbub.com/authors/sarah-echavarre-smith
    facebook.com/groups/sarahsmithbooks

Printed in Great Britain
by Amazon

46066196R00209